5000 NIGHTS OF OBSESSION
A TWISTED GATSBY STORY

DRETHI A.

Created with Vellum

Author Note

This book contains nonconsensual sexual scenes and a dubious extramarital affair. Depending on your comfort zone, the content might disturb you.

To Moms and daughters and their complicated relationships.

BLURB

This dark book isn't a fairy tale romance. There is no Prince Charming, only an irredeemable villain and the object of his desire. His OBSESSION.

I felt his eyes on me everywhere I went.
I recognized his smell lingering within my home.
I even sensed his presence in my sleep.
It was too late by the time I found the monster hiding under my bed. He had wedged himself into my life, cornering me with nowhere to run.

The worst part?
The world adored him, but no one knew the devil lurking underneath the beautiful mask—no one except for me.

Manipulative, cold, and remorseless, Axel Trimalchio was a certified psychopath hiding in plain sight. He was fixated on me and would never stop chasing me.

He was determined to make me his... even though I already belonged to someone else.

Axel shouldn't be considered a hero. Check the author's content warnings before proceeding.

PART ONE

The Fall

CHAPTER
ONE

*Karens ignore trigger warnings, only to complain about said
warnings. Don't be a Karen or kink-shame others. This is intended
for readers exploring their fantasies in fiction while exercising
sound judgment in real life. This isn't a fairy tale romance. It
contains nonconsensual sexual scenes and an extramarital affair.
Please don't read if that triggers you. Your mental health is worth
more than this book.*

May 30th, 2022

Piya

"IT'LL BE FUN," JAY DECLARED.

"No, it won't," I countered. "My argument is based on the very rebuttal; it won't be fun. Jay, why do we have to go out tonight? It would've been the perfect night to stay in."

My sentiment was countered by the gust of wind sweeping over us since Jay had taken down the top of his convertible. It was the perfect night to go out instead of staying cooped up. The baby hair on my forehead danced along in agreement. The intense cold of New York winter was replaced by cool spring weather. A night out was a reprieve while the weather was cooperating. I merely disliked our destination, as I'd much rather stay home with my husband.

Unfortunately, business calls.

Jay owned a hedge fund company based in New York. We were both born and raised in New York but decided to make Chicago our home following our nuptials. Jay relocated his main operations to Chicago while maintaining a smaller client base in New York. After a decade away, we found ourselves in a bind and moved back.

Since our return to New York, Jay has been preoccupied with re-strengthening his previous business connections. The best way to do so was by attending parties and socials, though I knew he despised the pageantry of these affairs more than I did.

We had been invited to a party in Long Island tonight. While Jay didn't know the host personally and was initially reluctant, he changed his mind upon realizing the event was basically in our backyard and the perfect opportunity to network. Some rich guy had been throwing these extravagant who's-who affairs all summer. Invitations to these parties were strictly through word of mouth but not as exclusive as expected. In fact, people were discouraged from showing up alone, the motto being *more the merrier.*

It made sense. Loners raised suspicion amongst the elites, and they steered clear of social pariahs. Not to mention, a word-of-mouth invitation could hardly fall into the wrong hands. The rich and powerful ran in similar crowds and would only bring along like-minded individuals. These social events were incestuous cesspools dominated by identical people.

Tonight would be no different.

My husband tilted his head, his dark hair partially covering his eyes. "Why are you being grumpy, babe? You used to love being social."

"I still love being social... with you." I placed my hand on his thigh suggestively. It had been months since we had sex, and I worried about our rift. Jay had always been driven, but lately, he had been working nonstop, traveling to Chicago at every opportunity since establishing connections there. Despite the beautiful home we purchased in Long Island, Jay was yet to spend a night in New York. I didn't understand his sudden motivation to magnify our wealth. It wasn't as if we needed it. He was home for only one night, leaving tomorrow on yet another trip. I stupidly assumed we'd spend the night alone.

Jay removed my hand from his thigh but kissed my fingers to soften the blow. "It'll be good for you to get out of the house more. Don't be a Debbie Downer," he chided softly.

"All Debbies will take offense to your statement," I retorted, brushing off the rejection with a forced smile.

"My guilty conscience will live to see another day." Jay shrugged, unaware of the large population of women named Debbie he insulted. "It'll be nice for you to see old friends."

There was only one friend of mine attending this party, Jordan. I met her at a time when I was young and a rebel. At this stage of life, I'd much rather be a social pariah and a recluse. Pretending to be happy at a swanky event had plastered a semi-permanent pout on my face.

Jay seemed unfazed by my lack of enthusiasm and switched on the blinkers to turn left, the flashing light indicating the end of our short journey. My exasperated sigh turned into a gasp when Jay passed the gate. The gold-rimmed sky-high metal gates were wide open, presumably for convoys of guests. It led passage into the larger-than-life driveway curling for over a mile. Something familiar niggled in the back of my brain at the sight of this path, but I couldn't place it, so I banked it away.

"Wow," I hummed hypnotically. "Do we know who owns this place?"

Jay shrugged. "No owner was listed online for this property, only a corporation. But I heard it's some guy trying to expand his connections."

Aka, new money.

"Apparently, he is a celebrity."

"Doesn't that narrow it down? If we see a celebrity at the party, we'll know it's him."

Jay shook his head. "There have been numerous celebrity sightings at these events. It's impossible to know which one of them is behind it. Given that planners and PR representatives manage the parties, the only way to find out is if the PR company cracks." He smiled at me wickedly, the insinuation evident.

Jordan.

My best friend ran a PR and Talent Agency, a legacy passed down by her father. She was the one who insisted we attend tonight's event. Her firm likely organized the events and knew the answer to the million-dollar question.

Who owns this property, and why have they been throwing parties all summer?

Nonetheless, I'd never pressure Jordan to reveal the identity of this mystery man. She managed big-name stars and was notoriously secretive about her list, especially if the client wanted to remain anonymous. I knew all about it from first-hand experience because I was one of Jordan's clients.

"Hm," I said absentmindedly, inspecting the stone mansion towering over us. Actually, calling this place a mansion was a misuse of the word. The term castle was a better fit.

Jay pulled the car up to the cobblestone roundabout. A valet scattered to us on cue, exchanging our keys for a paper slip. Jay pocketed the claim ticket, handing the man some cash before he drove away with the car. We entwined fingers, turning a couple of heads in the process.

It wasn't abnormal for people to gawk at our odd pairing. The peculiarity didn't stem from my five-foot, three-inch, petite frame against Jay's six-foot, one-inch, muscular build. It was the seventeen years between us that was so striking.

Some might peg me as a gold digger upon learning of our vast age difference. It couldn't be further from the truth. Jay was as out of my league at fifty-one as he had been at thirty-eight. My husband didn't use age as a reason to let himself go and saw a personal trainer four times a week. It contributed to the solid block of muscle under his custom-made suit, further distinguishing his handsome features.

Women salivated after my husband, and despite Jay's constant reassurance, I wasn't impervious to the yearning gaze they cast his way. We had been together for over a decade, but the stares hadn't subsided. Most eyes were on him tonight, especially since Jay wore his show-stopping navy blue suit.

I was over the exhibitionism of elaborate affairs but still dressed accordingly. Appearances played a significant role in Jay's world, and despite my reluctance to attend, I didn't want to embarrass him in front of his colleagues.

With my pastel cardigan folded over my right elbow, I smoothed the skirt of the conservative cocktail dress that flared around my knees. I generally wore muted colors but couldn't help pairing the outfit with sparkling Jimmy Choo pumps. Taking stock of the well-dressed attendees enjoying a glass of champagne or a smoke outside, I was relieved to discover the shoes didn't stand out.

"You look beautiful," Jay whispered on cue.

My skin warmed under his gaze. "I'm not the one everyone is staring at. Those two haven't taken their eyes off you." I stared down the two women smoking next to the grand staircases. They shamelessly eye-fucked my husband and weren't deterred by the scowl on my face.

Jay smirked. "You mean I have other options? Hold on, girls.

I'm coming." He made a show of sprinting toward the leering women as I playfully tugged him back. It was enough to lighten my sour mood, and I broke out with a toothy grin. He always knew how to get me out of a funk. He had been there for me throughout the most challenging times of my life, and despite the recent disconnect, there was no one I'd rather be here with other than him.

I giggled in response to his playfulness, diminishing some of my previous annoyance over attending this party. Squeezing my hand, Jay led the way.

"Shit," one of the women ogling my husband cried out.

My neck twisted in her direction to find the front of her dress ruined by cinder-colored dust. The cigarette ashes had fallen on her bodice, and when she hurriedly brushed it off, the color stained the front of her chest.

We stopped next to the woman, and I held out my cardigan. "Here."

Flustered, she glanced at my outstretched arm. "Oh. Oh, no. It's okay." She reddened, realizing I was the woman who'd glared at her for checking out my husband.

I internally shrugged. Everyone checked out my husband. I could hardly hold it against the poor woman, especially knowing from personal experience that these types of incidents were mortifying. It took me years of practice to eventually exercise grace. Before then, I used to be an impatient free spirit, leaving behind a trail of clumsiness.

"Really, take it. You won't be able to fix that with club soda." I nodded at the front of her dress. It was ruined beyond what

9

could be repaired tonight. The only cure would be a trip to the dry cleaners. "If you button up the cardigan, it'll cover up the stain."

"That's so kind," she murmured, finally grabbing the cardigan. A warmth radiated from her that hadn't existed a few moments ago. "Thank you," she said, shrugging on the delicate material.

"You're very welcome."

"I'm Greta, by the way," she offered. "And this is my friend Rachel."

Jay nodded in acknowledgment as we exchanged handshakes. "Jay Ambani. This is my wife, Piya."

We politely chatted with the two women, sharing small talk. Soon, the conversation turned to the inquiry about our elusive host.

Neither of them had seen the mystery man we sought. There were hushed rumors that an enigmatic celebrity had bought and renovated this property. He had been hosting these spectacular events for the surrounding community. This was a dream for anyone searching for investment or networking opportunities or simply to party and climb the social ladder. The speculations for the host's vague reasons remained at large since he was yet to make an appearance.

As we bid goodbye to the women and turned away, Greta called after me, "Wait. How do I return this to you? Should we exchange numbers?"

I smiled. "Keep it. Looks better on you, anyways."

Jay guided me up the grand staircases and through the

opulent entranceway. I stopped short upon reaching the top of the stairs, the view taking my breath away.

The foyer opened to a large ballroom with a magnificent set of stairs smack in the middle. A giant chandelier hung off the ceiling, while two smaller ones accompanied it on each side. The walls were painted white, with large windows covering much of the room. They were draped with elegant curtains in cross-cross fashion, and even from here, I could see a beautiful courtyard connected to the ballroom.

The ballroom was too exquisite to simply exist inside someone's home. The whole affair was past ostentatious. The theme was *a night in Paris* with appropriately reflective food, décor, and music. Uniformed servers passed hors d'oeuvres. There were multiple bars with exaggerated champagne towers for show. A live band sang in French, and the room was packed with guests. Spiral staircases led to the second floor of this majestic ballroom. It was the only unoccupied area as it didn't hold the same festive atmosphere.

I whistled under my breath. "Exactly how rich is this guy?"

"Good question," Jay agreed.

Our pondering was interrupted by a server holding a silver tray. "Champagne, madame?"

Did all the servers have a French accent, or was it a façade because of the theme?

"Oui, s'il vous plaît," I chirped. Jay grabbed two flutes and passed the second one to me. Raising my flute, I clinked it with his. "Cheers."

The first sip of the refreshing drink barely hit the back of my throat when I noticed Jay fixating behind me. I followed his gaze to find that Jordan had spotted us, rushing over with enthusiastic glee. The word on the street was that she had been courting the mystery celebrity responsible for this event and handling his parties to sway him to sign with her firm.

Despite skipping town shortly after my wedding, it didn't impact my friendship with Jordan. One reason was because of what we both did for a living. Before getting married, I wrote corny jingles and sold the soundtracks for a profit to various lingerie and racy ad campaigns. After my wedding, I considered giving up music because my brand was on the spicier end. Jay's family was prominent, and he had often reminded me that being an "Ambani Wife" came at a price. Neither of us could shake those expectations, and creating music for indecent commercials did not fit the bill.

Jordan, whose vocation was in Talent and PR management, vehemently protested the decision. She devised a stage name for me to hide behind, so my family and Jay's business associates wouldn't discover my alter ego. Jordan had maintained my secret identity for years while ensuring I remained relevant with consistent jobs. The persona allowed me to work remotely on soundtracks based on client specifications. I loved the steady stream of income and loved Jordan more for not letting me give up. More than propelling my career, she'd helped me maintain financial independence. For that, I'd be eternally grateful.

Aside from professional aspirations, Jordan was my constant upon return, helping me embrace life in New York. Tonight was no different.

"Hello, Jordan." Jay nodded.

"Can you believe this house?" Jordan exclaimed instead of acknowledging Jay's greeting. Her long blonde hair was styled in beachy waves, bouncing over her shoulders. She wore an asymmetrical white dress, accessorized by Carrie Bradshaw's famous, blue-studded Manolo Blahniks. It gave her five-foot-six frame an additional boost. At thirty-three, Jordan looked more like a model than a PR powerhouse. As usual, I was struck by my best friend's beauty at first glance. Numerous eyes were glued to her with similar approval.

"Hello to you, too, Jordan," Jay repeated. He hated when people dismissed manners. My husband and best friend were as different as night and day. She was easygoing, whereas Jay epitomized formal and polite culture.

Jordan waved off the *hello*, unaware and uncaring. "Did you see the courtyard?" she asked.

"I haven't been out there yet," I replied, quickly hugging her.

"There is a string quartet outside," she gushed.

Jay rolled his eyes, giving up on correcting Jordan's manners, and gestured at the bar. "Oh, I see a friend of mine."

"Lies," I berated. Businessmen like him had little interest in personal relationships, focusing instead on making connections. "You have no friends."

Jay laughed softly at the jab. "Fine. It's an investor. Do you mind if I say hello?"

I sighed at the question. I thought we'd at least hang out together at the party if Jay refused to stay home. However, I couldn't argue. "Not at all."

"Do you ladies want anything from the bar?"

We shook our heads in unison since Jordan already had a drink, and I was still nursing my champagne. As soon as Jay left, Jordan filled me in on everything that'd happened at the party thus far. After she grew tired of giving me the latest gossip, we made the short walk outside. Fresh air impaled my senses while the laughter in the beautifully manicured courtyard was indescribably jovial. There were bars outside as well, along with the coveted string quartet. I realized it was so the guests could enjoy drinks and music while filtering in and out for a smoke break.

The attention to detail astounded me. I had attended many extravagant galas and affairs, but this party made the rest look like amateur hour. The event's magnificence was something out of The Great Gatsby.

There was only one dilemma. The bars were packed, and the servers with champagne trays were inside making rounds. Instead of flocking to the overflowing bar, I stopped beside the giant champagne tower. "I'm not standing in that line." I stared determinedly at the coupe cocktail glasses, feeling daring from the bubbles fizzling in my veins.

"I think those towers are for display only," Jordan argued.

"Then they shouldn't have made them look so delicious."

Jordan giggled. "You're crazy. Oh, guess who I ran into earlier?"

"Who?" I asked, distracted. As if playing a dangerous game of Tetris, I carefully worked on extricating two champagne coupes.

"Tina," she replied. "She is divorced now. I'd feel sorry for her if she wasn't a giant bitch."

I suppressed a laugh. Tina was a name I hadn't heard in years, but I shouldn't be surprised. It seemed many of our mutual acquaintances were in attendance. Tina was the mean girl equivalent in Jordan's former clique.

"Not to mention," Jordan continued, "Tina getting divorced means you owe me a thousand dollars."

This time, I couldn't hold back the giggle. "Oh my God, go away while I do this. You're going to make me spill."

"Whatever, drama queen," she tsked. Nonetheless, she played with her phone, giving me space to figure this out.

My fingers hovered over the tower's topmost level when a sinking feeling of being watched overcame me. The stare was forceful and so potent that my neck craned on its own until settling on the second floor of the building. There was a window to the second-floor hallway, with the curtains drawn back. Only one man stood atop, and his eyes were trained on me.

A gasp spilled out of my mouth.

Time slowed around me, the moving bodies around the courtyard seemingly coming to a halt. All of the universe had stopped in place except for my heart, which was suddenly pounding at an alarmingly increased pace. My gaze roamed over the man, and I only had to narrow my eyes to catch every detail about his features, and the intensity etched on his face.

My breath hitched.

Electricity shocked through my body next.

My feet tingled as if pricked by fire ants, and I stumbled.

I should be worried about knocking over the champagne tower, but I couldn't tear my eyes away from the man. Forceful gaze honed in, stripping me bare and telling me he was all things wicked. He was tall, handsome, and definitely dark in an obsidian suit that matched his eyes. His hair was perfectly styled, and though there was no other disarray about him, his expression was wild. The chiseled jawline set as the liquid pools of darkness devoured me.

Captivated, I held his inappropriate gaze. At any moment, my best friend could look up from her phone and catch me in the act. I had to break contact, but my eyes refused to play ball.

My clammy hands brushed my hair out of my face. The slight effort lifted the hem of my dress' skirt, and his intense gaze landed on the strip of exposed skin around my mid-thighs. The break in our staring contest was the sweet escape I needed, and I finally blinked away.

Jordan glanced up from her phone. "One of those for me?"

"Right." My haze broke. "Yeah." I caught a glimpse of Jordan's perfectly filed nails as I passed her one of the coupe glasses.

I didn't have to look to know his lingering orbs still crawled up my body. Goosebumps broke out over my bare skin, and I wanted to shout, *Stop staring at me!*

Jordan sipped on her drink and gave me the dirt about everything I had missed out on. I nodded absentmindedly, and though I knew I shouldn't, my eyes darted toward the upstairs window where I had located *him*.

He was gone.

I returned to Jordan, who had polished off her drink. "I need to break the seal and touch up. Want to come?"

"No, that's okay. I'll get you another round." I gestured at the champagne tower.

Jordan laughed wholeheartedly. Shaking her head, she vanished inside the main ballroom, searching for a bathroom. Left behind to my own devices, I bent over to excavate another set of coupe glasses when I felt a hush fall over the courtyard. I tilted my head, caught a glimpse of the group nearest me, and found them staring in the same direction.

"That's him," someone whispered.

Who?

My silent question was answered by a deep voice reaching inside to squeeze my heart. "Hello."

I froze in place the way drops of water would in Antarctica. Once more, the crowd faded away. Slow like the sands of time, my body moved on autopilot. I straightened to be greeted by a pair of orbs that appeared lifeless and bored. If you paid close attention, you'd also find them holding a speck of curiosity. They were the blackest of the black shade, framed by thick brows, equally dark lashes, and a full head of hair styled to perfection. Sun-kissed complexion contrasted the otherwise ominous features. His generous lips were slightly camouflaged by his five o'clock shadow, which appeared groomed instead of unruly. A straight nose and a chiseled jawline completed the man who could only be described as a male model.

In a black suit, he fit in perfectly with the elegant backdrop while also managing to stand out. Not only was his beauty unequivocally unmatched, but his sheer dominance had an imposing presence. Everyone around us was staring at him as well.

"Hi," I squawked with an unspoken plea for him to go away. He didn't hear it. I steadied myself by placing a hand on the champagne table without tearing away my shameless appraisal. It seemed like an impossible feat to accomplish.

"The champagne towers are for display only." He nodded at the table next to me, though his eyes of bottomless pit never left mine.

I opened my mouth to make an excuse or lie that I wasn't planning to steal two glasses of champagne. "Then they shouldn't have made them look so delicious," I bit my cheek as the rebuttal from earlier tumbled out like word vomit.

He smirked. The otherwise flat, dull eyes changed from slight curiosity to slight amusement. He leaned closer, and my breath caught in my throat. "I didn't take you for a champagne drinker," he murmured.

"What's wrong with champagne?" I heard the breathiness in my voice. He smelled so unbelievably good, clean with a barely-there hint of something refreshing, but what?

"You are too interesting for a single-pour drink."

"What would you suggest?"

"Some sort of cocktail. Sex on the Beach during the day or a Dirty Martini at night." He licked his bottom lips, and my pupils followed the movement. "How about I get you one of those?"

The way he spoke, with double entendre, bordered on improper. I looked around, searching for someone to rescue me. I couldn't be trusted when left alone with this man.

Three women near us kept glancing at him while acting inconspicuously about spying. Yet, no one dared to approach him without permission. The most blatant of the three peeked from under her lashes, scanning his body leisurely from head to toe. She wanted him. All three wanted him, and they weren't the only ones. All eyes were on him as if he had lit the same fire under their skins.

My insides quivered when he stepped closer. The intimate space between us was beyond inappropriate, but worse was his intoxicating aroma. Feeling lightheaded, I lost my sense of right and wrong and unintentionally leaned into it. The scent was driving me crazy. What was it?

Hunger flamed behind his unfazed eyes, recognizing the same thrill coursing through my blood. If my husband saw us in this capacity... I needed to make a run for it.

"No, thank you. I prefer the simplicity of champagne." I regained my senses and hurried away as if I had been burnt. Any association with this man was dangerous.

There was an intense urgency in the voice booming behind me, something to the extent of a demand that I stopped. Even without turning, I knew he was at my heels and following me through the hordes.

My heart raced as I exited the cramped courtyard, only to end in the swarming ballroom. The progression of the night packed the room tighter than earlier. I didn't dare breathe until reaching one of the indoor bars. My short frame disappeared behind the taller ones surrounding me. The bar was the most jam-packed area, and losing him in this crowd was easier.

A bartender placed a gold and white cocktail napkin in front of me. "What can I get for you, Mademoiselle?"

I was at a loss for words. The bartender's expectant face put a ticking clock on me, and I blurted without thinking, "A Dirty Martini, please."

"Coming right up." He turned to grab a shaker before I could change my mind.

What had come over me? Why had I let that man get under my skin and order his suggested drink?

Get a hold of yourself, Piya. I chastised myself, closing my eyes.

My lids flew open when an abrupt grip landed on my elbow. Heat burst inside me, dizzying my senses. The hair on my arm rose on cue, and I knew who it was without turning.

A voice thick with desire spoke against my ear. "Don't run."

The order was short, concise, and commanding. Part of me knew nothing good would come from associating with this man. Nonetheless, the draw was so intense that I could do no more than stand in place and obey.

The bartender chose the precise moment to set my drink in front of me and announce, "Dirty Martini for the Mademoiselle."

Mortification flooded me when I felt his arrogant smirk warming the side of my face. "Dirty Martini," he noted, refusing to let it slide.

There was an immense desire to arch into the body heat enveloping mine from the back and confess I had ordered the drink because of him. I caught myself, realizing my involuntary reactions. What was it about him?

"You can try to run, but it's of no use. I'll always find you."

"I didn't *try*; I ran." Hit by the same recklessness as the first time I laid eyes on him, I found myself engaging to differentiate success versus mere attempt.

"Why?"

I tried to step away, hardly recognizing my voice as I stammered, "I—I...." But what reason could I give him?

His grip on my elbow tightened, refusing to let me run again. His other hand was on the bar counter, trapping me in place. Unlike the courtyard, there were more people indoors, so a presence like his had somehow gone unnoticed. The guests weren't paying close attention, and it was difficult to single out a familiar face in this crowd. It meant no one would think of rescuing me, and I was at his mercy.

"Piya. We have been looking for you." Jordan's jarring voice broke whatever spell he had cast on me. I jumped, snatching my arm back and finally glancing at the man to my right. His hungry eyes didn't bother hiding their fury from my sudden jolt. Unwavering and unblinking, he grew more intense by the second, nearly buckling my knees.

Jordan's steps faltered upon noticing my current company. "Mr. Trimalchio," she said excitably, a broad smile spreading over her mouth.

His expression closed. "Jordan," he greeted politely, though I caught the whiff of irritation in his voice. "I see you brought a friend."

"Uh, y-yes. This is my friend, Piya Ambani," Jordan gestured at me.

"Hello," I managed to croak.

"How do you do, Piya?" the immensely controlled voice asked.

Unexpectedly, a large hand grabbed my smaller one for an unwelcome handshake. The fireworks it set off made me want to crawl out of my skin. His thumb made circles on the back of my hand, eliciting an unfamiliar sound. I abruptly retracted my hand.

My rude action nearly dropped Jordan's jaw to the floor. The man remained unflustered by my demeanor. With a guarded pose, he mused, "I seem to have offended your friend."

"Piya," Jordan spoke with a bite in her tone, scolding me to play nice and be on my best behavior. "This is *the* Axel Trimalchio," she spoke with intention and raised her eyebrows pointedly. "I'm sure you've heard of him."

Who hasn't?

The world-famous Axel Trimalchio—a celebrity DJ and a powerhouse in the music industry. Even EDM non-enthusiasts had an inkling of "DJ Axel" because he was well-rounded. He frequently dominated charts for House Music and was featured alongside the likes of Tiesto, Calvin Harris, and Afrojack, to name a few. He also worked with other popular artists to produce mainstream music, immersing himself in every pop culture genre. Though a celebrity DJ, Axel wasn't known for flaunting in the limelight and was notoriously private. There were barely any photos of him online other than the ones taken by fans at shows and music festivals, and most details about his personal life were on a need-to-know basis.

However, you didn't have to be acquainted with his looks to have heard the name in passing. That's why everyone outside was staring at him. Surely, everyone inside would do the same if this place wasn't crawling. He wouldn't remain concealed for long, though. Jordan hardly gave anyone the time of day, and even she wasn't immune to his charms, batting her lashes and patting his arm occasionally.

"Who hasn't heard of him?" I asked with a dejected sigh.

Jordan nodded approvingly, casting Axel a sideway yearning glance.

"H-how do you two know each other?" I asked no one in particular.

"Mr. Trimalchio has been exploring his options with my firm. How—" She looked between us. It was clear we were deep in conversation when Jordan interrupted us, and though she was dying to ask how we knew one another, she changed directions. "How come you don't have a drink, Mr. Trimalchio?" she asked playfully.

Axel lifted a shoulder at the same time I revealed, "W-we met while waiting in line at the bar, but Mr. Trimalchio never had the opportunity to order." Though Jordan didn't vocalize the question, something told me an explanation was needed. No idea why it felt like I had done something criminal when absolutely nothing had happened.

Jordan's brows furrowed while Axel cocked his head, burning a hole in my face. Luckily, Jordan didn't read into it. "Oh, okay. Let me get you a drink then," she offered, scooting closer to the bar. All the while, Jordan carried the conversation for the group. "So, keep this on the DL, but Mr. Trimalchio is our secret host for the evening and the owner of this house. He's just too modest for acknowledgment."

Why wasn't I surprised? "You have a beautiful home, Mr. Trimalchio," I offered, mimicking his unruffled pose.

Axel didn't respond. This luxurious home wasn't erected as means of fishing compliments.

"What would you like to drink?" Jordan asked Axel.

"Whatever you're having," Axel responded dismissively, eyes glued to me. The leering was a dead giveaway, and I silently reprimanded him to take it down a notch. If Jordan weren't preoccupied with ordering drinks, the intensity would've set off alarm bells by now.

"Excuse me, excuse me." She finally caught the busy bartender's attention to put in a drink order. As he walked toward her, Jordan looked at us over her shoulders and spoke louder since she was nearly out of earshot. "Before I forget, I ran into Jay coming out of the bathroom. He was looking for you and recruited my help."

The temperature dropped by several degrees. "Jay?" Axel echoed.

"Piya's husband," Jordan replied absentmindedly without turning our way, distracted by whatever the bartender said to her.

Only a nanosecond passed as Axel's eyes trailed my left hand, landing on my wedding ring. I could no longer see those dark liquid pools but knew nothing good was written there. The air vibrated with meaning, and something ominous threatened to break loose.

"You're married," he accused, voice so low and dangerous

that it made me want to disappear. The hint of malevolence didn't indicate an observation but rather a threat over my marital status.

Something else ran deeper, though. An unspoken plea for it to be untrue. I doubted a man like him yearned for anything in life. Looking around this brick-and-mortar, it was clear he had everything. Fleeting as it might've been, I'd held the undivided attention of the man with everything, and now it was over.

I was married.

I set my Dirty Martini on the bar counter, stepping back to distance myself. "Yes. Yes, I am, and I better go find my husband. Enjoy the rest of your evening."

I never heard his response because I was faster about my escape this time. I sprinted across the ballroom and ran right into a brick-like body.

"Piya, watch out." Jay steadied me by grabbing my shoulders.

"Sorry. I wasn't paying attention. I-I was just coming to find you." Without looking back, I knew Axel's vigilant eyes had located me. The control it took to keep my cool should've been noteworthy.

"Are you okay?"

Slanting my head, I skimmed the crowd over my shoulders until fixing on Axel. *Shit.* He had started toward us. "I-I just have a terrible headache. Can we go home?" I spoke with urgency.

Jay followed my gaze and spotted Axel's larger-than-life body moving toward us. "Someone you know?"

"No," I replied hastily. My eyes were downcast, unable to withstand what Jay might see if he were to look closely.

My deflections didn't deter Jay. "He is coming over and looking right at you."

"He probably thinks I'm someone else. Please, Jay. Can we go home now? This migraine is killing me." I grabbed Jay's hand and allowed my eyes to dance back to the superstar making his way across the room. Axel froze in place the moment I entwined our fingers. His eyes focused solely on our adjoined hands, his jaw locked and muscles clenched as he ground his teeth.

I had never seen such wrath on a person's face. Something told me that if he reached us, he'd drag me out of here despite a roomful of people or my husband standing next to me. I decided to fast-track our exit, rushing out and forcing a silent Jay to match pace.

"Are you sure you've never met that man before?" My intuitive husband asked one last time.

"Positive," I confirmed, hoping Jay wouldn't see through the lie.

The truth was that I had met that man once before.

CHAPTER
TWO

Past - Milan's Wedding
September 20th, 2008

Piya

"FOR FUCK'S SAKE, PIYA. WHAT DID MOM TELL YOU?"
Milan was displeased by my presence. What else was new?

I held up my palms in surrender. "I just want to congratulate my brother on his wedding. Is that a crime?"

We were celebrating Milan's wedding at a beachside property in Long Island. The beautiful wedding venue, Chateau at the Hempstead, stood proudly on a cliff, a regal presence overlooking a private beach.

Close family and the bridal party were staying at a nearby mansion, and Milan asked me to stay put until the wedding. Lounging by the beach was dreadfully boring, and I ended up sneaking onto the grounds earlier than anticipated.

There was also one more reason. Jay Ambani.

Mom was worried about any idiotic stunts I might pull on Milan's special weekend. She coddled my brother and warned me against jeopardizing her favorite child's mood. However, she also instructed me to get better acquainted with Jay Ambani this weekend, rumored to be day drinking with my brother. The Ambani clan was practically royalty in our circle, and Mom was privy to Jay Ambani—Ari and Maya Ambani's only son— wanting the whole nine yards, wife, kids, white picket fence.

After informing me that I didn't have a shot with Jay— personality-wise—Mom had begrudgingly added, "But you're young and pretty. Maybe that's all he is looking for in a wife."

It wasn't the first time my mother tried setting me up with an eligible bachelor. However, it was the first time I gave in.

My track record with men was far from clean. My crappy list of ex-boyfriends included boys deep in the nightclub scene, those with loose morals, and all-around douchebag losers who treated me like dirt. After my latest ex-boyfriend, my will to fight my mother's attempts at set-ups waned. The bastard stole my wallet. Even I had to admit that I had terrible taste in men. I had been dating since I was thirteen, and the quality of my taste had only declined in the last eight years.

When Mom suggested meeting men with the intent to marry, I couldn't refute the logic. I was twenty-one and wasn't looking to get married right away. However, I wanted to date someone who saw a future with me.

Mom directed me to Jay Ambani, who was irrefutably out of my league. He might as well be playing "Bachelor," with the women in our community as contestants in this twisted game. Rich, hot as hell, polite, mature, educated... yeah, women circled him like hounds. The competition was stiff, and since I was labeled a troublemaker, I was at the bottom of the food chain. Nonetheless, I wanted to throw my hat in the ring. Perhaps if I dated a man like Jay, I could finally become a straight shooter and stay out of trouble.

Alas, Jay Ambani only thought of me as his friend's baby sister.

Mom was twenty-three when Milan was born, a planned pregnancy. She was shocked to find herself pregnant a second time at thirty-seven, this time with me, an accidental pregnancy. My brother mercilessly teased me about it while growing up. Milan was fifteen years older than me, and Jay was two years older than Milan. While I thought the seventeen-year age gap was what the doctor prescribed, it made Jay see me as a petulant child. Other than gently disciplining me for my rowdy behavior, Jay had never shown romantic interest. Not that I'd let it deter my efforts. After my latest... um... blunder, I was determined to change my taste in men.

Mom's instruction to not spoil my brother's mood while simultaneously vying for Jay's attention was too much of a contradiction. In any case, Mom was convinced I'd wreak havoc, and I didn't want to disappoint her. So, I snuck into the

venue grounds, hoping to run into Jay to further our...
acquaintance.

Except Jay hadn't arrived yet. My brother and a few of his
buddies were playing cornhole outside the groom's cottage next
to the main building. They were drinking beer, partaking in
"manly" things, and slapping each other on the back. Focused on
day drinking and getting high, they appeared surly by my unexpected presence. I wasn't welcome here and considered quitting
my ambitious plans when the axis of my world tilted. Literally.

"Watch out!" Nick, Milan's best man, suspended his fabric
bean bag in the air as he shouted from behind the angled cornhole
board.

Forest leaves and twigs crunched under my tennis shoes
before my foot landed on an uneven tree bark. Unbalanced, my
body tipped to the right.

"Whoa!" I shrieked, arms flailing to grab something that'd
restore my stability. I was the clumsiest human on earth.

My gaze drifted sideways, legs shaking from the effort to
steady myself from the awkward angle. Rain had turned the
uneven grounds muddy and slippery, so there wasn't much
purchase. Unable to regain my balance, I landed on my ass.

"Shit!" Joe, another one of Milan's groomsmen, outstretched
his arms in a seeming effort to grab me, though he was much too
late.

"Piya!" Milan exclaimed, coming over.

A stifled sob caught in my throat at the sight of blood. Sharp
rocks and twigs dug into the exposed skin on my legs and elbows,
resulting in endless minor cuts and scrapes. My brother and his

friends helped me stand and examine the injuries. Luckily, they were mostly superficial and could be easily taken care of with the help of anti-bacterial soap and bandages. It could've been a lot worse.

The nasty fall and inspection of injuries lasted approximately sixty seconds. Despite the short-lived commotion, my attention was suddenly laser focused.

I felt his eyes on me before noticing his shadow. It fell onto the ground ominously with the afternoon sun shining bright. Only one glance at the shadow told me something monumental was about to happen; I just didn't know what. An oddest out-of-body experience awoke something inside that I never knew had been sleeping. It forced my eyes to travel from the ground to the owner of the shadow.

Regardless of the day's heat and elegant setting, the figure wore jeans and combat boots. Although his clothes were all wrong for the chic atmosphere, the outfit looked right on his body. He was physically taller and more built than the guys out here. Veins stood to attention around his arms, and even the modest clothes didn't hide his raw masculinity, which he carried with an air of effortless confidence. With trepidation, I let my eyes travel north, moving languidly as if to savor each minute.

The sun behind him created a corona around his head. At first, I couldn't make out the face. He went in and out of focus as he strolled toward us while still maintaining distance. The sun bounced with his leisurely pace, nearly blinding me at times depending on his newest position. My first proper glance at the stranger happened during this dream-like sequence. A chill ran down my spine as our gazes finally met. Dark, unforgiving eyes stared back, dead set against giving away their secrets. Dark was an understatement. His eyes were pitch black. A vision imprinted in my mind—as if asserting its right to remain there for the rest of my life—burning into my memory.

My eyes squinted to make out the rest of his face, revealing a strong set jaw and plentiful lips pressed in unreadable lines. He regarded me—more like disregarded me—with unapologetic indifference. His unhurried movements made me impatient for something more, and I stepped forward absentmindedly to study a flicker of something I had noticed earlier.

This man was the only person unruffled by my fall and seemingly unaffected by the bloody outcome.

People's emotions shone through their eyes during pivotal moments, while his remained unconcerned. They perused me from top to bottom, assessing if I was worth the concern displayed by the group. Something told me that no matter the grandiosity of the outcome—whether I survived the fall without a hitch or I was covered in blood—it would've had no impact on him. There was an absence of... everything inside him.

Unease crept up my spine. Call it intuition, but his uninterested eyes had me deciding something on the spot, something I never thought of another person so instinctively: I was staring into the eyes of someone without a soul.

I was unsure what made me draw the conclusion, only that it was true.

Dry air frizzled the hair covering my eyes, forcing me to run my fingers to tame them so I could continue watching him with trepidation. My hands were clammy, and I rubbed them against my knee-length plaid skirt. Only when my brother spoke did I realize I hadn't taken a breath and let out a ragged exhale.

"Are you okay?"

"Who is he?" I asked without answering, nodding at the man who was clearly Satan's offspring. Cold eyes watched me remorselessly. He wasn't part of the group, a dead giveaway in the way he maintained distance.

Milan shot him a glance. "Who cares?" he snapped. "What the hell are you doing here? Didn't Mom tell you not to piss me off today?"

"Is he with your group?" I interrogated, disregarding my brother's inquiries. I had met all my brother's friends before.

"No," Milan said, thrumming with impatience. "He is probably the venue's audio or lighting tech."

Milan's sharp tone made me tear my eyes away from the stranger. "The venue has its own audio tech?"

"Piya, focus!" Milan chided, exasperated. "What the hell are you doing here?"

"Um—" Disobedient eyes returned to the stranger, except he had retreated inside the large truck in the parking lot. My brother was right. The demon lover was either the audio or lighting tech. A ramp was propped up as he unloaded items from the back of the truck.

I had a feeling the mystery man's sudden interest in work was unwarranted. He seemed far more engaged when there was a threat of me dying and was utterly bored by the turn of events. I watched him disappear into the truck and wondered if he also used it to store the chopped-up body parts of his victims.

Nick and Joe exchanged a look and snickered. Apparently, I was transparent.

"Go back to the house," Milan said icily, realizing his friends' insinuations. My horrible taste in men pissed my brother off beyond measure. "And I better not see you again until the wedding."

I opened my mouth but snapped it shut when the sound of a car approaching broke through the otherwise tranquil environment. Jay's Beamer came down the winded driveway and onto the parking lot. He pulled into the spot next to the oversized truck. The heathen exited the truck simultaneously, carrying a large box. Tattoos peeked out of his V-neck shirt, and his bad-ass energy vibrated with alpha male quality. He resembled every man who'd broken my heart, and I knew he'd shatter me if I let him. My brother and his friends knew it, too. That was why they were laughing—poor, predictable Piya with her terrible taste in men.

Like a prayer answered, Jay opened his car door with ease, a blaring contradiction to the man beside him. There was an aura about Jay, comforting and soothing with quiet confidence. Well-dressed in a custom suit and a crisp white shirt without a hair out of place, he molded into the role of a tycoon. He was domineering in a different way.

Jay buttoned his suit jacket and slanted his head as if searching for something. He stopped upon landing on our four-some. I knew it wasn't my imagination or wishful thinking when his gaze zeroed in on me, his intentions crystal clear.

The heathen with tattoos watched under hooded eyes as Jay walked toward me.

Screw.

Him.

Jay would've never thought it was amusing if I fell.

I smiled big as Jay approached me, making me feel like the luckiest girl on the planet. I gave my back to the Devil worshipper, finally making the right choice in men.

THREE

Present

~

Piya

"ARE YOU SURE YOU'RE OKAY?" JAY ASKED, UNLOCKING the door to our new home in Long Island.

I wasn't okay because running into Axel Trimalchio was unprecedented. Almost fourteen years later and I could still feel it when his gaze crawled over me. It was impossible not to when it lit my skin on fire.

However, I had a bigger problem to squash.

Jordan caught up to us by the time valet had pulled up our car earlier tonight. She casually mentioned my run-in with Axel, our host for the evening. I quickly followed it up with lame excuses. *Due to the onset of a migraine, it slipped my mind to mention running into the host.*

The way Jay stiffened next to me told me he didn't buy it. After all, why wouldn't I have mentioned meeting the mysterious celebrity when it had been the topic of conversation all night long?

I watched Jay, waiting for the other shoe to drop. No reaction. The ride home from the party was painfully quiet. The noiselessness in the car was only interjected by his polite inquiries about my migraine.

Jay held the door open to our home, and I walked inside monotonously. This new residence inside a gated community of Long Island was a better choice than Jay's condo in the city. It was family-friendly and less flashy than our home in Chicago. Our new home had six bedrooms, remodeled kitchen with granite countertops, a spacious living room with high ceilings, and a wood fireplace.

Although we lived in an elegant home, the atmosphere was bleak compared to our earlier rendezvous. The lack of music and champagne made the void in my heart more apparent. Even so, I'd never been happier to be home. If only Jay would join the bandwagon.

"You have barely spoken a word since we left the party," Jay said gruffly. "Do you still have a migraine?"

"No, the headache's gone."

"Just within that five-minute drive?" Jay never missed a thing.

"Are we discussing the logistics of a migraine?" I closed my eyes, taking my heels off. The newly installed heated floors were godsent on my sore feet.

"You looked like you saw a ghost tonight," he mentioned carefully. "You were shaking when I found you, and I don't think it had anything to do with a *migraine*."

"Jay, please," I cut him off sharply, my pitch startling him. Jay preferred civilized arguments, and I'd maintained mild mannerisms throughout the extent of our marriage. Considering Jay's demeanor, I didn't lead with my naturally confrontational temperament. I took a deep breath. "I'm sorry. I do still have a slight headache, but not as bad as before. I just want to take a shower and go to sleep."

"Okay," he tentatively conceded, though his eyes tracked me.

Ignoring the prodding look, I walked into the ensuite bathroom. Once inside, I hooked my hand back to unzip the dress, peeling it off, and letting it pool around my legs. While turning on the shower, I did the same with my bra and underwear.

As the hot water fogged the bathroom, I gazed intently at my elbow where Axel had gripped me. Unable to withstand the sight, I turned off the lights in the bathroom, instead lighting one of the many candles I kept purchasing to add a romantic ambiance. The water was scalding by the time I stepped inside the shower. I didn't mind it and instinctively leaned into it. If anything, I did further damage by scrubbing my skin vigorously with a loofah until my elbow turned red. I wanted to get his touch off me.

"What did that loofah do to you?"

I turned to find a naked Jay stepping into the shower with

me. "You are letting the steam out." I nodded at the shower door he held open. Swiftly, he closed the door behind him.

I couldn't help giving Jay's body a once over. He was tall with a runner's body; his thighs were contoured, along with his biceps. Men and women alike chased after him, yet he was humble, unaware of his physical beauty along with the immense intelligence he possessed. The traits only intensified his attractiveness.

However, it was apparent that our sex life had dwindled. When we first married, he couldn't keep his hands off me. Now I wondered if he even found me attractive. It sucked. There were walls between us, and I wasn't the one to put them there. I had no clue why things had shifted between us. Jay noticed the distance between us but was too preoccupied with work. This was the first time he had stepped into a shower with me in months, igniting a spark of hope.

I circled my arms around his middle as he did the same. "You okay?"

"I am now." I closed my eyes in relief, taking in his familiar scent. Dior Sauvage. I loved the scent and bought him a bottle every six months. A newly purchased bottle was waiting for Jay on my vanity. It warmed my heart that despite his extensive cologne collection, Jay wore the same one to appease me. He was a good husband.

Jay placed a soft kiss on top of my head. The tender affection suffocated me with guilt. Feelings of betrayal bubbled as the memory of Axel watching me from the second floor flashed through my mind. I couldn't chase the image out.

"If you want to talk about—"

I grunted with frustration, rising on my tippy-toes so fast that Jay withdrew his hands around my waist. Without giving him a chance to speak, I kissed him, silently imploring him to give in. My soft lips meshed with his firmer ones, my tongue lapping against his with desperation.

"Piya?" The question came out muffled against my mouth.

Jay used to be the aggressor in the bedroom. I loved that about him until he stopped, and somehow the tables had turned on me. He had started rebuffing my advances, whereas I craved his attention.

Tonight, I needed to forget everything. My mind was mush, and I needed my husband to solidify it.

"Please, Jay," I begged. I grabbed his shoulders. My lips moved along his wildly, fingers trailing his flat stomach, drawing circles as I reached my destination. With my eyes fixed on his, I broke the kiss to kneel before him. The water beat down my back, adding comfort to the setting. I placed two hands on his thighs and was shocked when he stepped back.

"Jay," I murmured, unable to hide the hurt in my eyes. What man rejected a blowjob?

One with a side piece, a filthy voice answered tauntingly.

"Piya... I-I got a call before hopping in the shower. I have to return to Chicago tonight. If we... you'll just be upset afterward when I leave."

"No," I whispered my protest. He was supposed to leave tomorrow evening. "Don't go, please."

"I have to."

Jay couldn't leave, not tonight. He knew tomorrow was an important day.

Oh god.

That was why he stepped into the shower. A consolation for his needy wife, except he still wouldn't fuck me.

"You can't leave tonight," I begged. "Tomorrow is crucial."

The reason we had to move back was because of our daughter, Poppy. She was recently accepted into a prestigious boarding school in Long Island, though some terms were pending. Her full admission would only be approved upon completing one successful session of summer school packed with a rigorous curriculum. Hence, we moved to New York to be closer to her. Though she'd live on campus for the summer and the subsequent school year, I wanted to live in the same city to visit her often.

We had already moved Poppy into her dorm, but tomorrow was the first official day of boarding school. She had gotten into some trouble in the past, and I had been feeling vulnerable about our daughter's obscure future. I had been turning to Jay all night for support while he had been brushing me off.

"I know. I'm sorry."

"You promised Poppy you'd be there."

"I'll call her in the morning to explain," he softly countered.

This time, my voice went up an octave. "It's our daughter's first day of school—"

One stern glance from him shut me up. Jay didn't care for high pitches or a difficult wife. It was part of the condition when we married. No drama. No complications. No dragging the Ambani name through the mud. That was the deal I had agreed to abide by. However, the rules had turned suffocating with the decline of our marriage.

"I'd stay if I could," he said sternly. "I have to pack."

Why bother? He hadn't even *unpacked* from earlier. However, I didn't say it and nodded instead.

Without another word, Jay peeled open the shower door and wrapped a towel around himself. He exited the bathroom, leaving me on my knees with the cold water beating down my back and wondering where it had all gone wrong.

CHAPTER
FOUR

Past - Milan's Wedding

~

Piya

"SHE DID THIS ON PURPOSE," MILAN SEETHED, FACE twisting in anger.

"It's okay, Beta. Don't let her spoil your day," Mom consoled, simultaneously looking down her nose at me.

Papa mumbled something, refusing to outright get in the middle.

After Jay's arrival, my day started to look up. He helped me clean up, then invited me to play a game of cornhole. When Milan protested, Jay easily dissuaded my difficult brother. My past relationships had left me jaded, and after being discarded so many times, I'd settle for a nice man like him who stood up for me. Jay was thirty-eight and only looking to date women he saw a future with. I didn't know if he saw it with a twenty-one-year-old, but I had an inkling he might be interested. Between laughter and easy conversations, the time spent with Jay was alluring. So much so it made me consider the list I had initiated after Dadi, my grandmother, passed away.

Although I was the black sheep of the family, Dadi always saw the best in me. I thought I had successfully hidden my debauchery, but her cunning eyes saw through the bullshit and badly wanted me to move on from the douchebags I dated. She was from a different generation and had an arranged marriage at twenty-one. Over time, she fell in love with my grandfather. They built trust, respect, a life. She wanted the same for me. Stability. Love. A man deserving of me. Unfortunately, I was an adrenaline junkie and engaged in shameless behavior that Dadi wouldn't be proud of.

The recent passing of my dear old Dadi, along with my ex-boyfriend stealing from me, changed everything. My biggest regret was that Dadi never saw me outgrow this awful phase. My determination to change myself strengthened upon discovering that Dadi left me with her remaining life savings. In a final letter to me, she asked me to use the money to live it up and get everything out of my system before settling down with someone worthy.

In other words, Dadi told me to go ham on a bachelorette

party for one, then grow the fuck up. As God was my witness, I'd do exactly that.

After spending the day with Jay, I wondered if it was time to throw myself the aforementioned party, then ask Jay out on a date. Milan mellowed out following Jay's arrival. Surprised by the attention I received from the reserved mogul, he took his cues from Jay and treated me like a human being. My parents also simmered down, bewildered by the interest their version of royalty had taken in me. Throughout the day, I felt optimistic about a brighter future and improving the deteriorating relationship with my family.

The hope had since dwindled. Jay was called back to the city due to a work emergency, and my family was back to hating me.

Milan and his soon-to-be wife, Dahlia, were born in America but were of South Asian descent. They incorporated our roots with an Indian ceremony. The theme was East meets West, Eastern clothes for the ceremony, and Western clothes for the reception. However, I fucked up on the order of attire. The wedding planners were seating the guests for the ceremony. The bridal party was instructed to arrive only ten minutes early to be lined up so we wouldn't run into the guests and ruin the grand reveal pre-ceremony. There wasn't enough time for me to fix the mistake.

"Just look at her, Mom," Milan spat, cutting me with a look so deadly I nearly crawled out of my skin. "She is not going to match with the rest of the bridesmaids. It'll totally screw up the pictures."

All elation from the day crumbled under Milan's narrowed

eyes. Mom's scowl was equally intimidating. Papa took off his glasses and wiped the lenses. It was a nervous tick. A man of medicine, Papa was far more interested in cutting people open and rearranging their body parts than partaking in family matters. He wanted to diffuse the situation from escalating with as minimal effort as possible.

"The instructions were so simple even a monkey could've done it." Milan hit his palm with four vertical fingers to list the order. "Bridesmaids wear sky blue Lehengas to the ceremony with rose gold Jimmy Choo heels, gold jewelry, hair up in a bun, and red lipstick. Then they change into baby blue A-line dresses for the reception with silver close-toed Louboutin heels, silver jewelry, hair down, and nude lipstick. What's so difficult to remember?"

My head hurt while Milan recounted the instructions. He was far too involved in fashion and was extremely materialistic. I had tried to keep up. While I remembered to wear Eastern clothes to the ceremony—a beautiful sky blue lehenga—I fucked up on the order of accessories and hair.

I wore silver close-toed Louboutin heels with the silver jewelry meant for the reception. A stylist was hired to do our hair and makeup. Everyone had scattered by the time I returned after spending the day with Jay. I thought we were wearing our hair down for the ceremony and had asked for my shoulder-length chocolate hair to be styled in big beachy waves—another blunder.

Milan nearly had an aneurism when he spotted me on the way to Dahlia's bridal suite to meet the rest of the bridesmaids. My parents were nearby, along with some of his groomsmen.

Milan didn't care about securing privacy for this conversation, ripping into me in front of everyone. None of his groomsmen stepped in, fearing the wrath of a stressed-out Milan. They averted their eyes and pretended this awkward family exchange wasn't happening.

Public humiliation was part of my punishment. This uncalled-for resentment stemmed from what my ex, Sean, had done to the family. The anger was justified, and so was my parents' lack of support to overturn Milan's ire.

"You could've paid a little more attention before running out of the house, Piya," Mom snapped.

I held in an eye roll. Milan was the ultimate groomzilla. The number of details that went into the wedding attire was exhausting.

Nevertheless, it was his big day.

"I'm sorry," I offered diplomatically. "I screwed up. Can we push the ceremony back by like twenty minutes? I can run to the house, change and be right back."

We were staying at the house on the other side of the grounds. It was only accessible through a narrow woven pathway and was a brisk fifteen-minute walk, ten if I made a run for it. I could grab the stuff I missed, throw my hair up, then run back. There were still five minutes to the ceremony, and surely all weddings started late.

Not Milan's wedding.

Milan hit the roof at the mere suggestion. "You want me to push my wedding back for *you?*" he thundered. "If it were up to me, you wouldn't even be in it. Dahlia insisted on it, and only because I didn't want to stress her out by telling her your *boyfriend* robbed us."

I flushed, looking down. Papa coughed uncomfortably. The topic of boyfriends was something I swept under the rug in front of Papa while Mom and Milan were privy to my dating life. There was no sugarcoating this matter, however. The bastard, Sean, hadn't only stolen from me but robbed my family as well. Papa decided to look the other way. Mom and Milan hadn't gotten over it, understandably so.

"Just go inside and sit with the rest of the guests," Milan hissed. "You don't need to be a part of the wedding party if you can't be bothered with simple instructions."

My chest throbbed with pain. I was ecstatic when Dahlia asked me to be a bridesmaid. I didn't have any sisters, nor had I been a bridesmaid before. Despite our differences, Milan was my only brother. How could he not want me to be a part of his wedding or the photos that would last forever? This was beyond hurtful.

"Come on, Bhaiya," I started, finding it impossible to believe my only brother wouldn't want me walking in with the wedding party, and prefer to have me seated with the rest of the guests. Milan was high maintenance, but this was beyond trivial. "No one's going to pay attention to my shoes or hair or accessories. Everyone will be looking at the bride and groom."

"Not if you stick out like a sore thumb." Milan stepped forward and raised an index finger pointedly. "The pictures will look ridiculous if you walk in looking completely different than everyone else. There is no point in ruining the coordination. Go find a seat. Or better yet, you're disinvited. Don't attend my wedding at all."

The blood drained from my face, eyes burning with unshed tears.

"This is unbelievable," he said to Mom. "She ruins everything. Do you know how humiliating this is for me?"

I choked. Dahlia had fifteen freaking bridesmaids. If Milan's only sister were left out of a wedding party so large, it'd be blatantly obvious it was a snub. And he thought this was humiliating for *him?* Not to mention, Milan could easily rectify this "humiliating" instance by letting me be a part of his day.

"I'm sorry—"

Mom held up a hand to shut me up. "You have said sorry so much in your lifetime that the word has lost its meaning. An apology means nothing unless you don't repeat the mistake. You have done the same things year after year, expecting different results, and you want us to believe you're sorry? Grow up, Piya," Mom said so sharply that I flinched.

While I looked like a younger version of Zaina Mittal, Mom and I were as different as they came. She was an accomplished CPA and owned an accounting firm, whereas I started writing jingles for racy ads during my senior year of college, a career choice Mom detested. Mom was driven and cutthroat. I was laid back and easygoing. She came from old money, just like Papa, and loved that they were a power couple. Other than to appease my family, I could care less about an ambitious partner. Mom expected more from me and could never accept the poor imitation I was of her.

"Even after everything you put us through, I asked very little of you today. To not ruin your brother's mood and look at what you've done." Unlike Milan, Mom was a first-generation immigrant and had an Indian twang to her accent. It didn't make her voice less menacing than my brother's. "You have no idea how lucky you are and take everything for granted. The privilege, the life we have given you, you squander it away on useless boys. If you had paid as much attention to what your brother wanted today, this wouldn't have happened. Learn to face the consequences of your actions, Piya. Either wait with the rest of the guests or return to the house. I don't want to hear another word out of you for the rest of the day."

The brutal words were shards of ice slicing my heart open. I shrunk back. Mom was right in her assessment. I did the same things over and over, expecting different results. However, today wasn't about what Mom thought of me. Weddings were a once-in-a-lifetime event. There had to be a part of Milan that wanted his only sister to be a part of it. "Bhaiya, I'm so sorry for not paying attention—"

"Enough, Piya," Mom dropped her voice as more groomsmen and bridesmaids started congregating around the elegant hallway. She turned to Papa. "Talk to your daughter." She dismissed me entirely, urging Milan to focus on his celebrations instead of me.

Papa, who had been quiet during this exchange and generally hated confrontations, gave me pleading eyes. "Just try to understand, Beta," he cooed. "There isn't enough time to go back and change."

"But Papa, I just—"

"It's Milan's wedding, Piya," Papa spoke more sternly because we were running out of time. "It's his choice if he wants you to be a part of it."

I closed my mouth, nodding. The planners had returned to round up the wedding party for the processional. Making a scene would only cause more distress. This discussion was over; I wasn't wanted.

Milan's jaw ticked as he mouthed, *Go.*

A sharp bite of devastation eviscerated the warm feelings Jay had incited throughout the day, and I left without a backward glance.

After the ceremony fiasco, I dashed home to change into the reception wear. Instead of dwelling in self-pity, I was adamant about not causing more issues. It took me thirty minutes to make myself presentable. I recounted Milan's list for the reception attire down to the shoes. Matte nude lipstick, smokey eyes, and high contours completed the look, and I was pleased with the finished product. It was only when I left the house that I stumbled in the dark and fell face down onto the muddy terrain.

Damn my clumsiness. I lacked the required patience for the grace exercised by the likes of Zaina Mittal.

This time, I didn't bother asking Milan if I could be part of the post-ceremony photos or walk in with the wedding party for the reception. There wasn't enough time to shower, change, and attend the dinner portion of the reception. The excitement over my only brother getting married had long passed from the day's rejections and this final disappointment. At this point, I simply wanted to stay out of the way.

I texted my best friend, Jordan, to tell her what happened and let her break the news to my family. Both of our families were from Sands Point, Long Island, servicing the richest of the rich. Amit Mittal, my papa, was a renowned plastic surgeon who manipulated and rearranged body parts the rich deemed unacceptable. Jordan's dad was a publicist who handled press releases and maintained the public image of New York celebrities. His PR firm dealt with scandals ranging from the latest celebrity sex tape leak to married stars caught with their pants around their ankles.

When Jordan's family moved next door, it was "best friends at first sight" for our fathers and us. Her family received automatic invitations to our vacations, mainly because Jordan was less of a rebel, and Mom hoped she'd be a good influence on me. Both Milan and Mom adored Jordan for that reason.

Jordan knew what had gone down at the ceremony and suggested steering clear of my brother until he cooled down. I agreed heavy-heartedly, returning home to change into a simple blue dress instead.

Re-entering the pretentious venue took all the willpower I possessed. Oversized centerpieces and ivory linens with baby blue napkins beautifully decorated the ballroom. Blue delphiniums and anemones peeked through large white hydrangea arrangements. White and blue uplights acted as pin spotters for every column in the room, giving it a magical glow.

Jordan nipped at my heels and followed me to the bar, refusing to let me stray while my torrent of emotions ran rampant. As I waited for the bartender, I took stock of the guests in attendance. My cousins were at the photo booth station. My parents were making their rounds with the *Aunties*, aka the gossip mongers of our community. And Milan was... shit... Milan was marching straight toward me. I knew he was still furious for fucking up both the day and evening outfits. Luckily, there was a buffer.

"Jordan! Piya!" Dahlia snapped me out of my stupor, embracing me tightly. "Are you guys having fun?"

"Of course," we replied in unison as I hugged back my new sister-in-law.

I quickly disengaged upon noticing my brother's rigid stance next to Dahlia. A scowl was painted on his face though I had hoped the open bar would've subdued it. "Drinks?" I asked. "Champagne for the newlyweds, please," I turned to the bartender without waiting for their response.

"You look so beautiful, Piya."

"I should be telling you that." I beamed at Dahlia. The newest addition to my family was the only one to treat me as such. Dahlia was a breath of fresh air. In an ivory mermaid wedding dress, she was a sight to behold. The makeup artist had done wonders, perfecting the minor blemishes of her deep golden skin. Her long dark hair was styled in a half-up with bejeweled hair accessories.

"How about you guys? Are you having fun?"

Milan made a gruff noise. "Considering everything that

happened today, we are making the best of it."

I suppressed an eye roll. Milan acted like things only happened to him. Jordan coughed uncomfortably, hating this friction more than Papa. Dahlia also knew of the drama to unfold earlier. Instead of further dwelling on my humiliation, she breezed past it. "Stop being a grouch." She playfully smacked Milan's stomach. "He is having the time of his life."

I smiled, appreciative of the reprieve.

Despite his uptight nature, Milan also gave Dahlia a rare smile. My brother was a prick, but I couldn't deny that he was smitten by his new wife. I stared between them and knew I was in the presence of true love. I wanted that so badly for myself. If my brother, the biggest elitist to live, could snag a ray of sunshine like Dahlia, there had to be hope for me, right?

I passed the champagne flutes to the blushing newlyweds and another to Jordan.

"Glad to see you can pass a drink without ruining another outfit."

I froze at my brother's backhanded compliment.

"Are you guys ready to tear up the dance floor?" Jordan quickly interjected to diffuse the situation, aware of my brother's glower.

"You know it," Dahlia chimed in, following Jordan's cue.

Jordan brightened, brushing past the awkwardness. "The music's been really good tonight."

I agreed with her assessment internally, though I was generally a music snob. The songs throughout cocktail hour and reception had been appropriately selected, oldies and newer hits, with some house music mixed in. Someone had curated this list with the utmost care.

"What company did you guys hire?" Jordan asked.

"We didn't." Dahlia shrugged. "The DJ was included with the venue's sound package. They have their own, so it was a nice perk."

Though we chitchatted in a group, it was mostly Jordan and Dahlia driving the conversation with neutral topics. Milan fumed, and I kept my head down to deflect his anger. We were all staying the night at the house, and the afterparty was supposed to be held there. I knew Milan's mood would only worsen upon seeing me at the afterparty. Hell was waiting to be unleashed.

Instead of chiming in, I hung back until I had entirely secluded myself off to one corner. Other people joined the conversation, naturally flocking to the bride and groom. With the crowd surrounding them, Jordan didn't notice me slinking away. She'd try to babysit me if she had, and I didn't want to ruin her night. She was also friends with Milan and deserved to take part in the celebrations. After all, she wore the right outfit and had done nothing to piss him off.

The dance floor opened, and I watched everyone bop to the music from a distance. Once more, I was pleasantly surprised by the DJ's picks. An unfamiliar song came on, quickly becoming my favorite of the night. There was a trace hint of recognition, and I strained my ear. I almost spat out my champagne upon realizing it was "Sweet Child O Mine" by Guns N' Roses. House mix and beat drops had turned the song into a virtually unrecognizable version. This was a sing-along type of song, but he had turned it into a danceable one. This DJ was exceptionally talented. If possible, more talented than some of the big names I'd heard and way too good for this gig.

I swayed to the music—they were all remixed versions of various Guns N' Roses songs—when I suddenly had the acute feeling of being watched. The feeling was so intense that it became unshakeable. Whipping my head from left to right, I searched for the source. The crowd on the dance floor parted like the Red Sea, revealing another lone figure across the ballroom by the DJ booth. I recognized him instantly.

Heathen!

Lord behold, Satan's child was our talented DJ for the evening. Dressier shoes had replaced combat boots. He wore a midnight blue sports jacket to not stand out from the well-dressed crowd. He tapped on his laptop sporadically, though his eyes were predominantly trained on mine. I was surprised none of the guests noticed the intensity he showered me with. It seemed the roomful of the wealthy and privileged didn't pay attention if the shoes weren't designer and the clothes were off the rack. The booth further divided him from the crowd. He was a lone wolf. *Like me,* I couldn't help surmising despite my animosity toward the stranger.

I had to hand it to him. Where I was in shambles over my isolation, he stood confident and composed, skimming me over indifferently with those deeper-than-dark eyes. He was probably waiting for me to fall for his amusement. I scoffed and met his crudeness stare for stare.

Despite my loathing of my newest archnemesis, there was an

enthralling draw to him... nope. No, Piya, you absolutely cannot go down this road. The last time you did, you ended up with Sean, which was supposed to be *the last time.*

Wising up, I hit up my supplier—aka bartender—for more champagne to distract me from walking toward my next heart-break. Knowing he couldn't see me with the crowd blocking his view, I ducked. I watched him from my secret position. Slight satisfaction warmed my blood when I found him looking around, searching for me.

"Stop it." Jordan's abrupt low voice put an end to my spying.

I cleared my throat. "Stop what?"

"Stop staring at the DJ." She nodded at the man across the room.

"Do you know him?" I asked, disregarding her warning. A throng of kids ran past the DJ booth, laughing with joy. He stared them down like he wanted to punch the children. I knew this man was the Devil. So why couldn't I look away from Satan?

"No, I don't know him. But I saw him staring at you like... Fuck. Why was he staring at you like that?"

"Like what?"

Jordan shook her head. "Never mind that. Do *you* know the DJ?"

I shrugged. "Not really. I saw him around earlier, setting up."

She narrowed her eyes. "That's all?"

"Of course. What's gotten into you?" I was used to the inter-rogation from my family, not Jordan.

"H-he," she stammered tentatively. "He was staring at you so intensely, like really intense. Fuck. I have never seen a man look at a woman that way." She glanced at the DJ and admitted after a hesitant pause, "He looked at you... the way all women want to be looked at by a man." Jordan turned her attention back to me. "Are you sure you don't know him?"

I laughed, though a thrill of electricity coursed through my spine. "Nope," I attested.

My best friend wasn't stupid and probably caught the twinkle in my eyes. "Whatever you're thinking, don't," she warned. "For God's sake, Piya. You're smart; you're beautiful. You deserve everything. Why do you keep chasing men who'll never be good enough for you? Do you even remember what happened with Michael?"

I closed my eyes. This was the closest to tough love I'd received from Jordan, and it was well deserved.

Until Sean, I hadn't dated for a year, and for good reasons. Michael was my boyfriend before Sean and was equally terrible. The asshole took my car out for a joyride and crashed it. I had been carless since. My loyal best friend gave him a piece of her mind. Things got heated, and Michael threw the car keys at Jordan. The forceful toss of the keys hit Jordan square in the mouth, busting her lips open. She ended up with stitches.

I broke up with the douchebag on the spot and apologized profusely to Jordan, plus I did her laundry for months to make up for it. It was dangerous to be associated with me because of the scumbags I brought around. Although Jordan never displayed animosity over the incident, I couldn't blame her for wanting to shake reason into me.

I opened my eyes. "Yes, I remember," I murmured defeatedly.

"You promised there wouldn't be any more of these guys after Michael. Then you started dating Sean."

With tattoos, long hair, and an edge, Sean was a DJ with bad-boy vibes. I told myself he was different from the rest of my exes. He was misunderstood. An artist.

At first, Sean was nice and invited me to his place often. We had movie nights, and he'd cook for me. I knew he didn't come from money, so I picked up the tab outside the home. Soon, it became an expectation.

Meanwhile, Sean gave me just enough to keep me on the hook while keeping his heart at bay. You could say there was an addicting thrill in taming an unattainable man. Chalk it up to my mommy and daddy issues. Persuading someone into loving you when they were only mildly interested had a charming allure I couldn't shake, and Sean was just the type.

Things took a nosedive when it became clear Sean only saw me as a walking ATM. I might be indescribably attracted to a certain type, but terrible taste in men didn't mean I was a pushover. I broke things off.

In retaliation, Sean stole from my family and me.

"I thought Sean was different," I mumbled, my eyes downcast.

"He wasn't." Jordan pointed harshly at the DJ. "And neither is that guy. He looks like every boy who broke your heart. The last thing you need is to develop an infatuation for a man like him."

"Infatuation?" I repeated indignantly, my gaze flipping up. "I'm only staring him down because Satan's spawn over there smiled when I fell earlier today."

Jordan bit her lips with a failed attempt to suppress her amusement. She quickly composed herself. "Seriously, Piya. Stay away from that guy. After what happened with Michael, you swore off those kinds of boys. You totally went back on your word when you started dating Sean and look what happened. It was a total slap in the face *after* I got stitches for standing up for your ass."

Mortified, I stared at my interlaced fingers once more. This sounded like an intervention, and it dawned on me how deeply I'd hurt my loved ones.

Jordan shook her head. "Babe, I love you, but I'm not picking up the pieces again. I'll take a punch for you any day, but not a slap in the face."

I knew exactly what she meant. Jordan ended up in the hospital for having my back. It was insulting to her that instead of being scared straight after putting her in a precarious position, I repeated my patterns by believing the best in Sean. What the fuck was wrong with me?

"I'm sorry."

"The only apology you can give me is being done with these boys who don't deserve you," she reflected the same sentiment as Mom.

Mom had hoped my taste in men was a phase I'd outgrow with age. After graduating college, I also thought it was a thing of the past until I met Sean at a friend's party.

It was the summer following my graduation. I moved back to my parents and was supposed to find a "respectable" job by the end of summer. Instead, I spent it writing music for lascivious ads and gallivanting with Sean.

My parents weren't happy, especially after valuables went missing from their home. After I broke up with him, Sean stole my wallet with my ID card, five hundred dollars in cash, and various items from my parent's house. No detective work was needed to figure out the "whodunit" mystery. Knowing my parents disapproved of Sean, I only invited him over when they weren't home and had trusted the bastard with the code to our house.

To make matters worse, Milan was visiting for the weekend, and Sean stole his limited-edition Rolex. When Milan proposed to Dahlia, my brother bought her the biggest engagement ring he could find. Thoughtful Dahlia proposed to Milan in return with an "engagement watch," aka the Rolex in question. The sweetest effort was tarnished by my lackluster choice of men. Though I offered to buy Milan a new Rolex, I knew it didn't matter because the watch was a sentimental gift and thus irreplaceable. Hence, Milan's current hatred of me.

The police report and a search warrant for Sean's house also came up empty. The money and items were never recovered, and my relationship with my family was ultimately frayed. The disapproving looks from my family hadn't dispersed—admittedly, they were well-deserved—and I decided it was time to move out. The jingles paid me enough to rent an apartment, but I wanted to wait until after Milan's wedding.

I shouldn't have bothered. No one had forgiven me, nor would they any time soon. A tatted-up DJ like the one searching for me would break the camel's back. He was every parent's worst nightmare.

Jordan nodded at the man across the room. "Your parents will never speak to you again if they find out you've got the hots for another DJ. For once, I agree with them. If you bring around one more of these guys, I'm out, too, Piya." She threw her hands up. "I give up."

My track record must be worse than expected if even my overtly supportive best friend was giving me an ultimatum.

My spine straightened. "Hell would have to freeze over before I date one more man like him. I'm done after this weekend. I promise. On Monday morning, you'll meet a new Piya."

"Good." Jordan sighed in relief. "Now, can we please be done with this stupid convo and hit the dance floor? The reception's almost over."

I waved my empty flute in the air and said I needed another drink. Jordan shrugged and returned to the dance floor. Reaching behind the bar while the server was busy, I grabbed a champagne bottle. I didn't plan on following her to the dance floor. The people I loved needed space from me, and the best thing I could do tonight was to make my presence scarce. It was best if I left and got started on my promise to Jordan and Dadi. Jordan's intervention worked. This weekend was my last act before I turned a new leaf, and it was time to get started on my list.

~~Steal a bottle of liquor from a bar~~
Shotgun a beer
Crash a party

Go to a strip club
Dance on a table in front of a roomful of strangers
Watch a live sex show
Compose your raunchiest song
Go to an adult movie theater
Have a one-night stand
Splurge on an expensive and irresponsible gift for yourself

"Didn't take you for a champagne drinker," a deep voice murmured behind me.

My pen suspended from furiously scribbling on the tiny notebook. Although I hadn't heard the DJ's voice before, there was an unshakeable feeling that the voice belonged to him.

"What's wrong with champagne?" I asked without turning, setting the bottle of champagne I had been chugging next to me.

After leaving the reception, I returned to the house and changed out of my clothes. The all-night-long afterparty was to be held there, which I wouldn't be joining. My parents were right; it was Milan's weekend. Currently, just the sight of me was pissing him off. My attendance at the afterparty would further incite his anger. There was nothing I could do to rectify the situation, and it was best if I left to salvage whatever was left of his wedding weekend.

Instead, I could use the weekend for the adventure I had been planning.

I changed into a bright pink cami carefully tucked inside a pair of black leather leggings. I kept on the sparkling heels because of my personal motto; *a pop of sparkle never hurt anyone.* A mini Prada backpack completed the cute, yet slightly edgy, look. It was also perfect for carrying the notebook and some essentials.

I had been sitting on a bench outside of Chateau at the Hempstead for the last ten minutes, waiting for my cab. While I waited, I curated a list for my last hoorah under a dimly lit streetlight. The things I wanted to accomplish this weekend weren't too raunchy. Sexual fetishes held no appeal for me, nor did drugs or violence. To be honest, my biggest folly was loving the wrong type of men. This DJ just so happened to be a blaring reflection of everything I vowed to avoid.

A large frame took the seat next to me on the bench. I kept my gaze forward and only watched him out of my peripheral. "You seem too interesting for a single-pour drink." There was no sarcasm laced in his voice.

"If I'm so interesting, why did you smile when I fell?" I retorted.

"I didn't smile," his voice carried amusement.

My jaw dropped at the blatant lie. "Yes, you did," I said stubbornly, turning to face him and immediately wishing I hadn't.

From up close, he was broader than I'd expected, and I tilted my head back to inspect his pitch-black eyes. They were so deep that they resembled a dark liquid pool you could dive into and disappear. Not a glint of human emotion flickered in them. I was convinced he could watch someone die without a morsel of empathy.

The imperious gaze returned my stare with a similar intensity. His impassive nature wasn't welcoming, but I refused to blink away first.

"I didn't smile," he denied a second time. "I was watching you."

Taken aback, I scanned my memories. Did he smile, or was that a figment of my imagination? I had been so sure he was amused by my fall. Was it possible he was merely watching me from afar like I'd been watching him?

Raw magnetism of the serial killer in the making was undoubtedly blindsiding me. Or perhaps it was his aroma. His smell was messing with the rational part of my brain. What the fuck was that scent? Citrus, lavender oil, jasmine? The intoxicating scent was making me dizzy.

Pushing my notebook off my lap, I quickly stood. "May I help you with something?"

When he didn't respond, I turned to find him scanning my notebook. The carefully crafted list lay dormant under the man's watchful eyes. He raised an inquisitive eyebrow. "Bucket list?"

"Hm," I grunted noncommittally without offering further explanation. My past list of boyfriends and the reason for my new mission was too embarrassing to divulge.

Amazingly, he didn't ask, either, merely standing to his full height. He'd returned to his earlier get-up with combat boots, jeans, and a black t-shirt. I blinked after his retreating form as he disappeared inside the venue's main building. He emerged within seconds, this time with two beer cans in hand.

Shotgun a beer.

It was the second item on my list, as I had completed and scratched off the first.

Tucking a can under his armpit, he reached into his back pocket and pulled out his keys. Beer sprayed from the can as he stabbed the side of it with the sharp end of his key. He pressed a thumb on the aluminum to make the hole bigger before passing me the can. I held the can horizontally, flabbergasted over this stranger's odd mannerisms.

No one in their right mind would've started on completing another person's bucket list without consulting them or asking permission to join the fun. Then again, I had long decided this man wasn't normal.

He punctured a hole in his beer can, then glanced at me. "Place your thumb over the tab and your mouth over the hole," he instructed. "Take a deep breath, then tilt your head back and chug fast. Open the tab with your thumb after you start drinking."

The man worked for a prestigious venue and regularly encountered powerful people. He knew the potential consequences of pissing off the wrong person. Fearing the same, even the snobs and gossips from my world acted with care while interacting with an unknown. Yet, he ordered me around like we were familiar, giving zero fucks about my standing in society or how he came off.

Whereas I should be offended by his bossiness, I found it amusing.

"Cheers." I raised my can as he did the same and tilted my head back.

Bitter malt cascaded down my throat. I chugged quickly, not allowing myself to think. My esophagus wouldn't comply, unable to keep up with the rapid flow of liquid. For a second, I didn't believe I could do it and considered lowering the can. Before I could, I felt his finger gently hovering over mine to pry open the tab. It let out the air inside the can and gave my goal a second wind. I sloppily glugged down the remaining content. Beer dribbled past my chin and onto my pretty pink tank top. I didn't care. Bursts of adrenaline surged through my system as I lowered my can. His was already empty.

I couldn't have wiped the smile off my face had I tried. This was the most alive I had felt this weekend, and all we had done was shotgun a beer together. It was so basic, yet I couldn't help the exhilaration it brought me.

"Thank you. That was… fun."

Instead of acknowledging my gratitude, he grabbed the can to dispose of it and threw another unsolicited curveball my way. "Zane Trimalchio."

Even the way he introduced himself was odd. I smiled. "Nice to meet you, DJ Zane. Or should I call you DJ Axl Rose?"

His brows shot up at my reference to the lead singer in Guns N' Roses.

Unveiled curiosity marred his beautiful face. "You picked up on the Guns N' Roses songs in my mix." He sounded surprised and… impressed?

A hot flush crept up my neck. "Axl Rose's voice is a hard one to miss."

His expression was unmoved. "Yet, no one else had caught onto it until now."

I lifted a shoulder. "No one else was paying attention."

He watched me under hooded eyes as if trying to figure me out. "You don't seem the type to like Guns N' Roses."

I tilted my head to the right. "What type do I look like?"

"Vanilla," he replied without hesitation. "I assumed you'd like something more," he gestured at my bright pink shirt, "teeny bopper."

"Both things can be true," I shot back without scoffing or denying my 'vanilla-ness.' It was true that I was sheltered, another reason why I gravitated toward men who were rough around the edges. Didn't mean I couldn't appreciate the flip side of the coin. "I like everything from classical music to teeny-bopper to heavy metal. The only thing I don't like are snobs who claim rights over a particular genre of music." I raised my chin at him pointedly.

The turn in the conversation didn't deter him. "Classical music?" he inquired curiously.

"Well, not so much as listening to classical music, rather playing it, I suppose." I weighed my words. "Guess I should mention that I play the piano."

"Professionally?"

I nodded. "I went to Juilliard for it."

It was the first thing that gave him pause. "And now you're in the music industry," he didn't ask but rather observed.

"Sort of. I write jingles for ad commercials."

His brows furrowed. "How old are you?"

"Twenty-one."

"And you already graduated?"

I nodded. "A few months ago."

"Hm." He grunted.

When I found him staring at me suspiciously, I straightened. Juilliard or not, it was atypical for a twenty-one-year-old to have such a career breakthrough. Each jingle I sold paid me anywhere from two thousand to ten thousand dollars. Depending on the demand, I'd be making six figures by next year. However, I could hardly take full credit.

Despite my parents' chagrin, Jordan forced her dad to help get my foot in the door since he owned a PR and talent agency. Pair that with my lifelong private piano lessons and an expensive education from Juilliard, I had a competitive edge off the bat.

That's how society worked, right? Those with money could keep it within the family since they could prepare the next generation for success.

Despite reaping the benefits—and the path privilege had paved for my quick rise to success—I could acknowledge the flaw in the system. Composers like me worked tirelessly to create music, whereas this DJ had played multiple originals throughout the night. After listening to his music all night, I was convinced he would've surpassed me by miles if he had one-tenth of my resources.

However, without proper resources, his career might never take off. Depriving the world of this man's endless talents was a depressing thought.

He didn't seem bothered, much too intrigued by our conversation. "How do you know the bride and groom?"

I froze at the mention of my family.

When I didn't respond, he recounted, "You sat by yourself at the ceremony."

I blinked, astounded that he saw me at the ceremony since I was sitting all the way in the back.

"If I remember correctly, you arrived after everyone else at the reception." Because I was knee-deep in mud, followed by a rigorous shower. "You didn't sit at a designated table, either, and missed dinner altogether."

Was he searching for me during the reception?

"You were alone at the bar for most of the night. I didn't see you speak to a single person at that wedding." When my eyes narrowed for a dirty look, he smirked. "You wedding crashed. It was one of the things on your list."

A tranquil look fixed on my face as I suppressed the pain in my heart. A total stranger thought I had attended my brother's wedding uninvited. That's how much I was left out of the fold today. Technically, Milan had also disinvited me earlier, so I might as well have crashed his wedding. I had unconsciously accomplished one task on my list.

Self-deprecation made me march to the open notebook sitting on the bench and cross off two items under the DJ's watchful eyes.

~~Steal a bottle of liquor from a bar~~
~~Shotgun a beer~~
~~Crash a party~~

My phone buzzed, saving me from the horrid reminders of the day. I glanced down to read the text from the cab company. They were waiting for me in the parking lot.

"I've got to go. My cab's here," I informed flatly and started gathering my items, slinging my mini back over my shoulders. "Thanks for the beer."

I jumped when the DJ stepped forward, brushing against my elbow. The heat evaporating from the nearness of his body was unexpected. "Tell me your name," he demanded.

Yes, he *demanded* instead of asking like a normal person. His mannerisms were so ridiculous that I could no longer help it. I threw my head back and laughed.

"Your name," he insisted.

Did this guy ever take a hint?

I shook my head. "Goodbye, DJ Axl."

CHAPTER
FIVE

Piya

THE FIRST AND LAST TIME I MET DJ AXEL TRIMALCHIO was at my brother's wedding. Why was he suddenly back in my life? What did he want? Most importantly... Did he know?

Tightening my black satin bathrobe, I placed two trembling hands on the bathroom counter and stared at the text that had popped up two minutes ago.

"You can run, but I'll always find you."

The number might be unknown, but the context was a dead giveaway about the identity of the sender.

Upon discovering he had adopted the name I dubbed him, I tracked Axel's rise to fame, granted he added an "e" to Axl. I assumed it was for copyright reasons, though the nod to the nickname I had dubbed didn't go unnoticed.

Axel started as a local DJ and gained enough following to do bigger shows. The big break came in the form of a DJ residency in Las Vegas. Axel's work ethic was renowned between the residency and playing tirelessly at festivals and international shows.

Despite the success in his chosen profession, Axel ventured outside the music industry to build an empire unmatched by others. Using fame as collateral, he created a brand and put his name on everything. Restaurants, hotels, clubs, e-commerce, you name it.

Once in a blue moon, Axel still played at select shows if the price was right. Otherwise, the recluse superstar had outgrown shows and focused on his ever-growing kingdom.

None of it explained his presence in Long Island, however. The sleepy suburbs were no match for glamorous Manhattan, only an hour away. It was difficult to accept Axel's sudden appearance was a coincidence. A small, terrified part of me screamed, *he knows,* although I stifled the paranoia.

I could hear Jay getting dressed for his flight on the other side of the door and prayed he couldn't hear the phone alerting me of another text.

> Axel: There is no point in hiding from me, Princess.

> Piya: How did you get this number?

Axel: From Jordan.

Bullshit.

I trusted Jordan with my life. She might not have recognized Axel from the minute glance years ago, but she'd never compromise my privacy. Refusing to give him an inch, I set a formal tone.

Piya: How did you really get this number, Mr. Trimalchio?

Axel: Using a formal tone doesn't create a wall between two people.

He didn't miss much, did he?

Axel: And it was easy to find your number once I learned your name.

On impulse, I hurried to the bathroom door and locked it, before putting my phone on vibrate. With my back pressed against the door, I tried to steady my racing heart.

Perhaps he'll stop texting if I don't engage.

I stared at the screen without responding. Minutes passed. The phone in my hand lay dormant, and I sighed in relief. I was ready to turn around and unlock the bathroom door when the phone buzzed. Dry throat, winded breaths, and the heavy rise and fall of my chest weren't enough to distract me from the incoming text.

> Axel: I also learned your home address. If you keep ignoring me, I'll come over, and we can have this conversation in person.

Oh fuck.

Swiping the unlock button, my fingers flew over the keypad as I furiously typed a response. Axel knew I was off-limits. We hadn't seen each other in years. Why was he suddenly fixated on me? Hundreds of women were enamored with him at the party tonight. Why not send these nondescript texts to one of them instead of tormenting me?

> Piya: What do you want?

> Axel: Many things. World domination, a space station, a private island. But if you're asking specifically about tonight, I want you to leave Ambani.

The phone dropped from my hand and landed on the heated tiles of my bathroom floor with a loud thud.

"Piya." Jay knocked on the bathroom door on cue. "Are you all right?"

"Y-Yup," I stuttered. "Just, um, I was washing my face and accidentally dropped my phone."

A pause on the other side of the door. I had been acting strange all evening, which hadn't gone unnoticed. Nevertheless, Jay's voice was kind when he said, "Be careful."

"I will."

I bent over to pick up the phone. The case and screen

protector were good quality, and my phone survived unscathed. Before Axel could send more preposterous texts, I put a lid on it.

> Piya: Please stop whatever it is you're doing. In case you don't recall, I'm married.

> Axel: How could I forget? FYI, Ambani no longer has a place in your life.

Laughter bubbled to the surface from his ludicrous proclamation.

> Piya: Oh okay, master. Since you declared it so, I'll simply inform my husband of thirteen years that he no longer has a place in my life.

> Axel: I'm glad we agree.

> Piya: Don't text me again. I have a family now, and this is highly inappropriate.

> Axel: End it with Ambani within the hour.

Seriously, what the fuck!?

> Piya: Are you hearing yourself? What is wrong with you?

> Axel: I also want Ambani's personal items gone by the end of the night. Throw them in a box when you kick him out or trash it for all I care.

> Piya: Go to Hell, Mr. Trimalchio.

> Axel: If you don't cut the formality BS, I'll get in my car and drive over.

> Piya: I'm done with this conversation. Goodbye.

I tapped on the number to block him when an inbound text debunked my efforts.

> Axel: If you block this number, I'll text you from another phone. I have a limitless supply.

I glowered at the messages and realized Axel was texting me from an unlisted number that couldn't be traced back to him. A burner phone, most likely. He had also been meticulous about not acknowledging his name during our exchanges. This conversation couldn't be used as proof of harassment.

My screen lit up with another incoming text.

> Axel: I'm a dangerous man to piss off, Princess. Trust me, you don't want to defy me.

> Axel: End it with Ambani and erase all traces of him from your life.

> Axel: You have one hour.

The texts glared at me like evidence of my new reality. Something told me Axel wouldn't be easily dissuaded. Unlike at my brother's wedding, there was a touch of madness in how he perused me tonight. It was as if he had fixated on me. The black eyes—ringed within an even darker shade of black—shone with greed. Axel seemed entirely unhinged. The perfectly placed mask shredded for a moment, baring his true identity and revealing the monster he hid in public.

Too bad my self-preservation instincts sucked against a deranged sociopath.

> Piya: Who the hell are you to show up out of nowhere and demand I end my marriage?

> Axel: Obviously, we'll have to expedite the paperwork for divorce.

> Piya: Obviously.

At this point, it was more humorous than outrageous. The man was a lunatic.

> Axel: I'll come over in a couple of hours. We'll grab a drink and talk logistics.

> Piya: You're crazy.

> Axel: Only for you, baby.

> Piya: DO NOT CALL ME THAT.

> Axel: Careful, baby. I don't respond well to capitalized texts.

> Piya: I don't care what you respond to.

> Axel: You should. Otherwise, you'll only make things more difficult for yourself.

I closed my eyes, willing this nightmare away. They flew open when I suddenly remembered a rumor circling Axel Trimalchio a few years ago.

The type of money Axel had accumulated in only a decade was equivalent to generational wealth, and it was unlikely hard work alone got him there. There was speculation that Axel's massive wealth came from his marriage to an heiress. In the end, nothing came of the gossip. If there was a secret rich wife, he had hidden her well since many tried to uncover her identity.

> Piya: Tell me, Mr. Trimalchio. Is it true you have a secret wife, and it was her money that helped build your precious empire?

Three little dots appeared on our iMessage exchange, indicating Axel was typing. They disappeared, and I was suddenly curious about the answer.

> Piya: It is true. You ARE married.

> Axel: Separated.

As if that was any better.

> Piya: I wonder how your rich wife would feel about these texts you're sending me, asking me to leave my husband.

> Axel: Angry, I presume.

Dumbfounded, I stared at his nonchalant message. I couldn't expect to have a normal conversation with a maniac.

> Piya: I don't have time for this, Mr. Trimalchio. Goodbye.

This time, I did block his number and soothed myself with the knowledge that our trusted security guards didn't allow anyone past these gates, celebrity or otherwise. The only people who could enter were premises were those visiting someone on the property. If Axel told them he was visiting me, they'd call me first, and I'd refuse his entrance.

I deleted the texts and left my phone behind in the chance Axel texted me from another phone. I re-entered the bedroom, gaze skimming over Jay's fully packed carry-on next to the door.

"Feeling better?" he asked.

I nodded. The semi-convincing smile turned into a real one when my eyes landed on the spread in front of me.

A giant bottle of my favorite red wine.

Two wine glasses.

Some romantic candles for ambiance.

"What's all this?"

He shrugged. "I have an hour before I have to leave for my flight. I thought we could have that romantic night in."

My heart warmed as Jay opened the bottle and poured two glasses. Drinking a bottle of my favorite wine was our tradition on date nights. Despite the abrupt departure, the effort was incredibly charming.

Yup, Jay Ambani had always been the right choice, and I was the luckiest girl on the planet.

CHAPTER

SIX

Axel

I MENTALLY SCOLDED PIYA FOR USING HER KID'S
birthday as the code to enter her home; 0703. The information
was easy to uncover, and it'd be the first thing any smart criminal
would try. People generally used birthdays as codes and
passwords.

I tsked, annoyed. Did she not realize the easy pin made her
unsuspecting prey? Silly woman. What if I had been a lunatic
breaking into her home?

I stepped inside, only to freeze in place when the wooden floor-
boards creaked under my weight. I carefully removed my shoes and

socks, treading barefoot on the boards instead. The hallway into the house was poorly lit, but it didn't dissuade me from taking a tour and searching for clues to her life. Despite the recent move, there were no signs of it or unopened boxes in any of the rooms. Things were orderly enough in the kitchen, dishes put away, and counters wiped down. Multiple oversized couches with throw blankets made the living room appear homey. It reflected a rich family's home, but nothing was over the top. Piya's personality shined through here and there with a sequined throw pillow and a grand piano with an uncovered lid. I ran my fingers lightly over every surface, taking in the life she had painted with the minor details.

Suddenly, something caught my attention out of the corner of my eye. Craning my neck, I took in the living room side tables. There were a few picture frames placed neatly on each one. One appeared to be of Piya's daughter, and the next was of Piya with her daughter. It was the last few photos that had my fingers curling and my blood boiling.

Piya on her wedding day with Ambani.

A family portrait of the three of them.

A photo of Ambani with their daughter.

The shock of seeing them together—pretending to be a happy family—stilled me in place, saving the frames from meeting their maker. I sharply advised myself not to throw the frames against the wall. If I followed the basic instinct of shattering the frames, it would wake Piya up. Then I'd have to deal with her screaming and would most likely have to tie her down to stop her from calling security. It'd be a whole thing because Piya was dramatic and wouldn't take me breaking into her house lightly.

No, it wouldn't serve me well to risk waking Piya up, not while the grand prize was within my grasp. Instead, I removed the photos from the frame and carelessly tore Ambani out of every picture before replacing them again. She'd pay the price for displaying his images. For now, she'd be freaked out after discovering the state of these photos. It'd have to suffice as punishment.

My instructions had been explicit; remove all traces of Ambani. I had a feeling Piya wouldn't be susceptible to the suggestion and tasked my head of security detail, Levi, with stirring up trouble for Ambani at his home office in Chicago. Asshole had to return on an impromptu flight. It would've been a cleaner break had Piya told him it was over before he left.

Piya will eventually learn I'll always be one step ahead of her AND have a backup to make things go my way.

I trashed Ambani's photos after ripping them to shreds, then picked up the picture of Piya and her daughter. It was a shame her daughter could no longer maintain a relationship with Ambani. Since Piya was mine, her daughter would belong under my care by proxy. Allowing her the fanciful notions of a relationship with her ex-father would only be cruel toward the child. Better if she forgot him as soon as possible.

I turned a corner from the main area to investigate the bedrooms. One of the rooms had been converted into a home office. The next one likely belonged to Piya's daughter, though it lacked the personality I'd presume a young girl to possess. The third room was my destination.

My footsteps remained deft as I entered Piya's bedroom. It was mildly cold, though the heated floors warmed the temperature. Soft lights streamed through the floor-to-ceiling windows since she had left the curtains open. It illuminated the room—though not by much—just enough to highlight the figure sprawled underneath the covers.

A good view of her was problematic under the dim lighting, so I lowered and sat at the edge of Piya's bed. It was still too dark, and I had to lean close to make out her features.

Chocolate-colored hair fanned the pillow while long lashes reached for her high cheekbones. Creamy olive skin made her racially ambiguous. It was the feature that had initially piqued my interest, and I tried figuring out her ethnicity. Even after I'd solved the mystery (she was Indian), I couldn't stop watching her.

Her skin was still smooth enough to wonder if she was made from porcelain, and her pink lips only added to the illusion of a life-sized doll. *A broken doll,* I surmised after taking in the large empty bottle of Chianti along with the equally drained wine glass on her nightstand.

"The parent will play when the kid is away," I muttered, gently brushing away the tangled hair off her forehead. She didn't stir, an aftereffect of the alcohol.

I was surprised Piya had polished off the bottle. Per my sources, the princess avoided drinking heavily. Our encounter must have shaken her. She wasn't accepting of her fate just yet, but she would be soon.

Piya clutched the blanket onto her chest, perhaps hoping to somehow regain control of her life in her sleep. To my annoyance, the pose hid most of her skin, and I could only gorge on the visible surfaces. I would have pulled the blanket off. Nevertheless, haste was unnecessary. The wine had done a number on her, and Piya was out cold for the rest of the night.

My plans of watching her for hours came to a halt when my gaze landed on another unwelcome perpetrator. A pretentious shopping bag with wrapping tissue sticking out of it sat proudly on Piya's dresser beside her beauty products. She had bought an expensive-looking gift, but for whom? It didn't look like something a child would appreciate, which could only mean one thing. I parted the shopping bag and found an unopened bottle of cologne, Dior Sauvage.

I stilled, my irritation rising by the second. This was unprecedented, even if she had purchased the item before our text exchange. There were no upcoming holidays, no birthdays, or an anniversary to celebrate. This was not an obligatory gift. *She was thinking about him.*

She did this to please him because he was on her mind.

My fingers curled around the bottle. Once more, I fought the urge to smash another item she owned against the wall. My lips curved as I settled on a better punishment. I did inform Piya about coming over, though I doubted she'd taken me seriously then. I had no plans of taking things further than observing her. However, she had pissed me off for the last time and had to pay the price for her insolence.

My hands shook, eyes locked on her unconscious body. Waking her up and damaging everything would be a colossal mistake. I should exercise self-restraint while everything is put in place. Even as I thought it, I opened the bottle and sprinkled on some of the cologne. I pulled off my coat, discarding the bottle and shopping bag in the trash can. Marching toward the bed, I unbuttoned my dress shirt en route and pulled it off my shoulders. I draped the shirt and coat neatly over an armchair before unfastening my belt. Reaching into my pant pocket, I pulled out my phone and turned it off. I gently placed it on the nightstand, doing the same with my wallet and keys. Undoing my pants, I slid them down my legs and folded them, once more stacking them over the armchair.

All the while I undressed, I devoured her with my eyes. It was unlikely I could look away when she was this pliant and vulnerable. Her lips parted in her sleep, and I wondered if placing my thick cock between them, then making her choke on it, would be punishment enough for displaying Ambani's photos and buying him unsolicited gifts.

Piya groaned softly and shifted to her side, exposing her slender neck to me. The blanket finally moved, revealing a flannel nightshirt. Without trying, Piya managed to ooze sexuality in an ugly, unappealing shirt. She had buttoned it to the middle of her chest, showcasing a stack of heavy breasts rising and falling with every breath. She didn't wear a bra, granting me access to her deep cleavage.

My cock jerked. I had barely touched her, and I was still rock hard.

"Will you sleep through this or wake up screaming?" I wondered.

Dropping my boxers, I crawled on the bed, lowering the

offending comforter down her body until she was entirely uncovered. It was clear this woman took great care of her body. Nothing suggested she had a kid except for the small C-section scar I found upon lifting the nightshirt to her waist.

"You really shouldn't have pissed me off, Princess," I whispered in her ear.

~

Piya

Sleep somehow found me despite the nightmare I was living through. I should thank the large bottle of red for the reprieve. After sharing only one glass, Jay stumbled and held onto the table to keep from falling. We were both surprised by his short-lived tolerance as he could generally hold his liquor. Although he tapped out, Jay insisted I enjoy the bottle since it was my favorite. After he departed for the airport, I did precisely that. I changed into a comfortable sleeping shirt, watched one too many episodes of a crime drama show, and drank one too many glasses of wine.

This was abnormal for me, but I was shaken by Axel's unprecedented return to my life. This couldn't be real. What happened tonight had to be a fluke. The text messages he sent proved otherwise. I drank enough to take down a small horse and wipe away the fear. Pacified by the false sense of security I found at the bottom of my wine glass, I dozed off and let the dreams take hold.

I couldn't make out the face. He went in and out of focus as he

strolled toward us while still maintaining distance. The sun
bounced with his leisurely pace, nearly blinding me at times
depending on his newest position. A chill ran down my spine as our
gazes finally met. Dark, unforgiving eyes stared back, dead set
against giving away their secrets.

I was unsure what stirred me from the alcohol-induced
dream. It was probably the menacing voice growling in my ear,
"You really shouldn't have pissed me off, Princess."

I trembled at the unrecognizable voice. A chill rolled down
my spine as I attempted to peel my eyes open. My intoxicated
brain had other ideas and refused to obey the command. I had
barely glanced at the top of a beautiful head of hair and the
shadowy figure caressing my neck when the dim—yet harsh—
lighting had me quickly shutting my eyes. The effort to reopen
them was significant, and I determined it wouldn't be worth it
since this was just a dream.

"Ugh," I groaned and tried to roll away when an arm locked
around my waist, holding me prisoner. A small voice warned me
that I was no longer alone, though I sensed no imminent threat.
If anything, a soothing smell grabbed hold of my senses. It was
musky and spicy, with an intoxicating hint of bergamot.

Jay.

I smiled. I was no longer in a deep sleep nor fully awake,
rocking back and forth between the land of the living and this
pleasant dream. He returned for Poppy's first day of boarding
school after all.

This is a dream; I convinced myself not to get my hopes up.
Not wanting this unexpected moment to be torn away, I

squeezed my eyes tighter and wished for the calloused hands to explore my body.

Vivid dream or not, my senses heated as the hand wrapped around my waist loosened to yank my shirt up, moving over my hips, past my waist, until he exposed my breasts.

I gasped.

Cool air hit my nipples, forcing goosebumps to the surface as his hand slid to my chest. His lips were on my neck—sucking and nipping—before drawing a line to my breasts. The hardness against my abdomen twitched on cue.

Was I awake or still dreaming? I hadn't a clue. All I knew was that my heart was beating wildly under his palm. My core clenched as he kissed my bare breasts, kneading them with his large hand and rolling a nipple between his fingers. My thighs squeezed in response, and I bit back a moan.

He slid his other hand up my thigh and pulled my panties to the side. His fingers lightly grazed my lips, and I wanted to die from frustration. I chanted in my head, begging him to touch me. Warmth engulfed me. It had been too many cold lonely months since I felt the weight of a man on top of me. The starvation for touch and affection stirred a frenzy. Madness descended, and I tilted my pelvis to chase the friction, never wanting this feeling to end.

Thick fingers parted my raw, swollen lips, answering my prayers. I shuddered on cue, a moan tumbling out of my mouth.

The wet mouth sucking my nipple, the expert fingers circling my clit, the hand kneading my breast, it was all too much. My body sparked from the various sensations, driving me insane with a need I never knew existed. I writhed, my body inaudibly begging for a steady flow of stimulation until reaching my peak. Ecstasy was within reach, and I hungered after it shamelessly.

However, Jay had other ideas and kept up the unyielding strokes that refused to end my torture.

"God," I moaned softly, grinding my hips against his fingers.

"Fuck," he reciprocated, sounding equally frustrated. The fingers suddenly disappeared, leaving me at the edge of the cliff. Before I could cry out in disappointment, a hard bulge landed on my sex in their stead. No lights were needed to realize it was a hard erection grinding against my aching core, parting my lips and spreading them wide open.

My eyes rolled to the back of my head behind my closed lids. *Fuck* was right. It had been so long, and the need inside me wanted to clench onto him with desperation. How long had it been since he touched me this way, or I'd had an orgasm?

"Don't stop," I moaned.

He worked me, building an unforgiving pressure on my clit with the head of his cock. He slid his cock, slicking himself with my wetness. It was hot and debasing all at once as he made me listen to the sounds of my arousal swishing around his cock. I grappled with the sheets as he continued, rocking my hips against him. At long last, he pushed the tip of his cock past the entrance of my pussy. Only slightly.

I shuddered, then groaned when he stilled. I heard the heavy panting as if he were inhibiting a primitive urge. As if he had been waiting a decade to do this, not months, and needed to savor this monumental occasion. I tipped my pelvis forward, wordlessly welcoming his cock. It broke his remaining restraint, and he suddenly turned frantic. He thrust forward so roughly that I cried out at the same time he groaned, "Fuck!"

He wasn't gentle, filling me to the brim. He grabbed my knees, roughly spreading them, as he pulled out slightly, only to slam inside with brutal force. His mouth landed on mine, and his tongue invaded swiftly. I would have groaned if his lewd tongue allowed the space for it. He devoured me with a hunger I had never known him to possess. Something about that blared an alarm at the back of my mind, but I ignored it. Nothing else mattered. Not when he was fucking me like a stranger while comforting me with the familiarity of the Dior Savage scent.

The blood in my veins fizzled as my body clawed toward the finish line. "Oh, God," I moaned, wrestling with my body to keep it locked in the needy position to reach my apex.

All at once, he pulled out, and the weight disappeared, leaving me hanging at the roots of desperation once more. *No, no, no. Not again.*

"Don't stop, please," I croaked.

To my surprise, he flipped me over on my stomach and lifted my shirt. I finally managed to open my eyes, wrestling with imbalance at the unexpected position. My palms landed on the mattress, and I tried to push myself to my knees.

The weight of a giant hand shoved my face against the 800-thread count Egyptian cotton sheets as he entered me from behind like an animal. In all the years I have known Jay, he had never fucked me like this. It wasn't how a respectful husband made love to his wife. This man was fucking me to oblivion with all the lascivious intents of a bastard.

My fears were confirmed when a silky voice and a pair of lips whispered against my ears, "How long has it been since you've been fucked like this, Princess?"

Wasn't that what Axel had called me?

The cobwebs of my mind from alcohol refused to clear. I craned my neck over my shoulders and blinked rapidly at the large hands grabbing my hips and holding me in place while he repeatedly slammed inside me.

Mind confuddled, my gaze languidly traveled up the veiny forearms. A bulky figure was behind me on his knees. Shadows masked half his face, though the muscularity of his body or the broadness of his shoulders couldn't be suppressed.

My eyes widened as the realization settled in. The whisper-scream, "What the—" was cut off when he pulled back only to shove inside me like a brute. "Fuck." I nearly toppled over, the protest all but cut off.

My mind raced to catch up. The combination of alcohol, sleep, and confusion had veiled my senses. Before I could procure another protest, a hand landed between my shoulder blades to press me into the mattress. He wrapped a hand around my hair and held my face against the bed, forcefully slamming inside me repeatedly with no holds barred. It was so primal and vulgar that my voice left me, and so did rationality.

He had kept me on edge so tactfully that a physical response was inevitable. He had roused a dormant beast in my sleep, and I was tethering at the brink, playing catch up. Right, wrong, and similar thoughts couldn't stop the thing building inside me, threatening to explode. My next breath had become impossible until the desperate ache he had surged was relieved. He knew it, too, and let loose a hunger I'd never known a man to possess.

My muscles locked without permission, my core tightened, and everything tensed. White flashed before my eyes when he pulled my hair to arch my back. A scream was locked inside my throat, and try as I might, I couldn't stop the explosion from happening. Broken gasps tumbled from my lips, and I wheezed to catch my breath. He kept fucking me through the excruciating high, the one that made me feel like I was about to die. It only made his growls more feral as he pounded harder, fucking my hole like a madman who had never heard of the word restraint or control.

"Look at me," he demanded. I could barely hear him over the ringing in my ear. "I said, look at me." He tugged at my hair when I didn't comply.

It took a monumental effort to open my eyes and look over my shoulders. Bizarre emotions circled my drunken mind. I watched the animalistic look on his face as he slipped out, only to pound back inside me.

"Fuck, I could do this forever. I could fuck you forever."

Oh God, I hope not; I might actually die from sex.

My pussy clamped around him like a vise. It milked him with desperation, an automated self-defense in response to the abuse he was inflicting. My heart was beating faster and faster until I feared it might break open my ribcage. It became impossible to keep the noises at bay.

His face contorted, and I felt his cock twitch inside me. He grabbed my chin and roughly tugged it to face him. "Look at me when I come inside you."

My eyes widened as I looked into the windows of a man's soullessness. Those lifeless eyes stared back, but they were no longer dead or unamused. They were lit with all things vile.

It happened right away. Waves and waves crashed and burned as another orgasm was wrenched out of me while his wet, hot cum shot inside me and out of me as well. In between heavy breaths, he declared I was his as his thrusts slowed, and his face landed against the back of my neck. I fell flat on the mattress, unable to remain on my knees. Neither of our breaths would steady, no matter how much we panted.

It was a few moments before it registered that a heated weight was wrapped around me like a gravity blanket, and this was the furthest from a dream. Like a bucket of cold water doused on me, I shoved him off and clutched the blanket to my chest.

Then I screamed at the top of my lungs.

CHAPTER
SEVEN

~

Piya

I SCREAMED AND SCREAMED UNTIL MY VOICE WAS
hoarse. The world spun when two large hands grabbed my biceps
and flung me backward onto the mattress. The first thought that
came to mind was of my husband, my protector, my knight in
shining armor. Jay would know what to do in such a situation.
Me? I was a fish out of water.

This shouldn't have been possible. We paid a small fortune to
live here and ensure a safe home for when my daughter came to
visit.

"How... how dare... how dare you?" I stuttered with panic
and opened my mouth to scream once again.

He slapped a hand over my mouth. "Don't," was the only word he uttered as my back hit the firm mattress. His naked body covered the front of mine, allowing me to feel every one of his taut muscles. Fear prickled my scalp over how quickly he had overpowered me, and the formidable brick wall silently communicated that I was at his mercy.

Trapped under his body weight, I found myself staring into obsidian eyes. The dim lights from outside clung to his body from behind like a fitted glove, illuminating chiseled pecs and biceps. My God. This man was bigger than I remembered and could snap me in half like a twig.

An eternity passed as we stared at one another, both still taking ragged breaths. Reality settled like a heavy pit in my stomach. A man broke into my house and fucked me... *and he got me off.*

"Don't scream again," he demanded. "I'd hate to wake up your neighbors at this time of night." Fingers flexed on my biceps with a crystal clear threat; he'd crush me if I dared to defy his orders.

As I stared into his dark pools of nothingness, I was positive he didn't care about the neighbors' sleeping health but only about how this might affect his reputation. He didn't possess the empathy required to care for another human being. Considering Axel broke into the home of a married woman and fucked her just because he felt like it told me how little he cared for other people's feelings, lives, or well-being.

I nodded to show my willingness to comply. "I'm not going to scream again." There was no need for it. These residential grounds required visitors to sign in. He had already left a paper trail, and I could easily make him pay the legal way, which I thoroughly planned to do. There was also a panic button on Jay's side of the bed. It alerted the residential guards about possible intruders. Once I pressed it, they'd be here in less than three minutes. Axel only had to avert his eyes long enough for me to reach over and press it.

Unfortunately, Axel's apathetic eyes didn't move from mine. At long last, his grip loosened. I quickly huddled toward Jay's side of the bed but didn't get far. Axel instinctively moved with me. My body trembled from fear—or maybe I was cold after losing the heat from the nearness of another body—and I lowered my flannel nightshirt to cover myself. It only came up to my mid-thigh. When his gaze landed there, I grabbed the blanket and brought it to my chest, cocooning into myself.

There was no way this was real.

A heated hand landed on my thigh under the blanket, proving otherwise with their unignorable presence. I shook my head, desperately trying to wake up from this nightmare. However, the cum trickling down my thighs confirmed this was no dream. He had taken advantage of my muddled brain during REM sleep and stemmed my arousal by wearing a familiar scent. Even now, the recognizable smell subconsciously brought me a fragment of comfort.

What were the chances he wore the same cologne as my husband?

The answer didn't matter, did it? It wouldn't erase the facts.

Under the influence of alcohol and terrible lighting, I had broken my marriage vows.

My eyes burned with unshed tears. I refused to let them fall because now wasn't the time to fall apart. I couldn't deal with the consequences yet, not while a naked man was on my bed.

"I told you I'd be seeing you soon." There was a dark threat in his whisper.

I broke eye contact to shove tangled hair out of my face. The shock had finally worn off enough to grasp that I wasn't out of danger yet. "Y-You broke into my house." I tried to keep the panic at bay. Was breaking into someone's house and raping them typical for him?

He cocked his head contemplatively. "I didn't break into your house; I walked through those unlocked doors to check if you were alive." He pointed at the bedroom glass doors overlooking the water. "You were passed out like dead next to a giant bottle of wine."

The grounds outside my bedroom door were adjacent to the water and stretched for miles, turning every residential home in these premises into waterfront properties. Although everyone shared the same stretch of land, designated lands were divided amongst the homeowners.

I steadied my voice to speak. "How could you have even seen me—" My eyes darted to the glass bedroom doors. It served as our entry and exit point to our designated waterfront land. The moonlight was illumined enough to display my bedroom if someone were to take a walk along the water. However, they would have had to cross into my property to see inside my bedroom. Even if he was granted rightful access to visit someone living on these premises, the land designated for our exclusive use was off-limits. "You were trespassing on my property," I screamed.

"Trespassing? I told you I was coming over. Even had the guards at the gate call you. They said you granted me access to the property."

I slapped the mattress so hard that my palm tingled. "I didn't." Fuck, did I? Had someone called me while I was drunk? Was it possible I told them to let Axel through?

No. I shook my head firmly. Axel was lying. I needed to sober up. Otherwise, I'd buy into his manipulations.

"You must've broken into this gated community somehow."

"I didn't," he countered calmly. "The guards let me in per your request. I parked my car but got lost searching for your house. I ended up on the waterfront side when I stumbled upon this scene."

"I don't believe you," I reiterated.

"Believe what you want." He shrugged nonchalantly, waving a hand over the empty wine bottle. "I thought you might have overindulged and ran inside to ensure you were alive. Luckily, those doors were unlocked." Once more, he nodded at the glass doors overlooking the water. "By the time I realized you were fine, you had started saying horny shit, begging me to fuck you. I'm a gentleman. I'd never deny a lady."

I gaped at the unfazed man. The only messy thing about this robot was his sex hair. Otherwise, he was unruffled and uncaring about upending my world with one lewd act, staring impassively.

"This was hardly my fault," he continued with indifference.

"I was just being a good Samaritan and trying to save you from alcohol poisoning."

My heart withered in shame. I never got carried away with alcohol, but I'd had a tough night. I was still drunk and unsure if the beginning part was a dream or how it had all started.

Nonetheless, I didn't reach for people in my dreams. Did he think I'd buy his horseshit? "If you truly believed I had passed out from alcohol poisoning, why didn't you call 911?"

He tsked. "We didn't have that kind of time on our hands. I took it upon myself to rescue you."

His blasé responses were on my last nerve. Anger took hold in place of fear. "Get out of my house. Get out right now, or I'll tell the entire world how their favorite DJ is nothing more than a rapist," I hissed, lowering my voice toward the tail end of the sentence.

"How will you say it to strangers when you can barely say the words to me?"

"You *are* a stranger," I spoke with measured steadiness.

"We are acquainted," he retorted.

He was arguing semantics? "That won't save your ass from going to jail!"

"Go to jail for what?"

"For breaking and entering and raping an unconscious woman," I listed his crimes.

"Rape? All I did was comply to fucking you after you begged me not to stop?"

I slapped my palm onto the mattress once more. "Only

101

because I thought you were my husband. Who else would come into our bedroom in the middle of the night?"

The nonchalance and amusement vanished from his face. His grip on my thigh tightened even as I tried to pry off those marauding fingers. "Ambani didn't care that you drank yourself to sleep," he bit out. "I was the only one who cared enough to check on you. So, how about you show a little less attitude and a little more gratitude for my heroic efforts?"

"What the fuck is the matter with you?"

"Lots of things. Should we discuss them over a nightcap?" His amused veneer returned as his glance migrated to the empty wine bottle. "Or perhaps a non-alcoholic beverage for you would suffice."

"Shut up!" I screeched.

"You're acting extremely dramatic for a woman whose life I ran here to save."

"That's not what happened," I announced through gritted teeth.

"Were you or were you not passed out from alcohol consumption?"

"Technically, yes, but—"

"Wouldn't you have done the same if you saw someone passed out from inebriation?"

"I wouldn't have fucked them. And I-I," I grappled with words, "I didn't have alcohol poisoning. Do you just go around looking for unconscious women to fuck?"

"*Woman.*"

"What!?"

"Woman," he repeated. "I fucked *one* unconscious *woman*. Singular."

I stared at him, feeling at a loss for words.

"So..." He phrased the word like a question while slowly rising from the bed. Axel grabbed his clothes—which I realized were draped over the back of the armchair—and dressed in meticulous precision. "How about that nightcap?" he returned to the earlier suggestion, buckling his belt. He spoke with ease as if it were normal to go out for a drink after what went down between us.

"You're out of your mind."

"Is that a *no*? Probably for the best if you're hungover."

I wasn't hungover; I was still drunk. Not that I'd admit it to him. "Most men usually buy you drinks *before* fucking you. Or, in your case, before forcing a woman."

He tsked again. "We have been over this. You came onto me, and I didn't deny you. To avoid future confusion, I'll ensure you're fully awake the next time I shove your face onto the mattress and take you from behind."

I banked away my trauma to deal with the words unraveling around my ears. "Next time? There will NEVER be a next time, not unless you force me again," I shouted, upset.

"That can be arranged as well."

Once more, I was at a loss for words. In a matter of a night, he had turned my life upside down. Why?

My shoulders slumped in defeat. "Please. Why are you doing this to me?" My fingers curled so tightly that my nails dug into my palms. He made me an accessory to his sinful ways and couldn't be bothered to give me a reason. "Whatever it is you're doing, stop. You can have anybody you want. Just pick anyone else. Any woman would die to be with you. You are a god."

He grinned wickedly. "You think I'm a god?"

I scoffed. "I meant that women, in general, think you're a god."

"I'm only interested in one *woman*," he drew out the a-syllable and smiled, though it didn't reach his eyes. I swallowed when he approached the bed and leaned over. "If it makes you feel better, I'm happy to start over and do this the right way. You know... buy you drinks *before* fucking you. But I'll forget the generosity if you keep giving me a hard time."

Dread coiled my spine because I knew without a doubt that he meant it.

"So, how about that drink, Princess?"

"Don't call me that," I snapped without thinking.

He gripped my cheeks, turning my lips into a pout. "I'll call you whatever the fuck I want, Princess, and you'll respond to it every fucking time. Now," he looked me dead in the eyes, "I asked, how about that drink, Princess?"

His hold tightened, and I realized he wouldn't let go or leave unless I acknowledged his term of endearment. I spewed hatred from my eyes but spat, "No, thank you."

"Your loss." Before I could rip my face away, he firmly kissed my lips and murmured, "Later, Princess." With that, he strolled away. Instead of using the glass doors leading to the waterfront, he exited through my bedroom door, the one leading inside the house.

I was out of bed within the flash and ran to lock the door from inside. Next, I buzzed the emergency button on Jay's side of the bed before running to the door leading to the waterfront.

It was locked.

It took several seconds for my hazy, still-drunk mind to realize Axel couldn't have come in through this door as it was never unlocked. He was already inside the house when he found me passed out drunk.

This man had access to my house.

Intoxicated tears were involved as I stumbled to dress, pulling on a pair of Uggs, a black t-shirt, and blue jeans. The security guards rushed to my house within the allocated three minutes. In a shocking turn of events, they confirmed Axel's story. They called my house number upon Axel's request for entry into the premises, and I granted it. Fuck. How was it possible?

I refused to be a sitting duck, waiting for another attack. There was no way I could stay at this house, knowing some madman had access to it. I had to get out in case he returned.

I grabbed my oversized Prada tote bag. It served as both a purse and an overnight bag when needed. Throwing in my toiletry bag, a prepacked travel makeup kit, a couple of outfits, along with underwear and bras, I called an Uber since I hadn't fully sobered. I sat in the backseat with blurred tears while the driver took me to the nearest hotel.

Despite being that it was the dead of the night, the concierge greeted me cheerily. There were only a few patrons lurking in the hotel bar. Otherwise, the place was empty. Lack of a crowd made the hotel seem grander and larger than life. Luckily, the vastness of the elegant hotel wasn't covered with gaudiness. Bright light fixtures highlighted modern furniture and chic décor.

The radiant ambiance and the cheerful greeting did little to improve my mood. Everything felt morbid as I checked into a corner room with a king-size bed.

It took me no time to find room 1450. As soon as the door shut behind me, I marched to the bathroom, turned on the water, and stripped my clothes. I scrubbed my skin under scorching hot water before crawling into bed like a coward.

What I should have done instead was go to the police and file a report against Axel. He was guilty as charged and belonged in jail. However, a few obstacles kept the idea at bay.

If Google search was an indicator, Axel was practically a champion for women, and none to cross paths with him had an adverse word to spare. In the ten years he had been in the music industry, not one female staff reported anything resembling sexual harassment or assault, calling Axel an exemplary boss in their testimonies.

I'd be the exception to the rule, the first and only woman to speak negatively about the elusive Axel Trimalchio. It didn't help that I was intoxicated when said event occurred. I could barely remember the details of our drunken fuck, and even now, my recollections were hazy at best. It'd be my inebriated account against a beloved celebrity known for practicing the utmost respect for his female liaisons.

I ran a palm over my face, pulling the comforter to my chin.

Going to the police also meant involving Jay, who'd insist on dragging Axel's ass to court. Between Jay's well-known company and Axel's celebrity status, a case like this would start a media frenzy. Did I want to put my family through that hell?

I'd be forced to take the stand and list the gory details of our tryst, which would further humiliate Jay. How could I tell the world I'd been so physically deprived that I responded to a man in my sleep, unable to differentiate his touch from my husband's?

Things would only go downhill once Axel opened his mouth and gave the public his defense. *He was out for a walk when he accidentally crossed into my property, only to stumble upon the not-so-picturesque vision of my unconscious, intoxicated body through the glass windows. With heroic adrenaline, he threw open the unlocked door to check on me. Except I had woken to kiss him and lured him into bed.*

I had no doubt where public sympathy would land once Axel professed his version of the story.

Bored housewife lures self-made celebrity Axel Trimalchio into her bed, then cries rape to cover up the affair.

Slut. The word bubbled to the surface despite my best effort.

Axel had the rags-to-riches thing working for him, whereas we were rich because of old money. The current culture hated generational wealth like ours and preferred self-made men like Axel. He was the green light at the end of the dock, guiding into port those hopeful of hitting the big time by toppling the social ladder. It'd better be foolproof if I pointed an accusatory finger at a beloved celebrity. Unfortunately, this story wasn't infallible and would only drag the Ambani name through the mud.

Worst of all, I feared Jay might believe Axel's word over mine. Our marriage had been rocky as of late, and both of us knew it, too.

I shoved away the depressing thoughts of my husband not believing me and stared at my phone. Maybe Jay would somehow understand what happened to me. He'd be furious, but perhaps he'd somehow forgive me. I grasped my cell phone and called him before I could change my mind.

"What?" came Jay's gruff voice.

My heavy soul dragged me down further. I hadn't expected such a hostile response off the bat. "Hey," I said softly. "How are you?" Could he hear my guilt or my raspy voice from all the crying?

"I landed in Chicago not even an hour ago and just got into bed," he stated, the unspoken irritation over a needy wife laced in his voice.

I cringed. "I thought you'd be happy to hear from me."

There was a long pause on the other end of the line. I needed Jay. I had to tell him I cared for him before I unfolded the rest of the story. But how could I when Jay was already acting like I was a nuisance? Could he not tell by my voice that something was wrong? Or perhaps he didn't care?

Ambani didn't care that you drank yourself to sleep. I was the only one who cared enough to check on you.

I refused to cover up Axel's vile act, play into his manipulations, or make excuses for his behavior. However, his words about Jay rang true in my ears.

My husband didn't care about what happened to me tonight. Anger clawed at my heart, and I bit my bottom lip to keep from screaming.

"Piya, it's late," Jay said with an exasperated sigh.

"I-I," I started hesitantly.

"Piya, it's the middle of the night," he spoke patiently, though I knew he was tethering at the edge of ire. "Let's speak later. Good night."

"I love you—"

Jay hung up. I held the phone loosely and closed my eyes, wondering if I was still the luckiest girl on the planet.

CHAPTER
EIGHT

Milan's Wedding

Piya

"You didn't answer my question." The DJ trailed behind me as I walked to the parking lot. "What's your name?"

"Mary."

"You're lying," he said automatically.

A small smile tugged at my lips at his intuitiveness. I immediately scolded myself. I needed to stay the hell away from this man.

Given my past, I was used to tough men and the bad-boy vibes my exes portrayed. Zane made my exes look like child's play. He was likely in his early twenties, but placing the word "bad" in front of "boy" didn't make him so. He was a bad *man*. And something told me this *man* could break me much worse than any of the predecessors.

His reserved appraisal further unseated me. I didn't want to impart any part of myself to a man like him, and I certainly didn't need him privy to my name. What if he told someone he had met me? If word got back to my friends and family about whatever this was with the DJ, I'd be finished. Jordan and my family had given me an ultimatum. They'd be done with me the next time a Sean look-alike came along. This man might be beautiful, but he wasn't worth losing everything over.

Ignoring him, I reached for the cab door after confirming the name of the driver. Zane's arm reached out and shut the door before I could climb inside.

"Name," he pressed.

My heart did a somersault as his intoxicating scent engulfed me once more. Silence stretched between us, neither willing to back down. He wouldn't remove his hand from the door, refusing to let me leave.

The cab driver broke the silence. "Are you getting in or not?"

Before I could respond, Zane reached inside his pocket and pulled out two twenty-dollar bills. He handed the money to the driver through the open window. "She doesn't need a cab after all. Thank you for your trouble."

"What the Hell!"

Zane pulled me back just as the cab driver took off at full speed, happy to be paid despite not having to give me a ride.

I tore out of his reach, spun in place, and blasted him at full volume. "Are you insane? What's wrong with you? That was my ride."

Could I kill him and bury him behind the building?

No, that wouldn't work. His body was too large to be moved by someone my size.

"Name?" Zane asked with the calm of a sane person.

What if I lured him to the back first, then killed him?

No. That wouldn't work, either. There might be witnesses.

"What the fuck is your problem? It took me forever to get a cab to come out here." I jabbed him in the chest. "You owe me a ride," I gritted out.

His response was to nod at a black Jeep parked a few feet away.

I snapped my mouth shut as my gaze fleeted over his car. While I still wanted to kill the asshole, we were in a remote location. If I wanted to get the hell out of here, my options were limited at this time of night.

"That's your car?" I asked tentatively, barely banking away my anger.

Another curt nod.

I looked back and forth between the car and him. We might've shared a beer and a few pleasantries, but it didn't erase my trepidations surrounding the man. Physically, his mass was bulkier than anyone I knew. Emotionally, he was unfeeling. Then or now, he hadn't so much as cracked a smile or done anything to put me at ease.

However, I was stuck since my sweet escape from my family drove away at full speed. What was bigger of the two evils?

Dealing with Milan's ire and ruining the rest of his special week-end, or getting in a car with a psychopath?

At long last, I held out my palm. "Show me your driver's license."

I was surprised when he reached into his back pocket without arguing and fished out his wallet.

"I'm showing you mine, now show me yours," he spoke without humor, handing me the card.

"Someone stole my wallet. I haven't gotten my replacement ID yet," I said while studying his identity card.

Twenty-two.

Gemini.

Organ Donor.

He stared at me impassively and must've decided it was true. Unlike the other times, he dropped the topic.

I took a photo of his ID and handed it back. "I am sending this photo to my best friend. If I turn up dead, she'll know you did it." I had no plans of doing such a thing. The lectures would be endless after Jordan specifically asked me to stay away from this man. Worse, she might wash her hands off me. Didn't mean Zane was impervious to empty threats.

"You've no plans of sending that photo to anyone. Stop lying, Princess."

I reeled back. How did he know? More importantly... "Princess?"

"If you won't give me a name..." he gestured at my pink and sparkly attire. "What else am I supposed to call you?"

"We don't know each other well enough for nicknames."

"Then tell me your name."

"Cassandra."

"Liar," he retorted.

"You know what?" I lifted my chin. "Princess suits me just fine."

He motioned a hand toward the car. "Then after you, Princess."

"Sounds good, *Axel.*" I enunciated the name on purpose, sounding it out as I followed him to the car. He didn't react, and I decided to call him Axel henceforth, verbally and mentally, to give him a taste of his own medicine.

Axel unlocked the car door, his eyes traveling over my face as we strapped in. "What ethnicity are you?" There was nothing civilized about the way he demanded answers. He asked whatever came to his mind with no regard for etiquette. "From the clothes you wore earlier, my first guess was somewhere from South Asia. Then again, you could've worn them to fit in and crash the party."

"Do you always ask this many personal questions?"

"No."

"So, why are you asking *me* so many questions?"

"Beats me." He shrugged. "What ethnicity are you?"

Axel was impossible. "I'm Indian. Happy?"

"Does your background have anything to do with why you won't tell me your name?"

I stared at him, dumbfounded by his abrasiveness. "What? Why would that matter?"

"If it isn't about your family or culture, what other reason could you possibly have for not telling me your name?"

My expression froze at the mention of my family. I had almost forgotten about them for a moment while quarreling with Axel over the ride situation.

"Are you not allowed to date someone outside your culture?" he pushed.

"We are not dating," I pointed out.

"Not yet," he retorted.

My cheeks burned.

Several moments passed while I processed his comment. The question wasn't a ludicrous one, considering my ethnicity. It was true that some Indian families preferred you to marry within the culture. However, my parents imposed no such rules, and my dating history comprised a rainbow of people. My family didn't care so much about race as they did about the quality of the man.

Successful.

Educated.

Old money.

Jay Ambani fit their criteria and then some. Being Indian and Hindu was merely a bonus. It was the same reason Milan and Dahlia hit it off so quickly. Similar cultures, religions, and social standings made things significantly easier. Superficially, Jay and I had everything in common.

All of that was way too much to explain. So, I gave him a recap of the truth. "Race isn't a big factor for them."

"If it's not your family, then what's stopping you from telling me your name?"

"Because I shouldn't be speaking to you at all, let alone give you more information about myself," I said firmly, remembering my promise to Jordan. "You were staring at me like..." I didn't know how to explain Jordan's alarming description of Axel's attentiveness.

He looked at you the way all women want to be looked at by a man.

"I could tell you were interested in me," I finished lamely.

"So?" Not a hint of shame or denial in his voice. Any other man would've been embarrassed or felt awkward if the object of your attention knew about your blatant staring. Whereas Axel took it in stride. Nothing daunted this man.

"I-I have sworn off dating," *the wrong men,* I internally added. "I... my picker is off. You're the wrong man for me. If the people I love catch me talking to you... they'll be upset."

"So, it is your family then," he surmised.

I looked out of the window. The last thing I expected was a pause from him as well. He had been the aggressor from the get-go. I felt his gaze moving over me during the lull in our conversation.

I broke the silence. "Do you think you can drop me off here?" I showed him the address I had jotted down in my notebook earlier.

The only answering response was the engine roaring to life.

"This is a strip club."

I grunted evasively as we pulled into the parking lot of a seedy building in Queens. A bright neon sign flashed "Boobie Lodge" over the entrance. The two o's were shaped like boobs with tassels coming out of where the nipples should be.

Clever.

"Thanks for the ride. Have a nice life. Bye." I climbed out of the car and heard Axel do the same. Two strong hands on my elbows pulled me back before I could reach the building. When my back collided against a hard wall, I whirled in place and stared up at lifeless eyes.

"Where do you think you're going?" he asked in that brutish manner of his.

I motioned at the neon sign above the bouncers. "Isn't it obvious? Bucket list." Surely, he'd read the entire thing when he glanced at my notebook. Strip club was next.

"If you want to go to a strip club, find one suited for..." he gestured to all of me, "someone like you."

I knew what he meant; Vanilla. Someone like me would never step inside a place called "Boobie Lodge." Outwardly, I appeared a bougie, pampered princess. The nickname he had given me was coined for a reason.

But tonight wasn't about doing the expected. I didn't want my last hoorah to be in a champagne room of an upscale lounge where the girls looked expensive. I sought the unsheltered experience, ones I wouldn't be privy to after settling down with someone like Jay Ambani.

I smiled, shaking my head. "This is the club for me. Don't worry. I'll be fine. The strippers are mostly trolling for gentlemen with single dollar bills. Not the likes of me."

I stepped toward the club. Once more, he stopped me. "Drunk perves are crawling all over the place. They'll eat you alive in there." The intensity of how he expressed the word had me stepping back.

The door opened on cue. A fumbling idiot and his bald friend were shoved out of the establishment. They landed on the concrete pavement and shouted what sounded like profanities at the bouncers. Their words were slurred beyond comprehension.

Okay. Perhaps I was more out of my element than I initially thought. "You're welcome to come with me if it puts your mind at ease," I informed Axel, apprehensively eyeing the two creepy men.

Axel smirked knowingly, having figured out I'd never been to such an establishment.

"Just so we're clear, I'm only letting you tag along to ease your conscience," I spoke confidently, simultaneously grabbing his hand in an ironclad hold. I hadn't meant to do it and was surprised Axel didn't pull away. He didn't seem like the hand-holding kind.

Axel's gaze landed on our intertwined fingers, and I wondered if the same thought crossed his mind. For this wasn't a simple touch; it was an experience. Every part of my body suddenly reacted in an unfamiliar way. My palms were sweating, my heart pounded irrationally, the hair on my neck was erect, and goose-bumps lined my bare arms. Part of me wanted to pull my hand back from an experience that was too intimidating to share with a stranger. I decided against it, however. Axel's larger-than-life frame provided comfort and security that was currently unmatched.

The problem was, he knew it, too. One cocky eyebrow raised to his forehead as he watched our interlocked hands. "Thank you for the opportunity to lighten my conscience."

"You're welcome," I replied easily. "Sometimes I'm too charitable for my own good."

The bald one sitting on the pavement caught a glimpse of us walking to the entrance and nudged his friend. They squinted their eyes, presumably trying to figure out if I was attractive or if they had beer goggles on. They must have decided on the first because they were suddenly staring at me like I was their last meal.

Axel's gaze followed mine to find the drunk idiots gawking at me. All previous amusement suddenly vanished. He watched the men with the most frightening back-off face I had witnessed.

He stopped a few feet from the two men, breaking their concentration. "You have thirty seconds to be anywhere but here," he spoke to them in the most apathetic tone.

"Don't worry about them," I whispered, not wanting things to escalate. It was hardly worth fighting over when they hadn't done anything past staring.

"Twenty-five seconds," Axel said to the men, ignoring me. "After that, I'm going to remove your eyeballs with my keys," he spoke informatively as if telling them the meal choices for their in-flight menu.

The calm, collected way Axel spoke, paired with his serial-killer eyes, erased the smiles off the men's faces. I also gulped, wondering if I was more scared of Axel or the drunk fools. Them, I could outrun. Axel, I wasn't sure.

Having realized the same, the men clumsily scrambled to their feet, holding each other for support. When Axel pulled out his keys from his back pocket and stepped forward to make good on his threat, they found their balance and scurried away.

Dumbfounded, I watched them disappear around the building and heard them hurling from where they'd vanished.

"You're mental," I murmured.

Instead of responding, he pulled me toward the line for the club. The bouncer sat on a bar stool with a podium in front, playing the role of gatekeeper. As we approached him, something dawned on me. Fuck. I didn't have my new ID yet. Would they still let me in?

Apparently, yes. Sleazy strip clubs were only interested in one thing, which wasn't identification for proof of legal drinking age.

"Cover's ten dollars per person," the large man grunted.

I took my arms out of the loops of my backpack's straps when Axel slapped a twenty on the podium. Before I could protest, his hand on my lower back pushed me forward.

"But I wanted to pay for us." I suspected Chateau at the Hempstead didn't pay Axel a hefty salary. Despite getting off the wrong foot, I didn't want him spending his hard-earned money on my mission.

Instead of acknowledging my protest, Axel held the door open with a hand above my head so I could go inside first. A shrewd feeling told me Axel's haste to go inside had an ulterior motive. He was staring daggers at the ogling men standing in line, and I got the distinct impression he was seconds away from starting a fight with... well, everyone.

Fucking Christ. I didn't even know the man. What's up with this possessiveness?

Nerves rattled; I marched forward as he fell into step next to me. We moved through the dark hallway without speaking. There was a comfortable silence and a natural rhythm to our pace that I hadn't expected.

We stopped upon reaching the main floor. Half-naked women of all shapes and sizes walked around with drink trays in hand while two fully nude ones danced on a stage with stained carpeting. The poles were on their last leg and seemed unsafe for the stunts they were performing. Leering men were spread sporadically on grotesque tables that would likely give you clap upon sitting. Unflattering red lighting illuminated the otherwise dim room. The floors under our feet were sticky from either spilled drinks or a variety of fluids. The entire place reeked from the smell of tobacco, alcohol, piss, and cum.

It was magnificent.

"Eek." I squealed, beyond excited.

"Let me guess," Axel said dryly. "You've never been to a strip club before."

I rolled my eyes, glad the music wasn't so loud I had to speak over it. "With your lack of excitement, I'm guessing you're a regular."

He regarded me for a moment before admitting, "First time."

"No way!"

He shrugged. "I don't see the appeal."

"Oh, come on," I gushed. "Admit this is more fun than the stuffy wedding you DJ'd earlier." When he didn't respond, I dragged him to the bar. "At least let me get us a round of drinks. Everything's better with liquor."

"So, not champagne?"

I couldn't help my smile. No, champagne wasn't my drink of choice, but it was what I drank around my family. "What do you think is my drink?"

He tilted his head. "Nothing. You're too restless to like only one thing."

During the car ride, I had changed the station numerous times before Axel banned me from touching the radio. He'd easily deduced it to my restlessness. The way he'd been reading me throughout the night unnerved me. He was the first person to push me for answers and find out things about me. I was pretty sure that if I still had my ID, Axel would've reached inside my backpack by now to find out my real name. No one else in my circle would've compelled me to share if I was unwilling to impart information. Axel gave no fucks about societal norms.

He was right in his assessment, too. I didn't have a particular drink of choice and blanked whenever bartenders asked me what I'd like. I was grateful when Axel turned to the bartender and ordered for me, "One of these." He tapped on their cocktail of the night: A Dirty Martini. "And whatever beer's on tap."

This time I was faster with my money, slapping a twenty

down on the counter. Axel shoved it away and handed his cash to the bartender instead. I had noticed the way men had been perusing Axel since our arrival. They edged away from him and his threatening presence. The bartender was no different. He read the ire in Axel's expression and accepted his money instead of mine.

"No way," I objected. "I'm paying for this round."

"Save your money for the strippers," he grunted, grabbing our drinks and leading us toward one corner of the room.

I followed him, leaving the twenty behind for the bartender as a tip. I noticed the man's reluctance even though Axel was no longer shooting him a death glare.

"Do you always boss people around?" I asked from behind.

"Yes," he spoke without looking at me, setting our drinks at a circular booth. It wasn't as grimy as I had expected, without any mystery stains on the red leather fabric. Axel motioned for me to climb in first and settled in next to me. Cornered inside a booth, I was suddenly hyper-aware of how secluded we were. Prey that'd walked into a lion's den.

I had promised Jordan to not only steer clear of men like Axel but specifically him. Instead, I ended up at a strip club with the very man. Even as I tried to justify my reasons (safety concerns and needing a ride to leave the premises so I'd stop pissing Milan off), I knew Jordan would hit the roof if she knew I was here with the DJ.

My leg bounced nervously when another whiff of his indescribable aroma assaulted my senses. Fuck, what was that scent? Musk? Vanilla? Bergamot?

Ugh.

"Thank you for the drink," I mumbled. "But you really should have let me pay. This bucket list is for my benefit. Otherwise, you wouldn't be here."

"Trust me. I don't do things unless I want to."

"I'm assuming you generally do whatever you want."

"I *only* do whatever I want."

"And tonight, you wanted to help me with my bucket list. Why?"

"To find out your name."

I shook my head. "Not gonna happen. What if you blab to someone about meeting me, and word gets back to my family?"

"But your family doesn't care if you date someone outside your race."

"We aren't dating," I reminded him.

"I picked you up, brought you here, bought you a drink. That's a date."

My jaw dropped. The man was delusional. We weren't dating, nor were we friends. We were nothing. "I hardly consider going to a strip club a date."

"You chose the venue," he countered.

"Even if this were a date, which it isn't, one date doesn't mean *dating*. The latter is a continuous term referring to a long-term situation."

"Semantics." He waved it off as if the matter about the status of our relationship had been settled. His index finger waved between us, returning to his previous point. "If it's not about cultural differences, why does it matter if I tell someone about us?" He speared me with his prominent orbs of dark liquid, calculating the possible reasons.

I smoothed my mien. Revealing any expression to this man was dangerous. He paid attention to every detail, the tiniest hints, and kept drawing conclusions with unyielding accuracy. I cursed upon realizing his large frame took up so much of the booth that there was no room to move away from his concentrated attention.

Taking a sip of my dirty martini, I carefully averted my gaze. Gin might inebriate my senses, but my hearing remained impeccable.

"I'm guessing your family is rich and pretentious," Axel speculated. "And wouldn't approve of the riffraff you enjoy hanging out with."

The shrewd way he deduced the reasoning hit home, and my eyes threatened to round at his explicit but accurate assessment.

To be clear, I considered the two drunks from the pavement to be riffraff. From everything I gathered about Axel, riffraff was an inaccurate description of him. Nevertheless, my family and friends would take one look at his tattoos, nonconformist clothing, and job title and declare him a risk.

I took another sip of my drink, allowing vermouth and gin to soothe my taste buds and gather some liquid courage before speaking. "They wouldn't be happy with my present company," I admitted. "I-I have fucked up a lot. So, the only decisions of mine they trust are the ones they've vetted and approved."

He caught onto my flat tone. "And I wouldn't be someone they'd vet and approve?" he guessed.

"You wouldn't be someone they'd even consider vetting. If anything, they'd veto you on the spot simply because you were my selection. Unless you look and speak just like them, or they know of you, they have no reason to trust my judgment." My mouth twisted for a self-deprecating smile. "I have made the wrong choice so many times that I've turned into the girl who cried wolf. Even when I do make the right decision, they no longer have faith in it."

I grimaced when he didn't react to my words. Anyone would feel rejected upon hearing such a statement. Just because we'd never see each other after tonight didn't mean I wanted to put the guy down.

I wanted to soothe the blow somehow. Tell Axel he was good enough to date any women or that my family and friends were pretentious for dismissing him based on superficial reasons. As much as I wanted to blame them, I couldn't.

I cringed, remembering the stitches Jordan had sported on my account, and all she asked in return was to stop my self-destructive ways. They were within their rights to demand that I stop dating men like Axel. Neither Jordan nor Milan would bring this type of calamity to my life.

To my surprise, Axel didn't seem offended, though he had every right to be. If I wasn't mistaken, he didn't seem to agree with my assessment, and his curious tone prodded for more information. "What are these supposed mistakes?"

Oh, God. I really didn't want to divulge the history of my failed relationships. "My inability to weed out crappy humans is what ultimately cost me my family's respect," I said tentatively, struggling to phrase my answer. "I'm a poor judge of character."

Disconcerting gaze moved over my face. "How so?"

I sighed, giving in. "You know how everyone puts their best foot forward to make a good first impression? While I buy into the façade, others seem capable of differentiating genuine versus disingenuous people during the initial vetting phase." I gestured at the stage where Missy Lusty was currently performing a chair routine to Christina Milian's "*Dip it Low*." "See that woman? Others in my clique would take one look at her and have the preconceived notion that she is bad news. Whereas I don't see the problem in us becoming the best of friends."

I shook my head, imagining the look on my mother's face if I introduced Missy Lusty as my new friend. Oh, the travesty.

Then again, I had been proven wrong so many times. So perhaps Mom had a point in her evaluation.

"I hate judging a book by its cover, but I'm starting to think maybe I should," I admitted quietly.

"There is nothing wrong with giving people a chance."

I scoffed. "Not if you're too optimistic. No matter how much I believe the best in people, they let me down."

"What's the common denominator?"

"Pardon?"

"You said people keep letting you down. What seems to be the common turning point in these situations?"

No one had phrased that question before, and I considered it for a moment. "I guess I'm generous with money. If someone I care about doesn't have much of it, I'm happy to chip in.

However, it's caused numerous bad habits to develop in the past. People start expecting me to pave the way, and soon I can't tell if they like me or they are using me."

I looked away at the painful reminder and caught the end of *Missy Lusty's* performance. A perfect set of tits stayed in place even though she was upside down on the pole. It was an impressive move. The masses shared the sentiment and cheered her on, throwing singles on the stage.

The only eyes not on Missy Lusty belonged to the man next to me. My heart slammed against my chest when I found him staring at me. "Why are you looking at me?"

He shrugged. "I like looking at you."

No matter how often he had done it tonight, I was dumbstruck by his constant brutal honesty. Sometimes I didn't know what to make of it.

"I envy your lack of filter," I admitted.

"You can become just like me," he alluded. "No filters. No hang-ups. Become an open book, Princess. And you can start by telling me your name."

I threw my head back and laughed wholeheartedly. I couldn't believe it. My incredibly shitty day had been replaced by a somewhat tolerable one. In fact, I was now laughing so hard that it left me with tears. "You never give up, do you?" I said, wiping the moisture from the corner of my eye.

My laughter hardly dissuaded him from his objective. "If you won't tell me your name, then tell me everything else about you."

"That'll take all night. I am supposed to finish this bucket list by Monday."

"Are you dying on Monday?"

"Well, no..."

"Then I suppose we have time. Talk."

The assertiveness in his voice made me want to divulge. What was it about him that was so domineering yet comforting?

With a couple more rounds of drinks, I found myself unraveling, starting from my childhood.

Zaina Mittal only wanted one child but accidentally ended up with a spare. She was supposed to be done with that portion of her life since Milan was grown. The last thing she expected to do was take care of a little one while her career was on the rise. As a result, most of my childhood was dealt with by nannies.

There had been a rift in our relationship from the beginning. Mom and Milan already had an established bond I could never infiltrate. Milan aspired to become a CPA, like Mom. They excitedly spoke about colleges and later which firms he'd apply to. Meanwhile, I had shown an early interest in all art-related things. Art wasn't regarded as a respectable profession, and Mom pushed practical career choices, such as asset management or medicine. It didn't take. Mom never saw the value in attending Juilliard, and even after the prestigious degree had helped put me on the map, she often expressed her dissatisfaction over my choice.

Amit Mittal, in turn, was a meek-mannered man. Dad never criticized me, which I appreciated. He was disinterested in interfering with family affairs and often followed Mom's lead the times I was shunned, which I hated.

Despite the discrepancies in my relationship with my parents, my childhood was all around satisfactory, with both good and bad memories. My privileged life hadn't endured real hardships until the passing of my Dadi. She was a great cook, and I learned to do the same by following her around in the kitchen. I had a weakness for Prada and Louis Vuitton, sparkly items, and all things pink. I had no long-term goals and when Axel asked about my five-year plan, the only thought to pop into my mind was purchasing this collector's edition piano that had caught my eye.

Axel didn't tear his gaze away while I unloaded. He listened with such intensity that my insides quaked during various points of the conversation. Something unfamiliar amplified a fear in my chest. This night would be over before I knew it, and so would this man's undivided attention. A strange grief gripped me by the chest, already mourning the loss of it. Axel's undivided attention was unlike anything I had experienced before. Despite the half-naked servers and the fully naked women on stage, his gaze never wandered. He was single-minded, focused... almost to the point of obsessive. Had he blinked even once?

I was vaguely aware of the announcement welcoming Stuffed Candy to the stage. Hoots and cheers echoed around us, but they appeared hazy and in the backdrop of a more critical conversation happening at this red corner booth. Axel still hadn't taken his eyes off me when a woman missing her top approached our booth. Her ass jiggled in a pair of yellow bottoms and matching high heels. Long, dirty blonde hair was styled to one side over her shoulders, shimmery glitter covering her exposed breasts.

As I said, a little sparkle never hurt anyone.

She put her hand on the booth behind Axel. Batting her lashes a few times, she said in a syrupy sweet voice, "Hi guys, I'm

Thick Cupcake. How are the two most beautiful people at this club doing tonight?" Though she asked both of us, her attention was solely on Axel. In fact, most of the female staff's attention had been on Axel since our arrival.

"We're good," I responded upon realizing Axel wouldn't acknowledge her. He genuinely did *whatever the fuck* he wanted.

"Do either of you good-looking superstars want a lap dance?" When Axel didn't glance away from me, she followed up slyly, "Or perhaps a tour of the private room?"

"Um."

I didn't care to do either of those things but realized we had done a poor job of participating in the debauchery of the club. I absentmindedly reached into my backpack and stuck a couple of twenties in Thick Cupcake's G-string, hoping a good tip would be enough of a contribution to the club's economy.

"Oh, thanks, sweetie," she gushed. Her focus was suddenly on me, the short-lived lust for Axel all but forgotten. "That's enough for the special treatment. Buckle up."

Before I knew it, Thick Cupcake had climbed abroad the circular booth. I meant the money as a tip, but she took it as an invitation to perform a lap dance. But hey, when in Rome, right?

I cheered her on as she started gyrating on my lap. Approximately two seconds was how long it took for Axel to be out of his seat, rip Thick Cupcake off me, and shove her aside.

"Touch her one more time, and it'll be the last thing you touch in your miserable life," he growled with so much menace that everything came to a screeching halt.

The MC broadcasting the announcements and playing the

songs, along with the guy shining spotlights on the girls, ceased on both accounts. With the music coming to an abrupt halt, all eyes landed on us. I had no doubt that we were seconds away from being thrown out. The only favorable account was the bouncer's absence from the floor. He had been going back and forth between the private rooms and the main floor all night. Lucky for Axel, the bouncer was currently in the private room.

Thick Cupcake appeared mortified, and I was out of my seat in a flash. "Dude, what are you doing?" Clearly, I misunderstood the tipping structure and gave Thick Cupcake an amount equivalent to the cost of a lap dance. Even if it hadn't been my intention to get a lap dance, I didn't protest once she started dancing. This was hardly her fault. "She thought I wanted a lap dance, and hello, this is a strip club. What did you think we were going to do?"

"Apparently, not let random women ride you for their entertainment."

"Oh, my God. Are you seriously jealous? The poor woman was just doing her job."

He ignored me and turned to the woman, seemingly angrier at Thick Cupcake because I defended her. "I better not see you again," he chewed out.

"Leave her alone." I tilted my head toward the woman. "I'm so sorry about this." I handed her a couple more twenties to make up for whatever loss of business this drama had caused her. She clutched my hands as she took the money and held onto me, most likely out of fear of the giant man towering over her, ready to tear her limb from limb.

Big mistake.

Axel appeared homicidal. "What did I tell you about touching her? Get your filthy fucking hands off her." He took a step forward. Thick Cupcake didn't need to be told twice. She retracted her hands and bolted.

I shoved at his chest. The temporary truce we had invoked while disclosing my life story was all but forgotten. "Where do you get off bullying people? She can touch me if she wants to; it's none of your fucking business."

"You think so?" he growled back. "How about I prove you wrong?"

I stared at Axel with round eyes. "How about I ditch your lunatic ass? You don't get to be possessive over me; we aren't dating."

"Yet," he added.

My temper threatened to break loose. The urge to walk away from this maniac was overwhelming, but so was my willpower to defend a fellow female. Girl power, girls stick together, and all that jazz.

My temple prickled from the danger of his large frame towering over me, but I held my ground. The MC and lighting guy caught my eye, appearing equally terrified of Axel. They presumed the situation as Axel being my uber-possessive boyfriend and, if I wasn't mistaken, were apprehensively concerned about me for taking on the big bully.

With my team of cheerleaders backing me, I glared at him with hell's fury pulsing through me. I didn't know what overcame me. Possibly, it was because I couldn't physically take him out but wanted to stick it to him for scaring the shit out of Thick Cupcake. Without thinking, I jumped on the red seat of our corner booth. Using it as leverage, I stepped onto the table.

Axel didn't move, shocked by my irrational behavior. I took his momentary lapse in judgment in stride and started dancing to non-existent music. It was the only thing I could think of to retaliate since Axel seemed hellbent on his possessiveness. The MC met my gaze simultaneously, and through sheer cosmic power, he read my mind. He grinned upon realizing I was sticking it to my supposed possessive boyfriend and whispered something to the lighting guy. The music returned to full blast, and his voice boomed through the speakers right as the spotlight fell on me.

"Ladies and gentlemen, we have a very special surprise for you tonight. Please welcome, Ms. Pink Siren." Courtesy of my hot pink cami?

All eyes at the club turned to our table. I flipped my hair on cue as the dancers had done and flipped it back, keeping in rhythm to the music. The patrons started cheering and hooting, and I twisted my butt to one side... that was as far as I got.

Axel, the force of nature, charged at me. He grabbed my hips and lifted me off the table, flinging me over his shoulders. A round of *boos* bounced off the walls as Axel moved at an alarming speed.

"Oh my god!" I shouted. "Put me down, you psycho."

Aggressive energy emanated from him. "No."

Fall weather cooled my heated shoulders as we exited the club. "Put me down! Put me down! Put me down!" I shouted, scratching his back.

"Why the fuck should I when you purposely pissed me off?"

"Because you're pressing down on my bladder, and I'm about to pee my pants."

Axel set me down on the pavement, and though his eyes remained impassive, he was as close to smiling as I had seen all night. Notwithstanding our livid argument and tendency to push each other's buttons, I started giggling.

Just as unexpectedly we had gotten caught up in a heated argument, the anger passed equally swiftly. I threw my head back and laughed openly while my bladder threatened to give. When I stopped, I found his eyes trained on mine with a smirk.

My mind suddenly went startlingly blank. I couldn't interpret his thoughts in the way he was looking at me, but the unfamiliar sensation from earlier returned with full force. The intimidating feelings were so overwhelming and so bipolar that I wondered if I'd lose myself in this fog. Part of me wanted to make a run for it. The other part wanted to lean into the fear to see what it would unveil.

In the end, I did neither.

"How do you feel about adult movie theaters?" I asked. "I'm sure they have bathrooms."

His mouth quirked. "I suppose you have a place in mind."

I nodded, smiling sweetly. I picked Boobie Lodge because it was within walking distance of my next dodgy destination.

"After you, Princess."

Steal a bottle of liquor from a bar

~~Shotgun a beer~~
~~Crash a party~~
~~Go to a strip club~~
~~Dance on a table in front of a roomful of~~
~~strangers~~

CHAPTER
NINE

Milan's Wedding

Piya

"You can put your stuff here or leave it in my car." Axel nodded at the blanket laid out on the soft sand. The bonfire cackled with charge, illuminating the deserted beach.

"Here is fine." I set my backpack on the blanket and reached for the fire to warm my fingers. Fall weather might be gorgeous, but not enough to fight the chill in the dead of night.

Axel retreated inside Chateau at the Hempstead with promises of libations and more blankets.

After the strip club, we went to an adult cinema. I couldn't stop giggling at the ridiculous notion of grown men jerking off inside a theater. Had they never heard of internet porn from the comfort of their home? We lasted five minutes before I caught some dude's attention, and an infuriated Axel dragged me out. We got into another argument, and I told him to go to Hell. He responded by throwing me over his shoulders again.

Next, we landed at a BDSM club. They let us in without the usual vetting process because Axel knew someone. It was the only place he was well behaved as voyeurism consisted of limited inter-action with others. We walked along a hallway lined with two-way mirrors, giving us a peek into various unobserving patrons frenzied by their niche of fetish. Room after room of leather, whips, and chains had been forever ingrained in my brain. It made me realize I had no kinks. Nothing I saw turned me on. The only thing heating my insides was the man walking beside me with his all-consuming presence.

As we exited the building, Axel insisted we break for food. My growling stomach didn't put up a fight since I missed the dinner portion of the reception. I was stumped that he remembered, whereas he was amazed I never had New York jumbo-slice pizza.

Two giant-sized slices later, I dragged him to a male strip club, another seedy establishment with questionable hygiene. We were cast out after Axel started a fight with a male stripper for getting too close. I told him he was insane. He told me I was a brat. I smacked him over the head, and once more, he threw me over his shoulders.

I spent mere hours with this man, yet it felt like days had passed from the rush of the night. Axel joined the debauchery in crossing off the items on my list, and I got the distinct feeling he enjoyed it equally. Upon prodding, he mentioned what his bucket list items would hold. Axel's list sounded evil rather than thrill-seeking like mine because he was a heathen, after all. Prank-calling an old college roommate. Convincing someone he was from the future to make them do terrible things. Speak in a made-up language in public. Jump into a taxi and scream, "follow that car." Those sorts of things.

Unlike the men from my past, Axel had been adamant about paying my way throughout the night and wouldn't let me pick up a single tab. He wasn't intimidated, either, upon hearing my family would reject him before meeting him. It stirred an alien emotion inside me. I ruefully admitted the night wouldn't have been a success (or safe) had he not tagged along, although, at times, he was the bane of my existence with the slivers of jealousy he displayed. It was apparent Axel had some form of antisocial personality, and like many with the affliction, he had started to view me as his possession and had claimed a right over me.

It would've been alarming had there been more of a future between us. There wasn't. With each item we crossed off, I was one step closer to the promise I had made to Dadi, Jordan, and everyone else in my life. Each glorious experience tonight was diminished by the impending panic of what was to come after. It was strange. We barely knew one another, and Axel was an emotionless, untouchable man. But the thought that there'd be nothing more with Axel once this list was completed left my insides with an unfathomable void.

Instead of dwelling on the inevitable, I focused on the night.

Axel didn't know Milan was my brother and mentioned in passing that the groom from tonight's wedding had organized fireworks at the end of the afterparty. Milan's bougie move didn't surprise me, and I asked Axel if we could return to Chateau at the Hempstead. Although I had no plans of returning to the house until after the bride and groom retired for the night, I loved fireworks and didn't see the folly in enjoying them from afar.

Luckily, we had a cozy setup. The staff at the venue had constructed a bonfire on the private beach for the guests to enjoy, though no one had ventured here since it was a walk away. The bonfire was supposed to be put out following the fireworks. However, when I enthusiastically dragged Axel to the beach, he texted the owners, offering to put the fire out so I could bask in it for longer.

Axel had his moments, didn't he?

He reemerged from the main building with two beers in one hand and his laptop in the other. Two blankets were flung over his shoulders, and a portable keyboard was carefully tucked under his arm. He gracefully maneuvered the items and set them down one by one. If it were me, I would have fallen face down by now.

"Thanks," I said as he passed me a beer and took the seat next to me. I wrapped one of the blankets around myself, staring inquisitively at the portable keyboard he placed next to me.

"Sometimes couples want live music for their ceremony instead of a DJ," he explained. "The Chateau has a portable keyboard, a harp, and a whole closetful of items for that purpose."

"Along with blankets and booze." I raised my beer to clink with his.

He nodded. "Perks of the job."

I smiled, grasping he'd snagged the keyboard so I could write a *raunchy song,* another item on my list. Leaning my palm against my cheek and wrapping my other hand around my elbow, I stared at the stranger. Despite our differing backgrounds, we were bewilderingly compatible.

I was an adrenaline junkie. He had no inhibitions.

I loved creating music. He loved mixing it.

I loved speaking my mind. He loved provoking me to bare my soul.

Social standing-wise, religious-wise, and racially, we had nothing in common... except for one another. The comfortability between us was one I hadn't shared before, and the impending loss of it was overwhelming.

"Tell me everything about you," I asked out of nowhere, rephrasing his question from earlier.

Axel's brows shot up. Throughout the night, he had pressed me for answers while giving very little of himself. *Just like Sean,* I mused. I hated comparing, but you become jaded after your heart's been broken so many times. Boys like him never revealed much about themselves, always keeping you at bay.

"Everything?" He scoffed predictably. "That'll take hours."

"So?"

"So, we'll never finish your bucket list by Monday."

"Are you dying on Monday?" I asked with a straight face.

"Wasn't planning on it."

"Then I suppose we have time. Talk."

Just when I thought Axel would disregard me, he stunned me by telling me his life story.

Smalltown boy whose ambitions superseded his resources. Unsupportive, alcoholic parents. Dead-end career paths. Lack of opportunities for musical aspirations. Not surprisingly, Axel didn't believe in family values or buy into the idea of a loving family. He preferred solitude and dug his way out with an impromptu college scholarship at sixteen. He said goodbye to his previous life in hopes of bigger and better things. Upon graduating college, he landed a job with this venue, and he'd been with them for three years.

"So, what exactly do you do for the venue?" I asked tentatively.

"AV. They sell in-house sound and DJ packages for their wedding and corporate events. I run their lighting, sound, and everything else related to AV. And they give me thirty percent of the cut."

Those cheap fuckers. "But I thought the industry standard was a fifty-fifty split."

He regarded me carefully. "It is."

"Then why work for this venue?"

"I work with multiple venues. I have a laptop and software to make music." He nodded at the laptop he'd brought with him. "But I prefer venues with flexible hours and in-house equipment. Things like speakers, turntables, cables, a built-in sound system."

I heard a basic DJ equipment system ran a few thousand dollars. It wasn't an absurd amount of money. He could probably save that much within a few weeks. So... "Couldn't you buy those items by saving a few paychecks? Then you can cut out the middleman?"

"That's the plan, eventually. But the equipment I want," his back straightened, "it'll take me a while to save up for it."

Understanding dawned on me. He didn't want good enough equipment to play at some thirsty club on ladies' night. He wanted to pursue music professionally and wanted industry-grade products. Since Chateau at the Hempstead had a built-in sound system, it allowed him to keep working as a DJ and produce new music while simultaneously saving to buy brand equipment used by the likes of celebrity DJs.

"You're saving up to buy the best," I deduced.

Axel nodded, listing the array of equipment and the sound system he planned to purchase.

Unlike me, Axel was patient and disciplined. With his sights set on the long haul, he wasn't opposed to paying his dues first. He had mapped out the next several years of life, including his rise to success. The undeterred ambition stumped me. He graduated from college at nineteen and saved every penny for the last three years. He still had ways to go if he wanted to do things the right way. Producing music in soundproof recording studios. Pricey equipment. An equipment van. Cost of roadies for setup at shows. Travel cost for shows. Fuck. There were so many costs for start-up artists.

I mentally calculated the total as he spoke. It was a lot of money. With New York rent prices, and based on what I presume he made at each gig, it would take him a few more years to reach his goals. I didn't have to say it, however. Axel was aware; this was a well-crafted five-year plan.

"I hope you do it," I spoke meekly, feeling deflated over the long road ahead of him.

Axel tilted his head in acknowledgment. I knew without a doubt he'd accomplish his goals. He was a man with a lot to prove, teeming with potential. He wasn't the kind to let his dreams wane.

"So," I nodded at the keyboard, "shall we?"

We spent the next forty-five minutes with me at the portable keyboard and him messing with his DJ software. A tempo I had been fiddling with seemed appropriate for the theme of this night. Beside the fire, the only available lighting was the hazy green glow from the beach's dock. I presumed the light was strategically placed so guests could find their way around the beach at night. Under the faint light, I put my fingers on the black and white keys of the board and played the beginning portion of the composition. He listened for a few beats. Tampering with his DJ software, he swiftly crafted a backdrop beat.

I listened for several seconds but didn't recognize the song.

"That's an original," I said almost accusatorily. I had an inkling Axel wrote music, but the guitar track in the background surprised me. "You play the guitar?"

He nodded.

"But you said your town didn't have a music program at school."

Another nod. "I taught myself."

Holy shit. I had never taught myself anything in life. Not only had Axel taught himself how to play the guitar, but he also incorporated it into his music... and mine. He had simply listened to the jingle I had been working on for weeks and thought of the perfect song to complement it. Then he remixed it and compressed it into a perfect fit. He thought of it just off the top of his head. How? It took DJs weeks and months to produce songs. Even mixing music took time. Whereas he had a natural ear for it. He hadn't an ounce of human emotion, yet music poured out of him as if he were made of nothing but.

Something unspoken passed between us. Using his music as a base and the green light as a guide, I started playing my tune and was shocked when it led me to the natural composition of the next notation I had been struggling with. The remixed version of the old song blended harmoniously with each chord, and I had to admit it was sexy as hell. Sexier than anything I had written before; the tune dripped with erotic energy.

We played in synchronicity and argued three more times before settling on the right combo. Fight and make-up seemed to be *our* synchronicity and felt like our natural habitat. Nothing with Axel felt forced, even fighting.

I pulled the small keyboard off my lap and set it aside as he did the same with his laptop.

He perused me thoughtfully. "You attended Juilliard."

"Hm."

"How can your family not trust your judgment after you graduated from the best music school in the world?"

"They don't see music as something to be proud of," I replied flatly.

"Your family hates music?"

The question was phrased so callously that I started laughing. "No, they don't hate music," I spoke after the laughter subsided. "They just don't think it's practical as a career choice."

"But it is practical. You're earning a professional income at twenty-one."

Only because Jordan got my foot in the door, I disputed internally, giving him a tight smile. Guilt of sorts took hold, and I couldn't meet his eyes. If I wasn't born into a wealthy family, received the best education money could buy, and had rich friends to further my career, I wouldn't be successful.

After listening to Axel, it was clear the world deserved to know him, not me. Anyone with an ear for music could tell that this man had the instinct to produce and compose and could probably do my job in his sleep. Yet, here I was, shy of making six figures, and here he was, climbing his way out of a hellhole. He persevered despite never being given a chance or having one person who believed enough to bet on him.

My heart sank because Axel still had a long way to go. The *rags to riches* phrase was true because all I had done to be successful was be born in privilege. It was an utter disgrace.

Sensing my melancholy, Axel's eyes tried to dissect me. I concentrated on the fire, unable to shake the hollowness spreading inside my chest. He followed my gaze.

He spoke suddenly, most likely to pull me out of my

thoughts. "There was a fire incorporated into today's ceremony. Is that a part of Hindu Wedding ceremonies?" Axel asked.

Unprepared to meet his gaze, I stared into the bonfire and said absentmindedly, "Yup. Do you recall the stage where the ceremony took place?"

He nodded.

"It's called a mandap. It's the wedding altar for Hindi ceremonies."

"There was a square box in the middle with open fire," he commented.

I nodded. "Fire is integrated into Hindu wedding ceremonies for numerous reasons. One of them is to signify the sacred occasion of marriage."

"They must not have seen my parents' marriage if they think marriages are sacred." He scoffed.

I smiled. "Shut up. I think weddings are romantic."

"Of course you do," he said dryly.

"You don't think so?"

He said nothing.

"Well, the wedding today was very romantic."

He raised an eyebrow. "Yeah. Nothing says romance like open flames in an enclosed space."

I tsked. "The only reason you didn't think it was romantic was because you didn't understand the ritual. I'll explain it to you." I grabbed his hands and pulled him to stand before he could object. "During a Hindu ceremony, you take *Pheras* in front of everyone."

"*Pheras*?"

"Do you remember when the couple from today walked around the fire?"

He nodded.

"Fires are significant at Hindi wedding ceremonies. The bride and groom walk around the fire seven times. Each time they circle the fire, it represents a different vow, aka a *Phera*. By the seventh time they walk around the fire, their union is sealed, and they are declared one for not only this lifetime but seven lifetimes."

"One circle for each lifetime?"

"Isn't that something? Why be with the love of your life once if you could do it seven times over? Many Hindus believe in reincarnation, and each time the bride and groom walk around the fire, they commit another lifetime to the other."

None of my friends outside the community asked me about my religion. Axel was the first to ask and was hell-bent on learning everything about me. He watched me unequivocally as I excitedly explained the various steps of the ceremony and what everything meant.

I rambled about fire and weddings for minutes before realizing that a guy like him probably didn't find this sexy. I groaned internally, then jumped at the sound of a sudden loud boom.

"Holy shit." I turned my head in search of the source. "What the fuck?"

"Easy, Princess," Axel's buttery voice soothed. "Just the fireworks."

I hadn't realized so much time had passed that the afterparty had officially ended. I glanced up and marveled at the sight.

The dark sky over the water lit up with glee. Green coils jetted to the top, blue hues chasing after. The sparks tumbled down upon reaching their destination, painting the September sky with northern lights. White whirls of dazzling sparklers shot to the sky next, shattering like a sparkling silver shower. Various shapes of sparks kept reaching for the heavens, only to tumble like fallen angels. Sparkling rain surrounded us as their ashes fell to the beach like gray snow.

The zig zags and zooms of lights had me mesmerized. I couldn't look away from the perfect night with an imperfect man, admiring a world of what could be. As always, I could tell when he was staring at me. I let my gaze fleet sideways for a moment to find him watching me, unblinking. He hadn't glanced once at the sky, and I realized he was using the light from the fireworks to see my face in the dark.

Before I could tear my gaze away from the sky entirely, Axel had closed the distance between us as if no longer able to stand it. He wrapped a hand around my throat and suddenly tugged me to him for an unyielding kiss.

The movement was so abrupt, so possessive, that I stumbled unexpectedly, my palms landing on his hard chest. I yelped in surprise, which he took full advantage of. His tongue lapped against mine ferociously, devouring me with promises to come.

I had never been kissed like this before.

It was impossible to catch my breath, and if he hadn't been holding me up, I would have fallen onto the soft sand. My lungs burned from the same all-consuming smell—rainforest, musk, vanilla, ugh, what the fuck was that scent of his—as he pulled me so close there wasn't an ounce of decency left between us. He refused to break the kiss even though I was running out of breath. Feeling lightheaded, I fisted his shirt, and he finally let up.

He yanked at my hair harshly to tilt my face to the side. "Tell me, Princess. Do you think your family would be pissed if they saw us kissing?"

"Yes," I breathed.

"And what if they saw us like this?" His lips trailed my neck, teeth sinking in to taste my flesh.

"They'll kill me," I moaned, eyes fluttering, mind blank.

"And what will they do if they see their little princess being fucked by the likes of me; right here out in the open?"

"They'll kill *you*."

I glanced around stealthily, guilt washing over me. My family would never speak to me again if they saw what we were doing right now. But no matter how much my brain ordered my body to stop, it had the opposite effect. An animalistic charge was leading this inquisition. No matter how many promises I made, my mind wasn't the one in control.

"Just this once," I rasped out. "I want to know what it'll be like with you."

In the dark of the night, with no witnesses, we could do this just this once. Please, God, let me have him just this once, and I'd never do it again.

Axel didn't need to be told twice. He grabbed me with unyielding speed, his mouth ravaging mine. Fireworks louder than the ones lighting up the sky burst inside me. He kissed me with such absolution that it wiped my mind clean of anyone to come before him.

With a hand wrapped around my middle, Axel lifted me off the ground. My back hit the blanket on the soft sand before I could form another thought. He undid my pants without ripping his mouth off me and yanked them down with incredible accuracy. He didn't bother taking off my underwear, most likely due to impatience, and simply moved the fabric to the side. Two thick fingers intruded.

A pitiful-sounding moan tumbled out of my lips. "Oh, fuck," I bit my lips and tilted my hips toward the sky. He had barely touched me, and my body had come alive as if it had never known a man's touch. Everything awoke inside me at the same time. My skin was on fire. My body vibrated with shots of ecstasy. Every nerve of mine stirred. My heart thumped against my chest, and I worried for a moment that I might have a heart attack.

"Oh god, oh god," I chanted, blood pumping in my veins so hard that I could hear it up to my fingertips. Slick wetness dripped off me and onto the blanket underneath. My ass was shamelessly soaked, and it only egged him on.

Axel's hardened face was unforgiving in the dim, bonfire light as he grabbed my right breast and squeezed. "I've been thinking about this from the moment I saw you," he murmured, sending tremors down my spine. It was followed by the sound of his belt unbuckling and the zipper of his pants. Within a second, he slammed inside me with such force that had his mass not been holding me down, I would have slid off the blanket.

"Fuck," this time, we both gritted in unison.

My moan was from a mixture of pain and pleasure. The sheer size of Axel's body reflected in the rock-hard length inside me. He was only halfway in, despite the force he had used to pummel inside me. I couldn't take more of him and shook my head as he charged ahead.

"All of it, baby," he said from behind clenched teeth.

"Axel, please." I placed a hand on his chest, asking him to slow down.

"I said, all of it," he growled, forcing every inch of himself inside me.

"Fuck," I cried out again before biting my lips in fear of someone hearing us. He was thicker than anyone I had taken before, and I had to breathe in and out several times to adjust.

Axel turned frenzied the moment he slammed home. My spaghetti straps came down, revealing a pair of bouncing tits. His black shirt was off, revealing an assortment of tattoos. He bit my breasts and neck, sucking and licking as if he couldn't get enough. Meanwhile, his cock battered me with such force my mouth hung open for an inaudible gasp.

My legs hung limply on either side of his hips, unable to hold onto him. He slammed in and out mercilessly, his fingers swiping over my clit and his mouth paying homage to my breasts.

The orgasm happened so suddenly that I was caught off guard.

"Oh god, oh god," I didn't know if I was crying to be saved or asking for more. I ignited more violently than the fireworks, and like the sparklers, my insides lit up with a type of bliss I had never experienced before.

His fingers wrapped around my throat and squeezed simultaneously. I reached for the hand, gripping my throat in a reactive response to pull it off. It made him squeeze tighter until my hand fell away, and my eyes flashed white. My back arched off the blanket, and I screamed until the veins in my neck popped, no longer caring about who might see us during this lewd act.

I gasped for air, head lolling to one side, when I vaguely heard Axel in the background.

"Hell no, Princess," he growled. "We aren't done. Far from it." Lifting me like a rag doll off the blanket, Axel sat up and placed me on his lap. I realized the move was to wake me up though my sated body refused to cooperate.

Axel didn't care. He thrust into me from underneath, setting a new unmatched pace I could barely keep up with. His hold tightened on my hips for a bruising grip as his mouth moved over my neck and chest for little bites. I knew I'd be feeling this for days to come as his five o'clock shadow scraped over my delicate skin. I realized he was leaving souvenirs on purpose, marking me for himself. I glanced down at the artwork he had created and opened my mouth to protest. All that came out was one more moan at his possessive marks of ownership. A craving I had never known burst inside me, followed by another round of unmatched elation.

My head tipped back. "God," I gasped, lips parted, hair in beachy unrulable tangles from sand and sex.

He fucked me through my second climax, speeding up more and more. I wanted to tell him to slow down, but words refused to escape me. At long last, he planted himself deep and held me there. I felt his cock twitch, and warm semen spread inside me.

"Fuck," he grunted, his mouth landed in the crook of my neck.

By some miracle, he maneuvered our non-operating bodies without pulling out and positioned us horizontally onto the blanket.

I groaned, covering my eyes with my hand, trying to understand what had just happened. Never in my twenty-one years had I experienced anything similar. What the fuck was that?

Neither of us moved or spoke, though we should straighten ourselves before one of the venue staff or guests stumbled onto the private beach for a late-night stroll. Once our breathing evened out, I tapped his chest.

"Axel, you're still inside me."

"So?" he asked without moving.

I pushed at his chest, though my eyes had fluttered shut.

He responded by grabbing my hand and pinning it to the side.

"Dude," I groaned. "Come on. Get off me." Try as I might, I couldn't get my eyes to reopen.

"No, my cock's staying inside you," he replied in a matter-of-fact tone. "I'll give you fifteen minutes to recover; then I'm fucking you awake."

What was with him and the ticking timers he put on people? I would have blasted him had he not fucked the heat out of me. Instead, I fought my lids against closing, mumbling incomprehensively. My eyes fluttered against the dim, green light at the beach dock before sleep won the battle.

Fifteen minutes later, Axel fucked me awake.

Dawn rays bothered my flapping eyelids. It took minutes for the cobwebs of my sleepy mind to clear and peel my eyes open.

We had hours of sex on the beach, and my body was paying the price. Axel insisted on sleeping with his cock inside me during the fifteen to twenty minutes he gave me to recover in between. The last we fell asleep was thirty minutes ago. I was on top of him, and Axel had covered my naked body with one of the blankets. He was finally sated enough to sleep longer than twenty minutes, and I took it as a cue for my sweet escape.

My pussy screamed in protest when I lifted off his cock, flinching from the pounding I had taken throughout the night. The bliss rivaled the pain it brought, and I stumbled to gather my clothes. With the break of dawn, guests staying on the property would likely be venturing outside soon. If they saw us in this position... I was pretty sure my family would insist the venue fired Axel.

Blinking my eyes against the first rays of the day, I dressed as quickly as my weak muscles allowed. I averted my eyes, refusing to glance at Axel again. Despite all the warnings, I had walked into another heartbreak, and fuck, why did it hurt so much more than anything I had experienced before?

It'll pass, I told myself. *It always does. You made a deal. You had one night, and now you're done.*

Forcing my gaze on anywhere but Axel, I gathered my items. I knew waking him up to say goodbye would end poorly. I saw glimpses of this man's possessiveness and knew nothing good would come from saying goodbye. He'd probably throw me over his shoulders, then jostle me out of here.

I smiled sadly at the image.

Shaking my head, I grabbed my notebook to leave him a note instead. Upon realizing the notebook was empty, sans the list from last night, I decided to leave him the entire notebook plus a souvenir meant for him.

I reached inside my purse for the souvenir, placed it inside the notebook, and wrote a message for Axel after a moment's hesitation. Carefully, I put the notebook next to him and stood. Still, I refused to look at his beautiful face because I knew what I'd find there. Heartbreak.

The sun had risen, and the spell had been broken. It was time to return to our real lives. The shitty weekend had been replaced by one I'd never forget. It should make me happy, but God, it hurt worse than anything imaginable.

I walked away that day without glancing at the beautiful stranger, and a month later, I became Mrs. Jay Ambani.

PART TWO

Rise from the Ashes

TEN

Present

~

Axel

"MR. TRIMALCHIO, WHAT ARE YOU DOING HERE?" PIYA asked sternly. Dark sunglasses barely hid her alarm upon seeing me at her daughter's boarding school.

Loose tendrils hung off Piya's high bun to tactfully frame olive skin that glowed in the afternoon sun. She wore minimal makeup with lips in some shade of pink. I lazily perused Piya's body, using the momentary lapse while she was caught off guard by my presence. A white blouse hugged her torso with a perfect hint of cleavage. The shirt was tucked into a brown leather pencil skirt that ended at her slim waist. A slit showcased a sliver of a toned thigh elongated by her heels.

Fuck, she was sexier at thirty-four than she had been at twenty-one, though now she screamed of refined old money rather than a wildcard princess. Nonetheless, both versions of Piya stirred my libido the same.

I repressed an image of fucking her out in the open. Probably not a good idea while we were at a high school surrounded by parents, teachers, and students. Nott Academy was built on five acres of land with an admissions office off to one side and a giant Hogwarts-style building in the middle with resident halls and classrooms. I ran into Piya in the courtyards of the building.

I hummed contentedly, without a hint of cocky disposition. "This is my school. I thought you knew." She didn't because I only bought this school earlier today.

"Oh, yeah?" Piya scoffed. "Are you like totally excited about the first day of school?"

A sly grin spread across my face. The brown-eyed beauty went into hiding after our impromptu meeting in her bedroom. She checked into a hotel last night and hadn't ventured outside her suite. I did the only thing any rational man would do under the circumstances; I sent an enormous bid to purchase the hotel. The offer was accepted on the spot.

As a secondary precaution, I instructed Jordan to organize a party and invite all the guests from last night. I couldn't be blatant and outright demand that she bring Piya along. Instead, I encouraged Jordan to bring *all* her friends. The efforts to lure Piya out of her suite were in vain, as she declined the invite.

It was possible Piya was simply busy with work tonight. Apparently, she became a recluse, locking herself away for days whenever private patrons commissioned a project. It was one of the many things I had learned about her new life.

Successful jingle and songwriter who worked under a pseudonym.

Recently moved back to Long Island after spending years in Chicago.

Married for thirteen years to the extremely wealthy Jay Ambani.

Of all the things Levi had uncovered, Piya becoming a mother to an extremely gifted twelve-year-old had been the most interesting part of the update. It had been years since I last set eyes on Piya. I had expected drastic changes. Nonetheless, the news of her daughter was unforeseen.

Did it complicate my plans? Yes.

Did it change my goals? No.

If anything, I found a way to work this to my advantage. For one, there were only so many ways of guaranteeing regular sightings of Piya. She lived inside a fortress, and entering the premises was near impossible by car or foot. There were four posts outside the fenced-in gates of her residential grounds, with a guard at each station. The security guards were the only ones with the code to enter the premises. However, these weren't regular old guards who could be bribed. These were highly trained ex-operatives. They were paid a handsome salary and received exclusive benefits from the influential residents to retain their loyalty. Ambani bought the best for his family, and it took Levi hours to figure out a minor glitch for a window of opportunity.

The only accessible points were the posts outside the fenced-in gates. Levi snuck into one of them while the guard assigned to it was using the restroom and tampered with the system. The guards manning the various entry points had the residents' home phone numbers listed on their computers. Levi changed the number registered for the Ambanis to a burner phone. When I went through the security check post, the number they called was directed to Levi instead, who obviously welcomed my entrance with open arms.

However, this would only work temporarily. Levi informed me that four guards also patrolled the grounds inside the tall fences. The residents had panic buttons hidden in plain sight around their homes, and if they pressed it, the guards would report in under three minutes. Time wasn't on my side once Piya discovered my presence. Now that she knew I had access, she'd investigate further and eventually determine the number they had on file was incorrect.

To see her regularly, I needed a better backup and tracked down Piya's daughter. Poppy was why they moved to New York, though Ambani still primarily resided in Chicago.

It appeared Poppy's academic accomplishments allowed her to skip a few grades, landing her in high school. Brilliant as she might be, Poppy's track record rivaled a criminal in the making. She was gifted, bored, and rich; a toxic combination for entitled brats. In the last year, Poppy had been expelled from two private schools, landing her at the gates of boarding schools. She was expelled from that as well, and Ambani paid a fortune to get his spoiled daughter instated into Nott, the only school willing to take in the troublemaker. Even so, Nott Academy required Poppy to complete one summer session without any incidents before granting her acceptance. Hence the Ambanis moved to New York.

Although boarding schools meant parents lived out of state, it turned out Piya was much too attached to her daughter. This school was also Poppy's last chance at a normal childhood; by extension, it was Piya's final opportunity to give her daughter a normal life. This school was the key to inserting myself into Piya's life.

Was using a child to chase a married woman an awful thing to do?

I had no idea. Guilt wasn't an emotion I was capable of processing.

I was three when I realized I was different from the "normies." By age four, I learned that assimilating was imperative to survive in the normies' world. Except, I didn't want to simply survive in their world; I wanted to dominate it. I ventured out early by starting college at sixteen, cutting ties with my wayward family. My goals were simple.

Power.

Money.

Control.

I needed the first two to gain the third because a life without control was unacceptable. Then along came Piya, and my objectives became vital instead of mere goals. Fame allowed me the necessary shortcuts to achieve them. It made me rich, but more so, my celebrity status established the necessary ethos to solidify the investments I needed to build my empire. If I wanted to open a nightclub, ten investors would jump on board simply to get in bed with a famous DJ. As a result, I managed to get my name on everything, bars, restaurants, real estate, hotels, and now boarding schools.

"I own this school. What are *you* doing here?" I asked nonchalantly.

Piya reeled back, dumbfounded. Agitated eyes stared at me blatantly. "Y-You own Nott Academy? How is that possible?"

The slight tremor in her voice and the way she recoiled, as if my presence wasn't worthy of hers, made me want to lock her in a room with me for the rest of her days. The visual of Piya at my mercy, and nothing standing in between, ran a line to my cock.

Great.

Now I was getting hard in the middle of the day.

I looked away from Piya, nostrils flaring as I thought of all sorts of boring things to cool my blood. Murder. War. Blood and gore. Anything that wasn't Piya bored me to death. How did she have this effect on me? She fit the mold of what I had avoided my entire life—someone who made me lose control—yet here I was, seeking her out.

For years, I had done a great job applying the learned behaviors from "normies" and successfully masking this part of me. The world saw me as some hero, a rags-to-riches story come true. This façade helped me hide my true personality in plain sight.

Piya was the first and only "normie" to stare into the eyes of darkness and dive in head-first. The glimpses into my darkness didn't scare her away. Instead, she embraced it, using it to her advantage. She thought someone scary like me would safeguard her while she ticked off some list filled with visits to shady establishments. She forgot to account for one thing. Who'd keep her safe from me?

My fixation on Piya stemmed from what some might consider a one-night stand. Except one taste wasn't enough. More than a decade had passed, yet I could still smell and taste what she aroused and set free within only a night. I had been searching for years to recreate the same high, and the inability to understand what this forbidding woman invoked in me only pissed me the fuck off. She had unknowingly enticed a monster and fed it. She shouldn't be surprised by the consequences it brought along.

"It was a recent purchase," I said mildly.

"That's impossible," she spoke mainly to herself, hoping it to be untrue. "I would have seen your name on the paperwork—"

A flash went off, stopping Piya midsentence. I glared at the perpetrator and saw him visibly gulp before lowering the device surely to be responsible for his death.

Fame uncomplicated certain parts of my life while becoming cumbersome in other aspects. No one dared to bother me in the sanctuary of my infamous home parties. They were thrilled to receive an invite with no intentions of rocking the boat by upsetting the celebrities in attendance. If you gave people what their hearts desired, their submission in return was too easy.

Outside the home perimeters, however, was a different story. A small herd of paparazzi had been tipped off about my appearance at Nott Academy, and they were gathered outside the fenced-in gates.

"Mr. Trimalchio, who is this lovely lady beside you?" Another man with a camera spoke from the other side of the railing gates.

Piya briskly walked away, pulling her gold Hermes scarf over her hair and firmly pushing back the sunglasses sitting on the bridge of her nose. The curiosity over my presence was trumped by her need to get away from the limelight. It only piqued the paparazzi's interest in her identity, and the cameras flashed away.

While being renowned was necessary for my success, this was tiresome. I waved politely like a regular old normie. The control it took not to rip the cameras out of their hands and smash them was one I had perfected over the years. Lacking impulse control was unacceptable; it was the reason my kind often landed in jail. Prison was crawling with anti-socials. Unlike those idiots, I'd never allow something trivial like a reflex to rob me of my goals. There were much more satisfactory ways of quenching the bloodthirst.

Piya Ambani, for one.

The *thing* to quench my thirst hurried away, opening the door to the building. I shoved my dress shoes in the crack before she could slam the door. I followed her inside while she tutted. Tiresome teenagers and their equally miserable parents buzzed around us. Caretakers settled overindulged teens into their rooms before the big send-off while the brats complained about their allowances.

There were a few discreet glances upon my entrance.

Otherwise, no one took photos, hassled, or approached me. Nott Academy was the birthplace of old money and reeked of it. Harassing celebrities wasn't part of the culture. Not to mention, there were numerous kids here with Broadway stars as parents, and if I heard correctly, two child actors had enrolled for the year. The teachers, students, and parents alike had all become accustomed to celebrity sightings.

Piya strode confidently down a particular hallway, pulling off her scarf and stuffing it inside her purse. I followed leisurely and smirked upon realizing she had quickened her pace to lose me. Didn't matter. The headmaster had given me a tour earlier, and I knew her destination. This corridor led to the cafeteria.

"You didn't answer my question. What are you doing here?" I asked.

Piya tried to ignore me with her chin in the air. When she realized she couldn't lose me, she spat icily, "Please leave me alone, Mr. Trimalchio."

"Let me guess. You're here to see your daughter," I stated matter-of-factly.

Piya froze in place, muscles tense. She spun and pulled off her dark sunglasses, brown orbs flaming. Evidently, I had hit a nerve. "How do you know I have a daughter?" She jabbed a finger at my chest.

My pupils followed where her nail dug into my flesh. What was it about this woman that caused such elementary effects?

Don't get hard.

Do not fucking get hard inside a high school.

"The only adults here are parents, teachers, and people who

recently bought this school." I pointed a thumb at my chest. "Seeing that you don't look like a teacher, it'd be weird if you were here unless you had a child attending this school," I calculated.

She opened her mouth as if to ask why I'd assume she wasn't a teacher. I cut her off, pointedly nodding at a lady with a top-knot-bun and button-down cardigan. The woman crossed something off the list stapled to her clipboard, a dead giveaway of her role. Piya rolled her eyes as if to say, *I get it.*

"But you specifically assumed I had a daughter? How did you know?"

"I have my ways."

"What the hell?" Piya appeared livid by my discretion. "Are you following my daughter as well? I'm telling you right now, don't you dare come near my child. Ever. Do you understand me—"

"Jordan told me about your daughter," I informed as her voice rose. It snapped Piya out of the hysteria.

Her eyes widened as if our mutual link hadn't crossed her mind, and she seemingly accepted the answer. Piya uncomfortably fixed her conservative knee-length skirt to compose herself, far from hanging up the suspicions.

"Let me get something straight, Mr. Trimalchio. We haven't seen each other in nearly fourteen years, and suddenly, you're everywhere. I ran into you at a party, and you followed it up by asking me to leave my husband," her voice dropped toward the end of the sentence as she looked around for witnesses to our conversation. "To top it off, you broke into my house, and you... y-you," Piya stammered, unable to voice the occurrence.

"I fucked you?" I offered helpfully since she seemed at a loss for words.

Piya reddened but refused to back down. "And I'm supposed to believe it's a coincidence you bought my daughter's school the very next day?"

"Let *me* get some things straight," I berated indignantly. "*You* came to my home without an invitation. As mentioned last night, I ran inside your house to save *your* life. I informed you that I'd be coming over, and *you* granted me access to your home. You're sending some serious mixed signals here."

Piya opened her mouth, though I swiftly cut her off.

"Now I find out your daughter attends the school I just bought, yet you're turning the tables on me. How do I know you didn't enroll your daughter in this school just to get close to me?"

"You're crazy if you think you can engage me with these ridiculous accusations," she snapped. "Goodbye, Mr. Trimalchio." Her chin lifted into the air as she continued her strides. I fell into step next to her. "Will you stop following me?" she scolded.

"Stop flattering yourself. We are going in the same direction."

"Why are you going to the cafeteria?"

"To check out the food quality. I hear the parents at this school are nuts." I looked at her pointedly. "I'm not giving them the chance to complain about underfeeding their kids."

Piya blew out an exasperated breath, her steps faltering as we reached the cafeteria. The retort died when her gaze landed on a figure off to the corner.

The cafeteria was packed from the lunch hour rush and move-in day crowd. Nonetheless, the ambiance was laid-back. Kids freely interacted with their parents or each other around the round wooden tables with padded chairs. Every table was occupied sans the corner one. A lone wolf—dressed head to toe in black—had commandeered it with a stack of books spread out in front of her. She reverberated "fuck-off" body language with earbuds on and an open laptop. With quiet determination, the kid had made it known she was unapproachable.

I would've done the same if no one were paying attention to me. Chosen a table far away from useless people, blocked out their garbage noise with earbuds, and made myself unapproachable to the normies. However, as mentioned earlier, it was the normies' world. The kid was making herself a blaring target with her standoffish attitude.

Piya noticed where my attention had landed. "Axel," her voice lowered, all previous hostility disappearing in favor of a pressing matter. "Can I speak to you for a moment?"

When I blinked in acquiescence, Piya looked left and right in search of spectators before leading me to the empty buffet line. She grabbed two trays and passed one to me.

The net worth of this cafeteria's current population equaled one percent of America's future GDP. Considering the clientele, the food was surprisingly unpretentious—hot dogs, fries, burgers, pasta, and salad—laid out in buffet-style chafing dishes. Piya scooped pasta and some salad onto her plate. I inattentively did the same, my curiosity piqued by Piya's sudden interest in a civilized discussion.

"It's been a while since we last saw each other," she started, her eyes fixed on something in front of her. "Things have changed for me since then."

I realized then why Piya chose the food line for a conversation. It was the least inconspicuous because it'd simply appear we were both patrons of the cafeteria food.

"I-I have a family now, and I'm here to have lunch with my daughter. She can't find out about—" Piya closed her eyes and took a deep breath. "Whatever happened last night, I-I'm willing to forget it. Maybe I did drink too much, and perhaps it was all a terrible misunderstanding. Let's call a truce and put it behind us," she spoke with intention, the insinuation crystal clear. Piya desperately wanted to keep me from meeting her daughter and didn't want her past trickling into her present.

I raised a pair of placid eyebrows. "You have nothing to worry about where I'm concerned." I held up a hand in surrender. She had a lot to worry about where I was concerned, but causing hysteria was hardly productive.

The longest exhalation of relief passed from her. "Thank you for understanding."

"Enjoy your lunch."

"Thank you," she whispered. "It was um-um... good seeing you again, I guess." She dilly-dallied uncomfortably, unsure how to end the conversation positively now that I had given in. "And congrats on, um, all your money."

My amused look only made her stutter further. In the end, Piya decided to end our conversation with a simple wave.

I watched Piya walk away, gave her a thirty-second head start, then followed behind to meet her daughter.

"Did you call Dr. Stevenson last night?" Piya sat across from her daughter at the corner table. I wondered how she felt about Ambani missing Poppy's first day, especially since he was unlikely to see his daughter for the rest of the summer. Hopefully, Levi's efforts caused an effective rift between them.

Panic crossed Piya's face when she glanced up to find me approaching the table. Her daughter had her back to me. When she saw the alarm in her mother's eyes, Poppy turned and looked right at me.

"Mr. Trimalchio," Poppy greeted without a hint of surprise in her voice.

My eyebrows shot up.

Very few things in life surprised me. Piya's change in marital status was one of the things to disrupt my generally collected veneer. I faltered momentarily, then regrouped and, as always, found a solution.

This was the second time something baffled me quickly. I hadn't expected Poppy's monotonous addressal without a lick of surprise laced in her tone. She had done the unthinkable; Poppy had managed to catch *me* off-guard.

The pest knew of me. How?

It was possible she was a fan and well-versed in House music. However, if she were a fan of mine, she wouldn't have sounded as disinterested as she had in the jaded way she addressed me. Poppy sounded like our acquaintance was overdue, and meeting me was already old news.

I should have expected it. Kids like her thrived on shocking adults. She was the poster child for surly preteens who didn't give a shit about the world. While the other high school girls in the cafeteria wore the designated uniforms—a black skirt with a white collared button-down shirt—Poppy had thrown a black cardigan on to cover her white shirt. Whereas they paired their uniforms with styled hair and designer heels, Poppy's chunky black boots and high ponytail stood out like a sore thumb. One look at her and I immediately knew to play along without acting caught off guard by her dispassionate voice.

"Ms. Ambani, if I'm not mistaken. How do you do?"

Poppy nodded curtly.

"H-hi, Axel." A baffled Piya glanced between us before focusing on her daughter. She was taken aback by her daughter's lackadaisical attitude at seeing me. "Did you know—"

"That DJ Axel just bought out our school?" Poppy retorted without missing a beat. "Everyone knows, Mother." The way Piya stiffened at the word *Mother* made it obvious Poppy used the term to antagonize her.

Interesting dynamic...

"Yes, but—" Piya held her tongue for some reason.

"Did you *not* know about it?" Poppy turned the table on her

173

mother since Piya also hadn't displayed bewilderment over my presence.

Piya's muscles went rigid. "I found out a few minutes ago."

"I read about it in the school memo hours ago," Poppy sounded bored. Every expression on her face was perfectly schooled. Impressive for a child. "Really, Mother, you should do your homework before sending off your only child to a school run by just anyone. For all you know, he is a serial killer and plans to murder me in my sleep."

Keep talking, and I might.

Piya gave her daughter a blank expression. "Poppy," she said tightly. "*You* begged us to attend Nott; that's why your papa did so much to get you admitted here."

"Hm." Poppy seemed to think that detail was trivial.

I cataloged their challenging relationship, wondering how to use this to my advantage. This was clearly a common occurrence between them.

"I'll save murder for another day," I cut into the mother-daughter battle, earning a glare from Piya. "For now, I'll settle for a seat at the table. This place is too popular to accommodate me." I nodded at my tray of food. A normal person would've invited the school's owner to join them for brownie points. However, Piya wasn't interested in playing ball.

"Um—"

Poppy read the hesitancy in her mother's eyes and immediately gestured to an empty seat at the table. "Go for it." The way Poppy pushed her mother's buttons surpassed the typical shit children did for attention. Albeit entertaining, I found myself wondering about her intentions.

The thought was quickly dismissed when I caught a whiff of Piya's scent, something floral and expensive. The hold on my tray tightened into a death grip. Fuck my plan and fuck weaseling into Piya's daughter's life. Instead, my eyes searched for the nearest bathroom I could drag Piya into.

A man's true testament of control came from the most grueling circumstances. Where others used singular exceptions to lose control, it was at those moments that I reveled in my ability to keep cool. Though when it came to Piya, she sure tested my limits to the maximum.

With more control than I ever exercised before, I blocked out the urge and set my tray down before losing the battle. According to Levi, Poppy was the most important thing in Piya's life. This was the surefire way of solidifying what I wanted. Without letting her figure out an exit strategy, I sat adjacent to a bewildered Piya.

"Umm, a-alright," Piya stammered. She looked between us as if half expecting Poppy to interrogate me or ask follow-up questions about my presence. When Poppy did neither, Piya's eyes drifted back to mine. For the first time since meeting her, I couldn't read what Piya was trying to communicate.

Piya speedily recovered upon realizing Poppy's attentive eyes were closely surveying our interactions and became determined to block out my presence. She turned to her side, reverting to their original conversation.

I enjoyed cafeteria lunch while pretending to be distracted by my phone. Whereas Piya's dismissal would've roused a need for destruction, it suited me perfectly fine in this scenario. Listening, rather than engaging in conversations, was a skill not employed by many. It gave me valuable insight into people, and I needed to level Poppy. More importantly, I needed to learn her wants and weaknesses.

"Is the Wi-Fi working in your room now?" Piya asked her daughter.

The little shit nodded, though her eyes perused me suspiciously. She didn't miss much and frowned when my attention drifted to Piya out of the corner of my eye. Poppy's demeanor shifted.

"And have you met your new roommate yet?" Piya asked Poppy, spiraling pasta around her fork. "Do you like her?"

"She is still alive and has all of her hair if that's what you're asking."

"Poppy!" Piya admonished but quickly shut her mouth when I looked up from my phone. She didn't want me to be privy to her troublesome daughter.

I shrugged. "Don't stop talking on my account. The headmaster sent over transcripts of all the students admitted to the summer session. I'm reviewing Ms. Ambani's permanent records as we speak."

Piya appeared to have stopped breathing, so I went in for the kill.

"I heard Poppy's last roommate left school in the middle of the semester."

Poppy's smile didn't reach her eyes, and that was when her weakness became abundantly clear. I was wrong.

The pest wasn't rich and spoiled.

The pest was rich and a non-empath.

This could turn into a problem. I had to figure out how to bribe her, and quickly. Distract the kid with what she wanted most in this world so she wouldn't create a spectacle during her parents' impending divorce proceedings. It had to be something Piya would approve of as well.

Given that Poppy's father was immensely wealthy, money wouldn't work. Using my fame and connections as bait was also pointless since Poppy hadn't inherited her mother's musical talents or interests. Instead, Poppy was an accomplished Mathematician. She was accepted into Mensa at the age of six, started coding by eight, competed in Mathematical Olympiad at eleven, along with a myriad of other accolades to her name.

Reviewing Poppy's track records, it was evident Ambani was grooming his daughter to take over his massive empire. He was from one of the wealthiest and most prominent families in India. They had their hands in every industry, but their most coveted source of income was hedge fund management. The stack of books before Poppy indicated everything Jay Ambani was known for.

Math whiz.

Investment guru.

Hedge fund tycoon managing billions of dollars in assets.

Piya was the momma bear type whose only desire was for her child to have a happy, healthy life. She wouldn't allow Ambani to dictate their daughter's future, not unless Poppy wanted it, too.

If I had to guess, Poppy was an ambitious kid who wanted to

take over her father's position one day. No one had this much interest in math, stocks, and investments unless they had a goal to achieve. I would know. Similar ambitions drove me when I was her age, younger even.

There was, however, one stark difference between us. Control. Poppy's behavioral issues were a dead giveaway that she lacked impulse control.

My attention drifted to another set of books cast to the side.

Master of Your Own Mind.

Rewire your Mindset.

Strategies to Effectively Calm Impulsive Reactions.

Hm. So, Poppy knew of her shortcomings and wanted to fix the issue. Not many with anti-social personalities would give a fuck... not unless their flaws conflicted with what they desired the most.

I scanned my mind about the details Levi had uncovered about the Ambani family. If you were from this family, you were automatically guaranteed a pampered life. However, if Poppy was like me, she didn't want a pampered life. She aspired to rule over them all. She couldn't do so at a company wholly based on family values. Someone unstable like her didn't fit their image.

The board members of their company were made up of Ambani's family members, which meant they were all aware of the little pest's troublesome past. The board approved the CEOs. If Poppy didn't clean up her act, they wouldn't allow her to succeed her father. Ambani didn't have enough seats on the board, so even if he wanted to, he couldn't give his precious daughter the reins.

There it was, the one thing Daddy couldn't buy for her and the only thing Poppy wanted in life—her father's empire and the family's respect.

This was my in with Poppy because getting ahold of my impulsive behavior was the first thing I mastered upon realizing I was different. Poppy desperately wanted to learn control, and Piya desperately wanted happiness for her only child. No one else could help Poppy in the same way. If anyone were to understand a neurodivergent, it was their own kind.

Just like that, the pieces fell into place. I'd offer to curb the little criminal's bloodthirst. She'd look forward to achieving the coveted seat at her father's side upon graduating college. The little shit would be grateful enough not to cause too much drama when her parents officially separated. And Piya would be forever in my debt for solving her daughter's behavioral issues.

As I said, give people what their hearts desired, and their submission in return was too easy.

"What happened with your old roommate?" I knew the answer but asked to remind everyone at this table where Poppy was lacking.

Poppy rolled her eyes. "Nothing. Everyone freaked out because I gave her a haircut."

"While she was asleep," Piya added with a hiss.

Poppy shrugged. "She touched my stuff after I asked her not to. She should've known actions have consequences."

"The poor girl has been seeing a therapist for months," her mother admonished, voice lowering in case of bystanders. "She still has nightmares about someone cutting off her hair in her sleep."

Poppy smirked.

"I don't want any repeats of last year," Piya warned. "Do you understand me, young lady?" Piya cringed as soon as she said, *young lady*. I doubt Piya thought she'd be the kind of mother who said, *young lady*.

Color me curious.

Poppy lifted a bored shoulder without verbally committing to her mother's demands. She stood and collected her food tray, along with any wrappers or trash.

My gaze coasted to the other tables in the cafeteria. The entitled brats ate their meals and left trash and wrappers scattered for the cleaning ladies in the cafeteria. Poppy was the only student who didn't expect anyone to pick up after her, nor was she turned off from getting her hands dirty. She even wiped down her side of the table with a napkin.

The kid was a future mogul. She was one percent of the upper one percentile demographic and likely richer than most kids here. While she didn't think twice about cutting someone's hair off, she considered the cleaning ladies at her school. Interesting. Maybe the kid wasn't too far gone, more motivation for Piya to heed my advice.

As Poppy put an empty water bottle on the tray, the little shit asked out of nowhere, "Mr. Trimalchio, can I look inside your brain?"

"Poppy! What are you saying?" Piya reprimanded, mortified. "That is not polite. Apologize."

"Right, sorry." Poppy nodded. "*May* I look inside your brain?" she rephrased, emphasizing the word *may.*

"Poppy," Piya tried again, sounding exasperated this time while holding onto her temple. "Sweetheart, you can't—"

"Relax, Mother," the pest cut her off. "You said you don't want a repeat of last year, so I have been broadening my horizon by learning about empathy."

Piya's eyes hastily glided over, once more uncomfortable with my knowledge of her daughter's... issues. Poppy was aware of the problem. It appeared that so was Piya.

"I'm writing a term paper about the part of the brain that determines empathy. I want to do a brain scan on Mr. Trimalchio to study the results," Poppy explained, taking her food tray to the nearest dispenser and throwing it over her shoulders, "You once mentioned he lacked empathy, so he's the perfect candidate."

My sharp glance shifted to Piya. *I'll be damned.* "You told your daughter about meeting me," I smirked.

"Don't read into this, Mr. Trimalchio," Piya leaned over to whisper while Poppy was momentarily absent from the table. "We saw you on television, and I mentioned to my daughter in passing that I had met you once. She asked what you were like, and I said you lacked empathy. Trust me, my words were never intended to be kind."

Well, well, well. Poppy's lack of response to me now made sense. When she found out I bought the school, she wasn't the least bit surprised that I sought out their table. Poppy thought I was a friend of her mom's.

"I have to leave for orientation now." Poppy returned to the table and gathered her items. "Was that a yes or no to the brain scan?" she asked me.

"I don't think we should bother Mr. Trimalchio with this," Piya interjected.

"When?" I asked Poppy, ignoring Piya. This certainly worked out to my advantage.

"Tomorrow, around this time, works for me."

Piya tuned out my wolfish grin. "I'm sure Mr. Trimalchio is way too busy to help."

"It's for science," Poppy countered, looking straight at me.

"Anything for science," I supplemented.

"In that case, I'll see you tomorrow." Just like me, Poppy ignored her mother, who was doing everything in her power to shut this down.

"I'll email your school email address with my contact information and any other details you need to prep."

A bewildered Piya couldn't hold back. "Wait a minute—"

"Sounds great." Poppy knew if she hung around longer, Piya would successfully ban us from keeping further acquaintances. "I'll see you tomorrow. Bye."

"Poppy—"

Piya's retort died when I reached over to squeeze her hand. A horrified Piya snatched back the hand and watched after her daughter, who was already halfway across the cafeteria.

I waited for Piya to scream or blast me. Interestingly, she did neither. Piya merely stood, her back straightening with accuracy, and said coolly, "Goodbye, Mr. Trimalchio."

CHAPTER
ELEVEN

One Year Ago

～

Piya

I WATCHED PATIENTLY AS DR. STEVENSON PICKED UP A
slab of the baked brie with pear and smeared it on a cracker.
Couple more bites, and he'd be in the mood to talk.

Dr. Stevenson was a family friend. He was also one of the best
child psychologists from New York and recently moved to
Chicago. After discovering this information, I was determined to
sign Poppy up for therapy. I was running out of ideas to get my
daughter on a better path and trusted Dr. Stevenson irrevocably.

He had no bullshit to spare and was a straight shooter. He was precisely what Poppy needed.

However, before signing Poppy up for sessions, I had questions of my own. Dr. Stevenson was diligent about patient confidentiality. Minor or not, he didn't discuss patients outside of sessions unless they thought of harming themselves or others. He especially disliked nosy parents.

I met him during his lunch break, hoping he wouldn't see this as helicopter parenting. I even brought a homemade lunch in hopes of bribing him with food. For as long as I had known him, Dr. Stevenson had never been able to turn down my home-cooked meals.

"Are you all right, Piya?" Dr. Stevenson asked.

"Of course. Why wouldn't I be?" I put on the biggest smile I could muster under the circumstances. Poppy got kicked out of school. I was scared shitless of it becoming a pattern and resorting to homeschooling. Poppy already had difficulty getting along with other kids. Isolating would further amplify her anti-social tendencies.

Poppy was young when I realized her interests differed from the other children. The Ambani family was large, with a multitude of aunts, uncles, and cousins. While her other cousins played dress up and tried on heels, Poppy used to memorize the serial numbers on the back of the Wi-Fi router for fun. Whereas they competed in science fairs, Poppy thought her competition existed in boardrooms. However, Poppy was never violent before, with some deep-seated appreciation of the macabre. She only wanted bigger and better things for herself. Poppy was only five when she walked into her papa's home office and announced, "When I grow up, I'll sit in Papa's chair in the boardroom."

Jay was so proud and excited. We championed Poppy's dreams until things took a nosedive. I no longer knew how to help my kid and desperately needed Dr. Stevenson.

"You barged into my office." He motioned at the spread on his desk. "And went to great lengths to bribe me." He bit into another cracker and brie, gesturing at me with it. "This will get you fifteen minutes of my time. Start talking."

See? Straight shooter.

"Okay."

Closing my eyes, I repeated the mantra that this was a safe space to disclose my greatest worries.

Poppy's uncontrollable reactive nature was turning sadistic, and I even caught her manipulating her cousins. One of them, Rayyan, was also gifted like Poppy and often boasted of becoming the next CEO of Ambani Corp. He once told Poppy that girls didn't become CEOs. That afternoon, Poppy told Rayyan there were nut products in the snack he just ate, which he was deathly allergic to. Poppy simply watched with blank eyes as a panicked Rayyan repeatedly stabbed himself with an EpiPen.

There were no nuts in the snack.

The extent of Poppy's obsession over her father's coveted head seat subdued her empathy. Her patience and impulse control persistently thinned with age. Poppy stopped connecting with kids her age, and her biggest rival to this day remained her cousin, Rayyan. When he got accepted into high school before Poppy, she nearly lost it. She was used to surpassing her peers academically and couldn't handle the disappointment of being bested. Poppy started showing signs of apathy and disengagement, and fights turned frequent.

"You know how some people can manipulate and exploit others without experiencing guilt?" I blurted. I feared that if Poppy couldn't generate empathy for others, she'd continue on this path and eventually end up in jail.

Dr. Stevenson observed me. "You mean someone with an Anti-Social Personality?" he asked nonchalantly.

I almost shushed him, though there was no one around. I wanted to learn more about Anti-Social Personalities without telling Dr. Stevenson this was about my daughter, not until I officially signed her up for therapy. Doctor-patient privilege didn't extend to you unless you were a client, and I didn't want private information about my kid falling into the wrong hands. Stigma was associated with kids considered psychopathic, and I didn't want anyone to treat Poppy differently.

I twisted my wrists. "What do you know about it?"

Dr. Stevenson raised his eyebrows. "Lots of things, I hope. Otherwise, I'd be a terrible psychologist." I rolled my eyes as he bit into another brie and cracker combo. "It might save us both time if you tell me what you want to know."

I decided to be a straight shooter as well and plopped onto the chair across from him. "From what I understand, people with..." I searched for the word before settling on the clinical term for Anti-Social Personality, "...ASPD struggle with violent tendencies." Would my daughter end up hurting people, too? I could no longer ignore the recent bout in violent incidents where

Poppy was concerned. How could I stop it? How should I help her? "Can they inhibit the impulse to harm others?"

Dr. Stevenson tilted his head, contemplatively assessing my words. When he showed no emotion, I tried to lighten the conversation so he wouldn't read into it.

"Or do they all turn into serial killers? Is there like a kill switch activation button?" I laughed uncomfortably.

He frowned, unamused at my attempt to make light of the situation. "That's based on an entirely unfounded theory. It's misinformation, thanks to societal oversimplification."

"You don't agree?"

He opened his mouth, closed it, then opened it again as if choosing his words carefully. "It's like saying everyone with depression will resort to self-harm. Do you find that statement to be true?"

My lips parted, not having thought of it that way. "Of course not."

"Did you know one percent of the population is considered psychopathic?"

I blinked. "I didn't know that."

"What's the population of America, Piya?" He was finished with the cheese spread and started on the second course. My time was limited, and I wished he would stop speaking in riddles.

"More than three hundred million," I said robotically.

"One percent of three hundred million is three million. Do you think there are three million serial killers in America?"

"No," I admitted slowly. Obviously, three million serial killers weren't walking around freely.

"Exactly," he concurred, unwrapping the foil off the salad container next. "Not every person to display antisocial traits is a serial killer, nor are they all prone to violence."

Hope blossomed in my chest for the first time since learning of Poppy's tendency to resort to violence.

"It's important to remember that social stimuli can manipulate ASPD," he continued. "If a kid with ASPD grows up watching violence, they're prone to imitate it."

But Poppy was part of a happy, healthy family without an inkling of violence in her childhood. Until recently, she hadn't exhibited these predispositions, either. So, what changed?

"If an ASPD kid grows up in a loving home surrounded by positivity," he continued, "they might deviate to academics instead of violence. i.e., instead of beating someone up for a thrill, they'll find it more exciting to excel in academics, business, or things that positively impact their lives. That's why many with ASPD pursue careers as world leaders and CEOs of large corporations."

Ugh. There was that stupid word, CEO. I hated the title, especially seeing what it had done to my daughter.

Ambani Corp was a family company, and while it employed endless people, only an Ambani could climb the ladder for high-ranking positions. The company was designed to encourage the kids in the family to grow up within a system deeply integrated within them. At the company, family days were highly encouraged, and opportunities were built-in for kids. Junior internships. Gifted and talented programs. A part-time job in high school. They had paid internships for all four years of college. Once these kids graduated college, you guessed it, they were offered high-salary positions to stay with the company.

Nepotism ran deep. That was how influential people kept the money within the family for generations. Even so, there was a larger evil. Ambani Corp was designed to control the upcoming generation. If you had a cushy, high-paying job, why would you have to leave it behind and move away from mommy and daddy? That was why Jay's family mainly lived in Chicago or New York. Those were the headquarters of operations.

I never pushed Poppy toward this company. Her dreams matured organically from being surrounded by the company culture. Poppy's self-inflicted stress of competing with her cousins and wanting to be the best was something I didn't under-stand, nor would I encourage this toxic behavior.

You could say I had grown to resent Ambani Corp and didn't want my only child tied to something for the rest of her life. I tried steering Poppy into less stressful environments numerous times, encouraging her to be a kid.

This sentiment of mine drove Poppy crazy. I wanted her out of this toxic environment where the kids were pitted against each other for some unforeseen future. Whereas Poppy resented me for not pushing her.

Why should I?

She was too young to be worried about a career. Even if she weren't, I didn't care what my daughter did for a living so long she was physically healthy, mentally happy, and safe. I wanted her to feel loved, and I wanted her to love hard. It was the most important thing in the world. Not to mention, she was only a little girl. Why was a child so preoccupied with becoming CEO when Jay wouldn't retire for another fifteen years?

We constantly butted heads over it. I no longer understood my child, and Poppy started viewing me as the enemy. Only one thing drove her anymore, the obsession with being the head of the company like her papa.

"Why would a person with psychopathy specifically pursue such a role?" I asked, tilting my head.

"Because they're good at it," Dr. Stevenson simply replied, setting the container down. "Let's say a large corporation has numerous locations. One of the branches is suffering, and the CEO must assess the long-term benefits of keeping it open. Though shutting it down would uproot workers, it would be fiscally irresponsible to let it drain the company's resources, costing more jobs in the long run."

"Okaaay. What's your point?"

"If the CEO is cold-blooded and lacks empathy, they can easily make the pragmatic decision of shutting down the branch. If their moral dilemma and overwhelming guilt for the workers were to get in the way, leading to an emotional decision, it might be more harmful to the company in the long run."

He picked up the container once more and resumed eating. I waited for him to finish chewing.

"Many CEOs, politicians, and leaders who lack empathy are better at their jobs because they think rationally when making the tough calls, rather than under emotional duress."

I nodded thoughtfully. "So, according to you, people with

this... affliction might even be more prone to success because of it."

He nodded. "With one percent of the population exhibiting these characteristics, it's likely we all know numerous people with antisocial personality traits, many of whom are leading perfectly normal lives."

My head snapped to meet his gaze. I did know someone else with psychopathy; Axel. Last I checked, he was leading more than a great life. How?

Dr. Stevenson answered my unstated question. "Just like with everything else in life, how someone chooses to deal with it depends on them."

"If it's so common, why is there such a stigma surrounding this?" I asked curiously.

Dr. Stevenson smiled kindly. "That's societal hypocrisy for you. Even after everything we discussed today, would you vote for a politician if you knew they couldn't understand your needs or desires, nor do they care about it?"

Good point.

Neither of us spoke as he finished the salad and dove into the next box with chicken risotto. I let him take a few bites before resuming our conversation.

"What causes someone of this nature to display violent behavior while others lead perfectly reasonable lives?"

He shrugged. "It's the same as any affliction. People with mild cases have some empathy, while severe cases lack it altogether. Non-empaths lack impulse control, and their reduced remorse allows them to pursue their desires without regard for others. But it's not their fault."

"Meaning?"

He stabbed at shreds of lettuce with a fork. "Meaning... ASPD is a result of biological predisposition."

A melancholy coursed through my veins. Lacking empathy wasn't Poppy's fault. Like my daughter, one percent of the population was susceptible to impulsive behavior from birth. Although she lost the battle occasionally, Poppy fought her natural inclinations because she grew up in a loving home. It hardly seemed fair to blame her for something she couldn't control.

This conversation had proved more positive than I had imagined.

"So, Piya," Dr. Stevenson said, diving into the last container with dessert. Chocolate chip cookies. "Are you ready to discuss Poppy's ASPD tendencies and how it's affecting your life?"

I smiled sadly and gathered my containers. He saw right through me, didn't he? "Maybe another day, Dr. Stevenson."

Before I left, I couldn't help throwing one last question his way. It was the one that had been bugging me the most. "Can a person without empathy love another human being?" I wanted everything for my daughter, but most of all, I wanted her to find love in her life. To feel loved was one of the greatest gifts on earth.

"Depends on your definition of love. If they feel a connection, they go to great lengths to take care of the person in the way they'd care for a precious item they possess. That often emulates what society defines as love."

I rephrased the question. "In *your* opinion, can someone with ASPD love another person?"

He didn't answer for several moments. I wondered if he'd give me another lecture for simplifying the word to the generalized version used by society.

Instead, he gave me a look of defeat and said, "No, they cannot love."

I closed my eyes before walking out the door.

CHAPTER
TWELVE

Present

~

Piya

MY INSIDES SHOOK WITH ANGER AS I RUSHED OUT OF the cafeteria. Axel didn't chase after me, but I wasn't about to leave it to chance. With my arms wrapped around my middle, I bolted outside.

Poppy was going through a rebellious phase where my very existence irked her. No matter what I did, I was Enemy #1, and she was dead set on defying me. She noticed that Axel agitated me and asked him to return.

My heart was ready to give out, and I pulled out my phone to call Jay. He needed to know what was happening, and we needed a strategy against the havoc Axel was causing in our lives.

One ring.

Two rings.

Voicemail.

I tried again and again. Voicemail each time.

Defeated, I stared at my phone. It was almost dead since I didn't pack a charger last night in my haste to leave the house.

Screw it. I didn't need Jay to handle Axel. I brought Axel Trimalchio into our lives and had to take care of it myself.

I spent last night hiding in my hotel room and drowning in regret over what happened. By the time morning came around, the effects of the hangover had subsided, and I had returned to the reality of being an Ambani.

Twenty-one-year-old Piya Mittal's natural inclination would be to cause a ruckus over Axel's actions, wanting to speak freely and get it out in the open. Thirty-four-year-old Piya Ambani was limited by the restraints in her life.

When we married, Jay told me there was no such thing as divorce for us. There had been numerous cases of infidelity within the Ambani family, all strategically hidden so as not to cause scandals. Yet, no one got divorced.

Jay and I could never leave one another, so telling him about last night would only hurt him and cause irreparable damage to our internal relationship. Instead of blowing up my marriage because Axel broke into my house and had his way with me, I had to do what Ambanis did best; repress. I didn't have the luxury to pursue this in court, so whatever happened, I had to put it to bed.

I was determined in my efforts until Axel showed up at Poppy's school, and now he had made follow-up plans to weasel into my daughter's life.

Oh God, did he know? Was he back in our lives because he knew of my and Jay's sordid secrets? Would he expose us to the world?

I was so distracted by my emotional turmoil that I didn't realize I was walking to the parking lot. Damnit. I had taken an Uber from the hotel, and the designated rideshare area was on the other side of campus.

I turned on my heels, ready to burn off my anxiety with a long walk. My brisk strides were cut short by an engine revving and a car veering to an abrupt stop.

"What the hell!" I gasped at the aggressive maneuver. A sleek, white BMW M2 pulled up beside me, and I knew the driver of the car a little too well.

Heathen!

Axel left the car running as he flung open the door. Satan's spawn bowed his head to emerge out of it. The non-threatening blue jeans and heather gray t-shirt didn't make him so. The tall man towered over me, biceps peeking out of his t-shirt as he ordered, "Get in the car. I'll give you a ride home."

I could have laughed. In fact, I did just that; I threw my head back and laughed wholeheartedly. Every time I thought Axel couldn't be more ludicrous, he proved me wrong. Did he truly believe I'd get in a car with him after what transpired between us?

Knowing Axel, he probably did. The fact only made me laugh

harder. Wiping the tears from the corner of my eye, I said sweetly, "No, thanks."

His jaw clenched. "I wasn't asking."

"I still feel compelled to respond with, no, thanks," I repeated.

A car honked from behind us. The driver had come to an abrupt stop because Axel had left his door wide open in the middle of the parking lot, leaving little room for other cars to maneuver past him.

Axel ignored the honking car. "Get in the car, Piya."

"No." I sidestepped the crazy asshole. He moved with me.

The sound of more honking tore through the air. Traffic swarmed as other cars tried to weave through the parking lot, also realizing they were trapped because of Axel's car. The pile-up of cars and honking escalated, but Axel was wholly unbothered by the chaos he had havocked.

"Hey! Move your car," someone shouted. I recognized the man as one of the dads from Poppy's school.

"Axel, move your damn car. You're creating a scene in Poppy's school."

"All you have to do is get in the car, and this scene will disappear."

My fists clenched. "You know very well that I'm never getting in that car with you."

Black orbs gleamed in the afternoon sun. "Get. In. The. Car," Axel enunciated as if I were an errant child he had to subdue.

"In. Your. Dreams," I spat back. When Axel stepped forward, my voice rose with hysteria. "Stop this nonsense. You can't just come into my life and turn it upside down. You certainly don't get to bring your insanity to my daughter's school—whoa, whoa, whoa, what are you doing?"

Axel threw me over his shoulders with a parking lot full of witnesses, including Poppy's teachers and the parents of her new classmates.

Oh.

My.

God.

"Stop it! Stop it! Stop it!"

My eyes darted around the parking lot to take stock of the witnesses. What if someone snapped a photo of Axel manhandling me, and it got back to Jay? I started thrashing, practically throwing a fit. I hadn't acted this unruly in years, but I couldn't get myself under control. Only Axel could incite such rowdy and wild behavior out of me.

"Axel, please, please, please put me down. I can't be linked to you."

"Then don't make this worse." Axel didn't bother opening the passenger side door. He leaned into the open driver's side door and tossed me inside. My butt landed on the center console. Ow.

I swiftly scooted to the passenger seat and pulled at the door handle. It was already locked.

"Everyone is watching," Axel reminded to stop any further escape plans.

Oh, God. My eyes scanned the parking lot. Numerous cars were backed up in the lot, with everyone watching the spectacle.

Their curiosity was piqued by a grown woman being manhandled in daylight. These people knew my husband and had kids in the same grade as my daughter. I didn't know if they recognized Axel or me while we were arguing outside. However, they were paying attention now that Axel had caused a scene by picking me up. Most likely, they had their phones out to record "woman pulling a jailbird escape." If I stepped out of Axel's car now, any one of them could snap a photo. Inside the car was safer with fewer chances of being recognized.

I buckled up as Axel slipped inside the car. "Drive. Fast. Please." I could only articulate one-worded instructions. I needed to get out of here and keep this situation from escalating. Axel was the lesser evil compared to what would happen if we were photographed together.

Axel pressed on the accelerator without buckling in. The car took off at full speed, leaving behind everything that could ruin our lives.

Those prying eyes had nearly caught us, and the anxiety from the escape had my heart thumping loudly. A crazy burst of energy surged through my system. My harsh breaths filled the enclosed space. A sensory overload sharpened my vision and heightened the touch of cool leather against my skin. My ears were sensitive to the soft music playing from the car's Bluetooth. Even Axel's non-recognizable scent hit me stronger than usual.

However small of a rush, the threat of getting caught in front of an entire school and having us exposed in public was a shot of adrenaline I hadn't experienced in years. I had killed this part of myself years ago for my daughter's sake.

I closed my eyes. Poppy. My little Poppy seed bagel. It appeared Axel had familiarized himself with everything, including the most crucial thing in my life. Why was he so determined to ruin the life I had built for her?

Enough was enough. I couldn't let Axel keep blindsiding me, especially when it came to Poppy.

"Axel, you can't see my daughter again." I got right to the point.

"Isn't that for your daughter to decide?"

"No, it's not," I stated calmly. "She is a child and doesn't get to do whatever she wants."

"We both know your daughter is much more than a child."

"Either way. I'm her mother, and I get to decide who's in her life. Whatever sick games you're playing, make me the target, not her. I can't have some celebrity barging into my daughter's life because I have become their flavor of the week. That's not how it works with kids. They thrive on stability, which you don't reflect."

"From what I hear, your daughter's not thriving at all."

My hands balled in my lap. "Say another word against my daughter, and I won't be so kind about forgetting what you did last night."

Axel seemed impervious to my threat. "A little touchy, aren't we? Is it because there is truth to what I said?"

Don't let him get to you. "You seem to think you know more about my daughter than I do, Mr. Trimalchio." I kept my voice friendly, knowing the formal addressing pissed him off.

Axel sped up on the deserted roads lined with trees. "I'll pull this car over to spank you on the side of the road if you use the formality bullshit again."

I swallowed at the gentle way he made the threat. "Fine, *Axel*," I emphasized his name, "What is it you think you know about Poppy?"

Axel didn't look at me, eyes steadfast on the road. "Detached. Single-minded. Emotionally reserved."

I glanced at him pointedly. "Sounds familiar."

"Lacking in impulse control," he added. "Does that sound familiar as well?"

I begrudgingly admitted that Axel didn't lack impulse control. He wouldn't have made it this far in life if he had.

As much as I wanted to argue with him, Axel had already seen enough of Poppy to identify the problem. Over the last year, I had hoped to make Poppy see reason with love. Despite my daughter's hard shell, she wanted to control her reactive nature but constantly lost the battle. The recent troublesome developments had vanquished my optimism as well. It was so unfair that some people thrived with ASPD while others gave in to their primitive urges.

Axel, for example, had no criminal records, no altercations, not even a parking ticket. I had Googled him obsessively, and there was nothing on the guy. Cool, calm, and collected, Axel Trimalchio was a downright Samaritan as far as the world was concerned. Other than while with me, he had immense control over himself and was as clean as a whistle.

I glanced at Axel as the thought jarred me.

He had immense control over himself and was as clean as a whistle.

Even though he had the same affliction as my daughter, Axel approached things differently. How was he doing it?

Perhaps I had been looking at this all wrong. I had been running from Axel, and for a good reason, but here was a rare window to learn about someone with Poppy's condition living their best life.

I had tried everything and hit a wall with Poppy. The universe had suddenly bestowed me with a resource otherwise unavailable. Axel was unhinged, sure, but he suppressed it well in public.

For once, I could turn the tables on Axel and use him for what I wanted most; a happy, healthy life for my daughter.

"It turns out your daughter's exactly like me," he spoke again.

I huffed. "I assumed someone like you thought highly of themselves?"

"I do."

"Then why would you claim Poppy isn't thriving by being exactly like you? It's not like she is doing something vastly different than you," I said as nonchalantly as I could manage, hoping he'd bite. The last thing I needed was for Axel to know he had something I wanted.

Axel stilled, the car coming to a slowed stop at a signal. Tilting his head, he watched me methodically, dissecting me piece by piece. The look was so intense, so possessive, my skin exploded with what felt like bites from a thousand fire ants.

"Except I can control my inner demons while she's a fish out of water... and you want to know how I do it."

Of course, he knew what I was up to; he was always one step ahead of me.

"Why don't you ask me what you really want to know, Princess?" he asked as the light changed to green. My upper body flung back against the seat as Axel took off at full speed.

"Fine. Please tell me how you control your reactions."

"Only if you tell *me* something first," he said amicably.

There was always a catch with him. "What do you want to know?"

I assumed he'd inquire about my new life, so it floored me when he asked, "Ever been to a rave or a music festival?"

I blinked, flabbergasted. "Those wild EDM parties where everyone is half naked and tripping on MDMA?"

His mouth quirked. "Yes."

"What does that have to do with Poppy?"

"Answer the question."

"My only experience with music festivals is the one I saw from my balcony last year." It was held around the waterfront across from our place in the city. I heard nothing but various beat drops sounding like *unch unch unch* for eight hours. "All I recall is hordes of nearly naked people, high on drugs, running toward Lake Michigan in zero-degree weather."

His lips curled. "Did you partake?"

I scoffed. "Are you asking if I partook in the drug-induced rave or the skinny dipping after?"

Angry eyes flipped toward me at the word *skinny dipping.* "Both," he said in a clipped tone. Axel was impossible. He couldn't possibly be angry after *he* asked the question.

I gave him an improbable look. "What do you think?"

An eerie glow highlighted Axel's face. I didn't like whatever thought was on his mind to cause the expression he wore. "Open the glove compartment," he suddenly ordered. I swear, he was the oddest man alive.

My hand shot up to find the glove compartment handle and pry it open. The car registration and documents sat in a neat pile. Underneath it was one of those flip notepads with a pen stuck inside the spiral spine.

"Grab that." He nodded toward the notepad.

I was too mentally exhausted to dissect his intentions and conceded.

"Write the items down," he instructed.

"What items?"

"Rave and skinny dipping. If you haven't done them before, they deserve to be on your bucket list."

I stilled, realizing Axel's intentions. "No," I said flippantly. "We aren't doing this."

"We are."

Axel drudged up a painful past I had buried six feet deep. I couldn't let him drag me back to the same state of mind. "No."

"Make the list, Piya."

I ignored him, glancing outside the windshield.

"Do you not want me to tell you the secret to controlling my impulses?"

Chin in the air, I kept my eyes forward instead of taking the bait.

"Did you know fifty percent of inmates have some sort of

anti-social personality?" he asked placidly. "But some psychiatrists believe it to be more. Closer to eighty-five percent."

I didn't reply, refraining from the urge to scream at him. My nerves stretched as his gaze burned holes in the side of my face.

"So many people with anti-social personalities end up in prison, though a select few end up in positions like mine. It's sink or float based on how they are guided in life. The question is, which way do you want to guide Poppy?"

Blood pounded in my ears, palms growing cold.

"Oh well." He shrugged. "I'm sure Poppy will look good in orange."

Seething with resentment, I flipped the notebook open. My little Poppy seed, if only you knew the things I was willing to do for you. "What do you want me to write?" I asked through clenched teeth. I knew Axel would milk this for all its worth.

"Attend a rave, skinny dipping," he listed in order, then contemplated for a moment. "I never did get around to convincing someone I'm from the future."

My pen came to a screeching halt. Laughter bubbled in my chest and I couldn't hold it in. I threw my head back, shoulder shaking as my chest rumbled with an unadulterated laugh. Only Axel could take me from ire to hilarity within seconds.

It would seem lightheartedness was contagious, and Axel cracked a smirk.

"How come you never got around to it?" I couldn't help asking.

Axel shrugged.

The night of Milan's wedding, Axel had mentioned his evil

bucket list and wanting to convince someone he was from the future. That was years ago. It was such a small pleasure in life, yet he hadn't partaken. Why not?

Perhaps he only liked doing these list items with me.

"I never ended up skydiving," I admitted reluctantly. It was another thing I had mentioned in passing, but it wasn't possible to accomplish that night.

"No time like the present to get started," he announced. "Let's kick off with item number one."

I huffed. "Where do you plan on finding a music festival at this time of day?"

"I am supposed to play at one," he hit the lock screen of his phone to check the time, "in about forty-five minutes."

My head reeled back, mouth agape in disbelief. "That's why you asked me if I'd been to a rave?" I should have seen this coming. "So, I'd go to your stupid music festival?"

Axel didn't bat an eye. "You want to learn how I control my quote-unquote impulsivity. What better way to do so than watching me in my element?"

His statement held a strange logic, but... "What if people photograph us together?"

"They'll assume we are friends. You're allowed to be seen in public with an old friend." He blew it off as a minor issue and not worth worrying about.

I would have believed Axel had he not acted so aggressively at Poppy's school and made a spectacle out of it. Nonetheless, he knew how to exploit my vulnerability.

"If you want to delve deeper into Poppy's psyche, you might want to start with mine."

Axel shot me a smug look, aware he had the upper hand. It only amplified my hesitancy.

He rolled his eyes. "If it puts your mind at ease, it's a day party. They aren't as large as the events at night. I doubt anyone from your crowd attends raves anyways. My security detail and roadies are meeting me there, too. If anyone does recognize you, you'll be in a group. It won't be out of the spectrum of possibilities that you're there because Jordan got you backstage passes. She is about to become my new publicist, after all."

It was a sound argument. Against my better judgment, I relented with a sigh and slumped against the seat. As we sped off, I tried to distract my troubled thoughts by doodling on the notepad. When I glanced down, I found that I had unthinkingly jotted down more items we had mentioned that night years ago.

Attend a rave
Go skinny dipping
Convince someone you're from the future
Speak in a made-up language in public
Prank call
Go skydiving
Jump into a taxi and scream, "Follow that car!"
Trespass on a private property

CHAPTER

THIRTEEN

~

Piya

THE RIDE WAS SHORTER THAN EXPECTED. IN LESS THAN thirty minutes, Axel's car had rounded an oval building toward the entrance in the back. The one considered an access point for staff and talent.

As soon as the car neared, earth-shattering screams of young women filled the air. I peeked through Axel's tinted window to locate the source of the commotion and realized a crowd had gathered at his behest.

Three large bouncers came out of the woodwork to shove the group back and barricade the car as it approached. It hardly made a difference. While both male and female admirers were in the mix, beautiful women seemed to dominate the group. Throngs of infatuated girls elbowed and pushed each other out of the way, the crowd thickening enough to stop the car door from opening.

Everyone was dressed in festival costumes. Glow sticks were sported in abundance. The guys wore tanks and ripped jeans. The girls wore rave outfits with fairy wings, see-through dresses, bedazzled bralettes, and covered in more stardust than clothing.

It wasn't the usual cocktail party crowd I had become accustomed to entertaining.

It was better.

I quickly shook my head. *Snap out of it, Piya.* This was no longer my scene. If anything, this was a threat to the life I had built.

Numerous phones in neon cases were held up high in anticipation of recording Axel's descent from the car. I swallowed the dread forming in my throat. I never considered myself camera-shy and fared well in front of an audience. However, unlike Axel's promise of arriving in a large group, I realized I would be the only one stepping out of his car.

Why did I trust Axel? This was bad for the Ambani name. Really bad.

As far as my and Jay's families were concerned, we were happily married. No one knew of the recent doom in our marriage, a predicament I'd hoped to reverse. It'd be an impossible feat to accomplish if I ended up on a viral video with Axel. Our families would see it as infidelity and a full-fledged affair behind Jay's back. Right now, I couldn't exactly deny the claims, either.

Unlocking my phone, I found my phone at ten percent battery. I shot Jay a text message instead of calling him again.

Call me. This is important.

No response. I waited until the last possible second of the car coming to a complete halt before giving up. I needed a Plan B. Fishing inside my purse, I pulled out my scarf and sunglasses. Swiftly, I put on the sunglasses and threw the Hermes scarf over my hair before tying a knot under my chin.

Axel glanced outside the window. "That's a big turnout for a day party," he mused.

"Big turnout?" His comment was the understatement of the century. I glanced at the gathering that could only be described as a mob. "Fifty people is a big turnout. There must be hundreds of people out there."

"Looks like the bouncers are clearing a path." He threw his car door open when a tall, thin man dressed in black pants and a cap-sleeve white t-shirt approached the vehicle. Presumably, he was valet or someone from Axel's team since Axel handed him the keys and instructed him to park the car. Axel rounded the car and opened the door for me. "Let's go."

I shook my head. "I can't go out there."

"You already agreed to do this item from the list," he reminded.

"Only because it was supposed to look like I was a part of your entourage. There were supposed to be more people."

"There will be once we go inside."

"But any of these people," I nodded at the hordes of girls screaming outside the car, "could snap a photo of us together."

Axel held my gaze. "So?"

"So?" I repeated incredulously. "So, it's inappropriate for me to be here with you. My life will blow up if we are photographed together."

"You'll be fine." Axel held out his hand, unconcerned.

I made no effort to reach for his outstretched hand and instead placed two fingers on my temple. "This is such a mess," I lamented. "I shouldn't have let you talk me into this."

Before I could follow up with how the world would paint me as a slut for gallivanting with another man while married, Axel swooped down and wrapped an arm around my waist. He plucked me off the seat as if I weighed nothing and held me to his chest.

"Axel, what the hell are you doing?"

He didn't respond, shutting the door after scooping me out of the car. Panicked, I struggled against him. Realizing he wouldn't let go, I pulled my scarf as far down my face as possible. I doubted the small disguise would work, but it was all the armor I had to spare.

"Axel," I whispered. "I can't. I can't do this. I change my mind. I have to leave."

Axel tensed as he carefully set me down. The slight frown on his forehead dictated his displeasure over my comment. A stipulatory hush fell amongst the masses simultaneously. They had expected Axel to exit the car but had instead bore witness to my unexpected presence. They were wondering about my identity, no doubt.

Axel answered their unspoken question by turning me to face him with a hand wrapped around the nape of my neck and the other around my middle.

"Don't!" I hissed. If we didn't have an audience, I would have told him off for holding a married woman this intimately. The right was reserved for my husband. Instead, I declared, "I don't belong here." If Jay or my family saw us entangled in this position, they'd assume I had run off with Axel. There was no other way of interpreting such a cozy embrace. The glint in his eyes reflected that he knew it, too.

Axel ignored me, pulling me closer to shatter any possible disillusions over the extent of our acquaintance. Just when I thought my life was over, he sealed the deal by swooping and kissing me in front of hundreds of people.

I pushed at his chest with ferocity. It only made him kiss me with such absolution that I momentarily forgot about our audience.

It wasn't an ordinary kiss but rather a display of possession in the way his tongue invaded my mouth, his hands exploring my body. I was breathless by the time he allowed an inch between our mouths to whisper, "This is exactly where you belong. Don't forget. You agreed to this, Princess."

I forced my eyes open to find my hands clutching Axel's gray t-shirt. Swiftly, I let my gaze fleet over the onlookers to assess the damage. Hordes of young women digested the scene, the pipe dreams of becoming Mrs. DJ Axel turning to dust. The silence remained for half a second longer until someone snapped a photo. It started a frenzy, and the crowd screamed with renewed zeal, snapping away with their camera phones.

Seething, I shoved at his chest. I could have saved my energy. Axel had already let go because he had accomplished what he set out to do. Excitable people narrated Axel's public display on their live feeds.

My smile was plastic due to the spectators, but the venom dripping from my voice was real. "You're such an asshole. I didn't agree to kiss you in public."

Fuck trying to get inside Axel's head. I was ready to make a run for it. The plan was nixed when Axel threw his arm around my shoulders to keep me latched to his side while walking us forward. "No, but you did agree to come to a rave with me. You haven't held up your end of the deal. So, the next time you try going back on your word, I'll pull the scarf down before kissing you in front of this crowd."

That shut me up. I forgot about my saving grace. The scarf, paired with my glasses, likely obstructed the photos taken.

Axel's menacing warning was still crystal clear. He could use his celebrity status and fans to ruin my life with only one kiss. I had to play ball and keep him on an even keel until I was out of his reach.

Keeping my head down, I prayed no one would get a good shot of my face. New bouts of wild screams ensued over Axel's presence. Confused and disoriented, I held my hand over my ear as the piercing shrills of the hundreds of people intensified.

The pack advanced on us, despite the fortified body walls

created by the venue security. They could barely restrain the masses blocking the way. Upon hearing the commotion, the patrons standing in line at the main entrance flocked to the back. People swarmed us, not allowing us to get through. Cameras with flashes went off from every direction as the crowd zeroed in like mindless zombies. Suddenly, trampling to death overruled my fear of what my family might think if they saw me hanging from Axel's arms. I had never seen such a spectacle.

Right on cue, a man with a large phone in hand broke through the barrier of security guards. He thrust his phone in my face in his missed attempt to take a close-up photo.

"What the—" I jumped when a flash went off, nearly blinding me.

"WATCH IT," Axel roared at the man, whacking the phone away so remorselessly it tumbled out of his hand. The phone met its maker when it landed on the concrete and shattered into several pieces.

Muffled murmurs echoed throughout the crowd following the aggressive display. Axel wasn't known for losing his cool. He was supposedly a man of the people.

I stilled, too, fully expecting the public to lash out at Axel for mistreating a fan. Nothing could have prepared me for what happened instead.

There were no reprimanding words or ugly comments directed at Axel. Angry fanatics abruptly started shoving and berating the man instead, the one who had barely assaulted a supposed celebrity's date.

I turned my head from side to side, baffled. Oh, God. Axel

smashed someone's phone into pieces, and they were cheering him on. They were publicly encouraging his aggression with positive reinforcement.

I wasn't the only one shocked by the turn of events. Moments ago, Axel used this platform to assert his dominance over me. The advantages of the unwarranted attention went sour for him within the snap of a finger. He was no longer amused about holding the threat of his celebrity status over my head. Axel curled an arm around my shoulders and shoved everyone out of my way before they could make contact.

"Where the hell have you been?" Axel chewed out angrily.

I thought Axel was speaking to me before finding three men jogging toward us from the right. They had managed to weave in and out of the throng without my noticing until they were right beside me. All three wore black suits and sunglasses, with an unironic take on Men in Black in their get-ups.

The leader of the group—I presumed based on the hierarchy of him standing a few feet ahead of his comrades—nodded at Axel. With olive skin and a bald head, he stood out from his fairer counterparts. He was also the tallest of the three, with a size rivaling Axel's.

"This isn't the usual day party crowd," Axel snapped at the man. "What's going on?"

The man squinted at his phone screen thoughtfully, all the while jostled side to side by the excitable crowd. "Seems the venue sold out on table service and tickets for this event."

I wasn't sure of the man's identity and glanced at Axel, who seemed unimpressed by the information. "So?" he asked impatiently as the security started moving people out of our way. "My shows always get sold out."

"Yes," the man agreed tentatively. "Only the venue manager let it slip that you aren't scheduling any new shows once you fulfill your remaining contractual obligations. People went insane after hearing the announcement."

Axel swore under his breath, appearing on high alert and tracking the crowd for danger.

I was seething over Axel's previous display but couldn't hide the bafflement over the stranger's news. I knew Axel had slowed down on doing shows but didn't know he planned on stopping altogether. I had followed Axel's career closely, so this must be a recent development. Why?

"I'm Levi, by the way." The man removed his sunglasses, revealing a pair of kind blue eyes.

Levi, I mulled over the name mentally. It sounded familiar. "Piya Ambani," I offered in turn.

"You're supposed to find out about these things before it happens," Axel icily snapped, interrupting our conversation. "What the hell do I pay you for?"

Axel's attitude didn't faze Levi. "Fans got frantic after hearing the news. These people never even bought tickets and just showed up to meet you in case they can't make it to another rave. What do you want me to do about it? You should have told us earlier that you planned to stop doing shows. I could've prepared better."

I liked Levi instantaneously. He appeared to be Axel's head of security, but clearly, they shared a camaraderie beyond that of employer and employee. Levi did as Axel asked but also gave it to him straight.

"This is your fans' way of saying goodbye," Levi concluded. A tiny bit of emotion was laced in his voice, and I empathized. I could hate Axel's ass but still recognize the end of an era.

However, only Levi and I found the moment bittersweet. Axel was immovable. "I'll break your face if you touch her again," he yelled instead, grabbing the shirt collar of another fan to bump into me.

"It was an a-accident," said the man, who could be better described as a teenager of eighteen or so. "S-Someone p-pushed me," he stuttered nervously, expecting to meet the same fate as the man who had been pummeled.

Oh God, he was just a kid, probably only a few years older than Poppy.

"Axel, what are you doing? Let him go." I held onto his forearm tightly as Levi surged out of the crowd, trying to stop the fight from escalating. The other two bodyguards pushed the people ahead, gaining us more ground.

Axel shot me a look before pushing the boy away, and I swiftly made my way toward the entrance to avoid any more drama. Although the bouncers and bodyguards had gotten the hang of crowd control, we struggled with the last few feet. We were shoulder to shoulder with the masses, many shouting, "I love you, Axel."

When we finally reached the door, Axel positioned me in front of him so I could enter first.

"We need more security," Axel grunted once the door shut behind us, drowning out the echoes.

"More?" Levi looked puzzled and I could relate. Axel already had a security detail of three big dudes plus the bouncers working at the venue. More seemed overkill, though hard to refute upon glancing at the increasing crowd through the rectangular window of the door.

"Find two more guys. Keep the regulars at the two entrances." He glanced at the two men standing five feet away from us. "Get somebody to keep watch of the backstage and someone else specifically for Piya. Find out if George is scheduled here tonight."

"George?"

"He is the usual guy manning the backstage entrance of this venue. He is the biggest guy they have; no one will try to go past him. I want him to be Piya's personal bodyguard and watch her between my sets."

I opened my mouth to say I didn't need to be watched but Levi cut me off. "Axel, those guys aren't here to be your personal security," he placated gently. "They are on crowd control and can't leave the dance floor to watch over your girlfriend."

My head whipped toward Levi, suddenly feeling lightheaded. *Girlfriend?* What!? I was married, hello! At best, Axel was a question mark for me.

So, I repeat, *Girlfriend?* When had that been decided?

My bewildered gaze fell on Axel next, who ignored it as if a bombshell hadn't been dropped. He calmly continued the conversation with Levi. "I would have asked you to hire more security for tonight had I known the venue announced my departure from shows. I'm guessing they're over capacity, too. I'm not leaving Piya alone when we have no control over this chaos." He nodded outside at the crowd, all desperate for another glimpse of Axel. "Any one of those people can sneak inside. Someone almost slammed into her earlier," his voice rose—irritated—with each word he uttered.

"Yes," Levi started slowly. "They should have told us beforehand so we could've taken appropriate measures. It doesn't mean they're obligated to provide security coverage."

"I'm walking if they don't give me extra security," Axel declared without a morsel of doubt. "The venue can explain the reasons for it to everyone who bought table service to see me play."

Levi let out an exasperated breath as Axel's anger heightened. He took a moment, then spoke calmly. "Walking away isn't an option. You know that. You signed a contract with them."

Axel stepped forward, leveling him. "In that case, I'll drag Piya on stage with me during my sets so I can keep an eye on her."

I glanced at Axel with horror in my eyes. Oh god, no. The thirty seconds it took from the car to the entrance had my nerves frazzled over being recognized or trampled to death. I had never experienced something like that before. The people outside were tripping on various substances and couldn't suppress their inhibitions. It generally wouldn't be a big deal as drugs were common party favors in New York. However, the odds weren't in your favor if hundreds of people were on drugs simultaneously and all those people were pulled in Axel's direction like a magnet. If I stood next to him, everyone would gravitate toward me as well and undoubtedly take tons of photos. I wasn't equipped for this.

Levi sighed. "Okay, let me see what I can do. Your roadies should be here and done with equipment set up. I'll circle back in a few." He pulled out his phone and started typing a text.

I tried to stray, needing a moment to understand what Axel was trying to pull. He only tightened his hold and dragged me along the backstage hallway.

The next few minutes were a blur. Axel had me latched to his side as various people came up with questions about the set list, equipment check, mic check, etc., etc., etc. He continuously referred to me as princess or baby. I lost count of how many times I blasted Axel for it or corrected someone about the status quo of our relationship. The backstage crew turned uncomfortable at my declarations and glanced from Axel to me, unsure of who to believe. They finally settled on it being one of those cruel jokes that stars played on the little people. Pitying the helpless souls, I gave up on the mission. This bit wasn't funny despite the shit we had pulled in the past. This was my life we were talking about, and Axel was at the cusp of ruining everything.

Levi worked his magic and found the tall, burly guard named George to act as my security, and Axel took his time specifying instructions to the man.

"If she needs to go to the bathroom, you need to stand outside the door. If she is out of my sight, I expect you to update me on where she is or what she is doing. Under no circumstance can she leave without me."

Axel droned on with instructions and managed to sneak in a

gentle threat to not look my way for long or touch me unless it was life-threatening, such as saving me from trampling to death. The conversation ended as jovially as possible for someone like Axel—with a curt nod of approval and the wad of cash he slipped into the man's palm with a promise of more if he did as instructed.

With a firm kiss I didn't see coming, Axel strolled off to the stage while I held my fingers to my bruised and swollen lips.

I needed to get the hell out of here.

I was insane to think I could turn the tables on Axel and learn a few things for Poppy's sake. I was in over my head by taking on a beast I couldn't handle.

I pulled out my phone to call an Uber before realizing Axel, Levi, and George's steadfast gazes were on me. I lowered the phone, realizing I had to bide my time until they were distracted. If I tried to leave, Axel would no doubt pull me on stage and kiss me without the scarf protecting my anonymity.

So, I parked my butt obediently when someone brought me a chair and a bottle of sparkling water. Unable to help myself, I scrolled through social media on my nearly dead phone. By kissing me in front of hundreds of people, Axel had started chaos in my life. I just knew there had to be a TikTok video or Instagram post floating around with one too many likes. I hated Axel for what he had done to my life.

Luckily, I didn't find anything promiscuous. Videos and photos of Axel kissing an *unidentified woman* were circulating, but his massive body had blocked my frame. I wasn't recognizable in any of the images thus far. I realized Axel had purposefully blocked out my face in the angle he kissed me and how he had led me inside the building. I heaved a sigh of relief. *Axel didn't sell me out.* It was the only reason I wouldn't be killing Axel Trimalchio tonight.

The show started with the typical "unch unch unch" thumping of House music. Relieved that the Ambani name would live to see another day, I sat motionless in perfect view of DJ Axel in his element. Except I wasn't watching him. Instead, he watched me intently, gaze never averting as he played and spun music.

The pounding of bass and the thrum of music filled the warehouse that had been repurposed into an event space. Axel's head was inclined backstage for the duration, unaware of the screeching fans or the live show he was hosting. Electricity crackled in the air as I held his gaze, the rapid rise and fall of my chest matching the eruptions of cheers from the crowd. The music filling my ears seeped inside, reaching deep until nothing else existed. When a hint of Guns N' Roses played in the backdrop of one of his songs, we smirked simultaneously. We were a symphony of our own.

A storm had ignited inside me since meeting Axel again. It also raged within him, communicated through Axel's unwavering attention. I didn't understand it, only sensed it was about to worsen.

When the last song was announced, I was determined to get ahead of the storm before it destroyed everything. Getting past the crowd outside, without security to clear the path, was an ordeal I was ready to face. Axel was preoccupied with checking the equipment settings. A brief window of opportunity had presented itself, so I leaped from my seat and rushed toward the exit.

George stood with a military stance, blocking my sweet escape. "Er..." I started hesitantly. "The show's almost over. I better head to the car."

"You can leave once Mr. Trimalchio is finished with the show." He nodded toward the stage where Axel was winding down. "Should only be a couple more minutes."

"It's fine. He won't mind." I tried to sidestep George, who sighed heavily at my petulance and barricaded any further attempts by outstretching his arms to resemble a giant, intimidating cross. I now understood why Axel had specifically requested George.

"Sorry, Miss." Despite his frightening presence, George kept his voice friendly. "Mr. Trimalchio clearly said you can't leave without him." The wad of cash had quite an effect on George. I wasn't going anywhere.

The tense muscles of my shoulders relaxed upon finding Levi hurriedly approaching me. "Levi," I said exasperatedly. "Can you please inform this gentleman," I motioned toward George, "that Axel won't mind if I head to the car now?"

Levi appeared equally uncomfortable by my suggestion. "You better wait for Axel," he said sheepishly. Had everyone lost their minds?

"I don't want to wait for Axel," I said through clenched teeth. I knew my fate would be further sealed if I waited for Axel. More opportunities to be photographed together. More opportunities for him to kiss me if I didn't do as he said. "Once he finishes his set, all the fans will rush to the back entrance again. Wouldn't it be safer if I ran to the car now to avoid the crowd?"

"That's a good question to ask him." With a hand on my lower back, Levi turned me toward my newfound jailor.

"What did I say about touching her?" Axel snarled, his gaze locked on Levi's hand resting on my back before the accusatory eyes turned to George, who was instructed to break someone's hands if they touched me.

Levi hastily retreated his hand while George primed a defense to show he had done his job as requested. "The lady was trying to leave. We told her she had to wait for you."

Unsure if the explanation placated him, Levi charged forward with an added justification. "She wanted to leave before the crowd thickened outside."

"What did I tell you would happen if you tried to leave again?" Axel growled.

"I attended the stupid rave, so why does it matter if I leave—"

Axel stepped closer until our chests bumped against one another, and his lips cut off my words as they collided against mine. I slammed my fists against his chest, beyond infuriated by the day's antics, while he pretended not to notice. He pulled my scarf down, exposing my hair and face, while his tongue dominated mine, hands moving freely over my body and groping as he pleased.

The intimate audience of two watched the blatant display of dominance, awaiting Axel's next instructions. Public lewdness or any sort of exhibition wasn't the Ambani way. Where I should

224

have been shoving at his shoulders, my brain short-circuited from the lack of breath he allowed me in between the wild kiss. My mind muddied somewhere between his lascivious tongue and squeezing my ass. My eyes only flew open at Levi's commanding voice.

"I'll have one of the guys pull your car up closer to the door."

Axel wrapped his arm around my waist to lead us toward the exit, motioning for George and Levi to follow.

"Axel," I protested shakily. "I did as you asked, but I can't walk through that crowd again and risk being seen with you. It was already too close of a call." I swiped the cold sweat off my brows. "I need to go home on my own."

"I told you I'd take you home."

I tried to pull free of Axel, except I should have saved my breath. "I'd rather call an Uber."

"Princess," he said tightly. It sounded like a warning instead of the usual teasing nickname.

"Please, Axel. I can't humiliate my family publicly."

His eyes narrowed. "I'm sure your family will survive the public humiliation of seeing you with the likes of me."

"That's not what this is about," I whisper-yelled. "I'm married."

Axel ignored my proclamation and mercilessly dragged me along, fingers digging painfully into my sides. "Either walk on your own, or I'll put you over my shoulders. Your call, Princess."

I stopped fighting immediately. Instead, I grabbed hold of the scarf dangling at the back of my head, once more pulling it over my hair and face.

Levi gave Axel an update as we walked, "I spoke to the venue. Barricades had been placed around the perimeters. No one will get close to you again."

Despite Levi's reassurance, anxiety returned as we neared the exit. To walk through that crowd was daunting, with or without the threat of being photographed. It suddenly dawned on me that was Axel's reality. What must it be like for him to live like this every day?

Is this why he no longer wants to do raves and festivals?

From the backstage gossip I overheard, it seemed Axel wanted to create music without being in the spotlight. He preferred to work behind the scenes.

The door blasted open with the flashes and cameras returning with full force. As promised, the fans were barricaded behind railings this time. Unsure where Levi procured those on such short notice, I stayed by Axel's side in case the barricades didn't hold. It did nothing to stop the paparazzi-style photography. The car awaited our arrival as promised, and Axel shoved me inside before rounding the car to get into the driver's side.

The engine roared to life with a deafening rumble. The vehicle darted toward the small opening cleared by Levi and his team. Upon realizing our escape was imminent, my fear melted away, replaced by relief and... excitement.

Like a high-speed car chase, we blazed to the next narrow street even as fans chased the car like maniacs. The car peeled away from the crowd, quickly accelerating to a dizzying speed. Tires squealed and screeched with an ear-piercing whine as they struggled to grip the pavement beneath them. I clung to the seat belt for dear life as the heady mixture of fear and adrenaline lingered in the air, along with the faintest hint of Axel's damn intoxicating scent. The concoction made me weak and stupid enough to breathe it in instinctively, making me lean closer to the driver's side.

Axel smirked, forcing me to straighten my back and glare at him. He pulled onto the highway toward Sands Point. I exhaled with relief. The bastard was actually doing what he said he'd do; he was taking me home.

"Well," I prodded.

"Well, what?"

"You promised to tell me how you control your impulses if I did the stupid item on your list," I reminded.

A pregnant pause permeated the air. "I focus on the end goal instead of getting sidetracked by the petty shit along the way."

I nodded, understanding setting in. He set goals for himself, and it kept him preoccupied and distracted from the primal way he was built to react.

"The promise of a reward at the end of your journey distracts you from losing your cool, is that it?"

His eyes flashed with dark excitement, tongue running over his bottom lip. "As long as the reward is worth it... something unforgettable so that nothing else matters."

My breath hitched when a pair of dark, smoldering eyes roamed my face before focusing on my lips. My mouth quivered in an automated response, my body tensing in an attempt to purse my lips. I quickly looked outside the window to keep myself in check. He was like the sun; if I stared directly for too long, he'd blind me.

The heat radiating from him was impossible to ignore, but I refused to let him distract me. I cleared my throat and spoke again, "But Poppy does have goals. So, why does she react so easily?"

"Because too many people are standing in the way of her goals, including those who're supposed to encourage her ambitions. Frustration often causes people to snap."

My neck twisted toward him to meet the side profile of his face. "What are you talking about—"

"Do you remember how I described your daughter earlier?"

I blew out a breath. "How could I forget? Detached. Single-minded. Emotionally reserved. Lacking in impulse control," I counted them off, wondering how to make Axel pay for each insult he directed at my kid.

He read my mind. "You speak as if I insulted Poppy."

"You did," I accused.

"What you consider insults are some of Poppy's greatest strengths."

"How so?"

"The fact that she is single-minded means she won't stop until reaching her goals. As far as I'm concerned, that's a good quality. She doesn't want a mediocre life, nor understands those who settle for less instead of achieving their full potential."

My shoulders slackened.

It was apparent Poppy didn't respect me the same way she respected her papa. Jay was a mogul with keys to a kingdom. As far as Poppy was concerned, I was overindulged and had never worked a day. She had no clue about my secret career or that I had a seven-figure income. I huffed in self-deprecation. I made one million dollars last year, yet my daughter dismissed me as if I didn't know the meaning of hard work. Poppy thought I thrummed on the piano for hours because I was *so bored* with my pampered life.

"I already knew that," I told Axel.

"If you know that, why don't you see these things as her strength? From the conversation I overheard between you two, it sounded like you want her to dream smaller. Do you not believe in your daughter?"

My jaw dropped in aghast disbelief. "Of course, I believe in my daughter. I just don't want her to be so wrapped up in her ambitions that she doesn't notice her childhood passing her by. Poppy is light-years ahead of her classmates and about to become a junior in high school. I don't get it. What's the rush to grow up? At this rate, she'll be in college by fifteen or sixteen."

"So what? I got accepted into college at fifteen."

"That's too young," I protested.

"Isn't that for her to decide?"

"I-I," I stammered, unsure how to voice my side of the argument.

"I finished my GED at fourteen and applied for scholarships to any college that would have me. I was dead set on getting out of my Podunk shithole of a town. I accepted the first college to offer me a full ride. But when I asked my parents for a loan to pay for costs the scholarship didn't cover, my father slapped me over the head. So, I worked and saved up for a year before starting college at sixteen."

Axel's words hovered in the air between us. Once upon a time, he had disclosed his alcoholic parents and how he'd severed all ties with them. I was glad he cut out the toxic components in his life. Nonetheless, it was heart-wrenching to hear.

Axel dismissed the sadness etched on my face. "Don't need your sympathy," he said in a cutting tone. "My point is that I knew what I wanted by the time I was ten, and nothing could stop me. If your daughter is like me, she doesn't care about living her childhood to the fullest. That's what *you* want for her."

There was no one else in this car, yet I felt ganged up on. "Why is it so wrong that I *don't* want to put pressure on my kid?"

Axel ignored my incredulous mien. "It seems Poppy likes the pressure. Perhaps she thrives on it."

I was stumped. There was a truth in Axel's words that I couldn't refute.

"Like your daughter," he continued, "I wanted bigger and better things for myself. What I didn't want was people telling me I couldn't do it. Didn't you once tell me your mother didn't support your choice to pursue music? How did her advice affect your relationship?"

Oh God, had I turned into Zaina Mittal? Mom never believed in me, and it hurt. Badly. Whether or not I understood Poppy's dreams, this was a wake-up call that I had failed by not supporting her.

I didn't look at Axel as we took the exit and went down a familiar path, staring out the window for several moments.

"I called Poppy *young lady* today," I reluctantly admitted, running a hand down my face. Mom used to call me *young lady*, and I'd almost cringed when the exact words had slipped out. "I never thought calling someone *young lady* was even in my DNA." Yuck.

The corners of Axel's mouth quirked knowingly. It amazed me how he had given me more insight into Poppy's mind within less than a day when I hadn't achieved it through months of therapy. It was a breakthrough.

Perhaps I should call Poppy tonight to implement some of Axel's advice. This was a good start, but I needed more.

"Any other advice you'd like to bestow?"

Axel sped up without answering me. I stared at him expectantly until something in my peripheral made me realize Axel had driven past my street.

"Wait, you missed my street."

"I know."

My breath caught in my throat as a familiar-looking property came into view. "This isn't my house," I stated the obvious.

"No, it's mine."

CHAPTER
FOURTEEN

~

Piya

"Get out of the car, Piya," Axel repeated. He had parked the car in the underground garage of his mansion and held open the passenger side door, patiently waiting for me to exit.

Never. Trust. Axel. Trimalchio.

I couldn't repeat this mantra enough, yet here I was.

"No way in hell am I going inside your house. Take me home." I sat stubbornly inside the car, arms crossed across my chest. Nothing good would come out of following Axel inside. I wanted to learn how Axel's brain operated for Poppy's sake, but currently, self-preservation was more important. I refused to leave the sanctuary of this car.

Axel was a master manipulator and dangled my kid as bait, knowing I'd fall for it. I was distracted and didn't throw a fit when he sped past my house. He drove through the iron gates of his property, which closed immediately upon our entrance, then drove us into his underground garage, which also shut. Unlike last time, the house was fortified today with closed gates and surrounding fences. Even if I made a run for it, I couldn't get off this property without Axel's permission. I was trapped.

I glared at him. "You said you'd take me home."

"I will after I show you something. So, get out of the fucking car before I reach inside."

Fear trickled down my spine from the coolness in his voice. "I need to hear the words that you won't try any funny business."

"There is no danger to you," was his abstract answer.

Yeah, right. I had ended up at the stalker's lair, and no one knew where I was. Even my phone was dead. The perilous situation dawned on me, my insides quivering with fear. I was at the mercy of this man, and stirring his ire would only work against me.

At long last, I stepped out of the car, taking my sweet time brushing non-existent lint off my skirt. It allowed me a moment to take in my surroundings. The garage was just as ostentatious as expected from a home of this scale. Several shiny cars were lined up in perfect symmetry, begging to be taken for a spin.

Axel paid no mind to his expensive showroom, eyes lasered on me as he grabbed my hand. Before I could protest, Axel had already dragged me across the garage. He punched in a code to

233

call the elevator but was too quick for my prying eyes to catch the numbers.

Nerves rattled, I entered the elevator as the doors opened. His house was so huge that an elevator was required for a smooth transition between the various floors. According to the numbers listed, there were seven floors.

The security in this house was top-notch, and another code was required to operate the elevator. Axel let go of my hand to select floor five on the keypad, swiftly inputting a few more numbers on the second touchpad underneath.

The doors closed on cue, leaving me hyperaware of his presence in the intimate space. Per usual, I felt his heated gaze on me as we rode the elevator. We didn't bother with pleasantries. No more cat-and-mouse games were left to play; it was time for a frank conversation. Once and for all, I needed to know what Axel Trimalchio wanted from me.

The elevator doors reopened to the fifth floor of Axel's lavish mansion. Since I had already received a sneak peek of his home, I didn't think I'd be stumped during my second visit.

I was wrong.

This floor of the mansion was just as impressive as the grand ballroom downstairs, more so without drunk people stumbling around. The long corridor was furnished with tufted benches and paintings on the wall. Built-in bookshelves and hanging potted plants dangled from the ceiling, giving the modern space a homey feel. This house screamed luxury, and all I had seen thus far was the hallway.

My heels clicked against the expensive, polished marble as

Axel led me out of the elevator. To my chagrin, he suddenly turned talkative. Axel went into great detail, explaining the history of the land the house was built on. He stopped at each expensive piece of art hanging on the wall and disclosed vast information about the artists.

This was his grand plan for kidnapping me; he wanted to show me his home?

All the while Axel spoke, I tried, unsuccessfully, to locate the exits. The doors that could lead to an exit were sealed shut. They each had lock pads and it appeared you needed a code to open them.

Fuck. I was effectively imprisoned in this house. I quietly watched him out of the corner of my eye, trying to assess his mood. Axel gave nothing away, keeping up the "walking tour" and describing every facet of his home.

It made sense why the grand staircases Jay and I had initially taken to enter Axel's home were so steep. It was because they accounted for the three floors underneath the main ballroom area.

Floor one was the underground garage. Floors two and three were for staff use only—basement, kitchen, pantry, and staff quarters with separate entrances. Floor four was the foyer and ballroom where Axel held his parties. Floor five was our current location.

We passed numerous rooms to wherever our destination was while Axel divulged the purpose behind each. They were mostly empty guest rooms. Once we reached the end of the hallway, Axel led me to a set of staircases that only went up. Either the stairs to the bottom floors were masterfully hidden or they didn't exist.

According to Axel, the sixth floor was comprised of the "necessary" rooms to function. Library. Sunroom. Home theater. Gym. That sort of stuff.

I didn't say a word as he continued the tour, leading me to the final floor through another set of one-way stairs. Floor seven was for Axel's use only. No one was allowed access without his permission, sans a maid who cleaned it twice a week.

I realized the doors for each room thus far had been left purposefully open to allow sneak peeks. If I wasn't mistaken, Axel was either showing off or he wanted my approval over his home. Both seemed at odds with his character. Axel never struck me as the show-off type, and he certainly needed nobody's approval. So, why the diligent effort ensuring my endorsement of his decorating abilities?

The thought preoccupied me as we reached the end of the hallway. Axel ushered me into a room that appeared to be a music room from the threshold.

"After you." He held out his arm, waiting for me to step inside.

It was the first room he had encouraged me to physically enter. I bobbed my head past the doorframe without walking inside, checking for booby traps Axel might have set in place.

"If I wanted to kill you, I would have done so already," he mentioned a little too casually.

I inspected him with narrowed eyes and finally stepped inside.

The room was immaculately tidy and much bigger than visible from the doorway. It was disciplined and orderly like Axel.

The eggshell walls were beautifully decorated with musical implements. Numerous instruments, such as collector's edition guitars and violins in expensive cases, lined the walls. A mahogany table sat in the middle, with two office chairs on each side. The few orchids spread around gave the room life. The setting made it clear that this wasn't just a showroom for musical instruments; it was where Axel created music.

A guitar was off to one side with a stand for notes. A turntable was nearby with an open laptop beside it. The items were strategically placed adjacent to a bay window. I followed the view overlooking a beautiful beach and blue water. A dim, green light at the beach dock was barely visible in the distance. It called to me like a siren, as if I had seen it before, and made me envious of Axel for having the opportunity to create music here. The serene room was a muse in itself.

Without argument, the most impressive item here was a gorgeous ivory piano. It sat on a riser at the very corner, magnificently displayed as the pride and joy of the room. The matching bench only added to its charm. It looked absurdly expensive, and it wasn't until I got closer that I realized my assessment was correct. I knew without a shadow of a doubt that this was an absurdly expensive piece because I recognized the piano.

This piano was less of an instrument and more of a collector's item. It was a piece of art that cost millions of dollars. I had mentioned it to Axel years ago during our adventures around the raunchiest parts of Queens.

I spun in place, mouth dry. "What is this?"

"It's the piano you talked about." He tilted his head as if confused by my reaction.

My heart slammed against my ribcage. Jay tried buying this very piano for my thirtieth birthday but was disappointed to find out the collector had sold it to an anonymous buyer. That was four years ago.

Axel bought this piano years ago, not knowing if he'd see me again. Why?

"Why would you buy this piano?"

He shrugged. "Because you wanted it."

I didn't know what to think and stepped toward the desk, setting my purse down. I hadn't realized tears had seeped out my eyes until the moisture cooled my heated skin. Axel moved with me, brushing away a single droplet with a thumb swipe. He stared dispassionately at his thumb, where the moisture was drying against his skin.

"This doesn't make you happy," he assessed.

I couldn't breathe and turned away from him, furtively dabbing at the corner of my eye.

"Piya?" he pressed. His low voice sent a shiver down my spine. I swallowed several times when I felt his presence at my back, stalking me. I scooted forward, hitting my hipbone against the edge of his mahogany office desk. When there was no more space left, he grabbed my elbow and turned me to face him.

"I need a minute." I tried to remove my arm from his hold, for I'd fall apart if he said one more thing right now.

He examined me thoughtfully without releasing his grasp. "Tell me why you're crying."

"Because I'm touched," I whispered, unable to hold back. I tried forgetting about our night together, chalking it off as a beautiful dream. But the truth was that I had often thought about Axel throughout the years. Until we ran into each other at the party, I assumed he had forgotten all about me. I never expected to have the same profound effect on him or for him to remember the piano I mentioned eons ago.

However, it was too late for us.

I shook my head. "Whatever is happening here, it's wrong. We are both married," I announced the reminder to no one in particular. It needed to be said out loud and repeatedly.

He didn't dispute the proclamation, watching me with the same dispassionate eyes. It irked me how little Axel cared about our spouses, especially since his wife's dime paved the way for him.

I didn't know Axel's endgame, but I knew this much. No celebrity DJ in this world made the kind of money Axel flaunted. I looked around the elegant room. It took generations to build such wealth, and he gained access to that opportunity through his heiress of a wife.

I knew Axel had big plans for himself, but I didn't expect him to use an unsuspecting woman as bait. He most likely invested her millions into his various causes, turning them into more millions. Now he was living the dream and buying expensive gifts for his mistress—because that was what he intended on turning me into—with the money *she* funded. My heart waned with shame.

"You... you bought me this with your wife's money," I accused resentfully.

I knew Axel was wealthy on his own accord, but he wouldn't be *this* wealthy without her. He married someone rich to multiply his earnings. I couldn't stomach the thought and tried to step away when his hand landed on my arm.

"Axel, please just stop whatever it is you're doing."

Axel did the opposite and leaned into me. "From the moment I set eyes on you again, I knew you weren't happy with how life turned out."

"You know nothing about my life," I replied stoically because he truly didn't. Things might seem bad from his perspective, but there was a time when Jay, Poppy, and I were a happy family.

"You're suffocated by the facade you have to maintain," he countered. "You don't disclose your true profession to your family. Ambani has no interest in seeing you and your daughter can't stand you. Am I missing anything?"

Axel's crass summary of my life made it sound meager, as if my life had no meaning, except he knew nothing about the truth.

I tried shoving him away, but Axel's grasp was ironclad. "Let go," I hissed.

"You don't want to be with a man who leaves you behind at every chance." His voice dropped. "A man who makes you feel insecure and unwanted, the way your family used to make you feel. You crave to belong to a man with eyes only for you."

"I'm not a piece of property. I don't crave to belong to any man."

"Could have fooled me with the way you looked at me that night. You wanted to belong to me."

I once more tried to free myself.

When he spoke again, his voice was somber without the previous arrogance laced in it. "At first, I couldn't understand why you'd leave after what we experienced on that beach. We were two of a kind, and I knew I wasn't the only one to feel it. So, I searched for you everywhere, traced every step, looked into every clue you left behind, but I could never track you down."

I said nothing. My stomach twisted in knots, knowing he hated me for leaving that day. Had Axel and I met a few years later, he would have easily tracked me down. The hindrance in his path was the lack of social media in those days. Even Instagram didn't come around until the following year.

"I couldn't exactly look up the Instagram feeds of every person attending the wedding," he admitted my sentiment. "If I had, I would have known you were the groom's sister."

My eyes rounded. Exactly how much had Axel uncovered about me?

"Once I learned your name, it was easy to find every piece of information that ever existed on you," he answered my unasked question. "The more I learned, the more I understood why you left that day."

My stomach dipped in premonition, knowing I'd hate the next reveal.

"You knew your family would disown you if you were

found with some riffraff. You had no intention of leaving your cushy life behind and did what every spoiled princess does in your position. You bagged yourself a rich husband—"

My temper overtook my sensibility, and I tried to slap him. Axel was faster. He grabbed both my wrists and held them at my chest. He twisted my body and spun me in place, wrapping an arm around my waist with my back to him. With a lightning reflex, he bent me over the desk. Important-looking documents crumpled underneath us, but orderly Axel was unaffected by the chaos.

"Get off me!" I screamed. My efforts to push him off were futile. He didn't budge.

"You have regretted your choice every day since leaving me on that beach. Admit it. Let me save you from this life that's beneath you."

"Save me?" I screamed incredulously. "You are destroying the life I worked so hard to build."

"You're bored senseless and only live to make other people happy. Ambani doesn't appreciate you and only wants a wife for display. That relationship is nothing but servitude."

"It's not servitude when it's someone you love."

Axel stilled behind me. Throwing my love for my husband in Axel's face was a terrible idea, but the words had slipped out. The ominous quiet in the room lasted for only a moment before I felt the cool draft from the vent on my bare backside as he pushed my pencil skirt up with force.

"What the fuck are you doing?" I shouted.

A loud smack on my ass rendered me speechless. I froze before it registered that he had spanked me.

My temper hit the roof. "Have you lost your shit?"

Shock over the demeaning act hadn't subsided when another slap landed on my other ass cheek. My skin burned in protest, although the pain didn't drown out the sound of Axel growling, "How dare you marry someone else?"

I didn't understand him. Why did Axel act like my marriage was a personal attack on him? He got married, too, albeit Axel only married so his wife could float his dreams of making it big,

Axel's heavy hand landed on my ass again, and I screamed. "Fuck, Axel. Don't."

He ignored me, paddling me on the ass repeatedly with his large palm. My eyes watered with rage-filled tears. I threw every profanity at him, thrashing my limbs to break free. Pain exploded from the multiple strikes, and I screamed and yelled until my voice was hoarse. I fought him off with the last of my strength until realizing it was futile; he was too strong.

Winded, I sagged over the desk in defeat while the assault continued for what felt like forever.

Axel finally ceased his attacks, but only after I laid utterly placid. Sweat rolled down my forehead as I attempted to catch my breath from the heavy exertions. Of all the things Axel had done so far, striking me wasn't one of them. A tinge of betrayal evaporated from the remaining thread of hope I had hung on to where Axel was concerned. It hurt worse than the physical pain.

His motivations made no sense, and I no longer cared to figure it out. Instead, I wheezed over the desk, deflated from the energy I had exercised. Awareness returned when I felt hot breath tickling between my thighs. I let out a painful hiss when he sucked on my inner thighs, then used his relentless tongue to draw a path to my burning rear.

"Axel," I croaked weakly, languidly attempting to disarm his ministrations.

Axel grabbed the back of my thighs and pushed me forward in response, keeping my hips pinned to the edge of the desk. The persistent pain and the physical exertions had wiped me out, leaving me fatigued and nearly useless. He didn't have to try hard to keep me in place. Although a weak voice insisted that I donkey-kicked him and made a run for it, surrendering was easier. The energy to fight had left me. I couldn't even muster a puny protest as his hand dipped between my thighs.

"Why are you doing this?" I strained. My voice was beyond recognizable, an aftereffect of the screaming match from earlier.

"Because I can't stop," he replied hoarsely, the thirst in his voice making my heart leap to my throat. He alternated between kissing and gliding his tongue over the skin on my abused back-side as if trying to heal the throbbing pain he had caused. I tried blocking out his thorough attention. It was difficult when the moisture from his tongue had a cooling effect on my heated behind, relaxing the pain from the physical assault.

He slipped off my heels and massaged my sore feet with his free hand. My breathing evened out, relishing in the slight reprieve. He kissed each ass cheek before returning to my inner thighs. My protests died by the time he moved my panties to the side and his tongue slid between my pussy lips. There were no more thoughts when he probed for entry and sought out my walls. The soothing licks were the only available Band-Aid to subdue the hurt. I closed my eyes as he feasted, distracting my brain from the pain signals it received from my pleasure nerve endings.

Axel ate me with the enthusiasm of a starved wolf. His fervor shattered my control over my body, curling my toes. The distraction from the pain was too welcoming, and the reprieve had my pussy clamping before a scream tore through me in ecstasy.

His tongue disappeared, leaving me with feelings of emptiness. My thighs shook in the aftermath while the distinct clink of his belt indicated he had taken it out of its loops. The sound of his zipper followed it. Throughout the process of undressing, he kept a hand on my lower back to restrain me in case I tried to escape.

He needn't have wasted his energy. The elation had depleted any chance of recoupment from my previous exhaustion. My breathing was labored, ears burning by the time he grabbed my inner thighs and pulled down my underwear. Humiliation trickled down my spine as my natural lubrication allowed him effortless entrance past my opening.

I expected him to take me roughly. Instead, Axel fit himself inside me with controlled precision, stilling once fully sheathed. I would have mistaken it as consideration for my throbbing ass cheeks if he weren't the one to cause the alleged pain. Nonetheless, his heavy, steadying breaths did sound like an attempt to reel in the urge from driving into me.

I felt forceful eyes watching me while I closed mine to escape his intensity. "How could you have gotten married?" he phrased the question from earlier before letting loose on my body. The kindness he had bestowed on account of my pain subsided upon remembering my "betrayal" by marrying someone else.

Despite the subsequent cruelty to follow, Axel was careful not to ram his hips against my stinging ass. He parted my cheeks to minimize the impact of his brutal thrusts. Hot breath and Axel's five o'clock shadow prickled my earlobe as he tilted forward and buried his face in my hair.

Though the pain persisted whenever he made contact with any part of my sore backside, I didn't make a sound. My right cheek rested against the desk as he moved. He watched me, gauging every one of my body's reactions to find a weakness. I tried to block it out so he couldn't find more vulnerabilities to use against me.

Separating from reality only served to muddy my subconscious. I wasn't paying attention when his arm came around my waist, and his hand dropped to find my sensitive clit. It wasn't long before the overstimulated nerve bundles jolted awake. I bucked and tipped my head backward. He tilted his face to the side, avoiding the headbutt he presumed me to attempt. However, I was past caring about anything except for the orgasm within my grasp.

"Fuck," he growled, sensing my muscles contract.

My eyes opened at the unexpected sound of his voice. He ground his hand against my clit to send my overused body flying off the cliff once more. An impatient moan tumbled out of my mouth in response. "God."

His control to carefully fuck me broke entirely with the first scream I was unable to muffle. He pummeled into me, fucking me hard enough to have the legs of the table screech against the wooden floor. My hand slapped the tabletop at the same time he gave me one last thrust.

Axel's palms splayed next to my head as he loomed, breathing harshly, while I lay perfectly still. We stayed in that position for what felt like hours before Axel finally pulled out and smoothed down my skirt.

It took me longer to regain consciousness and accept that I was aroused enough to be thoroughly fucked during my debasement. I hung my head in place, unmoving. There was wishful thinking that he'd allow me a momentary reprieve based on the mortification etched on my face.

One should never underestimate Axel's lack of empathy.

Axel grabbed me and pulled me off the expensive desk, forcing me to face him. I flinched, recoiling when his hand reached for my cheek. "Please don't," I whispered.

Axel stilled at the rejection, turning the room quieter than before. I waited for whatever anger I had set off next.

I was surprised when Axel didn't react with fury. Instead, he clasped my face and yanked me to his chest. Our mouths crashed while my hands pushed against his chest for the distance I desperately sought. I was no match for him. His grip on my face remained firm though he kissed me with affection he hadn't displayed only minutes ago.

"Stop," I pleaded.

He responded by picking me up bridal style and carrying me

out of the room. My combative nature took a backseat, feeling deflated. I let him take me to what I presumed was his bedroom. I didn't utter another word as my back hit the soft mattress and he undressed me.

Fighting seemed pointless. This house was barricaded with lock codes at every turn, my phone was dead, and no one knew I was here. Who'd come looking for me? I couldn't get out unless Axel let me out, and agitating him only caused me harm.

I was defeated.

My eyes closed by the time he pulled a comforter over us. I wasn't surprised when Axel climbed on top and parted my legs. His lips landed on my throat, alternating between nibbling and sucking.

He is marking me with his teeth.

A natural fight reemerged at the primal act, and I swung my hand, unsure of my end goal. He grabbed my wrists and pinned them to the side of my head, once more slipping inside me. This time, it wasn't followed by brutal thrusts.

He moved a few strands of hair out of my eyes, resting his forehead against mine. I met his dark contemplating gaze and couldn't help murmuring one last defense laced with a guilt trip. "Imagine how your wife would feel if she knew you were fucking another woman in your bed."

He paused, head tilted to one side. In all the uncaring ways I expected Axel to respond, I could have never predicted his next words. "What other woman? *You* are my wife."

CHAPTER

FIFTEEN

Milan's Wedding

Piya

"THERE WAS A FIRE INCORPORATED INTO TODAY'S ceremony. Is that a part of Hindu Wedding ceremonies?" Axel asked.

I explained the significance of fire to Axel before grabbing his hands and pulling him to stand for a live demonstration.

"Fires are significant at Hindi wedding ceremonies. The bride and groom walk around the fire seven times. Each time they circle the fire, it represents a different vow, aka a *Phera*. By the seventh time they walk around the fire, their union is sealed, and they are declared one for not only this lifetime but seven lifetimes."

With my right hand grasping his left, I led him around the bonfire. I wanted him to experience the full effect and decided to enlighten him while we physically walked the circles. Interpretations of Pheras differed, so I could only explain how Dadi had described the ceremony to me.

"As we take the first *Phera*, we make a promise to help each other with things like food, shelter, and finances," I enlightened.

His brows furrowed. "That's oddly specific."

I laughed as we came to a stop. "That's because men are oddly forgetful."

We continued walking around the fire.

"In this second round, we promise to take care of each other in sickness and in health."

This time Axel didn't make a snide comment, nor did he come to a stop after completing the circle. Instead, he was the one to lead me around the fire.

"We take a vow of fidelity during the third *Phera*," I explained.

"So, no more strip clubs?"

I giggled before scolding him, "Shh. Pay attention." We circled the fire again. "With the fourth *Phera*, we ask our families to bless our union."

As if remembering family was a sore spot for me, Axel's hand tightened around mine, providing me with the support I unknowingly sought. Suddenly, what started as a lighthearted explanation about religion felt immensely heavy and meaningful.

He moved closer while we walked, heating the intimate space between us. The warmth he surged had nothing to do with the flickering fire.

"The fifth *Phera* is a vow to our future children to be good parents to them," I breathed, barely able to utter the words.

My heart was suddenly beating so hard that I could hear it. The hair on the back of my neck rose with some sort of premonition. My palms were also sweating, though I didn't let go of his hand. We walked around the fire for another full circle.

"In the sixth round, we promise a life of honesty."

Soft ocean breeze tickled my forehead, making me realize the temperature had dropped further. I should have been freezing after brushing off the blanket to stand, yet I felt nothing but him. He had put me in a trance, and I barely noticed my environment.

"With the final Phera, we vow to love each other and pledge a lifelong friendship. We are about to become each other's family and promise to be there through thick and thin."

We stopped walking and came to a final stop at where it all started. My lips parted to finish explaining but no words came out, nor could I meet his gaze. I was under his spell, mesmerized by the stranger captivating my heart. It had to be a dream because what else could make you lose rationality this way?

Something deep and meaningful passed between us though I couldn't put it into words. What the fuck had just happened?

We exchanged something unfathomable with a walk around the fire, and everything in the world seemed different afterward. The air was crisper, the ocean smelled saltier, and the sand under my feet was grittier. Everything looked different, as if I had rose-colored glasses painted on and couldn't take them off. Nothing would be the same again; nothing would feel the same again.

"The completion of the seven *Pheras* means that the couple has made a promise to be together for seven lifetimes," I hardly recognized my voice. "Hence, we walk around the fire seven times, once for each lifetime."

A cynic through and through, I expected Axel to fall to the ground, roaring with laughter. He surprised me by saying, "So, you're mine for the next seven lifetimes?"

I swore he could hear my heartbeat thumping louder than the crashing waves.

"I saw the groom put something red on the bride's forehead and hair after the... *Pheras*." He watched me through thick, black lashes. For once, he didn't mask the emotions on his face, filled with dark promises.

"Sindoor," I whispered as if it were a secret.

God, I couldn't speak or breathe with the intensity of his proximity. I had to snap out of this; otherwise, this man would take me with him to the deepest corners of the ocean, and I'd never reemerge.

I took the slightest step back and cleared my throat. "Sindoor is vermilion; it's this red-pigmented cosmetic powder. The groom places it along the bride's hairline to seal the deal. It's a sign of being officially married."

"We don't have the box of vermilion. Bride's family took it with them after the wedding."

An image of an old Bollywood movie unexpectedly crossed

my mind, and I couldn't help giggling despite the intense moment we were sharing.

"What?"

"Sorry. I just remembered this sappy Bollywood movie. The hero in the movie tried to marry his lover but didn't have vermilion. So, he cut his thumb and used the blood to swipe over her hairline."

The hero was a sentimental SOB, immensely in love with the woman in question. I couldn't hold back another fit of laughter as the ridiculous scene of him cutting his thumb and using the blood in place of vermillion replayed in my mind. I giggled without restraint, though I tried to subdue the sound with a hand over my mouth.

I was so caught up in humoring myself that I didn't realize Axel had moved to our setup on the blanket. His back was to me, and I had to slant my body to see past his massive bulk. He held one of the empty beer cans we drank earlier and stabbed the side of it with his keys like he had done when we shotgun beers.

I walked to him. "What are you—" I gasped when Axel pressed his thumb down the hole, puncturing his skin on the aluminum.

Red blood prickled, a drop falling on the sand to mar the previously pristine, white beach.

"My god, Axel. Are you okay—"

I was cut off by a determined Axel turning toward me abruptly. Just when I thought he'd fling me over his shoulders for some unknown neanderthal reason, Axel stumped me by pressing his thumb over my forehead and smearing the blood along my hairline.

"There. Now we are married."

Gah!

I was wrong to ever make fun of the sappy SOB from that Bollywood movie. It wasn't a corny move.

It was SO. FUCKING. SEXY.

"You're so corny." My voice was thick with desire, contradicting the comment.

He smirked. "That's not what you were thinking, Princess. You loved it when that man did the same thing in the movie."

I bit the corner of my mouth. This was the most romantic thing to happen to me. "It's unhygienic and gross."

His hungry eyes perused me since I was leaning toward him, practically offering myself on a silver platter. "You think it's romantic," he countered.

I do. God, why do I think it's so romantic? I was internally fanning myself. This had to be the sexiest, most swoon-worthy moment of my life.

This draw between us was so strong, so inescapable, that it was ripping my soul out of me. I had to somehow return to earth before he completely eviscerated me with his magnetism.

I cleared my throat and was relieved that my voice sounded normal when I spoke again. "It's just a way to seal the deal."

"Seems somewhat anticlimactic."

"Oh yeah? How do Catholics seal the deal?" He had mentioned that his parents were Catholic.

"How do you think?"

A kiss was at the tip of my tongue, but I dared not utter it out loud since he hadn't either. I rambled about fire and weddings for minutes before realizing that a guy like him probably didn't find this sexy. I groaned internally, then jumped at the sound of a sudden loud boom.

"Holy shit." I turned my head in search of the source. "What the fuck?"

"Easy, Princess," Axel's buttery voice soothed. "Just the fireworks."

Before I could tear my gaze away from the sky entirely, Axel had closed the gap between us as if no longer able to stand it. He wrapped a hand around my throat and suddenly tugged me to him for an unyielding kiss.

"*Now*, the deal's sealed," he murmured against my lips.

The Next Morning

Forcing my gaze on anywhere but Axel, I gathered my items. I knew waking him up to say goodbye would end poorly. I saw glimpses of this man's possessiveness and knew nothing good would come from saying goodbye. He'd probably throw me over his shoulder, then jostle me out of here.

I smiled sadly at the image.

Shaking my head, I grabbed my notebook to leave him a note instead. Upon realizing the notebook was empty, sans the list from last night, I decided to leave him the notebook plus a souvenir meant for him.

I reached inside my purse for the souvenir, placed it inside the notebook, and wrote a message for Axel after a moment's hesitation.

You better become a superstar with this money.
-Princess

It was a cashier's check for fifty-thousand dollars, the amount Dadi had left me upon her death. After finishing my "bucket list," I had planned on spending the remaining money on an extravagant and irresponsible gift to myself—a deposit toward a grand piano I had been eyeing for years. However, this was a much better gift to myself.

Throughout our time together, I admonished an unfair hierarchy that artists couldn't break through unless they had resources at their disposal. No one had given Axel an edge in life yet look how far he had come all by himself. So, what could he achieve if only one person believed in him?

This money was a drop in the bucket compared to what he needed to achieve his big dreams. I highly doubted he'd erect some massive empire out of it, but at least it was a sliver of an opportunity. Axel had gifted me a night I'd never forget. While the money wasn't enough in the grand scheme of things—Axel's goals were much too big—the true gift I wanted to impart was my faith in him. Axel had led a life without support, and I wanted to be the first person to believe in his greatness.

After all, I did make a promise to help my "husband" with things like food, shelter, and finances during our first *Phera*. I mentally shrugged. What better way to keep my promise?

Opening the notebook, I crossed off everything we'd accomplished together.

~~Steal a bottle of liquor from a bar~~
~~Shotgun a beer~~
~~Crash a party~~
~~Go to a strip club~~
~~Dance on a table in front of a roomful of strangers~~
~~Watch a live sex show~~
~~Compose your raunchiest song~~
~~Go to an adult movie theater~~
~~Have a one-night stand~~
~~Splurge on an expensive and irresponsible gift for yourself~~

When I placed the notebook next to him and walked away that day, even I couldn't have predicted what Axel would achieve if only given a chance.

CHAPTER
SIXTEEN

Piya

I COULDN'T MAKE OUT THE FACE. HE WENT IN AND OUT of focus as he strolled toward us while still maintaining distance. The sun bounced with his leisurely pace, nearly blinding me at times depending on his newest position. A chill ran down my spine as our gazes finally met. Dark, unforgiving eyes stared back, dead set against giving away their secrets.

I woke with a jolt from the same dream I'd had every night for almost fourteen years. Unlike the other times, where the face haunting me faded into the background, I knew Axel was staring at me.

Regardless, my eyes refused to open. They fluttered against the threat of the dusk sunlight streaming through the windows.

"Wake up, Princess."

The familiar-sounding voice lulled me back to sleep, though the intent was the opposite. He dragged a finger across my forehead, and I blinked several times to vanquish the gossamer constricting my vision. When the mattress shifted, I jerked, remembering someone else was in bed with me.

My vision finally sharpened, making me gasp when I found Axel on top of me. His face was mere inches from mine. We had sex over and over until I fell into a boneless heap against the soft mattress. Apparently, Axel wanted to make up for the last fourteen years with the number of times he fucked me. The fight in me had also waned in light of Axel's revelations. It felt like he was owed something for all he had been through, and the only payment he accepted came in the form of my body. I fell asleep with him still inside me, only to be awakened in the same position. We were equally naked, with a comforter haphazardly thrown over us.

"I can't breathe." I tapped on his chest lightly, his large body starting to lug heavily over mine. Taut muscles throbbed from the slight effort.

Axel pulled out in response, allowing my sore body the needed reprieve. He tilted to one side by putting his weight on his elbow. My skin burnt as linen slid across it, forcing me to glance down at my naked form. Bruise-like marks stretched from my décolleté to my nipples, covering the entirety of my breasts. Tracking down, I found my inner thighs also covered in love bites.

He had placed his mark on every intimate inch of my body. It dawned on me that he'd done it purposefully to ensure no other man would see me in a similar setting. At least not without witnessing the blaring proof of his ownership. A shockingly effective method. Axel had left me in a comparable state once before and I had to shield those areas from view. The act was calculatingly possessive.

Regardless, I no longer had the heart to be angry at Axel.

"How long have we been asleep?"

Axel glanced at the clock on his nightstand. "An hour."

"Oh," was my measly response.

Hazy bits and pieces returned from our earlier conversation, and ice set in my chest. With one claim, Axel had brought out emotions too painful to revisit. A symbolic exchange on the beach altered the course of his life. He didn't know it but I had been equally obsessed with the memories from that night. I thought about it daily, but I never let it consume me. I had other things to worry about, such as Poppy, my husband, and our family. I wasn't allowed to drown in my obsession like Axel had for years.

It worsened my guilt.

I didn't mourn Axel the way he had mourned losing me. I'd married, had a kid, and lived a full life with them.

Axel was frozen in time.

I clutched the white comforter to my chest to shield myself from the truth. Meanwhile, Axel leisurely pulled himself to a

seated position. Soft bedding swayed from his unhurried movement, exposing the slopes of his V running across the sides of his
cut abdomen. My eyes unwillingly lingered over his naked state
before I forced them away. Instead, they fell on my clothes neatly
stacked on the side table, where I then realized Axel had folded
each piece while undressing me. I grabbed the pile.

Allowing my gaze to wander while I dressed, I scanned the
unfamiliar room for the first time. I didn't take stock of it before
and was momentarily struck by the lavishness of the loft-style
room. The two-story bedroom had a set of spiral staircases
leading to an upstairs balcony. The wraparound balcony overlooked the bedroom instead of outside. Built-in closets lined the
walls of the upstairs area with suits I could see hanging from here
and shelves with more folded clothes.

While the upstairs was a giant closet, the downstairs was no
less opulent. Chic floor-to-ceiling windows posed as walls, with a
view of the beach. The curtains were drawn on some of the
windows, but even so, it was done with precision. A chesterfield
sofa, television, and fireplace gave the illusion of a separate area
for a living room inside the bedroom. Meanwhile, a small desk
with a chair neatly tucked into place created a separate office area.
A modern floor lamp stood perfectly straight and aligned with
the desk.

Each purchase, possession, and accomplishment of Axel's
stumped me. He had built an empire that rivaled Jay's, and all
with a measly sum I didn't think would get him far in an expensive city like New York.

The power of social media changed things for rising artists a few years after I met Axel. Those with talent were no longer handicapped by their lack of connections; they now had a direct platform to reach their audience. Instagram blew up with DJ Axel's name and he escalated from a club DJ to a superstar almost overnight. I heard his name on the radio a year after getting married. I thought I was losing my mind until I Googled him and found out he had already amassed wealth through various investments, one of them being his DJ career.

Never in a million years did I connect the dots; Axel had used the money I left to build all of this. At most, I thought he used it as rent money to float his music career. The things Axel had admitted before I fell asleep were both bone-chilling and heartbreaking.

"Axel..." I started in a soft voice. "I'm sorry for leaving that morning." It sounded pathetic even to my ears.

How the hell did one apologize for this? *Sorry for stranding you on a beach five minutes after you thought we shared something so profound.*

I had painted him as the villain and a thorn in my side. It turned out that I was the bad guy.

"I-I am very happy you accomplished what you set out to do," I continued, looking around the lavish room.

Axel turned to me, pulling on his jeans. "What I set out to do?" He gestured around the room with one hand. "I thought this would make *you* happy."

Speechless, I snapped my mouth shut. I had no idea how to respond and continued dressing quietly until I realized what my ensemble was missing.

"Do you know where my shoes and purse are?" I asked somewhat awkwardly. The room was immaculate. If my purse were here, it'd be easy to locate the giant tote or the glittery pink cell phone case peeking out of it. It was so sparkly that it could be identified from space.

"You left it in the other room."

"Right." Despite locating the coveted purse and shoes, I remembered another problem. My phone was dead. "Can you call me an Uber?"

"You're not leaving," he snapped.

Taken aback by the sharp tone, I parted my dry lips.

Axel swiftly smoothed out his frown, swapping the previous expression for an award-winning smirk. "I told you that I wanted to show you something. You haven't seen it yet."

I frowned. "But you showed me the piano. That wasn't the big surprise?"

Axel shook his head. "Let's go." He nodded toward the bedroom door.

I sighed and followed Axel without argument. My previous fury over Axel's misconduct and the guilt over inadvertently betraying Jay hadn't vanquished, but I banked it away for now. Raising Poppy had given me further insight into Axel. People with antisocial personalities often had a distinct sense of justice and what they were owed. According to him, I betrayed him, which came with consequences and irrational actions. While some trepidation remained, I was no longer scared of Axel. In its place, I wanted to pacify the rejection he must've experienced after that night and soothe whatever I had broken in him. I just didn't know how. He wanted me to leave Jay, but divorce wasn't an option, nor could I return to my marriage without disclosing today's occurrence to Jay. A single isolated mistake might be forgivable, whereas this was too big to repress.

With a heavy heart, I walked down the extravagant hallway with Axel and reentered the music room. It appeared someone had come by and tidied up. I was surprised because Axel mentioned that the staff didn't access this floor without his permission.

The room was once more immaculate, traces of our previous struggle miraculously erased. My purse and shoes were placed neatly next to the mahogany desk, and the scattered paperwork had been picked up and gathered into a neat pile.

Heat rose at the base of my neck as I remembered how the papers had gone flying. I turned away, spotting a cell phone charger plugged into the wall on the other side of the massive room. I must have overlooked it during my first encounter with this room.

There was one more deviation to the scene. A stack of manila folders sat atop Axel's desk, perfectly aligned in an orderly fashion.

Those weren't there before.

The way Axel deviated toward the files and told me to give him a minute—despite his previous resolve to show me something important—confirmed my suspicions. Someone had dropped those folders off per Axel's instructions, and judging by his interest, they held important information.

Axel methodically opened every folder, reading the documents from cover to cover. Considering how meticulously he reviewed the information, I realized it'd take Axel some time to go through all of them. So, I grabbed my sparkly cell phone and crossed the room. I plugged it into the wall charger and watched with relief as my phone lit up with life. If I wanted to read my messages, I couldn't disconnect it from the charger, so I stayed huddled on the opposite side of the room, next to the wall.

For once, Axel didn't complain or demand that I stay next to him. Seizing the opportunity while he was intensely concentrated on the documents, I decided to call Poppy. This was the most distracted I had seen Axel, and I was too far away for him to eavesdrop on our conversation.

After a momentary hesitation, I unlocked my phone and hit Poppy's name. I heard the ringing on the other end and wondered if she'd decline my call. I was surprised when my daughter's voice came through.

"Hello?" Poppy sounded reluctant since I generally called around her bedtime.

"Hi, Beta," I said softly.

Axel glanced at me from across the room when he heard me on the phone. He returned to the paperwork upon realizing I was speaking to Poppy, giving me the privacy I sought for this conversation. I tried to snuff out the emotions Axel had roused today but felt them creeping up my throat, nonetheless.

"How are you?" I asked.

There was a pause on the other end. Poppy had never been one for small talk. "Fine."

"That's good."

I tried to fill the silence by asking how orientation went. Poppy answered in a clipped tone, like always, but I didn't let it deter me. Not today. I continued to prod, asking about various topics until we landed on her remote internship with Ambani Corp.

I had been so resentful of Jay's company that I never brought up the company unless forced to. While I kept up the front of a dutiful wife, I hated discussing company business in the privacy of our home.

I was starting to realize this approach didn't suit Poppy. She considered me unsupportive of her dreams because I refused to discuss the company outside those perimeters.

"How is the internship going?"

Poppy's surprise was warranted, and I heard the restraint in her voice as she said, "It's fine. It can be time-consuming, I guess."

My previous inclination would have been to suggest dropping the internship if it was time-consuming. After speaking with Axel, I realized how detrimental the suggestion would sound to Poppy. It would seem as if I didn't believe in her abilities. For the first time, I tried a different approach.

"Oh yeah? What do you have to do for the internship?"

Taken aback, it took Poppy several seconds to respond. "They usually send me companies to research. I can do it remotely, but finding details and why they are a good fit for investments can take time."

It was the first time I had taken an interest in *her* interest, and it was working. These were the most words Poppy had spoken without sarcasm. Why hadn't I thought of it before?

Grabbing the opportunity by the horns, I asked another follow-up question. To my surprise, Poppy responded. With each question I asked, Poppy answered in slightly more detail than the last response. By the time I asked the seventh question, I realized this was the most my daughter had opened up in almost a year.

"I'm proud of you," I said truthfully when Poppy told me about applying for Ambani Corp's upcoming company-wide junior competition.

Poppy was silent on the other end before saying, "Thank you."

I was floored by the genuineness in her voice. I had never been supportive of my daughter's ambitions and understanding ultimately dawned on me that rather than protecting her, it had made her feel how Mom used to make me feel. Maybe Mom's intentions weren't unfounded, either, just misunderstood. Perhaps I owed my mother a call as well.

I mentally scoffed. Axel had unknowingly fixed three generations worth of mother-daughter relationships.

"I told the school lab about the brain scan for Mr. Trimalchio tomorrow," Poppy said out of nowhere. "If you aren't doing anything... you should come by and watch. We can have lunch afterward."

Oh. My. God.

I was always the one making plans, asking Poppy if she wanted to grab lunch, or forcing my way into her life when she refused. My daughter hadn't initiated one activity with me in almost one year. This might seem trivial, but only someone with a preteen knew how crucial this moment was; the moment your daughter stopped giving you the evil eye and returned your affections.

Okay, affections might be a stretch for Poppy; however, beggars couldn't be choosers.

Be cool, Piya, be cool. Don't blow this by coming off too strong.

"Sure, whatever," I said, feigning as if it didn't matter one way or the other. Internally, I was dying of glee and went to great lengths to suppress my excitement.

"Okay. I'll see you then."

"See you then." I hesitated for another moment before going in for the kill. "I love you."

Poppy usually said *okay* whenever I told her that I loved her. So, imagine my surprise when I heard a soft-barely-there *'love ya too'* before the phone disconnected.

The phone would have dropped to the floor had I not been clutching it with an iron grip. Holy shit. Did that just happen?

A mixture of emotions flooded through me. Of all the ways I expected the conversation to go, that wasn't how I thought it'd end. Poppy hadn't said she loved me in almost a year. Sadness, happiness, trepidation, it all mixed together, and I had Axel to thank for this moment. I might forgive the bastard for all his assholery just for giving me this one moment with Poppy.

Love ya too.

I replayed the words in my head over and over, wondering if she'd say it again tomorrow.

My elation was difficult to suppress and I practically skipped back to the other side of the room, feeling high on nonexistent drugs. Since Axel was still engrossed in the manila folders, I used the time to slip on my shoes and admire the view from the bay window. The scene outside was of an idyllic beach with white sand and pristine water. The sight seemed familiar, although I couldn't place it. Once more, my gaze was drawn to the barely visible green light at the far end of the beach dock. It was microscopic from this distance, so I stepped closer for a better look.

A punch in my gut landed as soon as I recognized the dock. It almost knocked the wind out of me.

"Is that the beach—"

"Yes, it's Chateau at the Hempstead's private beach," he confirmed without missing a beat as if he'd been waiting for me to recognize it.

My mind went blank. For several moments, I couldn't get myself to react. This area had appeared recognizable from the beginning because it was near Milan's wedding venue. The same reason the view from this window looked familiar; it overlooked the beach where Axel and I... I closed my eyes against an image that was too painful to recollect.

It was an endeavor to speak again. "How is this possible?"

Axel dropped the manila folders on the desk and stepped toward the window. "Properties around here rarely go on sale. When I found one across from Chateau at the Hempstead, I was instantly interested," he spoke mildly as if it were no big deal, unaware of how he had detonated my life with information that kept dropping like bombs. "But when I saw this view of the beach, I knew I had to buy this place no matter the cost." He stood beside me, staring at the same faint green light in the distance. I wondered if the same images were flashing through his mind.

The question *why* was at the tip of my tongue, but there was no need to voice it. Axel overlooked this beach while creating music because it was his muse, as his memories had been mine for years.

"Piya?"

I shook my head, realizing my trance had distracted me from whatever he had said. "Sorry, what?"

"Have a seat."

I glanced at the office chair Axel had pulled out. Vanquishing my melancholy with a heavy sigh, I marched over and took the seat. Axel set down the stack of documents—the ones his staff had gathered from the floor— with a loud thump in front of me and sat at the edge of his desk.

"What are these?" I stared at the pile and froze upon finding the words "Petition for Divorce" etched on top.

What the fuck?

"Divorce petition," he declared though I had already gathered as much. "Sign these, and we'll serve them to Ambani by the end of the week. My lawyers investigated his assets. They think we can expedite the paperwork and divorce procedures by declaring you don't want anything from him. Custody will be the bigger problem—"

My body reacted before my mind could process the words. I jumped out of the chair and cleared the stack of papers off the desk in one quick sweep, screaming, "How dare you?"

Axel watched coldly as the papers flew off the desk, landing on the floor.

"This is what you wanted to show me?" I panted, my temper rising with each word.

My blood boiled with rage. Every time I softened toward Axel and showed him an ounce of human compassion, he took it for weakness and tried to bulldoze over my life. He had the audacity to discuss the custody of my child, drafted a petition for divorce on my behalf, and wanted me to serve my husband. Really?

I thought we had exercised a momentary truce while reminiscing over a heartbreaking what-could-have-been past. It was all a farce. The moments of respite were nothing more than an elaborate trick meant to catch me off-guard. He was a master architect of manipulation. Of course, he had organized something deceptive behind my back. The thought only fed my anger.

My outburst made no difference to him, and Axel didn't bother picking up the pile of papers. "You might lose custody of your daughter if Ambani proves infidelity and that you're an unfit mother," he explained detachedly.

"I'm not an unfit mother," I shouted.

"You were so drunk last night you had no idea who was fucking you."

The room descended into a heavy silence. I clenched my jaw and uttered, "Poppy wasn't with me. What I do in my own time—"

"Will be brought into question during a divorce proceeding," he interjected. "How likely are you to win a custody battle if—"

"What custody?" I yelled, upset. "I'm not getting divorced!"

The way Axel's expression morphed told me that I had said the wrong thing. Perhaps I'd been hasty in not fearing Axel, after all.

Axel stood, and it took all my willpower not to cower against the tall frame towering over me. His muscular, broad shoulders and thickly muscled arms flexed with purpose, and I thought he might attack me like before. Instead, Axel reached behind to grab the stack of manila folders. They landed in front of me with a dull thud. Without needing instructions, I knew the files were meant for me to review. He confirmed it by raising his eyebrows at the one closest to me. "Why don't you take a look inside that file?"

I had no clue what the folders held, but I was certain it was something worse than divorce papers. That was why Axel was perusing those documents with such interest.

Anger swelled inside my chest. I wanted to retaliate by messing up Axel's perfectly aligned life. Maybe move his guitar or turntable by one centimeter to the right, which would undoubtedly drive him insane.

However, a part of me knew that lashing out against Axel wouldn't help my cause.

In the end, curiosity trumped my wrath. My heart raced as I slowly picked up the first file and read the label. Jordan Banks. Fear and uncertainty washed over me. With much reluctance, I eased myself back into my chair and opened the folder. Numerous pages of asset summaries and quarterly reports slipped out onto my lap.

"This is about Jordan's company," I whispered in bewilderment, unsure why Axel would show me the financial details of my best friend's company.

"Read it," he encouraged.

I glanced down and scanned the numbers, shocked by how bleak they looked. Jordan had lost numerous high-profile clients over the last several months, but I had no idea things had gotten this bad. Why didn't she tell me? While I knew little about numbers, I knew when I saw a company bleeding dry.

When I finished reading, I glowered at Axel, who had recouped his previous position at the edge of the desk. His eyes motioned toward the remaining folders, gently urging me to continue browsing.

I refrained from picking up another folder out of sheer fear. Judging by the first file, I had an inkling that the rest held information on more people near and dear to my heart. My unwilling eyes darted to the folder labeled "Poppy Ambani." My breathing turned labored, and I was surprised when my voice came out steady.

"What is this, blackmail information on everyone I love?" I challenged.

His silence and the slight tick in his jaw answered my question.

I wanted to scream and throw things at him, preferably heavy things. He had collected blackmail information on everyone in my life and couldn't be bothered to provide me with an admission of guilt.

The dusk lights from the window behind him fell against his form, creating a corona around his head. An eternity went by before Axel spoke again, but instead of answering my question, he said, "You should have never left me with that money."

Dumbfounded, my head kicked back. "What?" Why was he bringing that up now?

"Even if you hadn't left me that money, I would have hunted you down."

I didn't know how to feel about the turn in the conversation and stared at him blankly.

"There was a group surrounding you the first time I saw you. So, I thought you were a guest at the wedding, but it later appeared you had no association with anyone. I assumed the group had shown kindness to a random girl who fell and didn't notice when you crashed the wedding later."

I stood on cue, ready to scoot away. I didn't want to reminisce with Axel. He lost that right the moment he used my loved ones against me.

Axel's hand shot up to grab my elbow and keep me in place. "Imagine my surprise to discover you were the groom's sister. Your family rejected you that day, making a stranger believe you crashed your brother's wedding." Something unrecognizable flashed in his eyes. "You were like me, Piya. Someone who didn't fit into the world they lived in."

His eyes raked over my face, landing on my mouth. He kept his gaze there as he spoke.

"The more time we spent together, the more it became clear that the only world either of us belonged in was the one we created together."

My heart started beating erratically. A panic of sorts grabbed hold, and I wanted to scream and shout to drown out his voice.

"What I experienced that night... the thrill, creating music, the beach... I had never experienced it with anyone. You gave me a glimpse into something invaluable and I knew I'd give up everything for another taste. But then you disappeared on me with only one instruction. You left me, a stranger, with all the money your grandmother left you. All so I could achieve my goals. Why would you do that?"

"I don't know," I chewed out.

"Try again."

"I really don't know."

"Yes, you do." His voice was calm, though the grip on my elbow tightened. "Think, Piya. You were born in privilege and had no business with someone like me. So why would you do that for a man no better than the hired help?"

"Please stop this," I croaked, pushing at his chest for distance. It only made him drag me closer, overwhelming me with his looming presence. That ever-lingering smell suffocated me, and I begged for divine intervention. I didn't want to discuss the things he wanted to talk about.

"You wanted me to turn my life around and be worthy of you; is that it?"

"No!"

"Yes. You fell in love with a stranger and didn't know how else to help him."

"Stop!"

"Not until you admit it. Tell me why you left me with all that money?"

"I wish I hadn't," I shouted, frustrated. "Then you wouldn't be able to use the same money to destroy my family. You're not supposed to punish someone for being kind to you."

"On the contrary. No good deed goes unpunished."

He dropped my elbow, and I rubbed the spot he had gripped tightly with my other hand to circulate the blood flow.

"I taught myself music and clawed out of my fuck-forsaken town with a scholarship," he said quietly. "I was driven and hungry for success and had everything to prove. Even if you hadn't left me that money, I would have made it on my own."

"I know," I admitted in a whisper. It was the only thing I knew for certain. Axel wouldn't have led a life of ordinary. The money I left him might have fast-tracked his career, but even without it, he would have done it eventually.

"So why did you have to go and do that?" He ran a finger down my cheek, and I stepped back to disconnect the contact. Axel moved with me until we were close enough for our breaths to intermingle and the unique smell of his turned overpowering. "You have no idea what you started with one action. My goals suddenly changed to accomplish everything that *you* wanted for me."

Dark eyes flickered.

"Except you weren't there with me. You left me," he hissed. "Every time I tried finding you, it was another dead end. I went by the name you dubbed me and had my hand in every type of music, knowing you'd eventually hear the name and recognize it.

Despite my manager's prodding, I maintained a home and presence in New York. I had been famous for years and knew that if you had any relation to music, you would have heard my name by now. Every channel of communication was open to you. Still, you never reached out and made yourself scarce."

The ominous threat in his voice sent a chill down my spine.

"Then, one late night, after I got home from a show, this commercial came on TV. Imagine my surprise when the jingle happened to be the one you wrote while we were together."

I couldn't hold back a sharp inhale.

For years, I held onto the jingle we wrote. No advertisement proved to be a good enough fit for the song. Then Jordan brought me a condom commercial. While the ad was superficially comical, the setting hit me hard. It was of a couple sitting on a beach blanket, with fireworks in the backdrop. There was a caption printed on the bottom. *Only get caught up in the moment, not caught without a condom.*

Even the advertisement slogan was tailored to us, considering we hadn't used protection that night. I knew the jingle belonged only to that commercial. I was paying homage to our night together. However, never in a million years did I expect Axel to see the advertisement and remember the jingle.

"You contacted the agency who supplied the talent for the ad," I guessed.

Axel nodded. "Jordan's company."

His hand landed in my hair, tunneling through my locks in comforting strokes. This time, I didn't pull away.

"Despite multiple opportunities, you hadn't reached out all

these years. I realized either you changed your mind about us or you'd never wanted to hear from me, to begin with."

His fingers suddenly closed in my hair to make a fist. I held back a yelp when his grip tightened painfully.

"So, I had Levi reach out to Jordan without mentioning my name. He asked to meet with the songwriter in question for an upcoming commercial. But the artist refused to meet in person."

I didn't deny the occurrence and realized why Levi's name had sounded familiar. I did hear of a Levi attempting to schedule a face-to-face appointment with me. I worked under a stage name and never met clients in real life, petrified of someone from the Ambani family finding out about me. It'd only take one person to figure out what "Mrs. Ambani" did for a living and use it to bring down my husband.

So, whenever a client acted overeager about meeting me, I refused all future projects and contact. It was how I had managed to keep my secret career under wraps for years. I remember asking Jordan to block all future efforts from Levi, fearful it was someone from Jay's world meaning to do us harm. No one was this interested in meeting some jingle writer. Until now, I never connected the dots.

"Levi tried everything," Axel continued. "He offered to do the commercial without meeting the artist, assuming he could build rapport and meet you down the line. The artist turned down the offer. He also offered to invest in Jordan's company, promised to bring in high-profile clients like me, and even buy the company out. Nothing worked. Jordan mentioned her unmovable precedence to protect her clients at any cost. She was the type who'd go down with her damn morals instead of disclosing a name."

My heart warmed at the reminder. Jordan was stringent about my real name and would never sell me out if a client wanted my contact information or to meet me in person. She didn't even post about me on her social media.

"While I admired the ethics, it was tiresome to my cause. I had to take action. I had made connections over the years, most of them in the music industry. They were all too happy when I reached out and provided unsolicited advice on achieving success similar to me." Axel lowered the hand tunneling through my tresses to grab Jordan's file I had discarded on the desk. "It wasn't difficult to steer Jordan's clients in a different direction and drain her company."

I couldn't hold back the gasp.

Axel was bankrupting Jordan.

"Within a couple of weeks, Jordan turned desperate. That's when I came in as an interested potential client, offering a bailout in the form of a large commission. To gain my business, all she had to do was show me what she could bring to the table. I asked her to help organize networking parties and introduce me to everyone she knew in the music industry, along with all her remaining clients. It was unsuspicious enough, and she did it without a complaint. After that, it was just a waiting game. I threw party after party, waiting for you to walk through those doors."

I glanced at the folder Axel held in his hand.

"I now understand why she did so much to protect one

client. Because it was someone she loved. So how far are you willing to go for the best friend who refused to give you up?"

My lips parted, my dry throat screaming in thirst.

Axel's unflustered veneer made me want to beat my fists against his chest to break open his armor. I wanted to hurt him badly. However, as much as I wanted to throw a fit, letting emotions rule against a man like Axel was futile; he'd never respond to it. The only way out of this was with a cold, hard discussion.

I squared my shoulders. Instead of answering his question about Jordan, I let my glance peruse the documents on the desk. "Why don't you save us both the time and tell me what else you have gathered about everyone in my life?" I asked icily.

Axel was all too willing to accommodate, no doubt to show me how he'd corner me if I didn't bend to his wishes. He picked up the file that read Amit Mittal. A pit grew in my stomach with unfounded premonition. My parents still lived in Long Island, and my relationship with them had progressed significantly after my marriage to Jay.

"It seems Jordan's family and your father share similar clientele. His practice is made of repeat celebrity clients. Though occasionally, a surgery goes wrong, and your father has to settle with a lump sum."

This wasn't uncommon. While rare, plastic surgery could go south if a client didn't follow the protocols beforehand. Even if Papa wasn't at fault, and the surgery failed due to the ineptitude of following instructions, Papa took the hit and settled because it'd only take one incident to sink his reputation. Celebrities didn't visit plastic surgeons unless their reputation was impeccable.

Axel knew it, too. "One of your dad's ex-clients didn't sign settlement papers, and it turns out she is ready to scream 'botch job' at my cue and the promise of a brighter career."

When I didn't react, Axel picked up two more folders. Milan Mittal and Zaina Mittal.

Milan joined Mom's firm, and they have been thriving since. There was only one instant where Milan made the mistake of scolding me for something. We were at a family gathering in our home in Chicago. Jay had stood on cue, bringing the conversations to a halt with his foreboding presence. He approached my brother and said, "Don't speak to my wife that way again."

Jay's refined manners were reflected in the delivery. The words were spoken softly so as not to embarrass his in-laws more than necessary, but his voice of steel left no room for argument.

After the awkwardness of the day subsided, my family saw me in a new light. Henceforth, they spoke with respect I had never known them to possess where I was concerned. Paired with Jay's stance and Dahlia's kindness, our relationship had grown positively.

The last thing I wanted was for Axel to obliterate everything we had built over the years. If they found out another blast from my past had returned to ruin their lives, all the good faith I had earned over the years would be for nothing.

"What do you have on them?"

"I just signed with their firm, pending one stipulation. They drop half their clients to manage the vast empire I'd bring with me."

Tension coiled in my shoulders. "Half?"

"These are confirmations of them dropping their clients." Axel nodded at the folder. "If I pull my business now, they won't be able to recoup the losses."

My eyes widened. Exactly how much money did Axel accumulate that managing his assets was worth it for Mom and Milan to drop half their clients?

As if realizing where my mind had fled, Axel dropped the files on the desk with a dull thump. "I made aggressive investments with some of the money you left. The rest I used toward equipment. I knew I'd find you, but before doing so, I had to reach the goal you set."

I went rigid and blinked as the words registered in my mind.

You better become a superstar with this money.

Did he take my note as an instruction, like a task he needed to accomplish before we could be together?

That was when it hit me like a train.

Axel did all of this for me.

I looked around the room. Oh fuck. I finally understood why Axel had flaunted his home and possessions—to show what he had accomplished for me with the money I had left. Axel thought I wanted him to become rich so he'd be good enough for me, and perhaps my family would no longer think of him as a "riffraff."

My knees wobbled, threatening to give out underneath me.

With great effort, I regained my composure and snapped my mouth shut. There was nothing left to say. I could be proud of his accomplishments and be flattered by the motivations behind them, but I could do nothing more. Not while he was destroying my life.

"I worked every day, almost every hour, until my body crashed from exhaustion. There were days I didn't think I could work any harder, but I forced myself to work another minute, another hour, another twenty-four hours." A muscle ticked in his jaw as if reliving those moments. "I was obsessed with achieving what you wanted from me. Now that the time has come to collect the reward, did you think I'd leave anything to chance?"

Axel loomed over me. My body screamed with a need to flee, but running would be pointless. There was nowhere to go; Axel had infiltrated every part of my life.

"I assure you that Milan and your mom are getting compensated generously," he spoke again. "They wouldn't have been swayed so quickly otherwise. As long as you sign those papers, they'll continue to be paid. I'll have my contact sign settlement papers with your dad so he is protected in the future. I'll also sign the contract with Jordan and dig her out of this hole. I'll even bring her new clients."

Without breaking eye contact, Axel grabbed the next folder. Despite trying to imitate Axel's unruffled posture, my eyes once more roamed the label "Poppy Ambani."

I immediately shook my head. I wasn't ready for Axel to kick me while I was down, at least not with my one vulnerability; Poppy.

"Don't you want to know what I have on Poppy?" His words were like knives cutting through the air.

"No," I whispered weakly. My heart couldn't take whatever was inside that folder. "I don't want to know." *Please, anyone but Poppy.* My butt landed on the chair, and I started rocking involuntarily.

My weary mind tried to find a way out of hearing whatever Axel had uncovered about Poppy, and because I was an emotional cutter, I redirected his attention to another terrible lane.

"I'd rather know about Jay. What do you have on him?"

Axel's right eye twitched, giving him away. I glanced at the folder labeled "Jay Ambani" and realized, unlike the rest of the files, it was wafer-thin.

The first bit of satisfaction since starting this conversation coursed through me. Axel had little or almost nothing on Jay. If Axel kept his records squeaky clean, Jay was better. He was more than even-tempered and cautious. Jay wouldn't be susceptible to Axel's schemes or get into bed to do business with someone unless vetting them thoroughly. He was vigilant about protecting himself and about protecting us.

Guilt dragged me to the far ends of the ocean at the thought. While Jay had done everything to protect our family, I had brought this calamity into our lives.

"You've nothing on him, do you?"

"Only that I fucked you and could leak this information on Instagram to my fifteen million followers. How long do you think it'll take for the word to reach Ambani and everyone he knows? Should we take a wager on it?"

He always had an answer for everything, didn't he?

"You tricked me into it."

"Good luck selling it to the public that you were *tricked,*" he used air quotes around the word, "into sex with someone like me."

I drew in a ragged breath as Axel scooped up one of the pages that had landed on the floor. I recognized it as the signature sheet, the only page that needed to be signed to serve Jay.

Axel set the page on the desk and pushed a rollerball pen my way. "Sign the paper, Piya. It's the only way to save everyone you love." He spoke the words in a soft yet resolute tone, his threat explicitly clear. Leave Jay or watch Axel destroy everyone I love, including my husband.

"No," I replied robotically.

"Sign the paper, Piya," Axel repeated, this time with an edge. His words were sharp like daggers, threatening to pierce my soul if I didn't comply with his demands.

I clenched my fists at my side as if holding onto an invisible rope, watching as the world spun around me. My eyes darted in every which way, desperate for a way out of this. There was none.

"You can't continue a marriage while already married to another man; a man you have been intimate with numerous times already."

My hair fell limply around my shoulders like a curtain of sorrow, and my body slumped in defeat. Albeit the consent had been dubious at best, sex with a man outside my marriage was still an extramarital affair. If anyone found out about it, Jay would be ruined. Jay, Poppy, and I were the faces of a company based on family values. If this got out, his leadership would be called into question. It would be humiliating for everyone, worst of all, my daughter. Everyone would gossip about her and Jay nonstop.

I brought my trembling hands to clutch my chest for comfort as if it'd ward off the emotional onslaught. Axel had cornered me like an animal. There was nowhere to turn and my husband was MIA. There was no one I could go to about this, not without disclosing this dubious affair.

"This is the only way to set things right," Axel continued as if he were considering my feelings and offering this solution for my benefit, not his.

"You're crazy," I whispered. "I'll never sign that paper."

"Sign the damn paper." His voice was low and threatening, like a great storm about to break on the horizon. He was running out of patience and loomed over me like a steady brewing storm. "There is no point in wasting your breath on a man you don't love."

"*I do love him,*" I shouted, unthinking. "You know nothing—"

Axel grabbed my cheeks to cut me off mid-sentence. His face hardened, eyes narrowed with rage. The last time I brought up my love for Jay, it ended poorly.

I no longer cared. There was nothing Axel could do to overturn this truth; I loved my husband.

Axel was right, I did fall in love with him that night on the beach. I had relived our memories and mourned losing him. Years had passed since; years that I spent building a family.

I'd throw myself in front of a train if I thought it'd keep them safe. For years, nothing had been more important to me than those two people, and I wasn't about to let Axel turn my life into a lie. Axel could kill me, and I still wouldn't take back my love for Jay.

Axel's grip on my cheeks tightened, his jaw tight with unspoken fury. His dark soulless eyes were filled with unyielding fury, piercing my soul. He was a force of nature ready to unleash its wrath.

"Do you know that bigamy is illegal in this country?" he asked in the same low voice, but the venom dripping from his lips made me quiver.

My heart gave out. "Axel, I'm sorry if you thought what happened on that beach meant more. You have no idea how much I thought about it over the years. But it's in the past. Please, Axel, stop trying to destroy my family. Just leave me alone."

Axel's stance remained tense, body rigid and unmoving. There was a distinct smell in the air, an acrid mix of anger and determination. It reeked of bitterness and betrayal and broken promises, like smoke in a burning building filling up every corner of the room.

"You're signing that paper," he declared with cold finality. His presence was overwhelming, radiating a sense of dread in its wake. His hands threaded into my hair again, tightly curling into fists. They held my tresses with an unspoken rage, ready to hurt me if necessary.

I didn't make a sound. Axel was like a live wire, electrifying the air around him and ready to explode with the wrong move.

"Sign it before I lose my shit." He tipped my head up by

tugging at my hair, eyes seething. I would've jerked away but realized he'd probably pull my hair out instead of letting go. I sunk my nails into his bicep to force him to loosen his grip when a loud knock interrupted us. I jumped as if electrocuted.

"May I come in?"

Axel didn't react but let go of my hair and slowly lowered his hand. With his eyes still steadfast on me, he returned to his previous robotic version. "Come in."

The door to the music room opened with care and three men walked through the doorway. Levi and his comrades.

"Levi," Axel snapped. "I told you not to interrupt me unless it was an emergency."

Once more, Levi didn't give a shit about Axel's tone. "I have that update you requested."

Axel's frown smoothed out at the news. Whatever it was, he had been waiting for it. He nodded curtly and made for the door. "Watch her," he threw a haphazard order to the other men over his shoulders.

My shoulders sagged as soon as Levi and Axel exited the room, the door shutting gracefully behind them.

Oh fuck. Oh fuck. I need to get the hell out of here.

"He is keeping me here against my will," I declared to no one in particular. "Can you guys help me?"

Neither man made eye contact, keeping their gazes straight ahead.

"He kidnapped me after promising to give me a ride home. I need to get out of here."

I repeatedly pleaded with both men before moving on to the

repercussions of being an accomplice to kidnapping. My phone was charging in plain sight, so if calling the cops was an option without humiliating my family, I would have done so already. They knew it, too, and were unmoved by my threats and plights. I moved on to offering them large bribes instead and asked for their Venmo handles. The question fell on deaf ears.

In defeat, I slumped against my chair and suspiciously perused the men standing in my way. Their forms suggested they were from military or law enforcement backgrounds, and I knew it'd be futile to make a run for it. This house was on prison lockdown anyway.

Instead, I pondered on Axel and Levi's conversation. Axel seemed interested, which meant it wouldn't bode well for me. What I'd pay to be a fly on the wall while they chatted. It was information Axel wanted, which meant it was information I needed.

Axel and Levi returned shortly. This time, Axel held an air of relief that hadn't existed moments ago. He wasn't smiling or jumping for joy, but there was a subtle delight in his expression I had never seen before. Outside of sex, this was the most elation Axel had exhibited.

What the hell did Levi tell him?

"You can leave," Axel told the men, returning to his frustratingly stoic self. His glance fell on me as the men exited. "Let's grab dinner," he said briskly. "You must be hungry."

My jaw almost hit the ground.

"What the fuck was that?" I whisper-yelled, my hand pointing at the door.

Axel watched me like he had no comprehension of what I was referring to. "Nothing for you to worry about."

My head reeled back. Was he serious? Only a few moments ago, this lunatic was yanking my hair so I'd divorce my husband. Then he had a conspicuous conversation with his most trusted advisor—presumably, about more dirt on my family—now he was pretending nothing happened.

"Wait a minute. Five minutes ago, you were blackmailing me into serving Jay with papers. Then that man," I pointed at the spot where Levi had stood, "said something to you, and now you have put the conversation on the back burner." I braced myself, straightening my back. "Why?"

He was unperturbed by my demand. "I wanted to give you some time to think about it."

Of course, I didn't believe him. Since laying eyes on me again, Axel had turned my life upside down. He wasn't a patient man where I was concerned, and it was unlikely he'd give me time to figure a way out of this... not unless there was no way out for me.

"You're lying," I chewed out.

He shrugged. "Believe what you want."

"Tell me what Levi said."

"He told me the downstairs fridge wasn't working but a repairman should be here soon to fix it."

I grasped my hair with both hands, ready to tear them out. He made me crazy, fucking absolutely bonkers. Who behaved this way?

My blood was aflame, and my stomach was full of cement. With labored breaths and my voice barely a whisper, as if the words themselves were too much to handle, I said, "I want to go home. You promised to take me home."

"You are home," he replied placidly.

Ice settled in my chest, and I started to feel numb. I struggled to process what was happening, mouth partially agape for a silent scream that I stifled. Dread gripped my insides as my new reality dawned on me.

"Do you want to eat dinner here or in the dining room?" Axel moved on as if my concerns had been addressed for long enough. "Let's eat in the dining room," he decided. "You haven't seen it yet."

I stared at Axel blankly as he called the kitchen through the intercom. I barely heard his question, asking what I wanted to eat. When my stupefied self couldn't respond, he placed an order on my behalf.

I watched Axel with unfocused eyes as he let go of the intercom button and approached me. My mind was vacant and a stillness that spoke volumes kept me rooted.

Axel's heavy gaze lingered on my lips, languidly moving to the curve of my neck and the places he had marked me. The hunger in his eyes was ostensible, but the way his hands twitched at his sides told me he was holding himself back. Perhaps it was out of consideration for my apprehension while I absorbed the sudden changes in my life.

"Let's go skinny dipping while they cook," he suddenly suggested an item from our list, once more indicating his good mood. "Pool or the beach?"

A terrible forewarning festered in the pit of my stomach and my melancholy was reflected in my expressions. I suddenly knew why Axel was in such a good mood, but I refused to acknowledge it. Denial was easier.

"I can cut off my staff's access to both, depending on what you're in the mood for."

As if having an out-of-body experience, I heard myself say, "Let's go to the beach."

Axel's face might be expressionless, but his eyes betrayed the tinge of surprise at my easy acquiescence. The perfectly schooled features returned momentarily with an oh-so-telling smirk.

Axel thought I had finally succumbed to my fate and submitted to his will. He was wrong.

I'd fight him tomorrow, but tonight, I'd accept this distraction. Muscles tense and trembling, I was ready for this list, the only thing that could help make me feel alive right now. I needed to see the world in vivid contrasts of black and white, dark and light, all at once with clarity and intensity. I needed to smell the tinge of sharpness in the air. The blood in my veins was already coursing at the speed of an express train. My heightened heartbeat sounded like a river over rocks or a stormy sea crashing against the shore.

I was facing the enormous loss of everything I'd known for years, something that would drastically uproot my daughter's life, too. So, I needed this rush, the jolt that would shake my body and leave it trembling with charged energy.

Nothing else in this world could put my body on full alert like doing a list item with Axel. I needed the spark that created an all-encompassing buzz around my ears, energizing my body from head to toe with every passing second. The tingling sensation of my skin on fire, like electric shocks coursing through my veins. The vibration that made me feel I could move mountains.

I needed all those things more than my next breath. I needed a reprieve.

For I no longer needed Axel's response about what Levi had found. That sinking feeling already told me. Jay's folder was the thinnest of them all, and Axel had been scouring to find material on my husband. A blaring, nasty voice screamed that Jay was having an affair, despite the rational voice soothing that he'd never. And even if Jay were having an affair, infidelity wouldn't be why a high-profile marriage like ours would be allowed to end.

It could only mean one thing. Axel didn't simply find evidence of Jay having an affair; there was more. He no longer cared if I served Jay with divorce papers, and there could only be one reason why Axel wouldn't care about me leaving Jay.

It was because Jay was already leaving *me*.

CHAPTER
SEVENTEEN

Piya

THE NEXT COUPLE OF WEEKS MADE ME REALIZE THAT the initial glimpses of madness I saw in Axel paled compared to the real thing. He'd blown into my life like a hurricane, upending my existence. Whenever I tried fighting the sudden invasion, Axel threatened me with the utter destruction of everyone I loved.

My freedom became stringent in the subsequent days to follow. Most of my essentials magically migrated to Axel's home. The items I lacked, Axel bought in abundance and filled the upstairs closet of his bedroom.

On the day we visited Poppy so Axel could undergo a brain scan, I managed to ditch him afterward and return home. I was shocked to find picture frames in my living room with Jay's face torn out. It left me unsettled and shaken, forcing me to acknowledge that I wasn't safe in my home. I packed my bags and made a beeline to the same hotel nearest my home, contemplating my next move. If I called the police, Axel would destroy everyone I loved. If I told my loved ones, they'd sever all ties with me for bringing the likes of Axel into their lives. The only way out was collecting dirt on Axel, which seemed an impossible feat to accomplish.

Within minutes of checking into the hotel and contemplating my life choices, Axel came waltzing in through the doors of my presidential suite. The asshole had purchased the hotel and could gain access to any of the rooms. He reminded me I had nowhere to hide, and he held the keys to everyone's fates in his pocket. I had no choice but to grudgingly return to Axel's mansion.

No matter the walls I continued to put up, Axel tore them down without a second thought. Any resistance I displayed made him distrustful, further extending his tight grip over me. I could barely ward Axel from following me into the bathroom and finally took a page out of his handbook. I distracted him with promises of lewd rewards if only he gave me a few private moments.

Only one silver lining distracting me from the mess that had become of my life: crossing off items on a list with Axel. Despite loathing his coercions, I couldn't deny the exhalation from the coveted list.

Even so, Axel was an ass about it. A few days ago, he insisted on going skydiving. Before we were allowed to take off, we were debriefed on safety measures and protocols. When the instructor strapped me in, Axel marched over and punched him in the face. I detonated, calling Axel a neanderthal. In retaliation, Axel threw me over his shoulders (of course), telling me we'd skydive another day. Levi had to pay off the instructor, so Axel wouldn't end up in the news, his loutish behavior knowing no bounds.

Nevertheless, Axel kept his word to help Poppy. Luckily, she didn't read into Axel's sudden presence in her life and had chalked it up to learning more about someone like her. Following the brain scan administered at the state-of-the-art facilities of Nott Academy, Axel started joining our lunches—sanctioned by Poppy. He mentioned tactics such as elaborate plans to achieve his goals and distract himself from the immediate gratification of swift revenge. I watched like a hawk as Poppy asked him questions. She listened carefully, and I knew she was taking mental notes to apply the methods. There had been no further incidents at her new school, her roommate's hair was intact, and the headmaster seemed generally pleased by Poppy's conduct.

Heeding Axel's advice, I stopped trying to steer Poppy away from her goals. A tranquility I hadn't known in months set between us upon changing my perspective. Poppy stopped seeing me as the enemy and had been more amicable lately... or as amicable as Poppy could get.

Milan and Mom's company was also doing well, managing Axel's assets. Axel persuaded his friend, who had undergone a lousy surgery at Papa's practice, to sign NDA papers agreeing not to share detrimental information. None of them had a clue about Axel being the catalyst to their potential demise or that he was the

DJ from Milan's wedding. Who'd remember someone they'd met in passing nearly fourteen years ago?

Jordan's company had also been soaring since Axel signed with her. The new position as his publicist made Jordan a desirable commodity amongst his peers. She collected new clients and made connections, growing rapidly to compensate for the previous loss of business.

Jordan was none the wiser about my 'relationship' with Axel, and I kept my distance until I could sort out my personal life. I wasn't ready to admit this sordid arrangement, let alone reveal the details to my best friend. I was simply happy that her career had been sorted.

The only person still unaccounted for was Jay. At every chance, I snuck away from Axel and called Jay, begging for a conversation or to meet face-to-face, but Jay was uninterested. Our conversations lasted less than thirty seconds, and he always had to go. Even if our marriage was in shambles, how could it end over the phone? Jay refused to return to New York, and when I asked if he planned on seeing his family again, he was quiet on the other end before abruptly ending the call.

Shockingly, Axel didn't bring up divorce again. He was suddenly apathetic about the entire matter as long as I didn't mention Jay's name in his presence. It contradicted his personality because Axel's possessiveness knew no bounds.

So why was a man like him no longer bothered by my marriage? Jay hadn't served me divorce papers, nor did divorce make sense. When we married, Jay explicitly said Ambanis weren't allowed to divorce.

No, I didn't expect to return to my previous life willy-nilly. I'd reached a point of no return the moment I gave in to Axel's demands, but it didn't make me stop caring about my husband. I wanted to understand what was happening to Jay. I had called a few family members whose stories had been similar. Jay had been working around the clock like a madman, and no one had interacted much with him. Apparently, he stopped going to the office and was working from home. There was something seriously wrong here and I needed to get to the bottom of it before Poppy caught onto the discrepancy.

The solution came in the form of Axel's last show. He had decided to stop doing raves and festivals after completing his remaining contractual agreements. His last event was a two-day music festival. I couldn't go with him because Poppy's student-teacher conference fell on day one of his show. I planned to finish the conference and fly to Chicago to see Jay. We had been together for thirteen years and shared a child. There was no way to dismiss our situation without a conversation.

While I doubted my actions would please Axel once he found out, I needed closure. If Jay wanted to divorce me, we needed to discuss Poppy. What were we supposed to tell our kid about what was happening between us? I knew Poppy was in boarding school, so it wasn't a problem that needed an immediate solution, but it was unlike Jay to leave things to chance. He'd never reject Poppy yet hadn't discussed custody. There had to be something else at play. Both Jay and Axel were hiding things, and I planned to get to the bottom of it.

Nonetheless, each moment closer to the two-day separation put Axel in a fouler mood than the day before.

"Why can't you fly out after the parent-teacher conference?" Axel asked stoically, arms crossed across his chest. He leaned against the stylish white bookshelf in his bedroom, suspiciously watching the duffel bag I had laid on the bed. I'd encouraged him to pack and grabbed the first bag I could find in the closet. It propelled Axel to interrogate me again about why I couldn't join him this weekend.

"We talked about this," I replied, averting my face. "The parent-teacher conference will end so late in the evening, I'd have to take a red eye to L.A. The flight won't arrive until six in the morning. By the time I check into the hotel, you'll already be at the festival. It goes on all day and I'll be too exhausted to attend. What would be the point of doing all that just to spend a few hours together? It would make much more sense to see each other once you're back."

"I'll move the damn parent-teacher conference then. It's my school."

It took everything in me not to roll my eyes. "You can't do that. It was organized before you bought the school, and parents are flying in from all over the country, some even internationally, for the mid-summer check-in. It was planned months in advance, travel arrangements had been made, and to be honest, I'd like an update on Poppy's progress as well."

"Poppy's doing just fine," he said, irritated.

I shrugged. "I'd like to hear that from her teachers."

Axel's body language made it obvious he was thinking of more obstacles to put in my way, but I was determined. I needed a couple of days to regroup and extract an answer from Jay. I couldn't focus on anything until doing so, let alone rekindle a relationship with Axel. Perhaps if things had ended organically with Jay and Axel hadn't blackmailed everyone I loved, I'd feel differently about having him back in my life. As it stood, I was counting down to the moment until I could get away. Not to mention, I had to tell Jay about Axel before he found out in another way. It was the least I owed him.

Axel would cook something up if he knew of my plans. I had to keep him on an even keel until we amicably parted ways tomorrow.

Everything was in place. I had been planning this since learning of the scheduling conflict and had been meticulous about the details. Personal security wasn't allowed inside the school premises. Levi and his men would have to wait outside Nott Academy during the parent-teacher conference. I'd speak to Poppy's teacher and leave two hours before the conference officially concluded. I'd call an Uber to meet me on the other side of the school. I knew buying a ticket to Chicago would somehow tip Axel off, so instead, I'd only scoured online for a non-stop flight and would buy the ticket at the airport counter. Before the security detail realized I was missing, I'd be in Chicago. Of course, I'd text Levi upon landing to let him know of my whereabouts and face Axel's wrath later.

A normal human should be able to end their marriage face-to-face rather than over text. Whatever Axel was to me, I should be allowed to have that conversation with my husband. Thoughts of Axel might've often circulated in my subconscious, but the reality of our reunion differed from the fantasy. Despite our connection, my heart refused to give itself to Axel. Every part of me screamed that I couldn't be his while I was still someone else's. He knew it, too. Hence, Axel always wanted me within his sight and scarcely bothered hiding his feelings on the matter.

"If the parent-teacher conference can't be moved, then I'll skip the festival—"

"You can't," I said a little too quickly before I caught his narrowed eyes. I swiftly recovered. "Levi said your contract was binding. They could take you to court for refusing to play."

He scowled. "So?"

I closed my eyes, praying for patience. Trying to speak to him and make him understand was pointless; I had learned the hard way. "Axel, you are so close to getting out; it'd be stupid to jeopardize it now. I mean, you only have one more show left. It'll be over before you know it—"

"Then come with me," he said through clenched teeth.

"I can't," I gritted out.

"I'm not letting you out of my sight again!" he yelled so loud that I jumped. My heart rate accelerated, and I had suddenly never been more grateful for the clause in his contract to toss him in jail if he violated it.

"It's only two days," I said meekly.

"That's too fucking long."

"There is no other choice. I have to attend Poppy's parent-teacher conference, and you have to do your show."

His jaw ticked, acceptance tentatively settling in. "This is the last time. We've already been apart for too long," he said so quietly that I had to perk my ears.

I nodded in acquiescence, watching him carefully. Axel didn't have to verbalize what he meant; it was apparent in his words and actions. He had reached his goals and had finally found me. After this last show, nothing would keep him from his reward ever again.

PART THREE

Secrets

CHAPTER
EIGHTEEN

~

Axel

THE SUMMER SUN, MIXED WITH THE CHICAGO WIND, made for comfortable weather. I watched Piya strut around her sunroom with purpose, watering the hanging potted plants with a gardening can. She was dressed in black yoga pants, a matching tank top, and a headband with an unmistakable line of glitter along the edges. Her hair hung like a glossy black curtain down her back. I could almost feel the heat radiating off her body with every step she took. Despite my anger, the hypnotization she held was difficult to deny.

Fuck, she was beautiful.

It had been two days since Piya ran away. The hordes of text messages and missed calls from Levi didn't come through because the festival was held at a remote location, and I found out too late that Piya had fled to Chicago. I realized the extreme measures Piya had taken to deceive me. I called her nonstop, leaving every imaginable threat on her voicemail, and the moment my show ended, I flew to Chicago and drove to the Ambani residence outside the city.

The house sat at the end of the paved driveway. Unlike Piya's home in New York, it wasn't heavily fortified since it was surrounded by numerous acres of land. Perhaps Ambani thought the seclusion provided enough safety.

It was easy bypassing the large gate and round the house to inspect how to break in. Finding Piya hanging out on the sunporch was simply a stroke of luck.

I fought the urge to break down the door, march inside, and drag her out by her hair. Did she think running to a different city would keep her safe?

I had waited years to find her, only for her to run at the first opportunity. It was time to pluck her out of this life once and for all and further submerse her into mine. If she thought what I had done so far to corner her was bad, I'd prove her wrong. I had nothing but time to make her bend to my will.

The moment I'd found Piya again, I had put the word out that I'd no longer be doing shows. This festival marked the end of my last contractual agreement. Fame would be a hindrance to my new life with Piya. We couldn't go anywhere without being recognized, and I had a feeling Poppy wasn't the kind to appreciate the limelight. She'd definitely break one or two of the paparazzi's cameras if they came near her.

I'd only remained in the spotlight for so long because I knew Piya was in the music industry. My goal was to maintain a public presence so I'd stay visible on her radar, and she could get in touch with me. Now that I'd found her, the shows no longer served me a purpose. From now on, we'd only create music when we pleased without the hassle of deadlines or fulfilling demands.

With fame no longer standing in the way, only one obstacle remained. Ambani. In a shocking turn of events, the situation had resolved itself. Or so I thought. I had written Ambani off, believing him to be a lost cause. There was no point in beating a dead horse because Ambani had taken himself out of the game.

It turned out that my mistake was in downplaying Piya's loyalty to him. No matter how much I'd tried to eradicate the thirteen years they had spent together, Piya wanted closure. As much as I hate to admit it, I realized she might fight me every step of the way until receiving it. Piya must've seen Ambani by now and was privy to the situation.

My eyes burned with rage, jaw set firmly in a menacing grimace. I wanted to shake Piya until she stopped giving a shit about Ambani. My rigid body moved to the glass door, ready to lunge if she didn't open it.

Feeling the weight of my stare, Piya set down the green gardening can and rotated her head to locate the origin. A deep furrow appeared between her brows, and her back went ramrod straight when she looked outside the glass casement doors of her sunroom. She caught my gaze with her own when I stepped into view. Even from here, I could see her breath hitching. She shook her head as if willing my presence away or asking me not to do whatever I had planned. Piya assumed there'd be retribution for her actions. She was right.

"Axel," she spoke from behind the pane of glass. I expected her voice to come out muffled. Instead, I heard her loud and clear despite the door separating us. Glancing above the glass door, I saw the open vent to allow air circulation into the sunroom. It seemed the room wasn't part of the central air-conditioning system of the house.

Unlike the room, the air between us was thick with tension, hot and oppressive, and heavy. I stepped closer. Smooth skin, soft like velvet, made me want to reach out and touch her. Scratch that. I would touch her.

"Open the door, Piya," my voice was a low rumble like thunder, each word punctuated with a sharp intake of breath, trying to control my rage. I knew she could hear me perfectly clear through the door.

A pensive expression settled on her face after digesting the shock of seeing me in Chicago. She stood tall and defiant behind the glass of the cascade door, unfazed by my demand.

"Open the damn door before I break it down," like an omen of doom, my voice echoed through the door. I inhaled deeply, momentarily composing myself. "We have discussed this," I tried to rationalize, sounding calmer than the fury boiling inside me. "Running is pointless because there is nowhere to hide. You don't have it in you to watch me destroy the people you love."

Her eyes remained determined, her lips set in a tight line with unwavering resolve. "I ran away because I had to know what was happening."

I smirked at the determination in her voice. "Did you find out what you were looking for, Princess?"

"You know I did," she whispered. "I'm not going anywhere with you."

The corners of my mouth curled as I stared at Piya with serene tranquility. It was time to show her all the cards. I didn't want to resort to this, but she twisted my arm into it. "Are you sure about that, Princess? We never did get around to opening Poppy's folder. Don't you want to know what I learned about your daughter?"

Piya's eyes were no longer brown and determined but black like the stormy sea. Her fists clenched tightly at her side, arms trembling. The pressure in her veins seemed ready to burst at any moment.

My menacing eyes were unmoved by her unspoken plight to leave Poppy out of this. "If you don't make things worse, I won't tell the world what I learned about Poppy," I generously offered. "Just this once, I'll forget retribution for this step back. You've had your little fun. Now it's time to go home. Open this door."

A faint glow emanated from her body. Silence and a calm stillness was in the air. I knew what it meant. Piya wouldn't comply with my demand.

Why do people insist on choosing the difficult route? She had to know there was nowhere to run and was only prolonging the inevitable.

Piya's face turned stoic with an eerie determination I didn't know her to possess. "You're not going to do anything to Poppy," she spoke with unwavering confidence.

I raised my eyebrows as if to say, *challenge accepted, Princess.*

"There is no going back for me, Axel," she spoke softly. "Coming home and seeing Jay..." Her lips quivered, and she bit her bottom one to stop the trembling. She spoke again after composing herself. "See Jay has reminded me that I'm not the same person anymore. I'm sorry, Axel. I can't go with you."

I threw my fist against the door without thinking.

Fuck.

Leave it to Piya to break the calm I had perfected over the years.

I stared at the glass with maniacal intensity, filled with an intense emotion that couldn't be contained for long. I was about to lose control and slip up. I could feel it coming but couldn't force it down. My eyes were wild and unfocused at the idea that she might've found a way out of my hold.

No.

No.

Impossible.

The plan was foolproof. I hadn't left anything to chance.

Then why the fuck did she appear serene, as if she had found a way out?

Piya stared at me with eyes pleading for me to understand... as if she had a choice in the matter. "I'm sorry, Axel," she repeated. "I'm sorry we missed our shot, but too much has changed for me in the last fourteen years."

A dark shadow loomed over us at the words. A sly grin crept

across my face, allowing me to regain my composure. "Do you know how long I have been searching for you?" I asked mildly. "Because I do; I counted each day you stayed away from me. That's why I find it amusing when you keep saying it had been fourteen years since we met."

The blood drained from Piya's face. "W-what are you talking about?"

I stepped forward until we were face to face, separated by nothing but the glass door. "You purposefully keep repeating the time frame to instill the number into my subconscious. Isn't that right, Piya?"

Piya tried keeping an emotionless expression, but it was too late. I could sense the fear buried inside and the dread over her deepest secrets being uncovered.

That's right, Princess, I was onto your little game. "Do you know how long it has actually been since we met again?"

Piya's lips parted as if to reply to the rhetorical question, but instead, she chose to remain silent.

"Thirteen years, eight months, one week, and four days."

Piya's eyes were unblinking. Her skin paled as she stood like a statue, not making a single move.

"After that night on the beach," I continued without letting her recover. "I couldn't make sense of why you'd leave all that money if you planned on walking out of my life." Every word out of my mouth was filled with heat, reliving those days without Piya.

I wouldn't return to that life. Never again.

"At first, I thought maybe you were investing in me; perhaps you needed me to prove myself before you could be with me. I worked like a dog, determined to achieve everything you wanted for me. I started gaining recognition and even kept my job at the venue for a few extra months so you'd know how to track me down. Still, you were radio silent, and it started pissing me off. Over the months, I became fixated on your intentions for leaving me that money if you had no plans of reaching out. The months turned into years, and my obsession with the matter only grew. The more my obsession grew, the more driven I became... and the more I wanted to punish you for staying away. I counted each day to pass by, promising to make you my prisoner for the same number of days you'd made me yours for years. No matter where or what condition you were in, I would've hunted you down. Even if you were dead, I would have dug up your grave. Nothing, not even death, would've kept you from me." My razor-sharp words cut through the air like a blade, reverberating through the glass.

The world stood still as she confronted the extent of my obsession. As I said, there was nowhere to hide, not even behind death's door, let alone behind a glass door.

Piya's shallow breaths told me she knew it, too. Her gaze, intense yet melancholic, locked with mine. She pressed a palm against the forsaken pane of glass dividing us.

I met her hand with my own through the glass door. Piya's breath hitched as if she could feel the caress through the barrier, and the cold surface somehow felt warm. I stared at where our hands were linked through the glass.

"Do you know what thirteen years, eight months, one week, and four days equate to?" I asked in a low voice.

Piya stared at me as if she had no idea what to say or how to feel.

"It equates to the 5000 nights I spent without you."

Piya's silence was filled with the scent of uncertainty as if struggling to make sense of where I was going with this conversation.

"I counted each night I spent without you until realizing 5000 days had gone by in trying to find you. I was throwing myself a party, a memorial, if you'd call it, to the time I had spent searching for you. The last thing I expected that night was for you to walk through the doors."

Piya's eyes widened, her pupils dilating as the words registered in her brain. The edges of her mouth began to slope in an ironic smile. With a half-smirk of my own, I dropped my gaze at our hands connected through the glass.

"So, tell me, Princess. Did you think you could fool me into thinking we hadn't seen each other in fourteen years?"

Her eyes darted to the garden outside, dodging my stare and searching for an answer to alleviate the deception. "I-I wasn't trying to fool you. I was rounding up." Piya's body was tense, though I knew she was moments from falling apart.

I sighed as if explaining reality to a petulant child. "No, you weren't. You were worried about why I had returned to your life and were desperately trying to cover your tracks. So why don't you save me the breath and admit the secret weighing down your soul for so many years?"

Piya's eyes were wide and glassy, her face drawn. "Axel, I—"

"Say it."

"Please," she pleaded, eyes wide with terror and voice shaking.

"There is nowhere left to hide, Piya. I already know, but I want to hear you say it."

The heavy scent of fear lingered in the air, but her time was up. "I can't."

"Say it!" I shouted.

Piya's cheeks turned ashen, her eyes fading to a hollow stare as if the life had been sucked out of her. "Poppy is your daughter."

5000 Nights Ago

Piya

"You're pregnant."

Dread coiled around my spine. The doctor's words sounded like a joke, and I waited for the punch line. When it didn't come, I quickly resorted to challenging the results unearthed by modern medicine.

"No, I'm not," I declared.

The doctor in the crisp white lab coat stared at me through the black-rimmed glasses resting lightly on her nose. She was a tall brunette with shoulder-length hair pulled back in a loose bun. Her blue eyes gave off an aura of intelligence mixed with sympathy. "I'm sorry if this news is coming to you at a bad time," she offered kindly.

The OBGYN read the room and determined this was no joyous occasion. Instead of congratulating me, she glanced at my chart, likely calculating my age based on my date of birth. Twenty-one wasn't unceremoniously young. Nonetheless, I was too young to be a mother, so I grabbed denial by the horn.

"Nothing is coming to me at a bad time because I'm definitely not pregnant."

The doctor sighed. She didn't wake up thinking she'd spend her day defending science to a recent college graduate. "Blood tests are definite, Piya. You're pregnant."

"I have been on the shot since I was seventeen," I refuted, "so it's impossible for me to be pregnant." Though I knew my fate was sealed, I spoke with unyielding confidence. If I refused to be pregnant, it would somehow overturn results determined by twenty-first-century medicine.

"Birth control shots are only 94% effective. Your chance at pregnancy increases if there are delays between appointments, especially with consummation during the period when the shot is less effective."

I felt lightheaded as the truth became harder and harder to deny. Fuck. I shouldn't have pushed back my last appointment.

It had been two weeks since Milan's wedding. I spent the entirety of the time moving out of my parent's home and into my new apartment. All the while, I had been haunted by memories of Axel. Once the move had commenced, and I had nothing left to distract me, doubt had seeped in if I'd made the right decision. If walking away from Axel was the right call, why the fuck did it feel so damn wrong?

I succumbed to my inner demons and drove to Chateau at the Hempstead to track him down. I had to stop myself right before taking the plunge. Everyone else's words and my past drenched doubt in the seemingly magical night we shared. When you had been burnt by men as many times as me, you started questioning your ability to tell the good ones apart from the bad apples.

After the inner turmoil, something worse came to mind; I had unprotected sex with a stranger.

Did Axel do that often with other women?

We were so caught up in the moment that condoms seemed frivolous. Super self-destructive behavior—I know—but at least I was on the shot. Still... was Axel callous in general or only with me?

I had no idea if he slept around without protection and needed to take an STD test ASAP. If I were clean, it might mean that I was an exception for Axel as he had been for me, and perhaps there was hope after all. Once the results of my STD tests came back negative, and if I still couldn't stop thinking about the stranger, I'd drive back to the venue.

Instead of calling on Axel, I called on a doctor.

Well, the STD tests came back negative; it just so happened that another test came back positive. Considering how many times Axel had fucked me that night, should this really be a surprise?

When they administered the STD test, they also tested the

blood for a possible pregnancy. Now I wished I hadn't gotten tested, as if living in denial would somehow absolve me of this reality.

"If this isn't something you're ready to handle... we can talk about your options," she said pointedly.

My head snapped up to meet her gaze. *She means an abortion.* Fuck. I always assumed that termination of pregnancy was reserved for teenagers after prom night. It seemed like a bizarre choice for someone my age, a person with a job and a new apartment.

How did I get here? This was a predicament I had never faced or considered.

The doctor discussed various options and handed me pamphlets for clinics in case motherhood wasn't for me. All the while, I stared at her blankly. My hand splayed over my stomach, stroking the skin. I never possessed any superior motherly instincts. It seemed irresponsible for nature to put me in charge of another life. According to everyone, I was a mess. What did I know about taking care of another human? I had no business taking on such endeavors, so why had I been charged with safeguarding this life? I'd be held accountable if anything were to happen to it. It was terrifying... yet oddly beautiful.

"C-can I see it?"

"It?"

"The..." My voice trailed off as I searched for the word to describe the tiny being inside me. Baby would sound too official, and I couldn't possibly entertain a different choice after acknowledging the word. Fetus sounded too clinical, so instead, I pointed at my stomach. I needed to confront the entity growing inside me before proceeding with a decision that would irreversibly affect him or her.

"You can do an ultrasound in a few weeks."

A few weeks was so far away. "Oh, okay. But... how do I know what it looks like?" I blurted.

"What do you mean?"

Once more, I pointed at my stomach.

"Small," she said softly.

"How small?" I held up two slender fingers to convey the size of the fetus. My thumb and index finger barely touched, with an inch of space between them. "This big?"

The doctor's blue eyes sparkled with amusement, and her lips twitched. "Smaller." She pressed my dainty fingers together, leaving no room, to indicate the size. "Fetuses are generally the size of a poppy seed at conception."

I stared at my fingers in disbelief. How could a poppy seed so small upend my life so majorly?

I tried to ignore the image of a single poppy seed flashing in my mind, but the visual kept popping back. A tiny, black poppy seed spun slowly on a never-ending cycle, forcing me to glance down at my belly.

Is that what you look like, little poppy seed?

Apprehension twisted my stomach. The tiniest, most delicate, and extremely vulnerable poppy seed had been entrusted to my hands. Me—the black sheep of the family—the one who screwed everything up and constantly wreaked havoc. The middle of my chest squeezed. Whatever mistake nature had made by doing this, I somehow didn't want to let it down. Most importantly, I didn't want to fail my little poppy seed.

I stared at my belly, petrified. It was the first time I felt a sense of responsibility to do right by someone else rather than indulging in my selfish desires for an adrenaline high.

"Piya?" the doctor prodded, concerned about my extended silence. "Do you not want those?" She nodded at the pamphlets for alternate options when I returned them to her.

I tried to smile reassuringly. "I don't need those."

Understanding crossed her expression. "Do you want me to provide you with some other information then? For a healthy pregnancy, the first thing I recommend is getting on prenatal vitamins. We can also schedule your ultrasound now. These appointments tend to get booked up." She continued listing the dos and don'ts while expecting. I listened carefully, nodding whenever she paused so she'd know I was paying attention.

I stood on shaky legs when she finished. We headed toward the door simultaneously. I wanted to exit, and her goal was the small sink to wash her hands.

"Oh, and Piya."

I paused at the door frame without turning to face the good doctor.

"Congratulations."

I froze at the word, surprised she said it considering my initial reaction. It was only when I glanced at the mirror over the sink did I realize my mortification had vanished. Instead, I appeared cathartic.

I needed a jumbo slice of a maple honey pecan pie. Satiating my pregnancy craving was the only thought I could focus on while running inside the twenty-four-hour diner located on the ground floor of my new apartment building. Pregnancy cravings didn't start a week after conception; I simply wanted pecan pie and needed a scapegoat to excuse my gluttony.

I was so preoccupied with thoughts of pecan pie that I almost missed the shadowy figure at the bar counter. Dusk peered through the window, covering the man with eerie highlights while he studied a plethora of paperwork. He had commandeered a good portion of the counter with his laptop and folders.

I came to a screeching halt, stopping two feet from the man.

Of all my wildest fantasies of running into Jay Ambani again, this one took the cake. I meant it in the literal sense. I was salivating after a piece of pie and had on my go-to gorging outfit, an oversized t-shirt with stretchy gray sweatpants. Dark circles surrounded my eyes, and my unwashed hair sat atop my head in a messy bun.

Meanwhile, Jay was a vision of perfection. He wore a dark gray suit tailor-made to fit his body. His hair was neatly groomed, and so was every aspect of him, down to his nails. I glanced at my own with dirt underneath the fingertips.

Why didn't I take better care of myself?

I considered turning around, but Jay had already sensed my presence and glanced up. My eyes widened while his remained neutral.

Since Milan's wedding, my parents have encouraged me to reach out to Jay. I had ignored their pushiness, busy mending my heart from the Axel debacle.

And to be honest, Jay unsettled me. I never knew what to make of him. Reserved, formal, he had an air about him that made you question yourself. I always ended up blabbing like an immature idiot around him, grappling for a topic that might interest him. Whereas he listened patiently because his parents had raised him right. He'd never tell a girl to shut up even if she was annoying, nor would he let on if he was bored with the conversation. He definitely wouldn't choke a girl during sex or indulge in the depravities I had recently been exposed to with Axel. No, that would be much too impolite for Jay.

I sighed mentally.

That day, it was supposed to be Jay and me. If he hadn't left, I would've stayed focused on Jay instead of the stranger who had upended my life. Jay would have used protection because it would've been impolite to knock me up before taking me out on a proper date.

The blunder in my most recent mistake was written all over my attire. This was by far the worst way of running into your former arranged-marriage prospect. As it was too late to make a run for it, I did the opposite. I strode to the counter, pulled out the chair next to him, and plopped onto it without explanation.

"Piya." The warmth in Jay's tone shocked me, given my unruly attire.

"Hey," I said meekly and glazed over the scattered paperwork, then met his eyes. "This is a nice surprise."

He nodded slowly, eyes roaming my face. "I work nearby."

"Oh." Despite spending hours together at Milan's wedding, we never spoke again. It seemed in poor taste to bring up how we had flirted shamelessly the last time we saw each other. Instead, I took my cues from him and let him lead the conversation.

"Do you live around here?" He glanced over his shoulder and stared out the restaurant door of the bustling neighborhood of East Village.

"My apartment is upstairs."

"Convenient. Right in the middle of everything."

Jay made a few polite inquiries, all appropriate for two people who grew up in the same circle. His impeccable class was effortless, and he never failed to deliver on his refined manners.

Dadi would've wanted me to marry someone like him, I couldn't help thinking with a defeated sigh.

If I had gotten pregnant with this man's baby, I wouldn't be gorging on oversized pie slices. He was born to be a father; loving, nurturing, dependable, trustworthy, even-tempered with a stable career. He'd set an excellent example for any child.

The thought sent me down a depressive spiral. It was all the things Axel wasn't. Axel hated family values and kids. He mentioned it multiple times during our time together. My throat constricted at the idea of Axel rejecting my little poppy seed.

After finding out I was pregnant with Axel's baby, I had considered driving to Chateau at the Hempstead. A pit in my stomach, a gut feeling, stopped me.

Instead, I ended up doing an intensive search on whether psychopaths could love their children. There were various platforms where psychopaths could answer anonymously, and a few chose to do so.

One of them said, and I quote, "No, I do not love my children, but I make them believe that I do."

Another said he viewed his children as possession, his to do as he pleased, and cared for them the way he would any other piece of property.

The responses left me shuddering to my core. You had to nurture something fragile like a poppy seed and fill it with love. But Axel wouldn't love my little poppy seed; it was a quality he didn't possess. At most, Axel would be proud of them if they met his expectations.

But he'd never love them.

The moment everyone found out that I was knocked up by a man like him—one who, on paper, was a carbon copy of my rotten ex-boyfriends—my family would also cut me out of their lives. It was the one thing Mom had repeatedly asked me not to do. *Don't get pregnant by one of those useless boys.*

Well, so much for that. I'd be ostracized and cast out from my family, and all for a man who had no interest in having a family or loving my child.

I tried to nod as Jay kept talking, even though I was consumed with worry over poppy seed's uncertain future.

Jay noticed. "I have never seen you so quiet," he said suddenly.

I wanted to give him a reassuring smile to dismiss his concerns but couldn't muster it.

Jay appeared suspicious of my demeanor. "Is everything okay, Piya?"

I shook my head, squashing the overwhelming urge to cry.

"What's wrong?" His arrested voice was low with meaning.

I blinked, averting his gaze.

Jay must've sensed my dilemma. "Piya, our families have known each other forever. You've known me all your life. You can tell me anything. If you're in some kind of trouble... I can help."

In theory, Jay was right; we grew up in the same Indian community. However, our lives ran parallel. He was older and was in a different clique. By the time our age difference didn't seem so large and Jay showed interest in me, I had become engulfed in Axel. We never got the timing right.

Nonetheless, I had known this man all my life. Could I trust him with this secret of mine? Jay wasn't the type to blab, and he was immensely mature. Perhaps he could help me find a way out of this mess.

"Is that a serious offer?"

His nod was curt, a tentative request for me to continue.

"I'm pregnant," I blurted.

If Jay was shocked, he refused to let it show. "I'm guessing there is more," he said without skipping a bit. The guy was unshakable and stable to the core.

I nodded my head and started listing my sins in order.

I slept with a tattooed bad boy after swearing them off.

I was pregnant with his child because I was careless about keeping my routine birth control shot appointments and didn't use protection.

I was on the brim of losing the spectrum of hope to smooth things out with my family because once they found out about this most recent blunder, they'd shun me forever.

I had walked into this diner to gorge on a giant pecan pie and planned to blame it on pregnancy cravings, knowing full well it wasn't the case.

Jay's expression was neutral throughout it all. "Does this man... does he know?" he finally asked.

My tentative expression answered his question.

"You don't know the baby's father well, and you're worried about his intentions," he phrased it as a statement rather than a question.

I composed myself. "He could be a good guy," I said diplomatically. When Jay didn't seem satisfied enough with my answer to stop staring, I let out a defeated sigh. "I don't know him very well," I admitted. It was the truth. There was something undeniable with Axel, but spending a night with one person didn't give you access to their thoughts.

I chanced a glance at Jay following my confession. Nothing. No reaction whatsoever.

"Well?"

"Well, what?"

"Aren't you going to reprimand me for getting knocked up by a stranger? Or at least give me false reassurances."

Jay regarded me thoughtfully. "I am thinking."

Thinking? Thinking of how one girl could cause this much trouble. I frowned but said nothing more. I shamelessly ordered two slices of honey pecan pie when the server approached me. Jay asked the waiter to add it to his bill without leaving room for me to argue. Otherwise, he was quiet.

"Are you still thinking?" I checked in after a while, to which he nodded. He watched me eat the pie. If he was disgusted that a hundred-and-ten-pound girl could pack away two large slices, he showed no signs of it as he packed up his paperwork.

Jay leaned back in his chair, scrutinizing me. "If you had to guess, do you think this man wants to be the father of your baby?" he asked at long last.

A vision of Axel glaring at the children at Milan's wedding flashed through my mind.

How would Axel react to this news?

Not well.

He had big plans for himself, and a kid didn't fit into the mold of the fast-paced life of a DJ.

Theoretically, Axel could step up to the plate, but then what?

It might start great, like every one of my past relationships.

It might also take a turn for the worse... like every one of my past relationships.

If life didn't turn out the way Axel wanted, his resentment would be directed at me for fucking up his future with a kid. It'd destroy poppy seed's childhood before he or she could explore it. My insides knotted at the thought, panic flaring as my arms instinctively wrapped around my middle.

There was a tiny creature inside me. It was pathetic that they weren't even born, and I was already failing them. I swallowed, taking deep breaths to steady my trembling fingers.

Jay suddenly took my shaking hands into his own, his strong hold stopping my fingers from quivering.

The unexpected gentleness of his reassuring touch had a gasp tumbling out of my lips. Jay wasn't an expressive man, nor had I witnessed him comforting anyone before. He didn't owe me anything, let alone use up his rare display of emotions on me.

Though Jay remained quiet as he tightly held my hand, it was the first time I sensed the strength in his silence. There was a force to it that didn't exist in words.

It was several minutes before Jay broke the silence. I realized it was because my breathing had evened out, and the shuddering had subsided.

"Are you all right, Piya?"

I nodded. "To answer your previous question," I said quietly, "if I had to guess, the man in question has no interest in being a father. I barely know him, but—" I bit my lip so I wouldn't break down into tears.

One night had sent me spiraling into the devil's lair. No matter how much I tried to claw myself out, a force of nature kept pulling me back to Axel. Now, there was something that would tie us together for life. Except, I didn't know if it was in poppy seed's best interest.

"What if he doesn't have to be the father of the baby," Jay suggested softly.

I frowned. "Too late for that, don't you think?"

"What if you had a way of getting into your family's good graces, didn't have to worry about raising a kid with a stranger who may or may not come through, and still had a stable father for your baby?"

"Oo, this is a fun game." I clapped my hands. "Let me try one. What if you won a million dollars, could live forever, and travel to outer space?"

Jay rolled his eyes. "I have many millions of dollars, and it's not all that it's cracked up to be. I plan to die young, and I have already been to space."

I jerked back. "You have?" Damn, Jay had lived a life I knew nothing about.

"We'll talk about it another time. Are you ready to listen without sarcasm?"

I closed my eyes, his tone bringing me down to earth. Jay wouldn't have made the suggestion unless he had a follow-up idea.

"I have a solution for all of your problems as long as you agree."

"Agree to what?" I asked.

"Agree to marry me."

My body reacted before my brain could catch on. I gripped the edge of the counter, threw my head back, and roared with a laugh so belly aching that it hurt.

Jay patiently waited for my obnoxious laughter to subside. When his expression remained solemn, I snapped my mouth shut. Realization swept over me. "You can't be serious."

"I am," he said simply.

I blinked as the two simple words sunk in. I didn't know what to make of his offer. We might have grown up around the same group, but we have never particularly hung out, been friends, or had any special bond that warranted this offer. Why would he go to such lengths to dig me out of this mess?

Yet, Jay seemed self-assured. He wasn't intimidated by the possibility of marrying a pregnant woman or becoming a father to another man's child. No hesitation. Not even a slight tremor of indecision.

My puzzled look gave away the unspoken question. "I've always wanted to be a father," he answered simply.

I scoffed. "No one's stopping you. Aren't you like the king of Indian Bachelor?"

"Indian what?"

I bit my bottom lip. "Um... I meant the whole... you know how my mom... you know how she was trying to get us to talk..."

He smiled. "Yes, Piya. I'm aware. Your mom wasn't exactly subtle."

"You..." I waved my hand, gesturing toward his perfect body and perfect face and perfect clothes, and perfect hair, assuming it'd be enough to get my point across. "You can have any woman to have your child. I mean, literally any woman."

"If only things were so simple."

I nodded thoughtfully. "Yes, I heard it's difficult being a rich, good-looking bachelor with women banging down on your door."

He grinned. "It's absolutely unbearable."

"I have no doubts." I watched him for a moment after both of our smiles disappeared. "Why resort to marrying a woman with a preexisting pregnancy condition?"

"Having a biological child isn't in the cards for me."

My lips parted, and I shot Jay a blank look.

The smile didn't disappear, though it turned somewhat morbid, "My father is sick."

I frowned at the unexpected turn of conversation. We weren't close enough for me to know the nitty-gritty details of his life, but Jay's father was a legacy in our community. I would have heard about it if it was serious. I still asked. "Is it something serious?"

My belated concern wasn't the reason he had brought up the topic. Jay nodded absentmindedly. "It's the reason I had to leave Milan's wedding. Baba took a turn for the worse."

How is that possible? "But I haven't heard anything about your father being sick."

"That's because most people didn't know. We wanted it that way." He watched me intently before glancing at the paperwork again. "A few years ago, Baba was diagnosed with a rare genetic illness. It's called familial ALS. It's a genetic condition."

I didn't know how to react. I had heard of ALS before, and I knew it was terminal. It was jarring to hear this news, especially with my limited encounters with death. However, something more disturbing niggled at the back of my mind. "Wait a second. If your dad was diagnosed with a genetic disorder, does that mean you're also at risk?"

He nodded. "Lucky me. I might carry on the family legacy."

My mouth fell open, taken aback. Thoughts of my family, unexpected pregnancy, and honey pecan pie all but vanished. My problems were trivial in comparison to his revelations.

"Jay, I'm so sorry. That's horrible." Unsure how to phrase the question, I asked softly, "A-are you sure you'll be affected the same way—"

He cut me off before I could finish, "No. Familial ALS means you have a fifty-fifty genetic predisposition to develop ALS. If I do, then yes, it's terminal."

My heart sank. I wanted to prod more but bit my tongue. Jay read into my tentative nature and explained.

"After Baba was diagnosed, they did a test to find out if there was a risk of him passing it on to his children. Turns out that there is a risk, but no way of determining whether I'll develop ALS in the future." Jay shook his head. "Maybe it's better if I don't know. If I were positive, I'd have nothing to look forward to but an awful death. Alternately, it'd be a relief not to look over my shoulder for a disease that might catch up to me. I constantly tell myself that I feel the healthiest in my life and that everything is fine. Living in denial is turning into a daily battle."

I nodded in understanding. Fuck, this was heavy.

"No one knows about his condition," he added pointedly.

I quickly nodded, assuring him I'd never reveal his secret.

"If the shareholders or board members of my company found out about a genetic disorder, they'd consider me an at-risk CEO and try to have me removed," Jay explained. "I took over after Baba got sick. I had been with the company my whole life and was an easy shoo-in after Baba announced his retirement. We plan to announce Baba's ALS, but if they find out it's genetic and can be passed down to me... well, you know."

I nodded in understanding.

Jay's father, Ari Ambani, had two affluent sisters and a

331

brother. Jay had six to eight cousins—maybe more—through his uncles and aunts. My encounters with them at various Pujas left unremarkable impressions. It shocked me to learn they came from the same stock as the likes of Jay, whose work ethic knew no bounds. None of his cousins wanted to put in a long day's work and split their time between partying and other entitled pursuits.

Despite their incompetency, their ambitions were limitless. If they spotted any vulnerability in Jay, they'd attempt to have him removed so they could climb the ranks and seize the position for themselves. Even if it was ultimately detrimental to the company, everyone wanted to be king. No matter how much their lack of qualifications affected the kingdom, people were inherently self-serving, selfish, and self-absorbed. I didn't blame Jay for not wanting to hand over the keys to the kingdom to people like that.

Preexisting wealth had crippled his cousins' personal growths, and I had no doubt they'd run Ambani Corp to the ground without Jay's oversight. It must be disheartening that vultures were prepared to squander away your life's work instead of honoring your legacy.

Jay took a relented breath, probably thinking the same. "My grandfather built this company. Baba managed to go public with it, and I took it to the next level. We are entirely family-based, and the company is meant to remain in my family for generations. That's why Baba used to encourage me to get married and have kids so that the company would remain with us."

I said nothing.

"After I found out I have a fifty-fifty chance of living a long life—" Jay took a sip of his drink, "I realized I had poured my entire life into something that I might not be able to pass on to my kids."

"You can still have kids," I said automatically.

"So, I can pass on this nightmare to an innocent? I'd either be sentencing a kid to death or a life worrying about death. No, thank you." I didn't miss the bitterness in his voice nor his unprecedented fear of harming children.

"But it isn't a guaranteed death sentence," I couldn't help mumbling. "You mentioned there is a fifty-fifty chance. Nothing might happen to you at all, and you can still achieve all the things you set out to do. Most people who develop ALS don't do so until later in life."

"I'm not exactly young, Piya," he pointed out.

"Thirty-eight isn't exactly old either," I shot back. "There is no way to predict how life will turn out. For all we know, you'll never be affected and have missed out on your entire life based on fear."

"Or I'll be screwing up someone else's life by starting something I can't follow through." Jay shook his head. "My biggest regret is realizing this company I worked so hard to build might be torn into pieces by fucking wolves." It was the first time I heard Jay speak passionately. This wasn't just a company for him; it was his family's legacy. "I always assumed I'd have kids I could groom to take over, the way Baba had done with me. When I found out about his prognosis—"

I sighed heavily. "You lied about his illness to buy yourself more time until you figured it out."

A curt nod.

My eyes widened. "So, everyone was misinformed then? You weren't competing in Indian Bachelor or trying to get married?"

A smile tugged at his mouth. "It's something I had wanted in the past, but after I found out about Baba, I wasn't so sure."

I shook my head, scoffing at myself. "Here I thought you were flirting with me at Milan's wedding because you were interested in me."

My ears burnt as soon as the words came out like word vomit, while his smile remained genuine. I was surprised he could be lighthearted while faced with a morbid death sentence. My kind of man.

"I was, and I am," he announced.

I averted my eyes, embarrassed, even though Jay was the one putting himself out there. I was right. If Jay hadn't left that day, things would have turned out differently.

"But then I thought maybe it was for the best if things didn't progress. I didn't know how you'd feel about... everything."

Is that why Jay never called me?

"Then why the sudden interest in marriage?" I couldn't help asking.

"Because it might be my only chance to have a family," he replied instantly.

I froze at the sincerity in his voice.

"You're determined to have this kid, but you don't trust the father of this baby. However, you'll lose everything if you have this baby without getting married, and your child will never have a relationship with their grandparents, your brother, or anyone else in your life."

The pain in my chest exploded. Growing up, I was immensely close to Dadi. However, little poppy seed would never have a dadi because I couldn't see a world where Zaina Mittal would be accepting of my baby in this current predicament.

"If you don't want to lose everyone in your life, you have to get married and establish a legitimate father," Jay declared. "I need to marry someone from my same background, and I don't want to father kids of my own. It isn't like I can adopt or surrogate, either. You know how close-minded that board is."

I nodded.

Different Indian families vary in their values, just like any other culture. Families like mine didn't care if I married outside the race or religion as long as the person was educated and came from a similar social hierarchy as us. Whereas Jay's family was traditional. No one in the Ambani clan had married someone who wasn't of the same faith and background.

The same rule applied to adoption and surrogacy. While it was no big deal in my family, it was a stigma in his. The board of his company—made up of his family members—would fight it every step of the way if there were even a hint of disqualifying the 'heir' after Jay.

Adoption and surrogacy could be unearthed, whereas... "No one knows about this child, not even the father," I muttered, the weight of his proposal settling in.

He nodded. "I get the feeling that you want security for your child. If you were to marry me, you'd have that, and your family would be happy. Do you think this guy might return to the picture or try to be a part of the kid's life?"

"He is twenty-two and looking to become a famous DJ."

Jay rolled his eyes. "Enough said. Marry me, and both of our problems will disappear. We can do this together."

"I-I... Jay, I can't let you do this. Raise another man's baby?"

"You said it yourself; you met that man after I abruptly left Milan's wedding. You wouldn't be pregnant if I hadn't left. I'm the reason this kid exists. You haven't told the father yet, nor is he interested in having a family. Meanwhile, I want kids but not my own. Then we stumbled into each other at some dingy twenty-four café."

"It's not dingy. Have you tried their honey pecan pie?"

"I don't like sweets."

"You're a sociopath." I didn't mean to sound judgmental, but only a man devoid of normal emotions could resist pecan pies.

Jay waved off my concern. "Tell me if fate has ever lined up so perfectly in your life before?"

A picture of Axel flashed in my mind, but I shook it off. Why go there? He was a man with big dreams, the ones I'd be stifling by showing up pregnant at his doorstep. Not to mention, I'd have to sever ties with everyone in my life to have Axel's baby. The same rules wouldn't apply to having Jay's baby. If Axel turned out to be a dirtbag like the men before, then poppy seed and I would be entirely alone in the world.

Jay's offer was clear. This deal was only on the table because Axel didn't know about it. As long as no one else in this world discovered the truth, Jay would give me and poppy seed every-thing. Love. Family. A future. Stability.

"No, fate has never lined up so perfectly in my life before," I admitted in a small voice. "It still doesn't sit right with me letting you raise someone else's baby."

"Why? This is my choice." He looked at me with determination. "I'm not cursing a life of uncertainty onto a child, but I also want a family. Here you are, with a family already on the way."

His words stunned me in a way I never expected. "It feels wrong. Like I'm trapping you."

He grabbed my hand again before the last word left my mouth. There was something so open, so authentic about Jay that I couldn't shake it away.

"You know what's wrong? I'm trying to convince you to marry me, knowing I might die young and leave you to become a young widow. I thought I missed my chance at having a family, and now I see a woman, one that I'd found myself drawn to repeatedly, in need of everything I could provide. I'm taking advantage of the situation, knowing the risk I'm putting you in. That's what's wrong in this situation. I might be dead in five years, but I want to die knowing what it's like to be a father and to have a family of my own."

The pregnancy hormones made me do it. I burst into tears, even as he reached over to wipe them away. I cried for Jay, and myself, too, but it seemed to accomplish nothing.

"This is all so fucked up."

"Or is it all meant to be?"

How could he be so unruffled at a situation so morose? "You don't know what you're saying?"

"I have never been surer of anything in my life. Say yes, Piya.

This is everything I ever wanted, and you need me as much as I need you."

I laughed in self-pity. "You don't need me. You have countless options."

"Do I now?" he asked dryly.

"Yes!" I insisted. "Possible ALS or not, every woman in our community is dying to marry you."

"My choices aren't as limitless as you might think."

When I stared at him, unconvinced, he pulled out the big guns. Jay, the math whiz, decided to explain things to me with the help of numbers. "Less than one percent of America's population is Indian."

"So?"

"So... it means approximately two point six million Indians live in America, and half are women."

Realization dawned on me. "It means you have your pick from one point three million women to get married to."

He shook his head. "Not so fast. Out of that one point three million women, we have to account for those already married."

Ah. Fair point. "Fine. Let's say half of them are married," I chimed in, distracting myself from the emotional turmoil with a math game to deduce Jay's perfect woman. "A quarter are children or the elderly. What number are we at?"

"Let's round it up to three hundred thousand."

"Half is likely already engaged, has a boyfriend, or is otherwise unavailable."

He nodded. "Now we are at hundred and fifty thousand. Of the hundred and fifty thousand, the potential woman in question must live in either New York or Chicago or at least be willing to move to either city."

That was right. Their headquarters were in those cities. "Let's say fifty thousand already reside in either city or are willing to move for your pretty face."

He rolled his eyes.

"That's still quite a large pool to choose from," I pointed out.

"We haven't finished yet. Out of the fifty thousand, they have to be from families like ours. Anything less would be unacceptable."

I knew what he meant; old money. Our families spurned anyone who had become newly rich. I sighed defeatedly. "Well, that eliminates everyone but the top one percentile."

He nodded thoughtfully. "Five hundred women."

"Wow." Slim pickings. How the hell was one supposed to find their soulmate from only five hundred women?

"Not to mention," he added. "I have to find the said woman attractive, charming, and preferably someone who is nice." He raised his eyebrow pointedly, making me smile and shake my head.

Jay leaned over, leveling me with his eyes meaningfully.

"And it'd be great if she was already pregnant by a man who doesn't know about it. So where does that leave us?"

"With me," I blurted. Holy shit, we just picked apart math, and he was right.

I was Jay's only solution as much as he was mine.

"Are we really considering this?" I asked, feeling lightheaded. We were proposing to dupe our families, friends, and the entire world. This sordid secret that we couldn't ever mention, nor could we risk people finding out.

"Do you see another solution where you can have everything you want for your baby and get to keep your family?"

"But I'm already a couple of weeks along. Did you know that your phones come with a calendar app? All people have to do is count the months we have been married and the months I was pregnant before childbirth."

His eyes moved over my face. "So, we'll get married right away. Something intimate; let's say five hundred guests."

I choked on the water I was drinking, letting the straw dangle near my lips. *Five hundred guests?*

"We'll move to Chicago before you start to show," he continued. "No one here will look into it if we aren't around, and we'll later announce that we had a preemie baby."

Oh God, why was I entertaining this? "Everyone will figure it out. We'll never pull this off."

"We will," he replied without a morsel of doubt. "People are surprisingly susceptible to subconscious messages. They'll believe it to be true if we keep repeating certain information. Such as the baby being a preemie and confusing them about the possible date of conception."

I held my fingers to my temple. I had gone from a surprise pregnancy to fake cravings to a marriage proposal. A lot had happened in the last twenty-four hours. "I-I need to think."

"So, think about it. Think about it all night and give me an answer tomorrow morning."

"Tomorrow?"

"If we do this, we have to move fast."

Neither of us spoke after his proclamation, eventually parting on a friendly hug and Jay promising to come by the following day for my answer.

At the end of the month, I became Mrs. Piya Ambani.

CHAPTER
NINETEEN

Present

∽

Piya

"DID YOU KNOW ALL ALONG?" I ASKED AXEL THROUGH the glass pane. I sat on the floor with my back leaning against the door and sucked in a ragged lungful of air to get myself together. My eyes drooped, and my arms were heavy at my side.

"Not at first. Ambani hid his tracks well; I'll give him that."

Axel sat on the other side of the glass with his back to me, leaning against the same cascade door. The glass pane in between divided us where our backs should be touching. The thought of leaning against Axel was comforting though it was one I could no longer indulge.

"The track records for the weeks after conception were miraculously well kept. From every angle, Poppy appeared as a preemie baby. But after meeting her... anti-social personalities are often genetic. My father was like that, too."

"How did you confirm it?" I asked curiously.

"After the first time we had lunch, I went to Poppy's school nurse. I swiped her blood sample that was on file and gave it to Levi to run a DNA test."

Laughter bubbled in my chest. Of course, he did. I now realized why it took my stalker more than five minutes to chase me down after I left the lunch.

"You should have told me," he spoke from the other side.

"Being with you wouldn't have been the right decision for Poppy," I replied truthfully.

"Right or wrong, it wasn't your decision to make," Axel spat back.

My head tilted to the side for one last look at Axel and commit the sight to my memory. Axel wore a breathable collared shirt with the cap sleeves slightly rolled up to display the array of artwork on his biceps. In khaki shorts and summer shoes, he looked like an Abercrombie Fitch model, bad boy 2.0 version.

"I never forgot about you after leaving Chateau at the Hempstead," I whispered, almost speaking to myself. "Before learning about my pregnancy, I thought about finding you because it felt like I was yours. After finding out about the pregnancy, it felt like I had become *hers*. For every decision, I had to consult *her* future, *her* needs, *she* was my priority. Before that test came back positive, I wanted to find you and make another list and tick off the items one by one. I wanted to go skydiving. I wanted to jump off a moving train with you. After that test came back positive, I could no longer do those things with you. I was going to be her mother, and that was my role. I had to choose between you and her. I chose her. It was the right decision for her because Poppy deserved everything the world had to offer."

I could hear the fire in his words as he argued between gritted teeth, "You didn't have to choose. I would have worked hard and provided for both of you."

"That's not what it was about. You were incapable of what she needed the most. Love."

Axel scoffed. "You think people like me can't love? You're wrong. We can love just fine."

As if feeling the weight of my stare, Axel tilted his head and looked me dead in the eye. His lips were pressed in a thin line, dark eyes silky like molten lava.

"We are just selective about *who* we love," he spoke with a muscle clenching his jaw. "I might not be able to love in the traditional aspect, but know this, Piya, I love the shit out of you. I love you enough to change my name for you. I love you enough to alter my goals for you. I love you enough to transform the direction of my life for you. Every single thing I am, every fucking molecule I'm made up of, it's consumed by my love for you. That's how much I fucking love you, so don't tell me I'm not capable of love."

The erratic beat of my heart thumped loudly against my ribs.

I could count each blow as it reverberated through my body and shook the air around us in a deafening sound.

I was touched—blown away, in fact—by words I never thought would be uttered by Axel. Nevertheless, it didn't change the facts.

I smiled sadly. "I didn't say you were incapable of loving me," I breathed. "You're incapable of loving *her*."

Axel was quiet on the other side. He didn't refute the words, and I didn't need him to. "Did you tell her about me?" he asked instead.

I nodded, a smile tugging at the corner of my lips. Jay and I sat Poppy down after her ninth birthday to tell her about her origin.

Poppy was much too smart. She knew her grandfather had passed away from ALS and started asking about possible genetic variations of the disease. We couldn't let Poppy live a life of fear and deterred that nine years was old enough to handle the news. In no way could I have predicted Poppy's response when she learned of her parentage.

"Do you think I can take a look inside my biological father's brain?"

Jay spat out the water he was drinking and didn't bother hiding his roaring laughter. Other than comedic relief, I knew he was reassured by Poppy's reaction. He had worried she might not think he was enough.

"Um... we don't keep in touch with Zane," I had replied mildly.

Jay knew Poppy's father was the DJ from Milan's wedding. However, he had no idea Zane was now the famous DJ Axel. Before we married, Jay wanted to discuss Poppy's father's genes, and I understood why. If Axel were blond, there'd be a chance of Poppy being blond, too, in which case we wouldn't be able to pass Poppy off as Jay's daughter. Luckily, I remembered Axel mentioning that everyone in his family had thick, dark hair. With Axel's dark eyes and my brown ones, I wasn't too worried about eye color, either. And I was almost as fair as Axel. Nonetheless, we sighed in relief when Poppy came out looking like me.

"Hm... that sucks." Poppy stood to walk away.

"Wait," I said hastily. "Don't you have any questions about what we just told you?"

"I do," Poppy replied mildly. "Can I take a look inside his brain?" she repeated, genuinely confused about where she had lost me.

"We meant questions about this whole situation," Jay clarified.

Once more, Poppy was confuddled. "What situation?"

Poppy hadn't even batted an eye after finding out Jay wasn't her biological father. Biology meant nothing to her, and she felt no connection to Axel. But when Axel randomly popped up on television one day, I stared at him like I had seen a ghost. Poppy caught on to my reaction and asked if Axel was Zane. I told her the truth and waited. Poppy's only reaction was asking me to ensure no one found out. Even then, Poppy knew the repercussions of her future with Ambani Corp if her 'legitimacy' was questioned.

When Poppy met Axel for the first time, I waited for her to voice questions but moved on when she didn't appear interested in getting to know Axel. Part of me initially wondered if Axel had returned to place a claim on Poppy. I watched him like a hawk to see if he knew. He didn't, nor did he care. Poppy and Axel mutually used each other. Poppy wanted to learn about someone with a similar neurodivergence, and Axel was using Poppy to get closer to me. There was no love between them, and it didn't matter.

Poppy didn't need Axel's love; she already had a father.

Past

~

I couldn't make out the face. He went in and out of focus as he strolled toward us while still maintaining distance. The sun bounced with his leisurely pace, nearly blinding me at times depending on his newest position. A chill ran down my spine as our gazes finally met. Dark, unforgiving eyes stared back, dead set against giving away their secrets.

I woke, gasping for air. Glancing sideways, I was relieved to find the bed empty. Jay had a home office, and it seemed he had already started his workday.

Two weeks had passed since our "small" wedding of only five hundred guests. The days since were spent moving out of my apartment and away from New York.

Jay proposed moving to Chicago until the baby's birth, then we could return to New York. However, I insisted on making the move permanent, so we bought a place in the suburbs outside the city.

Jay showed me a few houses. I made my decision by closing my eyes and picking a random one. I never even saw the house before moving in, but I knew a permanent home in Chicago was pertinent. I was a married woman now and needed to focus on my husband. I couldn't start a new life in a city that constantly reminded me of Axel.

Only one problem.

Axel seemed to have migrated to the new city and my new home through the power of my mind. I had effectively blocked out his thoughts while awake, but my subconscious was harder to control. No matter how much I chided myself, the dreams kept returning like the sun at dawn.

Every. Single. Night. Axel haunted me and refused to stop. I had become obsessed with shoving his memories out of my mind, but they always returned.

The start of my new marriage had gotten lost in the shuffle of the move, the accidental pregnancy, mending my broken heart, and now this newfound obsession of trying not to think about Axel (epic fail, by the way).

Jay worked around the clock, so we barely saw one another. I didn't mind it. Not seeing Jay let me escape the guilt over thinking about another man who wasn't my husband.

Jay was a saint and never made a move on the first night we spent together. Didn't even mention sex. He simply kissed me on the cheek and turned off the lights. Since then, Jay had respected my boundaries immensely, aware that my heart wouldn't be in it.

Jay had a good sixth sense because I had no idea what I'd do if he pushed me for sex. I wasn't ready for another man to touch me.

I knew life couldn't go on this way. I was married, and my heart needed to accept the truth the way society had.

With a dejected sigh, I rose from the bed and dressed for the day.

I strolled through our elaborate new home, scattered with unopened boxes. We had discussed hiring a few staff to help upkeep this large house. I had been dragging my feet because I disliked sharing my privacy with strangers. As I stared at the untidy boxes, I reconsidered my take on hiring staff.

With new determination, I started unpacking the boxes and separating the contents inside into neat piles. Décor items went on the various built-in shelves on the walls. Picture frames went on the side tables. Winter clothes were hung in the closet nearest the front door. With each box that was put away, my resolve strengthened to redecorate my new home and life.

It was almost the end of the workday by the time I finished opening all the boxes and putting away everything. However, I still hadn't heard a peep from Jay.

I knew Jay owned a "bachelor pad" in the city and had mentioned we'd stay there on the days he had to go into the office. As of now, he had been working out of the new home office. I had a feeling he was only doing this so I wouldn't be lonely in a new city. Jay's considerations made me want to make an effort as well. I didn't know how else to contribute and decided to cook dinner. Other than playing the piano, cooking was the only other thing I could do blindfolded.

After taking stock of the ingredients in the fridge, I decided on a cheese lasagna from scratch. Tantalizing smells wafted through the air within the hour, but still, no sight of Jay.

With a huff, I laid the meal for two on a tray and took it to him. The door to his home office was slightly ajar, and I peeked inside. Jay sat in front of a computer, looking at it so intently I wondered if there were naked chicks on the screen.

I cleared my throat, knocking timidly on the door.

"Come in," came a deep voice.

I suddenly felt apprehensive about the intrusion. Perhaps Jay wouldn't think barging in here with a tray full of food was cute.

I took a deep breath, steeling my nerves and pushing the door open with my shoulder. Jay's office was bright and airy, with windows overlooking the garden. A single desk sat in the middle, with a couple of chairs distributed around the room.

Jay glanced up from his desk. "Hello." He seemed unsure of my motivations since I had never interrupted him before.

"Er... um... I thought you might be hungry," I said lamely.

His eyes landed on the tray as if it were the last thing he expected. They flipped back to mine, then gestured at an empty space on the desk.

Jay pulled out a chair for me while I set down the tray. Why the fuck was it so awkward to have dinner with my husband?

I fidgeted. "I, um, I don't know if you like lasagna—"

"I like lasagna," he replied instantly. "Thank you, Piya."

With relief, I sat on the chair across from him, picked up my plate, and thought about conversation topics. Meanwhile, Jay wasn't bothered by the prolonged silence and ate without

350

complaint. I knew that even if he disliked the meal, he'd clear the plate.

Shaking my head to myself, I dove into my food when I noticed a picture resting on the corner of his desk. It was inside a wooden frame so small that I had almost missed it. What I didn't miss was the unmistakable smiling picture of another woman sitting on my husband's desk.

With a forced smile, I waved at the frame. "Friend of yours?"

Jay stilled, his fork suspended in the air. He dropped his fork on the plate so gently that it didn't clatter. He glanced at the frame and nodded. "Kat."

My heart dragged heavily to the center of the world. I knew we hadn't started this marriage with big declarations of love; I wasn't delusional. However, wasn't it customary not to cheat on your wife at least until the five-year mark? At the minimum, have enough respect to mess around behind my back instead of flaunting it in my face. Sheesh.

"She was my girlfriend."

Didn't make it any better. I didn't know how to feel about his ex-girlfriend's photo having a place on his desk. Jay picked up on the tension and stared at me for a few contemplative moments, wondering if he should share this information. He ultimately said, "She died a long time ago."

Aaaand I just went from a woman scorned to the worst human on earth.

"What happened?" I asked softly.

Jay glanced at his food and went back to picking at it. "Leukemia."

"I'm so sorry."

"Don't be. I knew it was bad and that she was dying. I knew what I was getting myself into."

"You knew she was dying but still chose to be with her?" I repeated in disbelief. A million questions flooded my mind. Why would someone choose to put themselves through such heartbreak?

Jay mulled over my words thoughtfully. "We grew up together, went to the same boarding school, then college. She was my best friend, but I was always crazy about her. You know... first love, kids' stuff." He shook his head. "But I stayed away because she wasn't Indian. Even if my family were to make peace with it, I knew the board members of my company wouldn't. There was no point in pursuing more when there couldn't be a future. So, I let it be."

Marrying outside of your culture and religion was the one thing you could do to get yourself excommunicated from the Ambani clan. I understood the dilemma. Though it wasn't about race, I had faced something similar with Axel. It would've driven a wedge between us if my family had found out about me dating another man from the nightclub industry. Giving up everything you know for the unknown risk was the scariest thing in life.

"But you said she was your girlfriend. What changed?"

I saw various shades of emotions crossing his face. "After she got diagnosed, I stopped giving a shit about what other people thought, and we got together. Death can do that to you, make you realize what really matters in life."

My heart ached, and I could feel his grief as if it were my own. Once more, I wanted to say I was sorry but held my tongue.

"I don't regret any of it. We shared many good years before she passed away."

"How come you never married her?" I couldn't help asking.

Jay shrugged. "Kat didn't want to. She knew if we got married, I'd lose everything I had worked for. She said she had no intention of leaving me worse than she had found me."

Both of us smiled at the comment.

"I didn't understand it then and was pissed off at her. We fought. I said she couldn't make this decision for both of us, but Kat was adamant."

"Do you regret it?"

"I understand it." His smile was self-deprecating. "If you know you're doomed, you want to die knowing everyone you love will be okay afterward."

I said nothing as Jay spoke, beyond touched by his story. I knew, without a doubt, that Kat would always have a part of his heart.

Shockingly, it didn't bother me. If anything, it was a relief because I was starting to realize Axel would always hold a place in my heart.

I had been boggled down with guilt, practically drowning in it, for being unable to put Axel in the rearview mirror. Hearing there was a woman Jay pined after as well made me feel an odd sense of solidarity with him.

"Do you miss her?" I asked. *Does this awful feeling ever go away?*

"Yes," he replied truthfully.

"How... how do you even go about dealing with something like that?" I prodded. How could I stop myself from drowning in the memories of the stupid heathen?

He shrugged. "If I ever miss her, I don't fight it. I take some time out of my day and think about the good memories we shared. The key is to grieve without letting myself drown."

How Jay spoke about Kat—honoring her memories and letting her have a part of him without letting it consume him—suddenly gave me hope for a brighter future. "You make it sound so easy about how you got through it."

He straightened, grabbing our now empty dishes and placing them on the tray. "It wasn't easy, but I had no choice. Too many people rely on me. I can't afford to be selfish and wallow in my sorrows."

I didn't understand Jay. He was so damn rich and was considered royalty in my community. Yet he couldn't even properly grieve because his 'subjects' were counting on him. Life had dealt him some bad cards, but he had no complaints and was perfectly content with life.

I looked at him thoughtfully, my eyes locked on his regal face. Jay was a king, but a lonely one, I surmised.

I didn't know what made me do it, except that I remembered the day in the diner when Jay grasped my hand when I felt the loneliest in the world. He'd held my hand, and suddenly, I wasn't so alone anymore.

I reached out and grabbed Jay's hands, taking them into my own. Jay's surprise was warranted since I had never initiated contact. I knew immediately that no one had comforted this man before. More so, I knew I wanted to comfort him again.

Jay stared at our interconnected hands and said, "I'm used to having this photo on my desk, but if it bothers you—"

"No," I said instantaneously. I shook my head firmly. "I understand how much she meant to you. She was your family."

Jay tilted his head and spoke as clearly as day, "You are my family now."

The sentence stumped me, moving me so deeply that I couldn't speak for several moments.

You are my family now.

There it was; Jay had put it in simple yet profound terms. I was his family now, and he was mine. Just like that, we had become each other's everything and came above everyone else in this world.

It suddenly dawned on me that the things Dadi wanted for me had come true. Trust, respect, and life with a man deserving of me.

I trusted Jay and shared the news of my pregnancy with him before anyone else.

We bought this house together to raise our family and build a life.

The simple fact that Jay was willing to box away the great love of his life for my sake solidified the last factor for me. Respect.

A camaraderie I had never experienced with Jay surged within me, and for the first time since our wedding, I started to understand the power of marriage. The connection. The bond. Weathering the worst storms together. Jay had agreed to raise another man's baby without a second thought and had gone to great lengths to ensure my comfort. He had asked for nothing in return, which was why I suddenly wanted to do everything for him.

"There is one thing you could do for me," I whispered.

"What's that?"

Before we married, Jay had mentioned the expectations that came from marrying into the Ambani family, expectations that even he couldn't deny. The Ambanis were part of a system, abiding by a set of unspoken rules. However, Jay also told me that if I wished, I didn't have to partake in the community more than necessary. I had finally made my decision about the matter.

"Can you teach me everything there is no know about being an Ambani wife?"

After that day in Jay's office, everything changed for the better. Instead of fighting the thoughts circulating Axel, I submerged myself in them. Every night, I dreamt of him. Every morning, I let myself relive thirty minutes of cherished memories.

Dancing in a club.

Eating jumbo slice pizza.

Fireworks on the beach.

Walking around a fire.

I didn't deny myself any longer, but I did limit myself. I understood what Jay meant about not letting yourself drown. I could live hours and days and weeks and years drowning in Axel. It'd be selfish when I had others relying on me.

Instead, I focused on my role as a wife and a soon-to-be-mother. We were the perfect couple in front of others and announced the pregnancy to our families, which brought many joyous tears. We were also the perfect couple behind closed doors and started being intimate.

We spent the first year of our marriage getting to know one another and building our friendship. After a few weeks into our marriage, I was touched to find my picture on Jay's desk next to Kat's. A few months later, I found a picture of Poppy's ultrasound in Jay's desk drawer. As the months passed, more pictures joined the collection, especially once Poppy entered our lives.

As expected, Jay was the world's best dad. Even if he worked all day, he was never too tired to change a diaper or take a night shift so I could sleep in. As a result, Poppy's bond with Jay was immediate. By the time she turned two, they'd developed a special routine. She'd stroll into her Papa's office and ask him to pick her up. Jay would place her on his lap while he scrolled through reports and numbers.

I'd sneak into the office, too, and together, we'd mess up Jay's schedule. I'd sit at the arm of his chair, watching Bollywood movies with my headphones on. Meanwhile, Jay would sit in front of the computer with Poppy on his lap. He'd read the end-of-the-day reports with his right arm wrapped protectively around Poppy and the left one around me. Every once in a while, he'd free the arm wrapped around me to scroll down the computer screen. Sometimes I'd worry about Jay's encompassing attention making him forgetful enough to loosen the hold around Poppy. Then I'd glance over and watch, astonished, at the iron-clad hold he'd have on Poppy, despite his eyes being glued to the computer screen. We'd do this little routine every evening.

One day, we were doing our same evening tradition in Jay's office. Jay thoughtfully read the screen while I sat on the arm of his chair. Shahrukh and Kajol were dancing their hearts out on my phone screen, my headphones blasting Bollywood music. Suddenly, we heard Poppy muttering the numbers on the screen. We were both so taken aback that we glanced at each other and shrugged the way parents do when they have no clue what's happening with their kids.

By the following year, Poppy had become enamored with any sequence of numbers, and her special gift came to light. She'd pick up numbers with incredible ease, and we started tutoring her at home.

During our evening tradition, Jay purposefully started scrolling down slower upon realizing Poppy liked to memorize the long sequences of numbers on the computer screen. I'd memorized our routine well and knew it took Jay exactly thirty minutes to wrap up at the end of the day. By slowing down for Poppy, it started taking Jay forty-five minutes to read the reports.

Jay was nothing if not a man of habit and conscious about time. Hell, he cared about time so much that he grieved his dead girlfriend for only a few moments at a time. Yet, the pragmatic man who even timed his mourning periods had suddenly succumbed to the unspoken demands of a three-year-old. Was there anything sexier in this world?

Jay cut back on work each passing year to spend more time with us. More pictures of Poppy and I appeared on his desk, the walls of his office, and every inch of his life.

And I... I. Was. A. Smitten-kitten.

I couldn't stop watching them together, enamored by their father-daughter bond. It never made me jealous that Poppy didn't share my interests. I was simply happy staring at the two people who seemed like the most beautiful things I had seen on earth. I never imagined it was possible to be so utterly and irrevocably in love to the point that I'd do anything for them. Like Jay, I was content with life, and for the first time, I wondered if this was what true happiness felt like.

Present

This story was the reason why Axel's deception hurt so badly. Still sitting on the sunroom floor, I tilted my head to the side and watched him out of the corner of my eye.

"If I hadn't run away from you, I would've never known."

"So, I guess you know the truth now."

I took in a shuddering breath. "How could you have been so cruel?"

Axel scoffed. "Cruel?" he asked tauntingly. "I planned on ruining Ambani, but after I found out... I showed him mercy. I let him off the hook and let nature take its course."

My face was a mask of anguish as I yelled, "Mercy? Jay should

359

have been with his family this whole time."

"His family?" Axel's voice was laced with mockery. "You're my wife, Poppy's my daughter. Where does Ambani fit into this equation?" The words sounded like a challenge, meant to goad me into action.

My skin was cold to the touch as my hands gripped each other until they became white from tension. "Poppy might be your daughter, but you'll never be her father," I declared. "Dead or alive, she'll only have one father, and she has made it clear. Jay raised your daughter, but you still planned to let him die without giving us a chance to say goodbye."

Axel didn't speak, nor did he deny it. It was what Levi had discovered that day about my husband. *That* was what put Axel in a good mood; the news of my husband's impending death.

Two Days Ago

"Why didn't you tell me?" My bottom lip quivered at Jay's horizontal body lying on our oversized sofa in our living room.

He glanced at me and smiled sadly. "There is no point in dooming us both."

I shuddered, remembering how the last time I saw him, Jay had grabbed onto the table after sharing only one glass of wine. He had diligently limited our time together so I wouldn't catch on. For a whole year, he had been hiding this from me, except his state had worsened. ALS came with sudden twitching, clumsiness, and falling. There was no way of hiding it any longer, so Jay stopped going into the office. I found him on the sofa upon returning to our Chicago home, and the paperwork next to him gave away his secrets.

I made Jay regularly test for familial ALS. The results of the last test came back positive, but he had hidden it.

My eyes were glazed, my jaw tight, and my mouth pulled into a thin line. I could barely whisper, "Why did you hide it?" My hand landed on his cheek, scraping over the full beard he sported for the first time in our marriage.

A trembling hand grazed my cheek in return. "Because I've already done this once with Kat. I cared for her until the end. It was awful. You can't spend your best years taking care of someone else."

"Someone else?" I shouted, upset. "I'm your wife. Who else should take care of you?"

"I already have a nurse and don't need another one." He shook his head; his kind, familiar eyes were adamant. "You're young. You can travel the world and fall in love again. You still have time to have another baby if you want. It'll be too late if you spend those years being doomed with me."

"Doomed?" My face was streaked with tears, shoulders slumped forward in despair. "How could you say that? How could you push me away like this?"

"Because I want you to have everything, Piya, but I'm also human. I can't watch the woman I love with another man."

Like a sinner, I sank onto the floor next to the sofa, sitting at the feet of my altar and begging for forgiveness. It turned out Jay had known about Axel all along. He tracked down the DJ from Milan's wedding in case Poppy needed an organ or such. He wasn't immune to the search engine history in the home, either, and was privy to my obsessive Googling of the same DJ.

Jay had been perfectly suited for me from the beginning, even in this. He knew what it was like to love two people simultaneously. He'd also had a great love of his life, but I never worried about his love for me. Throughout our marriage, Jay had showered me with affection. His love shone in his eyes and in every one of his actions. I knew Kat was to him what Axel was to me. A fantasy.

Jay believed the same... until he saw Axel charging toward me at that party. Suddenly the fantasy had become a reality. He did what Kat had once done for him. Jay knew he was doomed, and he wanted to die knowing that I'd have what I wanted the most in life.

Love.

According to him, I still had a shot at having another baby and another family. ALS could take years to deteriorate, and he didn't want me to spend them sitting by his bedside. Pushing me away was easier.

Pragmatic as always, instead of worrying about his mortality, Jay did a deep dive into everything he needed to accomplish before death. His priority was to give Poppy and me what we wanted the most. He started working endlessly on collecting clients, swaying board members, and finding a way to leave his number two in charge. Jay had planned everything perfectly. His number two was trustworthy but old, so by the time Poppy graduated college and had spent a few years learning the ropes, Jay's number two would be ready to retire and happily hand over the reins to Poppy.

After learning about Jay's diagnosis, I immediately called my mom. I asked her to pick Poppy up from Nott Academy and fly to Chicago. She needed to be with her father.

I must've dozed off by the time they arrived. When I opened my eyes next, I found the same brown eyes as mine staring back.

In the silence of the room, I could hear the faint sound of air rushing in and out of Jay's lungs as he slept. His right arm was hooked around my neck while my head rested on his chest. Poppy was also resting her head on Jay's chest across from me. His left arm had subconsciously wrapped around her shoulders, and I knew that even in sleep, he wouldn't let go on the off-chance she'd fall off the couch.

Poppy hadn't displayed affection, such as cuddling, in years. It could only mean one thing.

"Did you know?" I whispered so that we wouldn't wake Jay.

A curt nod.

My breath caught, eyes closing for a moment. "How?"

Her eyes perused mine for a moment. "Papa stopped seeing his personal trainer. So, I searched the downtown office to double-check his last test results."

Poppy frequented the office for various company events. I never visited the location in downtown, so it made sense that Jay had hidden the documents there.

"When did you find it?"

"Last year."

My heart shattered as the pieces fell into place. Last year was when Poppy's rebellious phase started, along with her intense ambitions and behavioral issues.

Was she acting out because she found out that her papa was dying?

Were her accelerated ambitions an after-effect of trying to achieve the dream Jay and Poppy shared?

"He lied to us," Poppy said in a small voice, breaking my heart. Her face seemed pale and drawn, not stoic like at other times. She seemed like a little girl, surrounded by a darkness that was pulling her down.

"Why didn't you tell me?"

Poppy was quiet for several moments before she replied. "Tomar kharap lagto," she spoke in Bengali, a language passed down to Poppy by Jay's mom.

Poppy was just as close to her dadi as I had been to mine. Although neither Jay nor I spoke Bengali, Poppy had picked up Maya Ambani's native tongue. Knowing we couldn't understand her, Poppy used the language as an emotional shield whenever she felt vulnerable and needed a way to fortify her walls.

However, I understood Poppy perfectly well today from the few Bengali words I had picked up over the years. *"You would have felt sad."*

My sweet, sweet girl. I reached over and started covering my daughter's temple with numerous kisses.

I knew then that Dr. Stevenson was entirely wrong about someone like Poppy being incapable of love. She loved her papa so damn much that she was devastated over the loss and had been drowning in grief.

Present

⁓

"I have heard enough." Axel's compassionless voice drifted through the door, interrupting my story.

I ignored him. "Jay had been pushing me away. Poppy had been pushing me away. Then you came along. After so much rejection from my family, your obsession, your desire, the feeling of being wanted, it made me weak and selfish. It made me forget that Jay had held my hand when I thought the world had deserted me. I can't leave him now that he needs me to hold his."

While sitting on the floor, I felt the tension fizzing in the air. Axel rose to his feet on the other side of the door, and I knew wrath like none other was warring inside him.

"I can't go anywhere with you, Axel."

The scent of burning anger hung heavy in the air with a mix of fear only a raging man could bring. However, I had no fears today.

"You can't stay in there forever, Piya. Open this door before I have my friend take your father's practice to court or bankrupt Jordan."

I didn't miss a beat. "You signed a five-year contract with Jordan." The contract was foolproof; I'd ensured it before agreeing to Axel's sordid arrangement. "And your friend already accepted the settlement from Papa."

"Then I'll pull my business from your mom and Milan's firm."

"Go ahead. Jay has already agreed to let them oversee Ambani Corp's large endeavor. They'll make up the losses."

Anger mixed with the tinge of fear and the faintest hints of desperation exploded into the air. "Then I'll tell the world that Poppy is my daughter. She'll never be approved for CEO if anyone discovers she isn't biologically Ambani's."

"You won't hurt Poppy, and we both know it," I announced without a morsel of doubt. Axel didn't love Poppy, but I also knew he wouldn't hurt her. It was the only thing he could do to forever sever our bond.

Realizing where the cards had fallen, Axel's collected veneer was starting to shred. His voice sounded more agitated this time.

"What's the play here, Princess?" he asked in a mild tone though I knew he was moments away from losing control. "You know that I'll never leave you alone. Even if you manage to solve these temporary problems, I'm going to come back harder and hit you with everything I have. I'll tell the world about us."

I smiled sadly and ignored his threats. "Over the last year, I couldn't understand what was happening to my perfect family. We went from daily dinners to Jay working all night and Poppy staying locked up in her room. I had no idea how to fix things and kept trying to find a solution, first by being the perfect Mrs. Ambani, then by being the reckless Piya Mittal."

I tilted my head to glance at him.

"You see, *that* was my big mistake. I couldn't help anyone by being only half of myself because I was both."

It was the truth I had known for years. A part of me belonged to Axel, just like a part of me belonged to Jay. Fighting either side only ended in disaster. Letting both sides live in harmony was how I'd found the solution to do right by my family.

"You were wrong, Axel. Jay never forced me into servitude or into playing the role of the perfect wife. Those things were my choice."

From the corner of my eye, I saw Axel's body shaking with rage. "Do not," he chewed out, "talk about another man."

I continued my story as if I hadn't heard him. "After we married, Jay struggled with my confrontational side because he grew up in a reserved household where people didn't scream their feelings at the top of their lungs. I saw the demands Jay faced from the world and didn't want to be another taxing person in his life."

"What did I just say about bringing him up?" Axel slammed his palm again the door, causing a deafening rumble.

I jumped from the noise but didn't let that stop me from telling Axel the whole story. He had to know to understand my decision.

"Not that it mattered. Jay never gave me a reason to be difficult. Perhaps because I was so much younger than him, he felt a sense of responsibility toward me. He was immensely attentive, catering to my every whim. At times, it felt as if his purpose in life was ensuring that I was taken care of."

Axel pounded his fist against the glass pane two more times. I wasn't concerned. These glass panes were bulletproof, and he couldn't break them. There was no other access inside this house, either.

"In turn, I wanted to be the partner that elevated Jay, not be his downfall. I adapted and made changes to fit in with his family and community. Instead of succumbing to my natural instincts, I aimed to blend in. I swapped out my hot pink camis for neutral colors to not bring unnecessary attention to myself. I hid away all the rotten parts of myself so they couldn't touch Jay negatively."

I ignored Axel as he shouted for me to open the door. He was getting more agitated with each passing moment.

"Everything Dadi had said came true, and we fell in love over time. It wasn't the all-consuming immediate blow that knocked me on my ass like you did. It was slow and crept up on us."

"Open this fucking door, Piya," Axel bellowed.

"You have to know that I thought about you and mourned you daily. I used to wonder if this unbreakable bond was because you were Poppy's biological father. I had many other theories on why I couldn't forget you, but by our fifth wedding anniversary, I stopped caring. You were a part of me, and the memories of you became the same as breathing oxygen. It no longer bothered me. It also answered the age-old question, could you love two people simultaneously? The answer is yes."

The banging on the glass pane intensified so loudly that my voice could barely be heard over it.

"I fell in love with you instantly on the night I met you. I fell in love with Jay over time as we built a life brick by brick. Loving you didn't mean I couldn't love him, too. It was incomparable, like apples and oranges."

Watching how Jay grew from his love for Kat and me, I knew the two weren't mutually exclusive. Despite his love for Kat, I never questioned Jay's love for me because both could be true. Jay's office was the proof. While Kat maintained five percent of his desk, Poppy and I ruled the other ninety-five percent. And that was why I had to make this difficult decision today.

"There is no one here," I informed. "I sent my family to our condo in the city because I knew you were coming for me, and I knew what I had to do next."

I grabbed my cell phone from my back pocket. My fingers dialed 911 and hovered over the call button. Axel's fists furiously pounded against the surface, leaving red marks in its wake where he made contact.

"Didn't you wonder why there was no security at this house when it isn't in Jay's nature to leave us unprotected?" I asked calmly, even though he could no longer hear me, lost in a world of chaos. "It's because once I call the police, it takes them less than three minutes to reach this house."

Rage radiated from his body as he slammed his hand against the glass and cursed loudly. I hit the call button and waited for someone to pick up on the other side.

"Hello. This is Piya Ambani. I want to report a break-in." I rattled off my address while Axel continued slamming his fists against the door in a never-ending cycle of ire, punctuated by the occasional scream of rage.

Axel took a momentary pause, seething. "You think the police will keep you safe from me? You're wrong."

I rose to my knees and turned in place. I leaned my forehead against the cool glass pane as if reaching toward him.

"Things haven't been right with us because I have unfinished business," I whispered. "You feel it, too. That's why you have been holding onto me so tightly, always looking over your shoulders for when I might run again. This is no way to live. Let me go, Axel, and I'll return to you the right way. I'll be your prisoner for as long as you want."

"I'll never let you go."

A single tear rolled down my cheek. Axel had made his choice. "Forgive me for what I'm about to do, but you left me no choice."

The cameras above the doors were recording this interaction with the proof of Axel Trimalchio threatening my family and me. I'd send it to Levi with a promise of not going public if Axel abided by the restraining order I'd attain through this video and the police testimony once they arrived on site.

I had watched Axel's new life closely. Levi was the only person who truly cared for Axel and wouldn't let him violate the restraining order. If necessary, Levi would track him conspicuously to ensure it.

Not to mention, Axel was so famous that it'd be impossible to return to Chicago without his whereabouts becoming public. That was how I'd found out he had landed in Chicago in the first place.

All these measures I had taken against Axel were Piya Ambani's doing. Powerful. Rich. Calm. Collected. In control.

However, I had to push Axel over the edge for this plan to be successful. Only Piya Mittal could bring out the beast inside him with a slightly reckless decision involving emotions.

"I love my husband, and I have to see him through this. You shouldn't have tried to make me choose between my family and you... because it'll always be them."

It happened then. The control Axel had been battling with since his arrival shattered entirely.

Uncontrollable anger thundered. His fist pounded against the door so heavily that it might as well have shaken the entire house. My hands fell on the ground as I watched the blood seep from his knuckles and the sound of fast-approaching sirens.

Even exhaustion didn't take him down as Axel continued pummeling the door, trying to break it down. Two large officers appeared on site and tackled him. It didn't take him down. He rose from the ashes like a phoenix and dispersed them. With his eyes on me, he charged at me like a maniac. Once more, he was at the doors, throwing his body against it with a primal fury to somehow get to me. His guttural voice sounded animalistic as he called to me while trying to break through the door.

I placed two hands over my ears, pain colliding against my chest. "I love you," I whispered to myself as I rocked back and forth. "I'll always love you. Please forgive me."

If there were any other way for Jay to peacefully live out his remaining days with his family, I would have taken it. But I knew Axel would keep coming for me until his last breath.

I watched as more police officers arrived on site, trying to take Axel down. The adrenaline wouldn't let him go down, and he assaulted the police officers without care.

I knew he'd hate me forever for this one action because I had finally taken the one thing Axel promised never to lose; his ability to avert the law and... his control.

CHAPTER
TWENTY

500 Nights Later

Piya

I'D HELD MY BREATH FOR 500 DAYS, DOING THE
dutiful things expected of a widow. Losing Jay was devastating for
both Poppy and me, but having the opportunity to live life to the
fullest decreased the bitter blow. Instead of focusing on the
inevitable, we had spent an entire year sailing around the world
on Jay's yacht, doing the things Jay loved most. Traveling and
spending time with his family.

It was hard at times. It took a toll even with the full-time
nurse we brought along, especially on Poppy, who hated

watching her big, strong dad wither away. Jay had both good and bad days, his spirit high at times and waning during others.

In the end, Jay went out the way he always wanted to, with his family. Poppy and I had cuddled up on either side of Jay for a nap and had maneuvered each of his arms around our necks so we could lie on his chest. That was how he passed away. Even in death, he never let go, and his arms stayed looped around our necks.

The doctors said it was a medical fucking miracle.

Since Jay's death, it had been days of sorrow, anger, and bitterness. It fluctuated for both Poppy and me. During our year abroad, Poppy finished her required curriculum under the supervision of the tutor we brought along and officially graduated high school at the age of fourteen. She was applying for colleges and was currently attending a non-credit internship program in DC.

Poppy planned to finish college by eighteen and start an internship at Ambani Corp afterward. It was unlikely she'd become CEO overnight, but her papa had paved the path for success. The board members swayed by Jay had held firm with Jay's interim CEO. It was an unspoken agreement that the position would be held until Poppy had finished college, completed an entry-level position at Ambani Corp, and proved herself to the board.

It was difficult to have Poppy fly the nest so early, but I had made peace and was confident in her abilities. I needed to believe in my daughter's abilities to make the best decisions for herself.

Meanwhile, Levi had kept his promise and hadn't let Axel come near our family or destroy everyone I loved. We traveled the world, and Levi alerted us whenever Axel tried tracking us down and put further obstacles in Axel's way. Not to mention, we also had the law on our side. A restraining order was issued for five hundred days, pending review for an extension. We managed to keep the whole thing under wraps, and it hadn't hurt Axel's status.

I knew the day would come when the restraining order would expire, and Axel would come for me. He'd make me pay for my betrayal and likely punish me for every day I had stayed away from him. If I thought the previous lockdown was worse, I was confident it'd pale compared to what he'd do now.

That's why I wasn't surprised to see the note on the fridge on the exact day the restraining order had expired.

~~Attend a rave~~
~~Go skinny-dipping~~
~~Convince someone you're from the future~~
~~Speak in a made-up language in public~~
~~Prank call~~
~~Go skydiving~~
Jump into a taxi and scream, "Follow that car!"
Trespass on a private property

There was also a message, and though it was unsigned, I knew who it was from.

We never finished the list.

It had been 500 nights since I last saw him, though I had felt his eyes on me since my return to America.

I had only just arrived at Jay's condo in Manhattan to clear it out. My heels clacked against the hardwood floors as I took a few steps to inspect my surroundings. I could feel his eyes on me and knew my stalker was somewhere close. He was watching me, waiting for my next move.

I should have been scared—petrified, in fact—but 500 days was too long to go without this feeling. I had been living with a dull numbness in my chest, and it was the first time I had felt alive in months.

Without thinking, I took off at full speed, barely grabbing the list and my purse on the way out. I didn't look back, running onto a street with oncoming traffic like a mad woman. Chaos ensued, and people screamed at me.

I didn't care. I barged into a cab and screamed, *follow that car!*

"Fuck you!" the taxi driver yelled back. He threw me out, taking me for another of New York's quirky personalities.

I jumped into another cab rolling at a slow speed due to the traffic. The driver pumped the brakes and kicked me out.

It took frantic searching and three more taxis for one to finally bite.

"Please, sir," I gushed to the man as I jumped in, "Follow that car." This time, I handed a bunch of cash to the driver in hopes of tipping the scale my way.

The cabbie shrugged and started following the random car I had pointed out. I couldn't hold back any longer. A manic laughter bubbled in my chest. I threw my head back and started laughing, unable to stop.

Pure, raw, explosive dopamine rushed to my brain. It was better than anything else that could trigger your pleasure receptors. Better than sexual kinks. Better than shopping. Better than drugs. Better than football players in tight pants. Better than your team winning the Superbowl. Better than hot jalebis in the cold rain. Better than McDonald's french fries. Better than oxygen. Better than life itself.

There was nothing in this world that compared to a list with Axel Trimalchio.

I laughed and screamed hysterically. "Go faster. He is getting away," I shouted at the cabbie.

"Who is getting away?" he shouted back, unsure who we were chasing. Even I had lost account of the car I had asked him to follow.

It was then I felt his gaze again, that distinct feeling of being watched. It was coming from the right, and the way goosebumps lined my arms, I knew he was in my direct peripheral.

"The car to my right," I said breathlessly. "Follow that car." Turning my head, I looked straight into a car with tinted glasses. He was inside, I was sure of it, and watching me intently. "Follow that car," I repeated.

The cabbie didn't argue and pursued the black car as it veered through traffic. Even before the car took the exit, I knew where we were going.

"Should I keep following?" the cabbie asked as we drove away from the city.

"Hell, yes."

We kept speeding, but I wouldn't let my eyes dart back to the black car. I knew, without a doubt, that his eyes were watching me. As soon as I saw the sign for Chateau at the Hempstead, my heart rate picked up.

"Faster," I told the man who was already flying through the streets over the speed limit. "In there." I pointed toward the private venue, knowing we were about to trespass and scratch off the last item on our list.

Shoving a bunch of cash in the cabbie's hand, I ran out of the car with my Prada crossbody bag slung across my chest. I saw the black car but knew Axel wasn't inside. He had a leg up on me as he'd arrived a few minutes earlier, and though I didn't see which way he had gone, I knew where he was waiting for me.

"Miss, stop right there. You can't be here." I turned to see a security guard from a distance. He pointed at me, signaling for me to halt in place. "This is private property," he yelled.

I took off at manic speed, ditching my heels when they became a nuisance. I heard the man calling the cops, but I didn't stop running until I was at the sandy beach and until the green light at the end of the dock came into view.

A tall figure was overlooking the water. I couldn't make him out from a distance, but when he turned, a chill ran down my spine as our gazes finally clashed. Dark, unforgiving eyes stared back, dead set against giving away their secrets.

I walked in a trance, hearing nothing else and seeing nothing else other than those liquid pools of darkness harvesting my soul from me. The hot sand under my feet pulled me toward the center of the earth, but the resistance was no match, for he pulled me toward him without my permission.

I heard the whistle from the security guards as they screamed at us. For a second, my attention threatened to deviate, but he distracted me with one sentence, "Hi, Princess."

Security guards and the venue owners were now outside, all screaming at us to get off their property and saying they had called the cops.

I smirked. "*Hi, Princess*; that's all I get after finally finishing this insane list? Seems somewhat anticlimactic after," I waved toward the security man running toward us, "all the chaos."

He raised an eyebrow. "What do you propose instead?"

"There needs to be something more official as a celebratory means. Perhaps something that seals the deal."

A wolfish grin spread over his face.

"You know, something like—"

Axel closed the distance between us, wrapping a hand around my throat and tugging me to him for an unforgiving kiss. I was unprepared, though my arms snaked around his neck by the time his tongue invaded my mouth. His tongue was just as lewd as I remembered and took what he wanted like a man starved.

We could hear the fast-approaching steps of the security guards, but neither of us let go. I was ready to be his prisoner for five-hundred nights, five-thousand nights, and all the nights to come afterward.

We both felt it when the guards grabbed our elbows, tugging to tear us apart and screaming, *"You need to stop this nonsense."*

Someone must have tackled us to the ground out of frustration from their inability to break the kiss. As our sides collided with the sandy beach, I heard continuous yelling. *"Will you guys cut it out?"*

Axel's heat embraced me into a cocoon against his chest, keeping me safe from external threats. Still, he didn't break the kiss. I had no idea what was happening outside of his tight hold, nor did I bother opening my eyes.

I felt it when the salty waves crashed onto our bodies and soaked us. Still, I didn't pry open my eyes, staying in the world we had created with each other where no one else could touch us.

Axel never disconnected our lips, kissing me with the same ferocity as three grown men screamed, trying to pull us apart. It wouldn't happen. We were already inside our world where only the sounds of guitar and piano mattered, where the thrill was never-ending, and where we had preserved our love for eternity.

~~Attend a rave~~
~~Go skinny-dipping~~
~~Convince someone you're from the future~~
~~Speak in a made-up language in public~~
~~Prank call~~
~~Go skydiving~~
~~Jump into a taxi and scream, "Follow that car!"~~
~~Trespass on a private property~~

~

I know. I KNOW. Don't hate me for not writing an epilogue. I tried writing an epilogue twice and deleted it because any ending different from this one felt unauthentic to Axel and Piya. However, if you still want more of Axel and Piya, turn the page to find out how to read a bonus scene.

You can also follow this couple in Poppy's standalone, Fatal Obsession, Book 2 in the Tales of Obsession Series.

Love,

Drethi

Afterword

~

Thank you for giving my books a chance. Several tragic love stories that emotionally wrecked me over the years inspired the Tales of Obsession Series. It haunted me that certain couples met terrible fates, and I wanted to give them a better ending.

The book that triggered me to write 5000 Nights of Obsession was The Great Gatsby. However, I'd be remiss not to mention the following books and movies that were also a source of inspiration: Love Me If You Dare, Casablanca, Rockstar, Gone With The Wind, Anna Karenina, and Indecent Proposal.

I hope you enjoyed this retelling and consider writing me a review on Goodreads or Amazon. A review for an author is like leaving a tip for your server. Each one goes a long way.

Feel free to sign up for my Newsletter for a bonus scene from 5000 Nights of Obsession, and find me on Facebook for signed paperbacks, giveaways, and more.

Last, but not least, be sure to check out Poppy's story, Fatal Obsession.

About the Author

Drethi Anis is a dark, contemporary author and prefers to write anti-heroes. Drethi's stories will always have angst, obsession, and a dark twist. Though toxic love and darkness are major players in her books, romance is still a priority. Stay tuned for future releases by signing up for her Newsletter. Connect with the author directly:

Linktree

OBSESSING OVER MORALLY AMBIGUOUS ROMANCE

Acknowledgments

Thank you, Lexi, Bianca, and Ash, for reading these pages as I wrote them, for crying with me, and for being late to work because I decided to drag my feet.

Thank you, Angie, for dealing with my procrastination. Nothing lights a fire like someone telling you, "I'll spank you, and not the good kind if you don't finish writing."

ALSO BY DRETHI

THE QUARANTINE SERIES

QUARANTINED

ISOLATION

ESSENTIAL

THE QUARANTINE BOX SET 1-3 & BONUS SCENES

THE CHAOS SERIES

ORGANIZED CHAOS

DISCORD

THE SEVEN SINS SERIES

LUST

TALES OF OBSESSION SERIES

5000 NIGHTS OF OBSESSION

FATAL OBSESSION